PENGUIN BOOKS

j

Last Judgement

www.johncarterauthor.com
www.facebook.com/johncarterauthor
twitter.com/JohnCarterAut

Last Judgement

JOHN CARTER

PENGUIN BOOKS

PENGUIN BOOKS

Published by the Penguin Group
Penguin Books Ltd, 80 Strand, London WC2R ORL, England
Penguin Group (USA) Inc., 375 Hudson Street, New York, New York 10014, USA
Penguin Group (Canada), 90 Eglinton Avenue East, Suite 700, Toronto, Ontario, Canada M4P 2Y3
(a division of Pearson Penguin Canada Inc.)
Penguin Ireland, 25 St Stephen's Green, Dublin 2, Ireland (a division of Penguin Books Ltd)
Penguin Group (Australia), 707 Collins Street, Melbourne, Victoria 3008, Australia
(a division of Pearson Australia Group Pty Ltd)
Penguin Books India Pvt Ltd, 11 Community Centre, Panchsheel Park, New Delhi – 110 017, India
Penguin Group (NZ), 67 Apollo Drive, Rosedale, Auckland 0632, New Zealand
(a division of Pearson New Zealand Ltd)
Penguin Books (South Africa) (Pty) Ltd, Block D, Rosebank Office Park,
181 Jan Smuts Avenue, Parktown North, Gauteng 2193, South Africa

Penguin Books Ltd, Registered Offices: 80 Strand, London WC2R ORL, England

www.penguin.com

First published 2014
001

The moral right of the author has been asserted

Set in 12.5/14.75 pt Garamond MT Std
Typeset by Jouve (UK), Milton Keynes
Printed in Great Britain by Clays Ltd, St Ives plc

ISBN: 978-1-405-91511-3

www.greenpenguin.co.uk

MIX
Paper from
responsible sources
FSC www.fsc.org   FSC® C018179

Penguin Books is committed to a sustainable
future for our business, our readers and our planet.
This book is made from Forest Stewardship
Council™ certified paper.

For Anthony.
Much of what you will read here is true. Probably
far more than you would like to admit.

'The lunatic . . . doesn't concern himself at all with logic; he works by short circuits. For him, everything proves everything else. The lunatic is all *idée fixe*, and whatever he comes across confirms his lunacy. You can tell him by the liberties he takes with common sense, by his flashes of inspiration, and by the fact that sooner or later he brings up the Templars.'

– Umberto Eco, *Foucault's Pendulum*

'History is the lie commonly agreed upon.'

– Voltaire

Prologue

Notre Dame Cathedral, Paris, France, AD 1314

The man's knees would be the first part of his body to feel the flames that would consume his life.

The pyre had begun to smoke long before the crowd saw the wisps of flame, but now the orange tendrils flickered through the branches into the cold March morning air. A cheer erupted at the first bright, fiery pillar that shot up through the bramble. But then, as the flame caught more quickly, the cheers began to die down. The crowd lowered its volume, expectant.

They were waiting to hear the screams.

Arnaud de Faulke did not wipe away the moisture that welled up in his eyes. He stood at the back of the mob at the entrance to a small alleyway that would provide a quick, unnoticed escape. He knew he was out of the public line of sight, and here his emotion could be expressed without shame or fear.

The orange flames dancing at the base of the pyre grew rapidly, a gentle breeze from the river fanning them into life. The moist air mingled with the smoke and a lingering expectation captured the mob, the only noise the crackling of branches as the heat began to consume its fuel.

Then the first longed-for scream came. In the centre of the massive gathering, made up of the old and the young, the rich and the poor together, was the pitiful form of an elderly man. He writhed, chained to an oak post. His body was naked, save for the legally required restrictions of modesty that warranted a dirty cloth secured round his midriff, and as his knees tightened to avoid the rising flames he howled involuntarily. It was the initial cry forced from his lips by a pain that would get far, far worse.

De Faulke closed his eyes, his lips offering up a prayer. He did not need to see the scene at the centre of the square: he'd witnessed the pyre often enough – sent men to it more times than he could remember. He knew the branches feeding the flames had been carefully prepared and arranged, and all the more so in this special case. Pitch had been applied thickly enough that the fire would turn the man's flesh to ash, eventually consuming even his bones. There were to be no remainders left at the end, nothing they could deem relics and carry away to treasure. Eventually, to make sure of this, the charred scraps would be ground and dumped into the Seine.

But the accelerant-soaked faggots had not yet been thrown on to the pyre. The court had ordered flames of a lower temperature for the commencement of their 'justice'. His death should begin slowly. The people should hear his wails. They should be able to see the humours beneath his skin start to boil, the charring begin to take form, the agony slowly rise to full intensity.

The few remaining knights in Paris knew the date of the Grand Master's public execution, but none would dare attend. As de Faulke blinked away his tears and scanned the crowd, he could see none of his compatriots, not one of his brothers. They had either fled or been killed. God save them. *God help them all.*

2

Another cry tore through the beautiful square, the towers of Notre Dame picturesque in the background. Arnaud de Faulke forced himself to look at the visage of the man who had led them through so much turmoil. He had been a gallant leader, a true nobleman whose final request – to be tied to the pyre facing the cathedral, with his hands bound in prayer – had at least been granted. Yet the world, even the Church, had conspired against what was right and good, and this morning's execution marked the final stage in their ungodly conquest. The Order, disbanded. The Grand Master, consigned to the flames. The glory of the knights, sullied.

'Enough!'

De Faulke's eyes, still wet with emotion, sprang open wider at the unexpected cry. The flames were now dancing at the Grand Master's waist, the flesh of his legs blistering from the heat. His hair was already melting, turning black against his scalp. But he had stopped his shrieks and now glared out wildly over the crowd.

'Enough!' he shouted again, agony in his voice. 'Enough of the world's lies and corruption!'

He tried to take a breath, but the heat seared his lungs and once more he howled from the agony. He had only moments left.

'*Dieu sait qui a tort, et a péché!* God knows who is wrong, and who has sinned!' he bellowed out over the sparks and flames. He stared up to the heavens, then back down to the crowd, his eyes wilder still. 'A curse upon you all! Mark my words, a great calamity will befall all those who have condemned us to such a death!'

A gasp emanated from the crowd. Defeated, captured

and seconds from death he might be, but a curse uttered by a man of God was still powerful. Those closest to the pyre took a step away, suddenly fearful. Whispers between the masses began to texture the square with new sound.

'Well, that's quite enough of all this nonsense,' a guard finally said, unhappy with the change in atmosphere. He stepped forward, grabbed one of the pitch-soaked bundles of branches and tossed it at the old man's feet. The fire instantly burst forth with new ferocity, flames burning white and reaching up to the condemned man's face.

'A curse upon you all!' the Grand Master screamed. '*Il va bientôt arriver!* It shall come upon you soon! *Soon!*'

The flames overtook him. The skin of his cheeks contorted, drew taught, then blackened in the heat. He lifted his eyes towards the heavens, closing them only an instant before the heat of the fluid inside removed any possibility of sight. He could no longer scream. His body roasted, his life burned away.

Its momentary, superstitious hesitation overcome by the sight of his death, the roar of the crowd returned. Cheers. Boisterous voices. Delighted in the spectacle if nothing else.

Arnaud de Faulke wiped his eyes, keeping them on the scene. He was here to bear witness, and as he watched the pyre disappear in the pillar of flame that consumed it, he stalwartly completed that duty.

He had borne witness to the death. But also to something more.

As the Grand Master's body blackened, crumpled and disappeared from the earth, the knight's sorrow fled.

De Faulke crossed himself, turned from the square and stepped purposefully into the anonymity of the narrow alley.

As he walked, he whispered under his breath only a single, sacred word.

'Soon.'

PART ONE
Encounters

I

Oak Island, Off the Coast of Nova Scotia,
Canada, Six Days Ago

'Lower the crane another two feet, then hold.'

Mud dripped over the wooden bracers, the smell of rotting peat nauseating in the dark, wet space. Operating at night kept them on their timeline, but made the dank, enclosed pit feel all the more constricting. The floodlights that hung over its surface were interrupted by the mass of equipment dangling down the shaft, casting as much shadow as light into the depths below.

Sean Blackburn shone a light at his ankles. He'd wrapped the three-quarter-inch rope harness round all four corners of the massive paver stone, and now re-checked each point of contact. A corner losing its grip would be deadly, and an uneven lift no less disastrous.

'Watch your head!'

He looked up as the warning was called out over the noise of generators and machinery far above, in time to see a four-hundred-pound hook at the end of the crane's winch slowly wind down to head height. He grabbed the steel clasp, called out for a halt when it was at chest level, and began wrapping the harness's leads round it.

Sean again surveyed the surroundings. Everything was holding. Mud oozed between the cracks of the retaining walls they had assembled as they dug down to the current

9

fifty-feet depth, but they showed no signs of buckling. Dozens of other explorers on the island had been thwarted, and lives lost, when pits in the notoriously soft earth collapsed in on themselves, but Sean's team would not suffer the same fate. The metal retainers they had purpose-built and brought from the mainland could hold back the collapse of a mineshaft's falling stone. The mud in which they were working provided no contest.

Satisfied that everything was ready for the lift, he backed himself into the northernmost corner of the pit. It was only twenty-six inches wider than the cover stone they were trying to raise – just enough room for him to stand clear, his back against the cold metal and nose full of the peaty, dank smells of the pit, as the two-tonne slab of rock was lifted above him.

Then, God willing, he would set his eyes on that which no one had seen in over half a millennium.

'Take it up,' he ordered. There followed a tense second of silent hesitation, then the rumble of an engine high above, and the ropes of the harness began to go taut.

The sound that came from the stone as the crane pulled at its weight echoed up through the pit. Sean smiled in the darkness. The suction noise of mud straining at an almost vacuum-tight seal was a good sign. There genuinely was a chamber below the stone, as they'd hypothesized. And the sound meant it wasn't filled in, that the weight of the earth over the centuries hadn't collapsed the medieval chamber they were here to find.

'Lower the sliders on my mark,' Sean instructed, switching to his radio as the noise of the crane filled the air. Topside, four of his crew manned the winches that would force down the sliding extensions of the retaining walls. The instant the covering stone started to rise, the muddy earth its edges had held back would start to pour into the chamber – an ancient trap, like others they had found all over the island. Forcing the extensions down would keep seepage to a minimum, protecting whatever was inside from being submerged and buried anew.

'Mark!' Sean announced. As the vast, flat stone rose, four metal planks were simultaneously thrust downwards at the edges of the mud. Ten seconds later, they hit solid rock. In-flow was blocked.

The cover stone rose to Sean's knees, but he didn't yet have the room to bend down and look beneath it. 'Keep the winch steady,' he ordered, anticipation almost over-whelming him. It even managed to hold at bay the mild claustrophobia that had always plagued him. The condition was more than an annoyance, almost a curse for a man who lived as Sean did, and would otherwise have threatened to take control of his senses in these condi-tions, a massive stone pinning him against the wall so far beneath the earth. Heavy, entrapping, like a tomb . . .

But the sheer excitement proved an effective antidote. After another fifty seconds had passed, the stone was at Sean's chest. It was just enough. Sliding his back along the retaining wall, he bent his knees and lowered himself slowly, his eyes coming even with the edge of the stone. The muddy wetness of its sides hung inches from his face, the rotten scent of moist earth filling his nostrils. Suddenly, the tightness of the space was compounded, terrifying, but Sean forced himself to hold his breath and keep his motion steady, sinking slowly beneath the cover stone. The cold metal of their retaining walls was firm against the red long-sleeved shirt that covered his torso as he slid himself downwards. Then, tucking his head forward as soon as he had cleared its lower edge, he shone his torch down.

A chamber. Intact.

And it wasn't empty.

Sean did a quick, anxious survey of the space. Four feet by six, the stone room was a good five feet deep and constructed of smooth granite walls. The cover stone, six inches thick, hovered above his head, still rising slowly.

'Sean, Chrissakes, wait till we get this secured!' A shout came down from above.

But he didn't wait. He couldn't. What he wanted was right before him, within his grasp. Even in the faint light of his torch, he could see it.

In the centre of the chamber was a small pedestal, made of the same stone as the walls. It stood two feet high, and atop it was the focal point of all their efforts over so many months.

Sean placed his hands at the rim of rock near his feet and lowered himself carefully to the floor. The sound of his boots echoed in the small enclosure, the noise of the equipment muted by the stone above him. He took his steps gingerly. A false floor would be entirely in keeping with their discoveries elsewhere on the island, but this small space seemed to contain no secrets except the one Sean was there to claim.

Slipping the torch into his armpit and approaching the centre of the chamber, he wiped the mud off his hands and reached them out gently. On top of the stone pedestal was a small onyx tablet, still shiny after almost 650 years in its subterranean solitude.

He lifted it carefully, brought it to the middle of his torch's round light and flipped it over.

The sounds of the dig evaporated. Time seemed to stop. Sean's eyes simply stared in wonder.

The tablet contained a series of runes that had been hand-carved into its surface. Though he wasn't able to read them, he recognized at once the familiar shapes.

What they meant, Sean couldn't know. But meaning would come soon enough. What mattered now, in the darkness of the reeking pit in the middle of the night, was one fact alone.

The tablet had been prepared by the last men on earth to have seen one of the greatest treasures the world had ever known. And now, Sean held it in his hands.

2

Jack Shepherd swerved his rental car hard to the right at the end of the freeway exit ramp, the engine of the space grey Mercedes C350 purring down to idle as he brought the car to a halt. Beside him, the remnants of his airport Starbucks run sloshed in a paper cup nestled into the dashboard holder, the aromas of the black coffee still in the air. Jack steeled himself for the unknown.

Arrival at the massive Blackburn Enterprises central complex was meant to intimidate visitors. Two security checkpoints had been required before Jack arrived at the front door of the facility, situated in the wooded hills off I-5 outside Seattle. The first had initially appeared to be a routine identification check at the edge of the property, but the handing over of Jack's driver's licence and passport had been supplemented with a request for a facial scan and full ten-point fingerprinting, all of which had been done from the car thanks to a custom-designed mobile tablet handed to him by a dispassionate but physically dominating gate guard.

'If you'd just pull ahead, sir, to the gate on the left.' The guard retrieved the tablet after Jack had completed the process by holding the ring and pinky digits of his left hand against its scanner. The guard motioned the way with what just about passed for a polite nod and nothing further.

Jack resisted the strong urge to make a light-hearted comment on security overkill, recognizing, as the words neared his lips, that the bulky guard probably had just as advanced a sense of humour as he did a way with conversation. Instead, he bit his tongue and pulled the car forward slowly, following the man's directions.

The bigger the billing, the bigger the toys. Jack Shepherd was used to security, albeit not necessarily with such advanced equipment. He was also used to men, or in this case, companies, wanting to make an impact when first encountered. He had been that way himself as a younger man, and he'd had the mentality drilled into him as he grew older. Impressions, impact, influence. A trio of professional showmanship he'd come to loathe. Maybe that was why he'd gone so far to the other extreme in recent years, insisting on letting the first impression he made make itself without being dressed up or crafted. Uniforms were a thing of the past, and he'd given away the only suit he'd ever owned last year. Everywhere he went, he went dressed as he was today: a pair of khakis, a comfortable shirt – usually a turtleneck – a windbreaker or jacket over the top. Himself, for better or for worse.

But Jack didn't begrudge his hosts today for the obvious show of technological savvy. If anyone was going to lay claim to futuristic, overblown security measures, it was going to be one of the biggest international names in defence contracting. He'd never been on their plush grounds before, but the strangely Disney-esque sculpted landscaping, combined with the mystery of what actually went on behind the floral hedgerows and concrete walls, were enough to pique a man's curiosity.

The 'gate' to which he had been directed turned out to be a complete-automobile scanning station, the like of which Jack had never encountered: a large, metallic enclosure without front or back, almost a drive-through garage, with interior walls of what looked like pale grey plastic. As Jack switched off the Mercedes's engine, following the instructions on a boldly painted sign, two new guards, each equally as bulky and fierce as the first Jack had encountered, emerged from a small station office. One had a dog at the end of a retractable lead, the other held an extended ground mirror, and together the two surveyed every inch of the car's exterior.

Jack had been offered a chauffeur-driven company car as part of his welcome package, but he'd always loved to drive and had turned down the offer in favour of the rental. For the first time that morning, he wondered whether that had been a mistake.

A moment later the guards completed their walkaround and two large yellow lights embedded in the archway began to blink. Both men quickly retreated to the station office and pulled the door closed behind them as a soft klaxon began to sound. The yellow lights became a flashing red.

'Do I need to get out of –'

'Please stay in your car, sir,' a voice announced over an unseen loudspeaker. 'The scan will only take a moment.'

Scan? Shepherd raised a brow, while the sound of cooling fans blowing across electrical equipment filled the archway, lasted a few seconds, then promptly ceased. A moment later the lights outside switched to green and the loudspeaker crackled back to life.

'You're clear to pull forward, sir,' the guard's voice sounded. 'Please follow the signs to Building K. Park in any of the green visitors' spaces. You'll be met at the entrance.'

Jack turned over the ignition and pulled out of the gate, conscious of the battery of no fewer than six cameras aimed at him as he pulled into the interior property. Though he hadn't come bearing any, he had the strong feeling that after the technology he'd just passed through, any secrets he might have tried to import on to these grounds would have been laid bare. For the first time in a long while, Jack Shepherd felt exposed.

Two minutes later, the grey Mercedes was parked in the second visitor's space outside the white concrete mass of Building K. Jack chirped the lock as he strode towards the glass doors at the entrance. He carried nothing with him. In his thirty-four years of life, Jack Shepherd had never been head-hunted for anything, and he genuinely didn't know what awaited him inside. He tousled his short brown hair and adjusted the half turtleneck beneath his jacket. They'd called him, he reminded himself, stepping towards the entrance. Never mind the fact that, even as he walked towards the imposing doors of the company, he still didn't know exactly why.

'Captain Shepherd.' An overtly friendly woman greeted him as the glass doors slid apart. She wore a name badge that simply read 'Tina' and a smile that positively beamed hospitality. 'Welcome to Blackburn Enterprises. We've been looking forward to your arrival.'

'It's just Mr Shepherd now,' Jack answered with a soft

smile, extending a hand. 'I left the Corps four years ago. Civvy dress, civvy classifications.'

The woman smiled back professionally. 'As you wish, Mr Shepherd. But you'll find we have a great deal of respect for uniforms around here, whether or not they're still being worn.' Her voice had a slight southern drawl, as if she'd grown up in Texas but spent most of her life elsewhere. Her figure, Jack couldn't help but think, just looked good, wherever it was from.

The look she shot back at him was rehearsed, but for a fleeting instant fluttered over his full physique, resting an extra millisecond on his broad shoulders and well-formed chest. And there was the faintest, slightest trace of a smile that went beyond the practised script of welcome.

Jack grinned inwardly and exhaled a relaxed breath. In a place of mystery, the familiar signs of basic human flirtation were reassuring. He felt his usual confidence start to return.

He surveyed the foyer as he followed Tina inside. Grey marble floors, sheen black walls. The reception desk was a fusion of stone and glass, and the pinprick lighting on the ceiling, soaring three storeys above, shone a bluish light into the large space. Two escalators, running in parallel at the rear of the hall, led up to unknown wings of the building. In the middle of the foyer, a glistening black table supported a two-foot silver statuette of the firm's logo: a globe surmounted by a shield, a single star at its centre.

No more revelations here than anywhere else. Jack had searched Blackburn Enterprises on the Internet after the first call they'd made to his home office, but apart from a sleek-looking website that identified it as 'one of the leading defence contractors to the US Armed Forces' and 'world leaders in specialist tactical technologies' the public materials offered very few particulars about the company.

'May I take your coat, sir?' Tina's soft drawl drew him out of his observations. Jack shook his head in the negative and took a step forward. What he wore was no longer a uniform, but he came as a complete package.

He managed no more than that single step before a security guard appeared from nowhere and came out to meet him. The man was enormous, with a head that seemed to emerge directly out of his shoulders; his neck, if there had ever been one, had long since retreated into the mass of muscles at the top of his torso.

'If you wouldn't mind, please follow me, Captain.' The man motioned to Jack's left, where he saw yet another security station configured in the foyer's corner. An X-ray arch stood next to a Plexiglas tower of what looked like one of the full-body scanners that were becoming more familiar at airports across the country.

Jack looked back at the guard, his own height and build imposing. 'If you really think it's necessary.'

The man simply stared into his eyes, his expression hard.

'We most certainly do.'

On the high-resolution CCTV feeds the newly arrived guest looked just like he did in the profile photographs. *Jack Shepherd, retired Marine Corps captain, six feet and one inch*. The cropped brown hair was slightly longer than in the military record photo, but not by much. Though he wore civilian clothes and moved with a less regimented formality than he would have during active duty, Shepherd still cut the figure of a military man.

Once a Marine . . .

Thomas Blackburn kept his eyes glued to the four video displays that filled the flat-screen monitor on his desk. *Concentrate. Focus.*

The encounter that would consume the next thirty minutes of his life, he'd been told, was important – though he still wasn't sure he was convinced of that. His son had assured him that this man's assistance would help them push past the last hurdles in their research, that Captain Jack Shepherd could offer another perspective to help them read the evidence that would be coming to them over the days ahead. They were at a threshold, and Sean was worried they'd grown too familiar with their material – that they were always thinking in the same way, that they'd lost some of the creativity that came when things were new. Sean's team would soon break the code, but that didn't mean they'd be able to make sense of what lay beneath it. He wanted a new set of eyes on board, and he wanted Shepherd. That meant Blackburn needed the man's help.

On his desk, the dossier on Shepherd lay open. The ageing CEO had read through it a dozen times, knew most of the details by heart.

Age 34, born to Harlan and Martha Shepherd at St Mary's Children's Hospital, Baltimore. Graduated summa cum laude *from Easton High School and joined up with the ROTC immediately on entering university at Virginia Tech. Graduated, again with honours, and went on to serve three tours in Afghanistan and Iraq before honourable discharge, followed by a post-9/11 GI Bill-funded master's degree at Duke, completed immediately afterwards.*

The eighteen pages of background detail continued in far more depth, but the broad strokes of the man's character were the most critical elements. Bright, honourable, well educated, and a man who had seen the world.

Perhaps those were the traits his son required. Of course, they were all the more inviting, given Jack Shepherd's fame acquired over the past two years. He'd earned a reputation, and developed skills since leaving the military, which clearly related to their work. And if the team needed him in order to help Blackburn reach his goal, then he was more than prepared to entice him.

He looked up again at the security displays. Shepherd was just stepping out of the Rapiscan Secure 1000 SP body scanner. The guard looked at the results on his display, which were mirrored on Blackburn's monitor. The man had come empty-handed: car keys in his right pocket, a wallet in his rear-left, a cellular phone in the left breast of his jacket. Nothing else.

No expectations, no preparation. Blackburn could have hoped for nothing better.

3

Blackburn Enterprises

As Jack Shepherd reached the top of the escalator, the shaded glass doors at its peak parted automatically. Beyond was a short corridor, no more than eight feet wide and fifteen in length. At the far end was a massive oak door that looked like it came out of another world. Two huge wrought-iron hinges were affixed on the left side, each with ornate flourishes that extended the fixtures at least a foot into the woodwork, and on the right-hand side was an equally monumental doorknob, also of black iron and at least six inches in diameter. The whole unit looked like it had been transported out of a medieval castle. The contrast with the sleek, modern foyer behind him couldn't have been more stark.

As Jack stepped forward, contemplating how to approach the bizarrely oversized handle, the door swung silently outwards on its vast hinges. The electronics that powered it were as well hidden as whatever camera had sensed his approach.

Stepping over the threshold, Jack's surprise at his surroundings intensified. As the oak door swept silently closed behind him, every trace of the technological, futuristic atmosphere of a moment before was replaced by what could easily have passed for the formal study of a stately home in upper-class Victorian Britain. The walls

22

were panelled mahogany to chest height, where they transitioned into burgundy-and-gold striped wallpaper that looked as fine – and expensive – as hand-crafted textile. The floors were covered in immaculate woven rugs that Jack assumed must be authentic Persian, and heavy pine-green curtains parted to either edge of three floor-to-ceiling windows that ran along one side of the enormous, oblong room. The opposing wall was covered in bookshelves, each chock-full of leather-bound volumes that looked as old as the history of the printed word itself.

At the far end, beneath a radically oversized oil portrait of a man Jack didn't recognize, was an equally oversized desk. Behind it sat the man Jack could only assume he was here to see: Thomas Blackburn, CEO of Blackburn Enterprises. One of the most reclusive yet most powerful individuals in the defence-manufacturing business, and the man behind the head-hunting that had brought Jack to the Pacific Northwest.

His host was already rising, ready to greet him; but it was what stood between the two men that truly captured Jack's attention. The long space was not filled with chairs and tables as he might have assumed, or even a conference space as a CEO's office would warrant. Instead, the room was home to two parallel rows of waist-height brass and glass display cases. The immense space was not so much an office as a museum, full of gently illuminated treasures.

'Welcome to Blackburn Enterprises,' the man behind the desk said, his voice exuding a comfortable authority. He spoke with elongated vowels that suggested having spent considerable time abroad, most likely in his youth. *England?* Jack's thoughts momentarily questioned.

23

'I'm delighted you could make it out on such short notice,' the man continued. 'I do realize Seattle is not exactly next door to Boston.'

'No problem.' Jack's reply was short, distracted. The surroundings had seized his focus.

Thomas Blackburn smiled and walked slowly towards him. As Jack finally forced his attention from the room to its occupant, he noticed the look of contentment on the older man's face, as if he were satisfied at the slightly spell-bound reaction of his guest.

'I trust the flight we arranged for you was satisfactory?'

'It was just fine,' Jack answered. He'd flown all over the world, but usually in the gutted bellies of C-130s or personnel transports, at best in the cramped economy cattle-stalls of commercial airlines. This morning was the first time he'd ever flown first class, which had made the journey an unexpected treat. But given the opulence now surrounding him, it didn't seem appropriate to mention the positive glee he'd felt on learning his fully reclining seat had a massage function.

The other man finally reached him and held out a hand. 'Thomas Blackburn. I'm honoured to have you here at the company, and to welcome you to my little retreat.' He took Jack's hand and shook it with surprising force for a man of Blackburn's age. The faint traces of an accent, at times almost absent, seemed slightly different now. *Not English. European?*

'A pleasure.' Jack shook back. 'I have to admit, after the mixture of Fort Knox and Silicon Valley I had to go through to get in, this isn't quite what I was expecting.' He motioned to the room's antique contents with a sway of his chin.

Blackburn laughed softly. 'A world filled with surprises is the only kind worth inhabiting, no?'

Jack answered with a silent smile. Blackburn's banter was friendly, informal, yet the man exuded a business-like formality that the light-hearted conversation couldn't conceal.

'Please, do come in. We'll sit at my desk.' Blackburn indicated the far side of the room and began to lead Jack through the cases.

They contained what Jack immediately realized was a remarkable trove of material. He noticed several pieces of medieval armour – if not original, then exceptionally convincing reproductions. Two illuminated manuscripts. A selection of folded, clearly centuries-old, garments. One case housed what appeared to be an ancient journal or diary in a remarkable state of preservation. It, like everything else in the collection, was meticulously presented, and it was obvious that no expense had been spared on the display.

'I've never seen so many medieval artefacts in a private collection,' Jack said as they walked, his eyes taken in by the sights.

'I'm something of a collector, Blackburn answered, continuing in step without looking back. 'Call it a heavily indulged hobby.'

'Not every day I meet a man of technology interested in history. It's usually one or the other.'

Blackburn reached his desk, itself an antique, and laid

a hand upon it gently. He turned to face Jack Shepherd. 'History as a whole doesn't interest me, just specific portions of it.' He let the comment linger in the air, his eyes slowly sweeping over Jack from toe to head as if performing some kind of unknown, personal scan. The silence grew, stretching out until Blackburn finally brought his eyes back to Jack's, his face transforming into a warm smile.

'The collection, it pleases you?'

An oddly phrased question, but Jack saw no reason to hide his answer. 'It's impressive. It must have taken quite something to amass all this.'

Another, briefer pause, and Blackburn motioned towards a richly upholstered chair that sat before his desk.

'Why don't we take a seat, Mr Shepherd? What is going to fill you with wonder this morning are not the treasures my collection already includes, but what I sincerely hope you are going to help me obtain.'

4

Blackburn Enterprises

'Is he really on the grounds?' Angela Derby set down a photograph atop a pile of papers perched centrally on her office desk. She asked the question round the pen clutched in her teeth, and snatched it as soon as her hands were free, promptly tucking it behind an ear. Her other hand steadied the stack of papers so that it didn't teeter and fall into the general mêlée of her desk.

The woman standing in the doorway didn't seem to take any special notice of Angela's organizational plight. 'Tina, over at Mr Blackburn's reception, said he arrived ten minutes ago.' The woman smiled suggestively at Derby. 'Said he's a looker in person, too, just like on television.'

Angela caught the other woman's deviously lifted eyebrow and shook her head. 'There are more sides to a man than just his looks.'

'I'll look at as many sides as he'll show me.'

That roused a chuckle and an exaggerated roll of the eyes. Angela's assistant was hopelessly flirtatious. She'd fawn over a rock if she could determine it was male.

Oh, to be concerned with nothing more than the latest potential conquest. The sigh in Angela's mind almost became vocal. She was only a few years older than Fay, almost touching thirty but not quite there yet, still very much in her prime. But she'd exchanged the carefree existence of her earlier life for a new regime of responsibility. Work. Authority. Things that just didn't feel twenty-something, no matter how hard you tried to keep up the spirit of youth.

She shook her head, but allowed her smile to remain. Angela might be a professional woman now, constrained by her position and responsibilities, but she could still appreciate a good moment of meaningless gossip when the opportunity came along.

The pile of papers under her grip wobbled. 'Help me with this, would you?'

Fay stepped forward and steadied the ridiculously over-sized stack. As Angela started to sort pages from the top, her assistant glanced around the room and gave the same loud, demonstrative sigh she produced at least twice a week. Angela knew precisely what it was meant to say, since Fay had said it outright so many times.

Your office is a shambles. It's hard to imagine how any work could get done in here. Your professional quarters are a tribute to the chaotic internal existence of the traditional absent-minded professor. Never mind the fact that Angela was not a professor, that she didn't yet hold a doctorate. These petty details didn't matter, and they only distracted from the scolding.

'Take these downstairs,' Angela suddenly instructed, lifting off a bundle from the top of the stack. 'I need that photocopied for every member of the next excursion team. Can you get it to them by the end of the day?'

Angela's assistant took the stack and eyed it. The pile of papers was over an inch thick and, as usual, contained a scattered assortment of printouts, hand-written pages torn out of a spiral-bound notebook, photographs.

'Sure, I can manage,' she answered. '*Just.*' She stressed

the last word, mimicking her boss's British accent as well as the little English expression she'd taken on as her own.

'Thanks, Fay.' Angela tried to flatten her Cambridge vowels to as American a shape as they would permit, reciprocating Fay's gesture. She gave a soft smile as the other woman exited the office, already humming the chorus of whatever she'd last listened to on her iPod that morning.

Angela relaxed into her chair, feeling content and satisfied as she watched the other woman walk away. These were the small trappings of authority. Her own office, her own assistant. A position in excursion hierarchies that far exceeded the pull of her CV's credentials. She'd come far for someone so young, and revelled in the scope of the work in which she took part. Work that, she could only hope, would have made her father proud – if only he could see her today. Teams would launch to far corners of the world based on her data and suggestions. They would seek what she told them they could find. Millions of dollars would be spent on tasks she helped develop.

That was more important than a social life, right? A fair trade? Not that a person could trade what they'd never had. The closest Angela had ever come to a full-on relationship was in silent, private moments late at night, when she would let her work slip from her mind and imagine the normal life that other people led. In those moments she lived all the stereotypes: the picket-fenced house in a leafy suburb, the pets, the children, the doting husband. The kind of marital bliss her parents had had long ago, in the earliest years of her childhood, which she could only recreate in her imagination, not truly remember. Things had changed as she'd grown. Marriage had come to look different. Life had come to look different.

And that's where her private reflections would usually end – culminating in the pessimistic memories of sickness and death and families that slowly disintegrated from the stress. And just like that, her solitary life, entirely consumed by her singular devotion to her career, didn't look so bad.

Angela looked down at her lap. Her fingers were dancing an anxious tap-step over her black jeans. She forced them to stop, surprised by her actions.

Why do I care if he's here? she questioned herself, and her thoughts came back to earth. She didn't harbour the flirtatious interest in Jack Shepherd's visit that inspired her assistant, but Angela was more than a little curious about his presence in the Seattle facility.

Shepherd's pending arrival had been announced at a planning meeting earlier in the week. An introduction, an interview, a lunch and a tour. The standard recruitment package. Angela had found herself more and more curious as the days brought his arrival closer. Sean Blackburn's sudden insistence on new blood and additional help had taken her by surprise. She knew he didn't doubt her abilities – they'd had far too many successes together for that – but bringing someone new on to their project, that meant . . . she didn't know what that meant, and that's what bothered her. Angela Derby had never met the famed Shepherd, but she knew enough about him to know that if he was being brought on board, things would change.

It's not an 'if', Angie, she scolded herself, employing the diminutive she almost never used, even in her own thoughts. Old Man Blackburn would greet him the same way he'd greeted her. Shepherd would be brought into the office, see the collection, and then he'd be told of possibilities no one could turn down. Real archaeologist or flash-in-the-pan sensationalist, he wasn't going to say no.

She sat forward, her fingers again dancing on her knees. Suddenly, meeting him was what she wanted more than anything else. She glanced at her small Tsovet watch. Twenty past eleven. Lunch was part of the package, and if the routine was the same as usual, that meant he'd be treated to an executive buffet at the Peaks Grill after his meeting with Blackburn. Two buildings over – horrible coffee but a decent salad. A good lunch could become a productive lunch.

She stood, grabbed her jacket from the peg on the back of her office door, swooped up her Tory Burch handbag from a chair, and stepped forward. There was going to be a new man on her team, and she wanted to know exactly what she'd be dealing with.

Embedded in the ceiling high above, little more than a pinhead-sized dot that effectively disappeared in the spotted foam tiles lining the ceilings throughout the office complex, a high-resolution camera took in the motions in Angela Derby's office in perfect clarity. A microphone, equally minuscule and just as well concealed, captured every sound, twenty-four hours per day, and was constantly monitored.

In a distant, windowless room, a man in blue slacks and a neatly ironed white shirt observed her exit. Derby's office lights flicked off as she passed her hand over the electronic control and pulled the door closed behind her, the camera automatically switching into night mode and the images on his display turning a ghostly green. On a keypad at his desk, the man entered the time and the required detail into the log. *11.22: AD departs office unaccompanied.* He hit 'send', and the line entry was immediately encoded, transferred up the wire and submitted to his supervisor, the timestamp linked to the video and audio records, should detailed examination of his log entry be desired.

He tapped the controls of another pad, and the camera view on his display switched to the corridor outside Derby's office. The woman buttoned up her jacket as she walked, moving towards the external door.

5

Lanier Heights, Washington, DC

'Get us inside, quickly.' A man, dressed all in black like his two companions, nodded towards the door as he whispered the command. A second, shorter man stepped up to the knob.

The trio had arrived at the house while the morning light was not yet burning. They had carefully studied the daily habits of its occupants. The father, an early riser with a work ethic that put him in the office hours before sunrise every day, was long since gone, but his wife and children had yet to rise. Just as they required. The home was silent, dark, inviting.

A slight click and ping were the only sounds that accompanied the lock to the kitchen door being forced. The house's alarm system had already been disabled: too easily done, given the owners' lackadaisical approach to security. They'd only had to patrol the neighbourhood a week, set up a few minuscule cameras in the garden, at just the right angles to capture the keypad as parents and children keyed in their access codes. They were all the same – not even variation among family members. Foolish.

'We're in.' The shorter man stepped aside and let the taller lead the trio into the house. The third ensured the door was gently closed behind them.

'The rooms are upstairs,' whispered the group's leader. They moved quickly and silently through the house. The stairway ascended from the front entrance, a broad, highly polished mahogany bannister offsetting the royal burgundy carpeting. Along the gently curving wall was a stereotypical collection of family portraits: wedding stills, travels, campaigns, births. Each was perfectly framed, a tribute in its unique way to a well-crafted and highly stylized life.

The men crested the first-floor landing and the leader surveyed the various doors before them. At the far left, a white-washed door was painted with stencilled flowers, a small wooden sign reading 'Anna and Bella' hanging at its middle. The central two doors were ajar, one a bathroom and the other a small office. The fourth door, to their right, was closed.

'The girls are there,' the leader whispered, signalling to his left. Then to one of his men: 'You take care of that situation.' He motioned to the other man. 'You and I will deal with the woman.'

He gave his first counterpart a few moments to move over to the children's door, then he and the other man stepped purposefully towards the master bedroom.

The woman heard the door open from someplace in her dreams, coming towards consciousness with the happy thought that her husband had forgotten something on his way to work, providing her the pleasant opportunity to see him once more before the long, customary day apart truly began. One more little kiss, pecked at her cheek as he grabbed his keys, or wallet, or whatever he'd left behind.

A rare extra second of domestic intimacy, so precious in their all-too-public lives.

The slamming of the bedroom door startled her out of her half slumber with a shock.

Two men burst into the room, both dressed entirely in black, balaclavas pulled down over their faces. They were sturdily built, gruff, with ferocious eyes that left no doubt they weren't here for a simple burglary. She could smell their sweat, acrid and angry, as shock convulsed her towards the headboard.

'Don't move, don't make a sound, or your girls die.' The first man into the room spoke firmly as he raised a black gun and aimed it directly at her.

She was frozen in place, her hands in knots round the beige bed sheet, pulling it to her chest. All she could hear was the thumping of her heart, the man's threat, the names of her daughters echoing silently in her mind. *Not the girls* . . .

The second man removed a small tote, unzipped it and extracted a handheld video camera, sliding his gloved fingers through the strap and fidgeting with the controls. His partner stood stoically, his gun unwavering.

'Please, don't hurt my —'

'Not a sound,' the gunman demanded, keeping his voice low but severe. He took a step closer, pointing the barrel of his pistol squarely at the woman's eyes. Her chest was heaving, a counter to his rock-steady gaze.

A moment later, the second man looked up. 'It's recording.'

The woman shot a terrified glance over at him. A small red light now blinked at the front of the camcorder, pointed at her on the bed. Its operator kept his gaze on the flip-out viewfinder.

'Tell me your name.' The first man made the demand clearly, his voice unnervingly calm.

The woman couldn't speak. Terror clenched her throat, an acid tinge of fear-induced adrenaline burned her tongue.

'Your name, bitch!' The man took another step forward, bringing the gun closer to her face.

In the blur of her fear she could see the weapon better now. The barrel started off square, but ended in a cylinder. *A suppressor.* The woman's fear escalated beyond her ability to control it, her whole body starting to shake.

'I won't ask you again,' the man demanded. 'Tell me your name, or your girls –'

'B-Beth,' she sputtered out, before he could threaten her girls a second time. 'M-my name is Beth.'

'And your children's names?'

Beth shook down her fear, but the names of her precious children came out only at a whisper. 'Anna. Anna and Bella.' She looked imploringly at him. *Please, leave my girls alone.*

The man with the gun glanced across at his partner. 'That good enough? It picked up the sound?'

'Got it,' the other man answered. 'Quiet, but clear.'

'Then we have what we need.'

The first man turned his attention back to Beth, who was shaking in her bed, tears streaming down her face. She looked up at his eyes: angry, cold, resolute.

Resolute.

Suddenly, Beth knew there was only one way this encounter was going to end.

'Please,' she said, pulling herself upright, a new strength in her voice, the inevitable now understood. 'Whatever you do to me, please don't hurt my girls.'

'That's not up to me,' the man answered. He started, as if he might say more, but seemed to realize there was no point.

Beth couldn't see his finger pull back on the trigger, but noticed his eyes tighten slightly. She took a breath, watched as the pinhole of black at the end of the barrel turned to a blinding, radiant sun.

Don't hurt my precious girls, became a single, clear thought as the whole room went a glaring, phosphorous white.

And then there were no thoughts at all.

6

Blackburn Enterprises, Seattle

Behind the desk, in a seat that over the years had become one of tremendous power, Thomas Blackburn became another man. The pleasantries of a moment before vanished into an air of business-like professionalism.

'You're here on interview for a rather specialist project,' Blackburn began, tugging open Jack's dossier on his desk.

'I know very little about it,' Shepherd answered honestly. 'I'm here more out of curiosity than any concrete knowledge of what you want me for. Your recruiters were . . . cagey.'

'We enjoy our secrets. To this point, it's been more important that we know about you.' Blackburn delivered the strangely evasive answer and let his iron gaze linger a long time on Jack's blue eyes. Eventually, just as the locked stare began to grow uncomfortable, he broke it and turned his attention to the files.

'Captain Jack Johnson Shepherd, US Marine Corps. Three tours of active duty, two in Iraq, one in Afghanistan. Had the unusual role of serving as translator and cultural liaison within the unit you commanded, based on your fluency in Arabic and Kurdish –'

'As well as French and German,' Jack interrupted. Blackburn neither looked up, nor seemed to notice the insertion, but Jack bore a certain pride in his linguistic abilities. He'd always considered them among the most useful gifts he'd inherited from his mother.

'Multiple commendations, including a Purple Heart for injuries received near Behsud, Afghanistan, taking hostile fire during a village sweep as part of a peacekeeping sortie. A leg injury that required three months' treatment, and a shrapnel wound within an inch of your left eye.'

'It was nothing,' Jack answered, immediately falling into the standard response he gave when questioned about his battle injuries. 'Others suffered a lot more than I did.' The second part, at least, were words he truly meant.

'Yet it marked you for life.' Blackburn lowered his sheet of paper slightly, inclining his head towards Jack's face, in that single motion drawing attention to what everyone else Jack met did all in their power to pretend they didn't see. The small crescent of a scar ran from just above the edge of his left eyebrow, down towards his temple. All these years later, the skin remained a soft, shiny pink, shaping the wrinkles around it when he smiled.

It had been so long since anyone had asked him about it, the more socially polite thing to do apparently being to pretend they didn't see it at all, that Jack for a moment couldn't think how to reply. Taking the moment for himself, Blackburn returned his eyes to his dossier and continued.

'Remained on active duty, despite the injuries, earning multiple further commendations. Promoted to O-3 classification just over four years ago, gaining the rank of captain and well positioned to make major in record time.

Yet you elected to retire from the Corps only two months later, for reasons listed in the paperwork simply as "personal".'

Jack adjusted his position in the chair, sitting a little taller, his posture more commanding. It was an uncomfortable thing to have his career narrated to him in this manner, particularly as he still did not know the nature of the interview, or of Blackburn Enterprises's interest in him.

'Honourably discharged four years ago,' Blackburn continued. 'A bright and promising military career over, without explanation.'

He looked up again, allowing his eyes to settle on Jack. From his silence, it was clear he was waiting for the explanation the files didn't contain to come from the man himself. There was a touch of impatience to his expression.

'Let's just say I'd seen enough,' Shepherd finally replied, more defensively than he'd intended. 'Spending time in two shattered cultures, all their legends and histories in tatters, with my own country's great ideals becoming less and less infallible, I'd seen plenty. I served honourably and I served with pride. No hard feelings, but enough myths had been shattered.' It was not the whole truth, but it was true enough for the moment.

Thomas Blackburn's eyes softened, the wrinkled skin round his eyes relaxing. It was as if a nagging suspicion had been momentarily relieved.

'That, we might say, is when your life became interesting.'

Blackburn again allowed his stare to linger far longer

than social norms would allow, drawing out the tension. Jack recognized the control technique and made a mental note. *The man has power, and he knows how to wield it to his advantage.* He forced himself to stare back – back into the green eyes of a man who sat comfortably with his authority. Blackburn's skin was creased with age, liver spots occasionally marking his features, but everything about him was immaculately cared for. His skin looked as if it had never gone a day without half Jack's monthly wages in creams sustaining it; his grey hair was perfectly coifed, every strand militantly bound into order with the others. He breathed long, deliberate breaths, and his hands lay entirely relaxed on the arms of his chair, only moving when he brought a well-manicured finger up to flip a page.

'On leaving the military, you took up studies under the post-9/11 GI Bill, earning a two-year master's degree in, of all things, cultural anthropology.'

'Seemed the right thing to do at the time,' Jack offered almost flippantly, before the other man could ask the question. He wanted to know where all this was going before he spent any energy explaining himself.

'And that's what set you up for your big claim to fame.' The dismissiveness was back in Blackburn's tone.

Jack had grown used to people dwelling on the sudden success he'd had two years ago, so the tendency to evasively shrug it off – 'fame' being something with which he was intrinsically uncomfortable – had long since passed. What roused his curiosity at that moment was that the CEO of one of the nation's largest defence contractors seemed more interested in his anthropological work than his military record.

'My success was more of an accident than an accomplishment. A bit of luck that attracted interest, given the subject matter.'

'Now, now, Captain, we both know it was more than that. Immediately following your postgraduate studies, you took your new anthropological interests out for a spin. A research grant right out of the gate, and directly into the realm of controversy. A year after Dan Brown is wowing readers with theories of Freemasonry embedded into British heraldry, you're in the field trying to prove such theories wrong.'

'Not trying,' Jack interrupted. His success was no secret.

Blackburn smiled wryly. 'Quite. No more than three months into your work you successfully refuted what had become one of the most prominent legends in the public consciousness.' He leaned back in his chair. 'Debunking the myth of a Masonic connection to Rosslyn Chapel doesn't happen merely by "accident". You were critical, engaged.'

Rosslyn Chapel in Scotland. Since modern-day Hollywood had re-stoked the public interest in Masonic conspiracy theories, it had become a hotspot of interest well beyond the confined ranks of scholars and specialists. It had been a perfect target for Jack's new interests; and as he had shown, its hype had amounted to little more than a very old, very elaborate hoax.

Jack sat slightly forward. 'I had time, and energy, and happened to be the one to unearth the genealogical record of the chapel's founders that laid waste to a tired conspir-

42

acy theory.' He'd only been starting out in his new field, but it had been a discovery that ignited media interest, and it had transformed Jack from an unknown to a voice whose thoughts on the subject seemed to be of interest to everyone.

Blackburn listened to Jack's answer in silence, then folded his hands across the well-ironed creases that ran down his lap. 'I have one more question for you. Just one more, and then we can get down to business.'

Jack restrained the urge to release the 'at last' that leapt into his mind.

'The world is full of experts,' Blackburn offered. His gaze was now direct, intent and surprisingly stern. 'Next to most of them, your credentials don't amount to much. You're a military man; this cultural stuff is a hobby, though obviously one you've pushed. Still, there are hundreds out there with far more qualifications than you – yet it's you at the forefront.' He stopped, letting his words linger.

'And?' Jack eventually asked. 'What's your question?'

'My question is *why*?' Blackburn almost snapped.

Finally, a portion of this interview-come-interrogation that wasn't just a survey of his past. The question actually made Jack think. He glanced at a small tapestry decorating a portion of wall to the side of Blackburn's desk. The legend of King Arthur, epitomized in a fading cloth rendition of the Round Table. A legend that, over the centuries, had evoked great hope but also profound delusion.

'I am not objective,' Jack finally answered. 'Academics are objective, weighing everything in the balance. That's their prerogative, but not mine. I have an agenda. I think these legends are harmful. I don't doubt, I disbelieve, and I'm able to justify that disbelief with proof, more often than not.'

Thomas Blackburn leaned forward, nodding. He appeared to approve of the answer, despite an air of dislike that Jack noted the man didn't strive hard to conceal.

'It is that, above all else, that has caused us to seek you out.'

'I don't know what my current work could possibly have to do with Blackburn Enterprises,' Jack confessed. 'There's nothing remotely connected to defence activity in my CV since leaving the military.'

'Look around you, Captain Shepherd. There is more to me than just our company's official activities.'

Jack glanced back at the museum that was Thomas Blackburn's office, an ancient breastplate from a suit of armour glistening in the carefully arranged lamplight. He turned back to the man. The gears in his mind were finally starting to turn. 'You've called me in to consult on your . . . hobby?'

Thomas Blackburn smiled, the wrinkles on his face spidering out from his eyes and lips. 'From one hobbyist to another,' he chortled to himself, 'there's something satisfying in that. But no, Jack, I've not called you here for hobbies or pastimes. I've called you in to take part in a mission. One that has, in one way or another, been the object of my whole life.'

Jack's body tensed. He'd left the world of missions behind him, and the two syllables of the once-familiar word now felt foreign and imposing. His face drew taught, defensive. 'Missions are outside my remit,' he answered firmly. 'The "ex" in ex-military isn't negotiable, and I don't appreciate being called out here for concerns that are no longer my own.'

'It's not your Marine background that makes you useful to this particular mission, Captain Shepherd, and I'm not proposing to send you into combat. Your relevance lies in your *current* interests.' Blackburn leaned back, his hands resting on his desk and his eyes as intense as ever.

'I am seeking, in, let us say, a personal capacity, one of the greatest legends ever known to man, and therefore something you won't believe could possibly be true, not even for a moment. And that objectivity is precisely what I, and more specifically, others in my employ, are hoping will help me to find it.'

Blackburn let the moment linger, then reached to his side and slid open one of the drawers of the wooden desk. He lifted an object out with what very nearly amounted to reverence, and shifted to set it on the desk before Jack.

Positioning the item before the former soldier's eyes, Blackburn asked the question that his demeanour suggested he'd been waiting to ask since their encounter had begun.

'Tell me, Jack, what does your historical mind make of this?'

Jack stared at the object, his mind a whirl of renewed confusion.

On the desk sat a folded piece of white cloth, old and stained with what looked to be dirt and ancient traces of blood. And at its centre, an unmistakable mark that Jack had only ever heard about in books or seen in artists' imagined sketchings.

A red cross of two equal-length bars, the ends slightly flared.

The legendary symbol of crusade, and of one group's crusades in particular.

7

Smoke still rose from the pyre as Arnaud de Faulke crossed the Pont des Planches de Milbray to the far side of the Seine, where his mount, tied, fed and watered, was under the care of his squire outside a small inn.

'Ready the horse, Alvain,' he ordered, the small form of the squire rising from a wooden perch at the building's corner, surprised to see his master back so soon. De Faulke walked with his usual slight limp, his right knee never having fully recovered from a battle injury sustained at Acre seven years ago. Most people didn't notice it – de Faulke took great pains, literally, to conceal what others would take as a visible sign of vulnerability – but around his squire he could let down his guard.

'We need to get out of the city immediately,' he continued. 'Obtain enough food and water for at least three days' travel. It will take us that long, perhaps longer.' He reached into a pouch at his waist and extracted a small coin, which he tossed to the other man. He had a very specific journey in mind.

De Faulke's thoughts were in disarray. On waking this morning, he had been convinced that the future was over, at least in terms of their noble fraternity. They had waged a battle against the encroaching arrogance of the Church's leaders for the past decade, but over the preceding ten

47

months each battle had been a losing one. When, a little over three weeks ago, Jacques de Molay had been condemned to burn at the stake, all hope had truly been lost. The last Grand Master, as history this morning had finally deemed him.

But the great man had given de Faulke a gift. His tormented screams from the flames had not been in vain. He had bestowed on the few who remained – Arnaud did not know how many there could still be – what they needed most. Hope.

'A curse upon you all! Mark my words, a great calamity will befall all those who have condemned us to such a death!'

The words rolled through de Faulke's mind like a mantra. He recited them over and over again as he stood in the stinking mud outside the inn, waiting for his squire to return with the foodstuffs for their journey. As they repeated, the words seemed to take on a sacred, prophetic air.

The squire emerged from the wooden building a few minutes later, his rough leather sack bulging with its new contents. He fastened it to the saddle of his own steed, then untied both horses. Interlinking his fingers and kneeling down, he provided a step up for his master.

'Where are we going?' the squire asked a moment later, mounting his own smaller animal. Both horses had been tied up all morning and were brimming with energy.

'We must escape the city first of all,' de Faulke replied. The streets here were far too dangerous, the risk of being recognized a constant concern. 'As soon as we do, we will head towards Troyes.'

'Troyes?' Whether the squire was more startled by the mention of the Grand Master's abandoned private retreat, or the thought of a day-long journey, was difficult to say.

De Faulke tucked himself further into the dirty commoner's coat he'd worn for the past two months. The heavy woollen garment stunk of cooking fires and human sweat.

'A great calamity will befall all those who have condemned us to such a death.'

Jacques de Molay, the man who had been a noble father as well as the Order's greatest leader, could no longer fulfil the curse that the heavens had spoken through his voice. But de Faulke could not escape the feeling that the Grand Master had meant him to hear those words, as much as he'd intended them for the entire crowd at his execution.

'We go to Troyes, Alvain,' de Faulke said to his squire, adjusting his position on the horse and lightly kicking him into motion, 'because the Grand Master died trying to tell us something. And I have every intention of figuring out precisely what it was.'

Outside Troyes, Two Weeks Later

'Let me in there with the key, mi'lord.' A dirty, burly man with broad shoulders and meaty worker's arms stepped forward, extracting an iron key from his pocket.

The door of the estate at Troyes was bolted locked with an oversized clasp on the outside of the door. The Grand Master had cherished the small retreat, a two-storey stone house, well over a century old, far from the centre of Paris. It had been a private sanctuary, nestled in the forested hills, where the great man could pray, think, work.

And keep his secrets.

Arnaud allowed the man with the key to pass. Jacques de Molay had been forced to abandon the estate four years ago, when attacks against the Order had begun to rise to their fiercest pitch and the full measure of his time was required in the capital. He had ordered the building at Troyes sealed, with instructions that none were to be allowed entry until he himself returned. The groundskeeper – a trustworthy man with a teenage son, both of whom were loyal to the Order – had been given the only key and charged with the estate's protection.

They had wept as de Faulke told them of de Molay's demise. A hardened man and a strong son reduced to tears. Their devotion was moving.

'Here you are, sir,' the groundskeeper announced, the heavy bolt unlocked and the door creaking open. 'Watch your step. Floor in this place 'as always been a bit shaky.'

De Faulke went forward. The darkness smelled of must and mould. As his eyes adjusted, the contours of a simple but elegant interior began to appear. A sturdy wooden table. A series of chairs. A painting, strung to the wall, covered with cloth and protected from view. In the midst of these sights, a sudden loneliness crept into de Faulke's heart. The estate had been abandoned as a temporary measure. Everything was left in place for a return that now would never come. For the first time since the Grand Master's execution, even as he stood now, surrounded by other men, de Faulke felt hauntingly, fearfully alone.

'Anything in particular you'd be looking for?' the groundskeeper asked.

'The Grand Master's study,' de Faulke answered, pulling his thoughts back to order. 'And, if there is one, the library.' He needed to find de Molay's notes, his journals – anything that could be of use in determining the true message behind the man's dying words. *A curse.* De Faulke knew the late Grand Master well. He would not have made a threat if it did not have substance.

'They'll be one and the same, them two,' the large man grunted back. 'Top of the stairs, second door on the left.' He motioned towards a wooden stairway at the back of the landing.

'Spent most of his time up there, whenever he was here.' There was a slight quiver to the man's lower lip. 'Shall I show you the way?'

De Faulke patted him on the shoulder. 'I thank you for your loyalty, William, and your kindness.' He looked towards the stairs. 'But now, I need to be left alone.'

8

Blackburn Enterprises, Seattle

Angela's breath hung light and white in the crisp air as she walked across the landscaped gardens between Buildings J and K. Her haste in leaving the office had been a moment of impulse, and she realized as she walked that it was still too early for the normal post-interview lunch to have begun. Thomas Blackburn was nothing if not punctual, and those lunches were universally on the interview schedule for 12.30 p.m. She had another thirty-five minutes before her intended intercept and espionage of Captain Jack Shepherd.

To her left, the windowless hulk of Building H loomed large, its concrete walls brightly reflecting the late-morning sun. Angela pulled the thick wool coat tighter round her and veered on to the connecting path. She had just enough time to check in with Sean and learn how progress from the previous week's expedition was advancing.

The expeditionary head of their research project, who, not coincidentally, was also Thomas Blackburn's son, commanded an entire hangar-like building for his work. It was not that his work was more significant than hers – Sean Blackburn could not function without the data, research and information constantly fed to him from Angela's side of the lot – but even she was ready to admit that his sphere of activity required more . . . space.

Everything from trucks to helicopters to remote drones were at his disposal, at his fingertips for a line of work that most in the company had no idea existed.

'I'm the brains, you're the brawn.' Angela had quipped the clichéd line to Sean as half jest, half testing-the-waters insult in one of the exchanges early on in their working relationship, two years ago. Sean had taken it entirely as a compliment. He had no pretensions of historical acumen or scholarly prowess. He was a young man entirely consumed with adventure, exploration, technology and work in the field. Their partnership had quickly become productive, friendly and efficient.

And Angela had come to know Sean's work ethic well. There was no question in her mind as to where he would be at this moment.

In the solitude of his office, a singular realization resonated comfortably in Sean Blackburn's mind. He had seen these symbols before.

The twenty-seven-year-old man sat hunched over his latest-generation iPad. On its display was an ultra high-resolution photograph of the onyx tablet he had recovered from the pit on Oak Island six days ago.

The rune sequence was unlike any other on earth. Or rather, it was like only one other on earth. The glyphs making up the two lines of encoded text were clearly of a common source to stone G-44, as it had come to be known – one of the multitude of strangely carved rocks that had been located, photographed and preserved on the eastern coast of the island. The stones there had been observed for centuries, though they had only been studied with any seriousness in the early twentieth, and even then they had proved more a curiosity than objects of any generally agreed historical significance. Incomplete Latin inscriptions, even English carved graffiti that had its source in mariner excursions and past explorations, were all ripe for speculation, but none of it interesting enough to have attracted more than local scholarship.

That was until Sean and his team had started to look at it with Angela's help. The runes met her hypothesis for the old encoding – the correct type of orthography, a promising collection of the right genre of symbols – and suddenly the vague curiosity of Oak Island had become their singular point of focus.

The past day had been spent carefully cleaning the stone they had retrieved from the pit, dusting it with gentle, electronically controlled puffs of air and submitting it to a subtle bath of misted water, pH-balanced to cause the least impact to the stone. It shimmered now, as if it had been carved yesterday. The main computer in the laboratory had already taken the high-resolution photo of the runes and broken it apart into individual maps for each character – twenty-four unique symbols, with some of the glyphs repeated to produce the full forty-two-character sequence of the tablet. What was important was sequence: the algorithm that would transform the cryptic symbols into meaningful text. When the inscription had been carved, so many centuries ago, breaking the encryption sequence would have been impossible without a key, and even more modern approaches had proven fruitless. The runes on stone G-44 were a case in point: they had been known about for nearly 200 years, yet had never been decoded.

But medieval man, and even more recent man, had not had the brute-force computing power of the twenty-first century. The supercomputer housed in Sean's purpose-built laboratory had the ability to process data at the sixteen petaflops level – slightly over 16×10^{15} floating-point operations per second, making it one of the fastest in the world, surpassed only by the Cray Titan at Oak Ridge. What was utterly impossible in the past was only a minor inconvenience in the present, that is, if you had an extra hundred million dollars to spare, a fleet of IT wizards and a crew of archaeological specialists at your disposal.

Which, of course, he did. Money was not an issue, and the supercomputer was but one among an arsenal of tools that would go beyond the wildest dreams of most archaeologists or explorers.

That computer worked now, and deep within its enclosed, liquid-cooled core churned through the ancient sequence with lightning speed.

As Angela walked into the hangar that housed Sean's quarters, passing through the double containment doors into the sanitized workspace, she responded with a gasp. The difference of atmosphere inside the controlled environment caused that reaction every time. The exterior air of the Pacific Northwest was cold, always heavy with the weight of the nearby sea and scented with pines and the forest vegetation that surrounded them, but the interior of Sean's laboratory was always kept a precise 78 degrees

Fahrenheit, its humidity a perfectly balanced 24 per cent. The air cycled through a series of purifiers and high-grade filters to remove bacteria and other airborne contaminants, and with them almost all the scents of the outside world.

Angela caught her breath, adjusting quickly, and walked to the far corner of the large concrete expanse. Sean's office was housed behind grey glass, well cleaned and suitably elusive. She tapped on the door and entered without waiting.

'Get anything yet?' she asked, motioning towards the iPad on which Sean's gaze was transfixed.

He looked up, smiled. 'Not yet, but they're working.' He made a swirling motion with his hand, his muscular arms covered, as always, in long, dark sleeves – as if this gesture somehow mimicked the inner activities of the vast supercomputer that sat two storeys beneath them. 'The computer will kick back something before too long.'

Angela took a seat in one of the office chairs. Sean looked the same as ever: the up-and-comer in a world of power and technology. His hair was tousled, whether by design or inattention Angela had never been able to determine, and he wore his long sleeves down to his wrists, as always. On only one occasion had Angela ever caught sight of Sean's bare arms, and she'd quickly surmised the reason for his particular dress sense. Both arms were covered in tattoos. She hadn't seen them long enough to study their subject matter, but at least one girl's name was permanently recorded there. Probably not the image of a serious, studious professional that Sean wanted to broadcast to his colleagues, or his father.

Angela had not been expecting results this early in the day and wasn't frustrated by the lack of new data. She had other things on her mind.

'You know your father's interviewing Jack Shepherd today,' she blurted out, the change of subject abrupt.

'Of course I know,' Sean answered, looking up from the tablet. He had something close to a grin on his face, though he was evidently trying to conceal it. 'And you know I know, since you've been giving me that look ever since I asked my father to bring him in.'

'What look?' Angela screwed up her nose, unhappy with the comment.

'That one,' Sean answered, not bothering to conceal his smile any longer.

'Am I not entitled to be disapproving of all this?' Angela waved off the taunt. 'This is Jack Shepherd, wunderkind of historical sensationalism. I recognize that an outside voice could be of help to us, thinking outside the box and all that creative management hype. But this?'

'Calm down. If it soothes you any, it's not an appointment, it's an interview. We don't know if he'll accept the offer.'

'Of course he'll accept,' Angela countered, shaking her head. 'The man who's glowing in his fifteen minutes of fame will be taken in by the surroundings, the collection, the intrigue – just like I was. Just like everyone.'

Angela wondered, only for a moment, whether she was being too harsh. Jack Shepherd had been in the spotlight for more than just fifteen minutes, and Angela had – though she would never admit it – watched him on a string of History Channel specials and morning-show interviews. 'The Handsome Anthropologist Who Could,' one show had captioned him. Public fascination with the debunking of ancient myths seemed to know no limits, and they soaked it up all the more readily when it was delivered by a man with the looks and charisma of Jack Shepherd.

'He's only in the business for the fame,' she persisted. 'Don't you think that he'll be interested in our project for the same reasons?'

Sean stood up, flipping closed the grey cover of his iPad. 'Maybe. But if that's the motivation it takes to get him working on our side, then so be it.'

Angela sighed. Macho men. She already had to work with one. The thought of another was nearly too much.

'Look, we need another head in the mix,' Sean added. 'You have your beliefs about the Templars, I have mine, my father has his. But Jack Shepherd is a sceptic. A man with abilities, but more importantly, without a theory to push or position to prop up – a man who can look at things just as they are, without baggage or expectation. We're nearing the end of our work. We could use that perspective.'

Angela nearly answered back, but Sean's points weren't without merit. Frustrating, probably fruitless, but not unreasonable.

'Where are you headed?' she asked, noticing Sean drop a few papers and his computer into a leather satchel and reach for a jacket.

'Since I made the staffing request, I get to host the lunch. Add my own grilling to the Jack Shepherd recruitment experience.'

Angela blushed, and Sean noticed. 'What is it?'

'I was planning to crash the lunch. Or at least get a table near by and try to listen in.'

Sean was smiling again. 'Better the enemy you know?' Then, motioning to the door: 'Come with me, and you can grill the man without subterfuge.' He touched her on the shoulder as they exited the room, something awfully close to a bemused wink fluttering at the corner of his left eye. 'We'll see if this man's as awful as you suspect.'

9

Jack's gaze rested for a long time on the folded cloth before he finally raised it, incredulous, to Thomas Blackburn.

'This is authentic?'

'One hundred per cent. It's been date-tested, its provenance confirmed. I can even trace out the lineage of its ownership, if you're interested.'

Jack waved aside the offer. He continued to scrutinize Blackburn's face, his mind trying to piece together what this meant for his visit here.

'If this is as authentic as you say it is,' he continued, 'then based on what you've said, there's only one reason you're showing it to me. You're interested in the group that produced it. You're interested in the Templars.' Jack swallowed hard, not quite able to believe he'd actually just said the last word.

Blackburn only nodded, keeping their gaze connected.

It was Jack who broke it, pushing back into his chair and releasing an exasperated sigh. 'You can't possibly have asked me here for this. It's a waste of my time, and yours.'

'And why is that, Captain Shepherd? I would think that for a man like you, no area of history would be out of the realm of your interest.'

'History, yes, but the Templars? That's the stuff of

insanity – what Umberto Eco called the final terrain of the lunatic. You can't even claim it to be legend . . . most of what's written these days is pure speculation and nothing more.'

'So, let's put aside the idle speculation, Jack,' Blackburn replied, a slight smile at the corners of his dry lips. 'Humour me for the moment. What do you know about the Templars?'

Jack reflected before answering. His morning had gone from mysterious to intriguing to surreal, and it seemed almost impossible to accept that he was sitting here, being queried about the Knights Templar.

'I know what everyone knows about them,' he finally answered.

'And what is that?'

'That they started off as a group of monks charged to protect pilgrims on their way to the Holy Land, but wound up leading the crusades and falling into disrepute.'

'That's a little generalized, even for the sceptic,' Blackburn rebuffed, his accompanying gesture dismissive. 'You can do better.'

Jack sat straighter in his chair. A fair criticism.

'They were founded in AD 1120, if memory serves, by Hugues de Payens, with the name the "Poor Fellow-Soldiers of Christ and of the Temple of Solomon".'

'It was the winter of 1119, for the sake of precision,' Blackburn interjected, but motioned for him to go on.

'They were originally intended to be nothing more than pilgrim guards. Protectors. And they started off their work that way. But the situation in the Holy Land changed, and so did their charter.'

'If by "changed" you mean became more aggressive, then you're right on track.'

'If I remember, it was marauders and thugs that started as the real threat to travellers, not the forces of outsiders.'

'Absolutely,' Blackburn affirmed. 'The Templars were an order of monastic knights precisely because a degree of military ability was required. Pilgrims travelled with belongings and wealth, but little in the way of protection against bandits and thieves, who knew only too well what routes they took towards Jerusalem.'

'But knights were among the best-trained forces in the medieval world.' Jack paused, reflecting. In its initial impulse, the creation of a knightly company dedicated to protecting faithful travellers was a noble idea. 'They would have been the best in protection that an empire could produce.'

'Though they were costly.' Blackburn waved towards the cases filled with armour, swords, shields and other attire. 'The accoutrements of battle come at a price, and the supreme skill of the knighthood at a higher price still. One that weary pilgrims travelling to the sites of Christ's earthly life could never afford.'

Jack stepped in. 'Which is why the Knights Templar were also a religious order, sworn to lives of poverty, in service to the Church's pilgrims.' He paused, his face scanning Blackburn's remarkable collection. When he turned back to face the man, Jack's expression was one of doubt. 'But that poverty was a myth. The Templars were one of the wealthiest groups in human history.'

'Not at first,' Blackburn interjected. 'In the early years

they lived out their ideal of poverty. Though they became known more for the red cross on a white mantle that they wore into battle, the mark of crusade, the actual symbol of the Order was two knights riding a single horse – a sign of poverty, sharing common resources rather than each possessing their own.'

'But how much sharing really went on? It's a noble idea, but history records a different side to the Templars.' Jack searched through his memory, seeking precise details to shore up his point. 'By the end of their existence, the Templars were some of the largest landowners in the world, were they not? With wealth sufficient to fund the rise and fall of empires. There's not much poverty in that.'

The vast wealth and power these 'poor' servants of Christ had accumulated had always been at the core of Jack's mistrust of Templar history.

'If poverty was part of their origin,' he offered, 'it doesn't appear to have been built into their way of life.'

'But it was,' Blackburn countered. He leaned forward on his desk now, his frame lively with enthusiasm. 'The Rule by which the Order was governed laid out strict parameters on possessions, on simplicity of life. Not only were the Knights Templar poor, they were ascetic, strict in their discipline and severe in their renunciation of worldly things. They kept to a daily discipline that began at four a.m., included a full cycle of religious services, and for all but the highest ranks theirs was a life of enclosure. They were not permitted to leave their enclaves, possess or spend money, or interact in social settings.'

'What happened?'

'What always happens,' Blackburn said. 'Whenever influence grows, so do temptations.'

'Temptations. That's a mild word for it.'

'It's the word the Templar chronicles themselves use. Their success on the field led to their expansion, and as their numbers grew, so did their popularity. They required more material resources to accomplish their work, and sponsoring the Templars became all the rage for the Holy Roman Empire's moneyed elite.'

'Material resources?' Jack questioned. 'You make it sound so innocuous.'

'Yes, Captain Shepherd. Initially, the sponsorship they received was directly related to their needs. Knights are expensive: they require horses, armour, squires, lodgings, food – not just for themselves, but also for their animals. Just like modern militaries, Jack. You know from experience how much rear-level support is required to send a squadron of men into combat today.'

Jack reflected back on his time on active duty. For every man on the battlefield there were dozens in research, intelligence, equipment, support, medical, tactical; not to mention the sheer quantity of supplies and equipment a fighting team required.

'It was said that, at the beginning of the Templars' existence, a single knight in battle required seven hundred and fifty acres of land at home in order to finance his missions. By the end of their existence, that number was almost four thousand acres per member. For each knight there were three horses, a squire, at least one sergeant, and perhaps three or four other men in support.' Blackburn spread his hands, gesturing an increasing expanse of involvement and cost. 'And that's before you financed in the need to build castles and fortresses, ships, armour, the fortification of cities and protectorates, and the costs of constructing living and training centres. None of these things are cheap today, and they were not cheap in the days of the Templars.'

Jack ruminated on the details. The figures were reasonable, explicable, but the shift from covering increasing expenses into radical wealth still didn't have a convincing explanation.

'I ask again,' he finally said, 'what precipitated the radical shift in the Order's standing? If the Templars were committed to poverty, if the vast resources funnelled their way by the aristocracy were required to support such extensive tactical work, as you say, then what changed, that they would be brought into the kind of wealth and influence they became known for?'

Blackburn pondered the question a moment, then sat back in his oversized leather chair, clasping his fingers together at his waist.

'Two factors. Practical ingenuity, and discovery.'

Jack waited. Comments that brief, made by men such as Thomas Blackburn, were always prefaces to something more.

'As to the first,' Blackburn continued, 'that's something for another conversation. But it's the latter, I think, that really strikes up your interest. And your ire.'

'My ire?'

'That ire against myth and legend that you're so keen to push. Because what I'm referring to is the discovery of something very specific.'

Jack immediately recognized where Blackburn was going. Where every Templar enthusiast ultimately went. Where countless wasted hours of research and popular books always wandered; where the insanity of legend always ended up.

The next six words out of Blackburn's mouth confirmed the point and caused Jack's stomach to sink.

'I'm talking about the Templar treasure.'

10

Blackburn Enterprises

There is no Templar treasure. There never was. It's a myth of the imagination. A lie. At best, a nonsense, and an idiot's game to put any stock in it.

Jack Shepherd's thoughts pulsed loudly, his frustration threatening to overtake the interest that he could not deny was present in the bizarre material Thomas Blackburn had shared with him. Curious though it was, it was a waste of his time. Foolishness, even if in the hands of a man of great power and wealth. Jack was not exactly an important man, but he did have priorities on his time and energies – and he didn't like them being wasted.

He walked the neatly groomed footpaths slowly, without enthusiasm, unsure whether he was really up for the lunch meeting that came next on the agenda. The pathway led from Building K to Building E, which housed the Blackburn Enterprises corporate social grounds, including the Peaks Grill at which the 12.30 lunch was scheduled to take place. More details, he'd been told, would be made clear to him throughout his visit.

A visit orchestrated to draw me into something that still has no obvious connection to this place. He looked around him. In the massive hangar-like structures that dotted the enclosed, hilly compound, the latest in satellite-guided nuclear cruise missiles were developed, the high-tech drones that operated over hostile combat zones – and now over US civilian territories – were conceived, crafted and tested; and these were just a few of the obvious technologies he knew about. Even with his military background, Jack couldn't imagine what secretive new developments were being designed behind these walls.

But Blackburn's personal interests aren't in secrets. They're in nonsense.

A man like Thomas Blackburn talking of Templar treasure seemed too surreal to take seriously. An executive with billions at his disposal, consumed with a myth that, even if it were not the stuff of conspiracy-minded dreamers, couldn't possibly amount to more material wealth than Blackburn already had. And yet he wanted it, and wanted Jack on the team he was funding to find it.

But what was harder to believe was that Jack found himself actually considering the offer. That was frustrating in its own right. Jack Shepherd was a rational man: educated, experienced, driven. Why was it that he couldn't seem to curb his interest in . . . everything? That he couldn't stop his mind from being drawn towards the unknown, even if the unknown was so obviously mythology, without substance? Jack was as annoyed with himself as he was with Blackburn.

Nevertheless, the old man had been right about one thing: Jack harboured an abiding dislike for the myths that moved people in odd directions – and if ever such a myth fitted that bill, this was it. Cultic fascination with the Templars had inspired Masonic foundations that continued, in the present day, to indoctrinate tens of thousands across the world. The same curiosity had grounded countless religious sects that attempted to recreate the Templars' 'glorious past', leading the unwary into ever darker circles of secrecy and back-room dealings.

A myth, yes, but a myth with power – and not a power for good. The fascination with Templar *treasure* was the real gem in the crown of the conspiracy theorist. With no justification other than a great question that had no answer, the myth had begun. The question that fuelled it was the same as Jack's query to Thomas Blackburn – how did the 'Poor Fellow-Soldiers of Christ' wind up in a position of unparalleled wealth and power? – and it was ultimately the lack of a satisfying historical answer to the question that had given birth to the tantalizing legend of treasure.

Surely, wealth like that could not have come by normal routes, the standard arguments went. *And as wealthy as a group might become, the power to influence kings and even the pope goes beyond any standard degree of richesse, power or might. No, the Templars must have found something – something important, something significant, something radical enough in the implications of its discovery that the highest rulers in the land were willing to bow and scrape before its possessors ever after.*

Of course, just what that 'something' was depended entirely on the theorist one asked. For some, it was the Ark of the Covenant, buried beneath the Temple Mount and discovered by the knights on their first victorious crusade. For others, it was the Holy Grail, the chalice of the Last Supper. For the more radical, or at least the more liberal, it was proof that Jesus had not really risen – his bones discovered in a secret vault, 'proving' that he had not been the ascendant Messiah. For others, it was proof that Jesus had married, had a family, had children . . . in any case, it was something explosive enough that popes and princes would give the Templars nearly unmitigated power in order to ensure their silence.

Jack sighed. *Maybe they had found evidence that the moon landing was faked.* It seemed to him just as likely as the other speculations.

Yet Thomas Blackburn, a man whose sanity and mental acumen no one could seriously doubt, was willing to fund the search for this 'treasure' to the tune of millions of dollars, and was willing to pay Jack a retainer that exceeded what he was likely to make over the next twenty years of his usual employment, even if Jack's stated belief was that such a treasure didn't exist, never existed, and was purely a myth that men used to give historical shape to their ignorance, greed and lust for power.

It made no sense. But then, few things intrigued Jack Shepherd more than a situation that simply didn't add up.

Suddenly, a voice broke through his reverie. 'You look like a man who can't believe what he's just heard.'

Jack looked up from the stone path. Before him stood a man, somewhere in his late twenties, dressed far more casually than most of the others in the complex. At his side was a woman of immediately striking features, though she wore an expression that was less than overtly welcoming.

'You must be Captain Jack Shepherd,' the man continued, smiling, holding out his right hand. 'I'm Sean Blackburn, son of the boss. This is Angela Derby.' He motioned to the woman, then quickly turned aside as his mobile phone began to ring. Before the introductions were even complete, Jack and the woman called Angela were left standing together, alone.

'Pleased to meet you,' Jack said, reaching out to shake her hand. 'But it's Mister now, not Captain.'

'We're here for the high point of your interview,' Angela Derby answered through a smile that Jack couldn't identify as sincere or forced. 'Lunch.'

She smiled again, and Jack tried to take stock of the woman standing before him. This was no ditzy receptionist with flirtation issues, that much was immediately obvious. Not that she wasn't beautiful in her own right – light brown hair that fell straight to the collar of her thick coat, green eyes that seemed to sparkle in the outside light. But she was more than just pleasant to look at. Something about Angela Derby breathed confidence, intelligence and a surprising degree of command for someone Jack assumed couldn't be more than about thirty years old. Her eyes seemed to probe him, and Jack felt, to his surprise, the slightest tinge of intimidation.

'You had a productive morning?' Angela asked, the cold air causing a slight clouding of her breath in the space before her lips, where Jack's attention was inexplicably drawn.

'Interesting,' he answered, forcing his eyes back to hers. 'I won't pretend I don't have questions to ask.'

Angela's mouth began to open, ready to invite him to be frank, and Jack's mind was already formulating his first question. But neither had a chance to act on their impulse. The tone of their banter was about to change.

'Your questions are going to have to wait.' Sean Blackburn cut into their conversation, turning back from his

71

call, his face broadcasting excitement and urgency. 'And so is lunch.'

He pocketed his phone and passed a glance to Angela. Her brow was raised, and Jack took note of the immediate change in her demeanour. Both she and Sean had the appearance of individuals who were expecting something, something dramatic. The anticipation was bare and unconcealed.

'They've got it,' Sean announced to her. 'The computer's done.'

The anticipation on Angela's face changed to a unique mix of wonder and joyful relief. For reasons he didn't fully understand, Jack felt himself growing anxious, almost excited, at the exchange.

'Got . . . it?' he questioned.

Sean turned to face him. He looked every bit as excited as Angela, and conveyed it without her quiet restraint. For an instant, the son of Thomas Blackburn, who obviously held clout in the firm, looked like a beaming teen at Christmas.

'Impossible to explain, Mr Shepherd,' he said with a knowing, conspiratorial smile. 'This is something you're going to need to see for yourself.'

11

'Get them locked up in the basement, then get the cameras live.' Commander Parker, the man who had led what was known internally simply as 'the retrieval' ordered the other two men briskly, then moved off into the kitchen and began removing the black garments they'd donned for the mission.

The little house on Atlantic Street had been chosen for its quiet location. Fully detached, in a poorer district where neighbourhood watches were 'something the rich folk did' and police security patrols as welcome as foreign invaders.

The other two men pulled the terrified girls down the steep set of stairs without ceremony. Anna, aged seven, and Bella, aged four, were still in their nightgowns, which were covered in kittens and unicorns and fluffed to a child-appropriate degree of cotton cosiness, but the additions to their attire made the nature of their situation clear. A strip of duct tape covered each girl's mouth, and their hands had been bound behind their backs with vinyl restraints. Their feet were bare, and their captors didn't pay any attention to the fractured wooden steps that burrowed splinters of old wood into their soft skin.

'Get back there,' one of the men said, shoving Anna with far more force than was required as she came off the stairway on to the cold concrete floor. The girl tripped into a small room at the back of the basement and her sister was pushed in after her.

The walls had been padded with thick, grey-coned foam padding – a simple yet effective means of sound-proofing. There were no beds, only piles of blankets and a pillow in two of the corners.

And two chains, each fixed to the wall by sturdy iron fastenings.

A moment later, the vinyl had been removed from Anna's wrists, then a steel clasp fastened round her ankles and attached to one of the chains. Before a minute had passed, the same had been done to her terrified sister.

The two girls were shackled to their new surroundings – captive, hidden from the world by sight and sound.

'Leave the tape on, for now,' one of the captors muttered to the other, nodding towards the girls' mouths. No point in risking the sound-proofing with energetic screams. Let them wallow a bit, get tired out from it all.

'You just get the cameras on,' the other man answered back. The taller of the two exited the room, and within a few moments three video cameras went live.

'We're recording,' he shouted from outside the walls.

The other man looked at the two girls, chained and crumpled in their respective corners of the small space, mouths covered but eyes wide, horrified, streaming with tears.

'Be good, girls,' he said, smiling a perverse smile. 'Daddy's going to look out for you.'

Five minutes later, the three men were assembled together upstairs. Parker had already changed back into normal

74

clothes and the other two were making ready to follow suit.

'Are we transmitting?' one of them asked.

'Only recording. Delivery will come in person.'

'Better that way,' the third man said, pulling off a sweaty black jumper. He threw it into a corner, followed by the black T-shirt beneath. He grabbed a white button-down shirt from a hook near by and began changing back into the business attire they all normally wore.

'When?' the second man asked.

'As soon as the Grand Master directs.' The leader sat at the monitor, watching the two girls in black and white. The older tried to reach out to hug the other, but the chains were too short. Physical contact was not possible. A little feature he'd thought up himself.

With a situation like this, paternal cooperation would be an absolute guarantee.

As his mind worked, his fingers passed over the small pin in his jacket lapel, its red cross barely shimmering in the kitchen light.

12

Fewer than five minutes after their outdoor meeting and the abandonment of their intended lunch at the Grill, Sean, Jack and Angela arrived at Building H and passed into the vast expanse of Sean's home turf.

'Welcome to my domain,' he said dramatically, gesturing to the bustle around him. At least a dozen workers were stationed at independently clustered workstations throughout the concrete and steel space, amidst a collection of what were obviously remarkable technological resources. Machinery that Jack had never seen before sat alongside computer terminals and work tables, surrounded by everything from small tactical four-by-four vehicles to a full-blown military helicopter, its rotors folded towards its tail, in the far corner of the hangar.

'My father will have told you about his aims,' Sean continued, beckoning Jack further into the space. 'We're the ones who try to accomplish them. And you're here because we want you to join us.'

Sean didn't allow Jack to respond before pressing forward. 'Our project is divided into two teams. Mine is responsible for tactical and expeditionary work – the digs, site research, exploration, that sort of thing. Angela's team is in charge of the research.'

'What sort of research?'

'Interpretive, theoretical,' she answered. 'Historical background on the Templars.'

'In short,' Sean cut in, 'Angela's team figures out where we need to go, what we need to look for, and mine is in charge of making sure we get there and find it.'

Jack took it all in, surprised by the expansiveness of the project. Thomas Blackburn's words had been historical and theoretical. What Jack was witnessing now was evidence of a vast infrastructure set on making those theories real. When Jack had delved into the history of the Freemasons in Scotland, the only 'team' he'd had at his disposal had been the regular weekday troop of librarians at the British Library, and his 'expedition' to Rosslyn Chapel had been a weekend road trip in a hire car with a scratch pad of hand-written notes and a few ideas. This, this was something altogether different. He wasn't sure, but he was nearly certain that the table to his left contained a portable ground-penetrating radar device.

'And?' he asked, more on impulse than by plan.

'And?'

'And if you're in charge of helping your father trace out Templar history, of "making sure things get found", what have you found? I'm going to take it as a given you haven't found the treasure your father's so eager to locate.'

Sean grinned. 'Not yet, but we're close. I can feel it. We've had successes in other areas.'

'What sort of successes?'

'That, my new friend, is precisely why we're here.'

Sean led Jack and Angela deeper into the complex, past

a small dividing screen into an enclosed area set apart from the larger-scale activities. The expanded cubicle had various pieces of technology round its edges, and at its centre a large table, meticulously cleaned. Atop it was a large glass case, twice the size of an average fish tank, in which a small object sat perched on a felt stand.

'This, Jack, is what we've found.' Sean motioned towards the case and drew him in close. The object on the stand was an oblong piece of black stone, highly polished and in excellent condition. Its upper surface contained two lines of strange symbols Jack did not recognize. They appeared to have been etched into the stone, then filled in with white paint to make the markings stand out.

Jack had been quick to dismiss Thomas Blackburn's interests as a mad idea less than half an hour ago, but this was obviously more than theory.

'What am I looking at?'

'This stone was buried in a small chamber fifty feet beneath ground level on Oak Island in Nova Scotia,' Sean answered, 'in a pit that included traps and obstacles that had to be carefully overcome before we could get to its base.'

'Oak Island?' Jack remembered hearing of some tangential connection of the place to broader Templar lore, but couldn't place the details.

'We've been digging there for the past eighteen months, at Angela's direction, though we finally laid claim to this only six days ago.'

'The island has been attached to Templar tradition for at least two centuries,' Angela cut in. 'It's one of the main sites associated with the hypothesis that some Templars, after the Order was disbanded by Pope Clement V in 1312, travelled north to Britain and Scotland, then westward across the Atlantic.'

'But I thought people had been digging on Oak Island for decades?' Jack questioned, some of the details he'd heard before returning to him. 'Didn't they name the main dig the "Money Pit", thinking the Templar treasure itself might be buried there?'

'The idea that the Templars would have travelled so far, just to bury their treasure in the mud of an island, is absurd,' Angela countered. 'People are far too gullible, and the Money Pit has yielded nothing since it was discovered, except for one fact: that the Templars definitely visited the island, and they definitely did create pits in which *something* was buried.'

'But it wasn't the treasure?' Jack pronounced the last word of his question with evident distaste.

'No,' Sean answered flatly. 'It was this.'

'And *this* is?' Jack asked again.

'We believe it's a set of instructions. Guidance towards the treasure's true location.'

'What makes you think that?'

'Because we know these markings, these runes, are related to the symbols on another stone found on the island – a stone that's been known about for years, lying on its surface.' Sean went to a desk at the side of the cubicle and produced a photograph of a rock, on which was a set of symbols, obviously similar to those on the black slab before them.

Jack merely stared at the runes, his mind utterly uncomprehending.

ᐁᐯᚷᐊᐱ ᐯ∴ᐃ ᛏ:ᒪᚷᐅ ᐃᐅᚷ
ᛏ∴ᒪᒪ∴ᚷᚷ ᚋᚷᛏᚷᗝᚋ ∙ᚥ∶ ᛏᛏᚥ∴∶ᗝ

'That's the so-called cover stone of Oak Island, which has been photographed and out in the public realm for decades,' Sean explained, allowing Jack to linger on the image.

'So you're dealing with samples written in some kind of runic language?'

'It's another language, yes,' Angela answered, 'but it isn't runic. The text behind what you're seeing is written in Latin.'

Jack stared at the photograph. Latin this obviously was not, but the confidence of Angela's words left him with little doubt that she and Sean must have found a way to read Latin through whatever he was looking at.

'So these runes are a cipher? Some sort of encryption system?'

'Precisely,' Angela answered. 'At first, no one knew what they were, but the symbolism of the individual glyphs was our first sign of a Templar connection. Look closely.' She pointed to the photograph. 'That small symbol is obviously a cross. That one is a Hebrew *aleph* – remember, the Templars were guardians of the Holy Land, where Hebrew has never fully given way to other tongues. That one has three dots, an indication of the Trinity. That one has two, indicating the human and divine natures of Jesus Christ.'

Jack scrutinized the image. The symbols could certainly be the sort to resonate with a Christian monastic order.

'Once we had a concrete Templar connection,' Angela continued, 'it didn't take long for us to realize what we were really looking at. The Templar banking cipher.'

Jack peered up from the photo. The technology Angela was referring to was mentioned in most history books. As a theory.

'A banking cipher. I know it's been speculated about by scholars,' he said. 'There's always been rumour that the Templars were essentially responsible for inventing the banking and lending system as we know it.'

'And that was something they needed to protect,' Sean said.

'And that's, that's this cipher?'

'It's long been believed,' Angela answered, 'that the Templars developed a code that allowed them to pass instructions through couriers across vast distances. The code was meant to keep the contents secure, as well as reassure the recipients that they were authentic and hadn't been modified along the way.'

'An instruction to provide the bearer with a hundred gold coins isn't going to be honoured if the instruction might have been for ten and the bearer had just scratched in an extra zero on his way to the Holy Land,' Sean noted.

Jack looked to Angela. 'But the Templar encryption system is hypothetical. You think this is actually it?'

'I'm absolutely certain,' she answered. 'Because we've been able to crack it.'

The surprise on Jack's face was hard to conceal. An ancient means of encryption had not only apparently passed from speculation to reality in front of his eyes, but two individuals whom he wanted more than anything to believe were involved in an extended bout of nonsense and were claiming to have broken it.

'My side of the project was instrumental in the crack,' Sean interjected. 'Two storeys beneath us is a company-built supercomputer, one of two that we have on site. Though we didn't have a key that we could use to decode the text, we did have a computer capable of a brute-force approach.'

Jack understood the terminology. In the absence of a password or decryption key, a powerful enough computer could launch a 'brute-force attack', which amounted essentially to guessing combinations until one that worked was found. An impossible feat for any human – even a simple four-digit PIN number, without any encryption at all, posed 10,000 combination options, whereas even only slightly complex algorithms raised this very quickly into trillions and quadrillions – but supercomputers whose processes-per-second capabilities were described with numbers followed by fifteen or even sixteen zeroes presented an entirely different set of possibilities.

'Though even that would probably not have been enough,' Sean continued, 'if Angela hadn't been able to provide us with some data about how the Templars originally encoded their material.'

'From the few sources that mention their equipment,' Angela stepped in, 'we know they used some sort of box with four rotatable dials. No one ever saw the interior, but we have one existing sketch of the exterior, which shows a series of levered input points and interconnecting gear works.'

'Not enough to recreate anything, of course,' Sean added, 'but it was enough to allow our computer to generate some virtual models of how their encryption algorithm might have worked – or at least to set some operational parameters based on the observable means of input. Some limits to how far and wide it had to search in its brute-force attack.

'It took almost three months of fairly constant computation, but the code on the cover stone from the island's surface was finally broken.' Sean allowed a pause, the suspense coming naturally. 'It was an instruction.'

He handed Jack another sheet of paper. The runes from the photograph ran along the top. Beneath them, a line of text in English. 'Between the two hillocks, seventy paces from the bay, thirty-five cubits deep.'

'The decoded text was in Latin,' Angela reminded. 'What you've got there is our translation.'

Suddenly, the pieces were fitting together in Jack's mind. 'This instruction. It was to another pit on the island. The pit that contained – that.' He motioned towards the glass case at the centre of the table. The onyx tablet shimmered in the blue light.

'Exactly,' Sean answered. 'We located the position the text indicated, then dug down thirty-five cubits, which translates to roughly fifty feet. It took a hell of a lot of doing, but we got there.'

Jack was amazed, despite himself. He motioned again to the black stone tablet. 'What does it say?'

Sean grinned. 'Question of the hour, my friend, question of the hour.'

'Since we still don't have a decryption key,' Angela

added, 'we have to decode this text the same way as the other: by brute force.'

'We'd thought it might come through later today, but, well, we interrupted lunch for a reason.'

The words weren't out of Sean's mouth before a young man, whose T-shirt looked at least a generation older than he did, entered the room and held out a sheet of paper. Sean snatched it up eagerly.

A moment later, he was staring up at Jack, a broad smile in his eyes.

'I know you said you had questions, Jack, but before we get to those, how would you like to read a text that hasn't been seen since the days of the Templars themselves?'

13

'Thou didst kneel a commoner. Thou risest now a knight.'

The sword that lay upon Michael Wyatt's shoulder seemed to bear down on him with more than merely the weight of the ancient tempered steel. Resting on the plain shoulder of his contrastingly contemporary garment was the weight of history – a force that, at this moment, had become tangible. It pressed into him, almost taking possession.

The blade rested on the beige cloth of his shirt only a moment before being lifted and transferred to his other shoulder.

The second touch, and it was finished.

Wyatt's breathing caught and halted, the significance of the moment literally taking his breath away. As the ceremonial sword was lifted off his shoulder, he knew his life had been forever changed. He was twenty-six, single, pure, dedicated. And he was well exercised in the most important virtue of the new ranks: devotion. His was limitless. By being taken up into an enclave that had been held at bay for centuries, becoming one of its restorers – it was where all his devotion culminated.

'You are ennobled; you are given the heavenly charge,' the Seneschal of the New Order continued, handing the sword away. His voice was as sombre and serious as his face, on which two bushy eyebrows stood watch over sunken, jade-green eyes. 'Rise, then, Sir Michael.' The eyes motioned a subtle reinforcement of the command.

He started. 'Michael' sounded just as foreign to his ears as 'sir'. He'd been Mike as far back as memory reached, and his sturdy, bulky build and cleanly shaved head hardly warranted the extra syllable that his mother had insisted made his name sound 'like something close to respectable'. But, then, this was the most formal, most respectable moment of his life. If ever there was a time to embrace that extra syllable of formality, this was it.

He rose from his knees. *Sir Michael Wyatt.* He stood a good two inches taller than the Seneschal, but the senior man easily commanded the greater authority. It was an authority to rival the Grand Master's own.

'Your knighthood is a new birth.' His green eyes burrowed into Michael's. 'A new baptism into a new life. As a sign of this commitment and heavenly benediction, receive the garment of your noble rank.'

Another man, scrawny with weasel-like features and mousy hair, stepped to his side and handed him a carefully folded vestment of bright cloth. The Seneschal unfolded it and draped it over Michael's shoulders.

The mere sight of it caused his breath to falter once again. *The white alb. At the centre of both sides, covering the chest and back, a bold, red cross.*

He, a new knight, was draped in the garment men had not worn for centuries, and he wore it not as a costume or memorial, nor as a sign of his own glory. He was one of them now, and their motto was his: '*Non nobis Domine, non nobis, sed nomini tuo da gloriam.* Not to us, Lord, not to us, but to Thy name give glory.'

'You have taken up the Cross.' The proclamation sounded like a heavenly report – the same words that the old knights had heard as they had left for Jerusalem, as they had taken up the mantle of crusade, all those centuries ago.

Yet not everything was the same. The Seneschal reached out a gloved hand. 'Now, take it off.' He motioned for Michael to remove the precious white garment.

'The next time you wear it will be in your grave.'

The New Order drew together as a whole infrequently, but when it did the knights gathered with gravity and solemnity. Particularly when a chapter gathering was called for the Charter Hall, where the documents that governed their lives were inscribed on ten granite panels that lined the plush space like shrines to a heavenly power – or, more poignantly, like the slabs of stone on which Moses was said to have received the commandments of the law directly from God. Their law, too, was divine in origin, and when the knights met in the revered space, they were made to remember that fact in potent terms.

'It is time to determine the will of God.' The Seneschal spoke firmly, his sturdy voice filling the room. His hand, wrinkled with age, fingernails well trimmed yet turning a slight yellow at the edges, gently tapped on the sword that lay flat on the table before him. The sign of office was required by their Rule to be visible at every convocation.

'Amen!' came a booming unison reply. The old iron and

crystal chandeliers that hung in dual rows from the ceiling shook slightly at the thunder of their cry.

No crusade was ever to begin without a royal charter. From the day of the Order's founding to its fall and later hidden history, not once had a sacred mission been launched by the fraternity without the clear determination of the will of God, manifest in a charter from His legate on earth. Nor would that tradition be broken today.

'Brother,' one of the most senior knights spoke, 'tell us what the Master has determined.'

The chief knights of the Order sat round the U-shaped table according to rank, the Seneschal at the centre. Each man wore a black suit, outwardly indistinguishable from the run-of-the-mill politicians, economic leaders or rank-and-file businessmen of the modern world outside. Only the tiniest of lapel pins, enamelled in the sign of the Order, marked them out in any way; and even that could easily be explained away – should anyone chance to express curiosity – as a simple signet of Christian devotion. Just like the crosses, taus or triangles that garnished countless thousands of lapels the world over.

Yet to those who knew, so very different.

Before the leadership table sat the collected ranks of the Order in sixteen straight rows of armless chairs. Over 150 men in total, each crested with the nobility of a knighthood that was among the most significant in all of human history.

'The Grand Master has seen into the darkness of our day,' the Seneschal answered, his green eyes slowly passing over the ranks before him, 'and has prayed for the Lord's will to be revealed.' The Grand Master was a figurehead, a leader by legend more than action. But these were the men in whom the New Order had its true life, and next to God's and the Grand Master's, no voice held more authority for its members than that of the Seneschal.

'The Grand Master has heard the divine voice?' The question came from another of the senior knights. None below the highest ranks dared speak at such a convocation, though they sat and listened with an attention that was almost electric in the sacred air.

'As so often before,' the Seneschal answered. 'And that voice leads us still towards our sacred goal.'

'The aim is pure? Righteous?'

The Seneschal turned his head slowly until it faced his brother knight squarely. His knuckles rested on the table top, his shoulders a firm support for his scowl.

'Are not the ways of God always so?'

Silence. A slow nod of pious agreement.

The Seneschal turned back to the gathered assembly.

'In our glory days, brethren, God's pious king would have given charter to our action. But the days of such governance are long behind us, and our Rule mandates that when no king may deliver God's will in righteousness, our Order itself must give it concrete form.'

'We are gathered, then, to nominate a charter?' one of the knights asked, though all knew that was precisely why they had been assembled.

'Amen,' the Seneschal answered.

'Amen!' thundered back the seated knights.

'And this charter . . . what shall it be for?' the questioner continued.

The Seneschal closed his eyes. They greying tufts of

eyebrow above them pursed together, deep lines making valleys of his forehead.

When he spoke, his eyes opened hard and firm.

'That for which our Order is always ready to shed its blood.' He paused. 'We seek a charter for war.'

14

Blackburn Enterprises, Seattle

Angela snatched the sheet of paper from Jack's grasp with an anxious impatience. He hadn't had a chance to do anything more than glance at the single line of Latin written across it in pencil before she'd grabbed it, and he found himself wondering what she must be feeling as she gazed at the surprisingly short text. If she and Sean were right, a remarkable amount of work had gone into keeping these words concealed in the past, and even more into revealing them in the present. But in the end, the line of pencilled text looked so simple, so . . . ordinary.

Angela's lips moved rapidly as she softly recited the text to herself over and again, appearing to run through the translation possibilities mentally as she went. There it was, Jack noted – that focus, that concentration, those signs of acumen and intensity that instantly made her intriguing. Jack took in the look of determination on her face, the way the whole room – the whole world – seemed to disappear from her attention as she concentrated. The tinge of intimidation Jack had felt at their first encounter returned.

He looked towards Sean. 'Your people couldn't translate it?' It suddenly struck Jack as curious that a team with supercomputers at their disposal and undoubtedly degrees from some of the finest universities in the world hadn't been able to manage a single line of Latin.

'We've got a translation,' Sean answered, 'but Angela likes to have things raw, to read them herself.' Jack couldn't tell whether Sean's expression was one of respect or mild annoyance.

Angela didn't seem to hear. She maintained her concentration a few moments longer, and then finally her head rose. She looked more puzzled than before she'd begun.

'What is it?' Jack finally asked. 'Doesn't the text translate?'

Angela was already shaking her head. 'There's nothing complicated about the text. It translates as, "To Henry's donation, and the tiered palace of the lord of the dance."'

Jack stared back in silence, biting down the urge to say something sarcastic. But he wasn't superhuman.

'The . . . lord of the dance?' he finally exhaled, incredulousness standing substitute for sarcasm. He turned to Sean, his face a question mark. Visions of dancing Irishmen performing to pop-refashioned folk music flashed through his mind.

'That's what we got, too,' Sean answered, matter-of-factly. He passed Jack a notepad on which the same rendering had been written out by hand. Jack read through it a few times. He wasn't surprised when he raised his gaze and saw frustration on Sean's face.

'It's not what we were expecting,' the multi-billionaire's son said flatly. 'The runes from the stone on the surface provided clear instructions. Where to go, reference landmarks, how deep to dig.' He sighed. 'We were expecting something similar from this. Counting on another set of directions.'

'These *are* directions,' Angela cut in, her tone at once energetic. Both men stared back at her.

'Of a sort,' she continued, stepping forward to the desk and laying her copy of the Latin text before them. '"To Henry's donation, and the tiered palace of the lord of the dance" – they may not be as clear as "Between the two hillocks, seventy paces from the bay", but these are directions all the same. I'm certain of it.'

'Explain.' Sean snapped the command with a mixture of impatience, frustration and optimism, and immediately offered an expression of regret for the harshness of it, signalling a more gentle prod with a push of his shoulders.

Angela turned full-face to Jack.

'Since you're here with a history background, take the first phrase, "To Henry's donation". What does that mean to you?'

Jack shrugged. 'It could mean almost anything.'

'No,' Angela rebuffed, 'not if you're thinking like a Templar. Put yourself in their place a moment. Which Henries stand out to you?'

Jack rubbed at the small scar above his left eye as he thought. Then, suddenly, the name clicked into place. A Henry who, according to the history books, had been key in offering support to the Templars in their foray into England and the north. The image of an old oil painting conveying his figure, produced in cheap photo reproduction in one of Jack's history textbooks, coalesced into his memory.

'Henry II,' he announced. 'The king.'

'Exactly!' Angela's face became brighter. 'King of England in the second half of the twelfth century. Now think about his reign, his influence. What would have stood out in the memory of the Templars, some 150 years later?'

'Henry II was the king that endowed the Templar church in London,' Jack answered, the fact well known to anyone who had studied the history, or, for that matter, anyone who'd been on a ten-pound tour of London tourist stops. 'The Temple Church, as it's known now, which still stands. One of the finest and most accessible examples of Templar presence.'

'"Henry's donation" in concrete form,' Angela confirmed.

'In England?' Sean asked.

Jack turned to him. 'The Temple Church in central London was built as the first permanent home of the Templars in England, only a few decades after the founding of the Order. It was modelled after the Round Church of the Holy Sepulchre in Jerusalem, whose patriarch came to England to consecrate it.'

'It was nearly destroyed in the Second World War,' Angela added, 'but the restoration works since have kept a great deal of the original structure, especially at its lower levels.'

'There's nothing quite like it anywhere else in the modern world. Even the other Templar churches and keeps that have survived hold nothing to its unique structure and history.' Jack found his own excitement growing and turned back to Angela. 'Your tablet seems to be pointing you to a very clear objective. Though I don't know what the second half of its inscription is supposed to mean.'

'Neither do I,' she admitted, 'but I have a suspicion that the answer lies somewhere within the Order's London temple.'

There followed a brief pause, broken by the sudden burst of Sean's voice. 'Thirteen hours,' he announced.

'Excuse me?' Jack asked.

'That's how long it will take to get us to London, figuring in booking and transportation on this end.' He paused a moment to finish his mental calculations. 'We could be there by morning.'

'You're going to England? Now? Just like that?' The speed of action surprised Jack.

'It's where this points, so it's where we're going,' Angela answered.

'The only question,' Sean added, gazing back at Jack with a smile that broadcast a foregone conclusion, 'is whether I'm booking two tickets, or three.'

I 5

US Capitol, Washington, DC

The transition from comfort to terror happened in an instant. It was a terror that US Senator Preston Wilcox had never known could exist, but one that tore into him and gripped him entirely.

The uninvited man had entered his office casually, Senator Wilcox's open-door policy for constituent visits a well-known standing practice. The visitor had waited patiently in the lobby until Preston's secretary had beckoned him in, then the man had politely spoken his thanks, shaken the senator's hand at the desk and taken his seat opposite him as the door slid quietly closed behind them.

He had worn a warm smile, every gesture and trapping professional.

'What can I do for you, sir?' Preston had asked, his own smile broad and every ounce of political warmth he could muster on full display. There was an Arkanasas tinniness to his voice that he'd never been able to eradicate, but he'd learned to soften it with long, drawn vowels and an unceasing smile from the first day he'd entered into politics.

'I won't take much of your time,' the man answered. He had not introduced himself, but that was not unusual. Visitors often forgot themselves in the majesty of the

Capitol, especially when standing face-to-face with a true-to-life forger of laws and shaper of the nation's future. The man would get to it eventually.

He opened the flap of a leather briefcase and extracted a small laptop. 'Do you mind if I show you something, Senator?'

'Not at all.' An unusual way to begin, but nothing really surprised Preston. He'd only been in Washington two years, but already he'd learned to expect everything and nothing. He swept aside a few photo frames and desk ornaments to make room for the man's computer.

A moment later, the laptop was illuminated and swivelled to face him. The visitor said nothing more, simply hit the space bar and a video file pre-loaded on the computer started to play.

And that was it – the moment of transition, when Preston Wilcox's world slipped away and terror replaced every other emotion.

The face frozen on the screen was his wife's, and at the man's key press it moved into life. She was on their bed, in their bedroom. Her eyes were wide, overcome with fear, as she pushed herself backwards against the headboard and gripped at the bed sheet. A whimper came from the speakers.

'What the hell is this?' Preston asked, his voice faltering at the sight but his eyes locked on the screen.

'I would advise you just to watch,' the man answered.

Preston couldn't move, couldn't breathe, couldn't believe what he was seeing. His wife was being accosted, filmed, terrorized.

'*Tell me your name.*' A voice spoke from out of frame,

somewhere to the left of the cameraman. Beth's eyes batted towards the voice, then slightly downwards.

And then Preston could see what she saw. At the bottom of the screen, a gloved hand came into view. It held a gun, complete with suppressor, aimed at his wife.

'Oh my God, no . . .' His heart was either racing, or it had stopped. Preston wasn't able to tell.

'*Your name, bitch!*' the voice repeated, the gun wagging slightly. Preston felt the tears well in his eyes, his wife staring at the gun, her body shaking.

'*I won't ask you again. Tell me your name, or your girls –*'

Preston's neck tightened at the mention of his girls, and he saw his wife's do the same.

'*B-Beth,*' she sputtered out through her fear. The man asked for their children's names and she managed an answer. Preston's fingers dug deep into his legs as the video fluttered, two voices talking to each other briefly off camera.

And then Senator Preston Wilcox's world seemed to end entirely. On the screen before him, the gun jolted. The laptop's tiny speakers ruffled to report the sound, but the image was clear enough. Beth's head slammed back into the headboard, a terrible smack sounding against the wood. A tiny red spot appeared on her forehead, and a second later blood poured over her shoulders. Preston's wife slumped sideways, her eyes vacant.

'What the fuck have you done!' he cried out, his wet eyes flying from the screen to the man behind it. The visitor sat calmly, his face as steady and polite as ever.

'I suggest you lower your voice, Senator Wilcox.' He

leaned forward and closed the laptop, placing it back in his briefcase.

'Now I want you to listen very carefully, as I describe what is going to happen next.'

16

In Flight, Between Seattle and London

The four Rolls-Royce engines of the BA 747-400 hummed steadily outside the windows as the flight that would take Jack, Angela and Sean to London Heathrow attained its cruising altitude and levelled out for the long haul over Canada and the Atlantic.

Angela's seat and surroundings were cluttered with files. They had left Seattle in such haste that she'd simply grabbed every notebook and folder that might be of use, readying herself to skim them en route.

'You obviously don't subscribe to the "cluttered-work-space-means-a-cluttered-mind" theory,' Jack said from the seat next to her. He'd noticed the chaos she'd brought from her office.

'Funny, funny,' Angela answered sarcastically. 'But if you don't mind, I have some reading to do. I want to gather together my notes on the Temple Church. I'll brief you and Sean before we land.'

'You can't talk while you work?'

Angela waved him away. 'Silence is a friend to thoughtfulness.'

Jack's brow rose. 'You're a thoughtful person, then?'

'That's a *professional* thoughtfulness I was referring to, Mr Shepherd.' Angela couldn't help but feel his features were warm, but too forward. She looked directly into his gaze and was reassured by the slight falter in his expression.

'Of course,' he answered, 'you're clearly that.'

'Clearly what?'

'Professional.' His smile broadened, and Angela sat back, comprehending. The man might not be as shallow as she'd anticipated – he'd absorbed the data about their Oak Island find and the decoded runes with surprising adeptness – but he was clearly still a flirt. *Just like all men.* The hesitation of the morning returned to her. Jack Shepherd was not her type – professionally or personally.

'You're aware now of our most recent discoveries,' she said, changing the subject as decisively as she could. 'We fully expect that the guidance from the runes is pointing us towards whatever it was the Templars who crafted it were so intent on concealing, whether in the Temple Church or elsewhere.'

'The "treasure",' Jack muttered.

'If that's what you want to call it.'

'You don't call it that?' Jack's face was a question. 'I thought Blackburn's whole interest was to find the fabled treasure.'

'Treasure's a name used by people like you,' Angela answered, and all too quickly realized how harsh she had sounded.

'And what sort of person am I?'

Angela could feel the blush in her cheeks start to return and tried to speak before it could show. She was not normally so aggressive, but she had put her foot into it now and it was hard to step back.

'A sensationalist. Words like "treasure" are not in the vocabulary of scholars or genuine historians.'

I sound like a bitch. For a moment Angela feared she'd been too blunt. It wasn't fair to be so harsh to a man who hadn't really wronged her, but maybe it was better that she get her thoughts out into the open now. If he was too easily offended by the truth, he wouldn't last long on their project anyway.

To Angela's surprise, the expression that swept on to Jack's face was not one of anger or defensiveness. He smiled at her with a strange confidence.

'So I'm *not* a real scholar or a genuine historian,' he said, 'but I *am* a sensationalist.'

The blushing threatened to return. 'I'm sorry if I was blunt, but –'

'No,' Jack cut her off, 'it's quite all right. Just trying to make sure I've got the categories right. Know where I stand, and all.' His grin positively beamed at her.

'I don't refer to what the Templar originators of this code wanted to conceal as "treasure",' Angela said, swiftly abandoning the uncomfortable exchange and getting back to the facts, 'because we simply don't know what the Oak Island deposit relates to. It could be anything. All we can reasonably say is that, given the complexity of how it was hidden, whatever we're aiming towards is something significant.'

Jack allowed a fair amount of time to pass in silence before he answered.

'Oak Island would have to be one of the western-most sites ever attached directly to the Templars,' he said. 'The standard theory, or at least the one I've heard about, since

I'm not a *genuine historian* –' he paused long enough to let the sarcasm of his tone sink in – 'is that whatever was left of the Templars migrated north from France after the disbanding, eventually to England and Scotland. Oak Island has been hypothesized to be a site of landing as they left Europe for what would become the New World.'

'That's the theory.'

'So you're expecting that this tablet will point you towards whatever those travelling Templars wanted to hide . . . presumably somewhere further west.'

Angela didn't answer. Jack had described the reasonable hypothesis that everyone on their team shared.

Everyone except her.

'No,' she finally said. 'No, that's not what I'm expecting.' She looked into Jack's face, and as he looked back, his expression was that of a man whose mind was furiously at work.

'Now that's interesting,' he drew out his words reflectively, leaning back in the airline seat. 'If you're not expecting it to point to something westerly, then your thoughts must be a lot like mine.'

Angela chortled. 'Yours? You've known about all this for less than a day. What thoughts could you possibly have had between our offices and the jetway?'

Again with the harshness, her thoughts immediately scolded herself. What was it about this man that caused these reactions?

Jack smiled calmly. 'Well, since you've been kind enough to ask this unworthy sensationalist, I would say that an entirely different interpretation would make far more sense. If I were a knight fleeing a Europe that had grown spectacularly hostile to my Order, I would want to do everything in my power to ensure people thought that I, that we, were gone. History.'

Angela watched Jack lean closer to her.

'I might even go so far as to travel far beyond the realm,' he continued, 'towards an unknown land, in order to plant signs of my presence there – signs that others could use to reassure themselves we were gone. Out of sight. And to provide sufficient misdirection, should any of the more zealous opponents of our cause extend their persecutions and try to come after us. I'd want them pointed as far from me as possible.'

As Jack continued to speak Angela could see the gleam in his eyes.

'So, my thoughts would be these, Miss Derby: that if the tablet you've discovered really does contain instructions for fellow Templars of a future generation who might, like you, have followed the misdirection meant for others and come as far as Oak Island seeking the remnants of their brothers, it won't be pointing them further west at all. I would guess it would be pointing them exactly in the opposite direction. It will be pointing them east.'

Jack's eyes glimmered as he spoke, but Angela hardly noticed. She was too concentrated on his words, and the shock she felt at hearing from this man, for the first time in her professional life, a reading of the facts that matched her own.

17

Troyes, France, AD 1314

The sun crested the French countryside with a shimmer
of gold that lit up the green and brown of the rolling pas-
tures outside the estate's rippled-glass windows. The
low-lying clouds that sat on the horizon glowed a bright
pink, radiating their colour upon the pastoral scene below.

It was a scene Sir Arnaud de Faulke had seen a thousand times in his life. So often, the peace of the morning
had been the prelude to battle, the green of the fields
turned a sour red by evening time, soaked in the blood of
the fallen infidel and too many lost compatriots. It made
even the serene beauty, silent before him today, haunting
in the way it could be only for a knight who had known as
much combat as he.

The Grand Master's study was a treasury, pure and simple. Jacques de Molay had kept meticulous journals, notes
on battles, reflections on significant encounters. He had
profiled his closest allies as well as his most dangerous
enemies. He had written accounts of every campaign,
every journey, during his long tenure at the reins of the
Order.

Including, Arnaud de Faulke had finally discovered,
after almost two months of reading and searching, notes
on one journey in particular. A journey he was now convinced was connected to the curse the Grand Master had

uttered with his dying breath, and the instructions de Faulke believed he had delivered to him from the pyre.

He turned from the window and walked into the building's oversized kitchen. The musty smells of the disused, vacant space had been aired out over the past months, and the stone kitchen now smelled of the boiled meat his squire was busy stirring through a richly seasoned broth that would suffice for a late breakfast. A good man, his squire. Faithful to a fault. Discreet. A simpleton, but he had seen much in his years of service. The man was worthy of the mantle.

'Tell me, Alvain,' de Faulke said, taking a seat on a wooden stool at the side of the room, 'what do you know of de Molay's private travels?'

The squire gazed up at him, squinting through the steam, unaccustomed to being asked such things. He thought a moment, returning his eyes to the iron pot before he spoke.

'The Grand Master travelled a lot, Master. Specially in his younger years.'

'And what do you know of those journeys? What have you heard?'

'Brothers say he travelled the whole world. Every edge of the empire, an' beyond.'

'Aye.' De Faulke knew the same stories. The Grand Master had been a man of means before he took up the Cross, known for espousing a wanderlust that had served him well in his later years. There had been few battle-grounds faced by the Order that de Molay hadn't witnessed first-hand before.

'Up north as far as the Scots,' the squire continued,

recollecting travel stories told knight to knight and brother to brother, 'down south to the mouth of the Nile. And we know his journeys out of the tip of Spain, you and I.'

'Too well,' de Faulke reflected. He and his squire had accompanied the Grand Master on his journey by ship round the cape of the Kingdom of Portugal many years ago – a route that had taken them through a storm that had nearly been the death of all of them. If de Faulke never stepped aboard a sailing ship again he would lose no sleep for grief.

'An' they say he went east, too,' Alvain continued. Then, abruptly, he went quiet.

De Faulke allowed the silence to linger a few moments, then prodded his squire. 'What of those stories?' he asked. 'What did you hear of his journeys east?'

Alvain looked visibly uncomfortable. 'No one talked much about those travels, an' the Grand Master never. They say he came back dark, angry. Disturbed. Told people never to mention it.'

In fact, de Faulke knew, de Molay's instructions on his return from a small expedition to the Far East had been more explicit than the squire recalled. *Not one question is ever to be asked, not one word spoken, so long as I live.* As firm a command as the Grand Master had ever given. He had intended to travel through Persia to the land of darker skins and strange pagan sorcery, and so he had presumably done; but he had returned silent, stilted, as if something had scarred him inside. Any discussion of the journey was an offence to be punished with the strongest possible sanctions their Rule would allow.

'Only heard he saw death out there,' the squire finally

added, interrupting de Faulke's recollections. 'Death like he'd never seen before.'

De Faulke nodded from his perch. He'd heard the same. Every knight had. Only now de Faulke knew why.

'I've discovered what we're looking for,' he announced abruptly. Alvain looked up from the pot again, surprised.

'Aye?'

'I've found de Molay's notes for that very journey. The one about which he never spoke. I know what he discovered, and what haunted him all these years since. And I know that it is precisely this he wants us to find.'

The squire's eyes widened. De Faulke smiled slightly, but the excitement he felt within was strong. The notebook containing the key information had been tucked away on a shelf containing dozens of others. It had taken work to find the entries he required, and that work wasn't yet done. The late Grand Master had clearly known that what he'd encountered on that journey held fantastic power, and knew that if it fell into the wrong hands . . . that it couldn't be allowed to fall into the wrong hands.

'That journey east is one we'll have to retrace,' de Faulke announced.

'Fair enough. Travellin' is better than just sittin' here.'

'But there's still work that needs to be done before we can depart. The route, the destinations, aren't yet known to me.'

'I thought you found his journal? Don' it tell you where to go?'

'It does,' de Faulke answered, 'in a way. But the Grand Master encoded the names of all the locations along his route.'

'Encoded?' Alvain looked confused.

'It's our way of changing text into –' de Faulke cut himself off. The squire was unequipped to understand such things.

'Don't worry about it, my friend,' he said comfortingly. A second later he rose, walking over to the pot and staring at Alvain through the steam.

'But when we're done with our breakfast, I'm going to need to send you back to Paris, to track down a piece of equipment that will show us the way forward.'

18

Unknown Location

'We are told we cannot serve two masters. This feels . . . uncomfortable.'

Sir Michael Wyatt stood solemnly, his body rigid with attention, but his face betrayed confusion.

'You are misreading your present circumstances,' the Seneschal replied. 'You do not have two masters. We are all the lesser brothers of our Master.'

'But you are challenging the Grand Master's orders. Why would you do this when we have a charter for war, which you helped us obtain?'

'I am not challenging him. I am merely ensuring the *overall* success of his plan.' The Seneschal looked over the young man. Wyatt was facing a moment that the New Order's second in command had imposed on only a few men before. The moment of choice, of loyalty and action.

'Tell me, my child, are there not times when loyalty demands betrayal?'

Wyatt looked confused, his face twisted in deliberation.

'Are there not times when, to serve the greater cause of which we are all a part, the will of one must be set aside – whatever his rank or position?'

'I . . . I suppose. Maybe.'

The Seneschal nodded. 'Of course, of course there are. They are rare, and only the greatest of men are able to observe that loyalty which stands above personality.' He drove his green eyes into the younger man's. 'I believe you are such a man.'

Wyatt's chest puffed out slightly at the affirmation.

'Our lineage, our history, demands more of us than the Grand Master is willing to recognize. It demands we look beyond ourselves. That we fulfil a higher calling.'

The younger knight pondered silently. Then, finally, he matched the Seneschal's gaze.

'What, precisely, do you want me to do?'

The old man handed him a printed file of the afternoon's surveillance records.

'You're going on a trip. The details of what I expect of you are inside. The number of people involved is growing beyond necessity and threatens to slow us down. You will help us to . . . eliminate that burden.'

He wrapped a hand round Wyatt's wrist as the younger man took the file.

'This work, it is essential. You cannot falter. And you must act with utmost secrecy.'

Sir Michael Wyatt drew back his hand and looked down. Three headshots stared up at him, and he felt his breath catch.

'These are . . . *targets*?'

The Seneschal nodded. 'You're to stay on their tails and monitor everything. Every word, every outing. Everything. And you'll do this until we have enough information, and then you'll eliminate them.'

Wyatt looked further down the page. The names printed beneath the photographs reinforced his surprise.

Sean Blackburn. Angela Derby. Jack Shepherd.

'And you will silence anyone they contact along the way,' the Seneschal added. 'We require complete security.'

The silence between the two men swelled. The Seneschal leaned forward, his gaze commanding and fierce.

'Can you be relied upon, Sir Michael, for this sacred task?'

Wyatt tucked the folder into his arm, shook away his surprise, and stood purposefully before the Seneschal. 'Consider it done.'

PART TWO
Expeditions

19

London

The call to sweep the small, nameless village outside Behsud, Afghanistan, had come through three hours previously. An advance strike team had cleared out the known armed insurgents, placed the village under control and monitoring, and moved on to its next target.

First Lieutenant Jack Shepherd's platoon was transported into the village twenty minutes after the call came. A house-to-house sweep to locate any combatant hideaways and secure the safety of the native villagers was standard protocol after a captive habitation was liberated. Jack had led his men on more sorties like this than any of them could count, each one still executed with as much care and precision as their first. They were usually routine, but the saying on the ground in Afghanistan held enough water to keep them constantly vigilant: 'The only things routine are the surprises.'

Twenty minutes to lunchtime. At 12.30 Jack's platoon was to be relieved by another, who would complete the action and release his men to other duties. A calm afternoon anticipated by all.

It was then that the gunfire started. The overlapping, woodpecker-like report of small automatic weapons fire. Old brick shattering at the impact of rounds hitting it at speeds faster than sound. An explosion came next, tearing through the afternoon air, rubble bursting out of the side of a nearby building.

'Cover!' Jack cried out. His men darted into nearby buildings, all eyes scanning the street front for signs of the insurgents targeting them.

Jack and two others took refuge in a small traditional Afghan home. That had been a mistake, he would come to think in the weeks that followed. An open central courtyard, rooftop terraces. The soldiers – if they could really be called that, they were barely more than kids with guns – had line-of-sight into the house from almost every angle. Bullets seemed to rain down on every side, shattering walls, courtyard planters and furniture.

Jack protected his men, the instinct of meticulously drilled training taking over. He spent half a clip from his M4 covering them as they made their way to a protected corner, taking out two of the rooftop shooters in the process. From their new position, his men took aim upwards and worked to eliminate the remaining attackers.

It was in the midst of all this that Jack spotted the child. Small, cowering behind what remained of a tired, battered desk. He couldn't have been more than four years old, trapped and isolated, a small ball by his side the only indication of the play that had occupied him until the attack had begun.

The boy would be dead in seconds if Jack didn't act – it was only a miracle a bullet hadn't found him already. Calling out to his men for cover, Jack lunged through the courtyard to the boy's position, pulling him to his chest and diving towards a nearby exit.

The explosion came as he was only feet from the door. A mortar, like so many others. The wall to Jack's left blew apart in a cloud of hot dust and stone. The world went black, then white, the shrapnel slamming into his body at full speed. A piece of plaster cracked into his leg, another flying into his face, nearly knocking him over; but Jack regained his balance and pressed forward, forcing himself and the boy to the safety of a side room.

The gunfire continued for another ten or twenty seconds before Jack heard his men call out the all clear. His ears rang and his vision was blurred, but he could stand and he clutched the child closer to his chest, tight and protective. He had to get him outside, into their transport and away to someplace safe. Jack would not allow the child to become the victim of his own people's anger at Jack's team's presence.

He began to hobble towards his men, the child gripped tightly, but the soldiers stared back at him with a look he couldn't place. He took a few more steps, his balance weak, but his men's expressions only grew more uncomfortable.

It was then that Jack looked down, and he knew at once the reason for his men's baffled stares. The mortar had injured his leg and the fragment near his eye had probably concussed him, but the innocent boy in his arms had fared far worse. A small wooden beam had impaled his abdomen, the red of the child's blood pouring down his legs. 'No!' Jack cried out, turning him over, but the boy's eyes were vacant and unmoving. They stared into Jack's with a hollowness that seemed impossibly inappropriate for one so young.

A boy, killed by one of his own.

Jack carried the child's corpse out of the house as his platoon reclaimed control of the street and village. He brought him towards an armoured personnel transport, lifted him into the arms of a medic as his own vision started to go light, his balance teetering, and then he felt himself starting to weaken, to fall . . .

Jack blinked hard, forcing the images from his mind. The nightmare was too familiar. It had been with him for years and threatened never to let him be. Even here, with the vastly different scenes of central London passing by his window, he couldn't seem to avoid the visions that crept up on him whenever sleep came at the end of a long flight, or the silence of a car allowed his mind to wander. Memory was a bitch.

He had located the boy's family, all those years ago,

even attended the burial. But something within Jack had died that afternoon with that boy. Though the scars on his legs and above his left eye had earned him a Purple Heart and commendations for the other men with him in the house, the psychological scars Jack had taken from Behsud went far deeper. They were the ones that still ached, the ones that still kept him bitter, and the ones that had shattered so much of his vision of the world.

'Not much longer now,' the driver announced, breaking through his reflections. Jack vaguely nodded, the voices of the others inarticulate behind him.

He watched the Thames give way to the impressive buildings of the Embankment and the Strand. This was the present. One day, God willing, he would be able to shake his past.

'Put the laptop away,' Angela instructed, smirking at Sean in the process. 'And your other kit as well. With all that technology on display, you couldn't look more like a snooping engineer if you tried.' They had reached the end of their drive a few minutes ago, and Sean had extracted his mobile electronics the moment they'd made their way into the stony courtyard tucked away from the main street.

'Am I supposed to hide my true calling in your properly civilized country?' Sean protested, smiling faintly, though he obediently slid his computer into his rucksack. Along with it went a duo of smaller handheld devices that had been holstered at his waist. Around them crowds of tourists huddled beneath umbrellas and plastic overcoats in the courtyard, their number occasionally broken up by a lawyer walking from the Inns to the courts.

'I'm not suggesting you mask your inner geek,' Angela continued. She had a smile on her face that suggested she felt refreshed to be back in her home country. 'But all that equipment makes it look like you're here for more than just a casual visit, and that's likely to create ... delays. Look up, the both of you. These aren't normal surroundings.'

Sean and Jack did as she beckoned. Before them stood the Temple Church, inhabiting the same plot of central London it had occupied for centuries. The buildings that had grown up around it over the course of history now dwarfed it, but the courtyard that surrounded the church had never been encroached upon, giving it the appearance of a medieval island in a sea of urban stone. At its east end the Master's House and Gardens presented a meticulously pruned vision of private paradise to passers-by through its gates, while sunken along the west end and north side were burial crypts and flagstones long since decayed to illegibility through generations of rain and pollution, marking the graves of their inhabitants with an eerie anonymity.

In the falling rain and grey light the brown limestone took on orange tones, almost of fire. The sight was, Jack thought, entirely majestic. For a moment, he could understand why people were drawn to the place and the legends associated with it. All speculations and wild wanderings aside, this really had been the English headquarters of the Poor Fellow-Soldiers of Christ and of the Temple of Solomon, and armour-clad Templar knights really had walked over the same stones on which his feet were planted now. It was a hard atmosphere to match. History seemed to linger here as the modernity of the city swirled all around it; it hung thick in the air and stuck to the ancient stones.

They moved across the courtyard, the sight building up an eagerness to enter the ancient church. Behind them, a limestone pillar marked out the centre of the elegant space, capstoned by a black iron sculpture of two knights, a common shield between them, riding a single horse and facing Jerusalem.

Angela gestured towards the small entrance a few feet in front of them, its placarded admission rates glistening in the light rain. 'Admission is only four pounds, to the *general public*.' She stressed her final words, tapping again on Sean's pack. 'Specialists and scholars tend to need special arrangements at London cultural sites. We're much likelier to be left alone, and free to snap a casual photo or two, if we're just tourists.'

'The whole we're-just-tourists bit is going to come off better if the two of you stop talking about it at full volume,' Jack commented half under his breath. The practical conversation brought his attention back from the sights before them to practical questions of his own, like why in God's name he was here. Jack had found himself surprised by the readiness with which he'd agreed to accept Thomas Blackburn's invitation to join this strange project, and to leave Seattle for England with two individuals he'd known for less than a full day. Though Blackburn hadn't seemed in the slightest bit surprised by his acceptance. When Jack had said 'yes' at the Seattle complex, his full contract for employment, non-disclosure paperwork, funding documentation and security credentials had been produced within minutes. As if there had never been any question as to what his decision would be.

And now here he stood, rain pattering lightly on his hair, outside the entrance to one of the oldest standing Templar sites in the world, in the centre of crowded London.

Jack pushed between Angela and Sean and stepped through the first set of wooden doors into a covered porch leading to the south side of the church proper. 'Why?' might be an open question, but he was here.

Another set of wooden doors was only a few feet ahead, and, shaking the rain from his coat, Jack stepped through them. To his left was a small table, covered in guidebooks and pamphlets – including, to Jack's horror, multiple copies of a small volume entitled *The Templars and the Secrets of The Da Vinci Code*. Behind the table sat a woman with a nest of hair carefully sculpted into an impressive, retro apparition of 1960s grandmother chic. The slightly horn-rimmed spectacles on her nose were inlaid with glitter and two plastic gems – a glimmer of a past that refused to be abandoned.

'Welcome to the Temple Church,' she announced automatically. The woman had a tinny, slightly raspy voice that went with the generally witch-like appearance, but she wore a sincere and welcoming smile.

'Admission for three, please,' Jack answered with as much warmth as he could muster. A few seconds and twelve pounds later, he had satisfied the entrance requirements and received a slightly apologetic nod from the woman.

'Sorry to have to charge for entrance to a church,' she said, motioning Jack and the others inward. 'We used to have donation boxes by the door, but a few years ago the treasurer counted up the contributions and worked out that they came to only about ten pence per visitor. Can't manage the upkeep that way.' Another smile.

'Could we have a printed guide also?' Glasses nodded *of course*, and produced a small tri-fold brochure from behind the desk. Jack took it and walked back to the others.

'Jack, I know the ground plan to this church backwards and forwards,' Angela whispered as she took a ticket from him and they made their way towards the doors. 'And after our review on the flight, so should you.'

Jack tried to keep his sigh hidden. The BA business-class seats that Blackburn Enterprises had not hesitated to book them for the long haul from Seattle to Heathrow had the unfortunate ability to transform each passenger's miniature cubicle into a meeting space, with seats for two and a table between. *Unfortunate*, Jack recollected, as Angela had taken advantage of the space to set up her computer and drill the entire history, architectural background and legacy of the Temple Church into him for well over half of the ten-hour flight.

'Just going along with the ruse,' Jack whispered back. He pulled at the zip on his windbreaker, tucked the pamphlet into the chest pocket and rolled back slightly on his feet. An abrupt laugh escaped Angela's lips before she could contain it, and Sean grinned broadly. Jack Shepherd looked about as stereotypical an American tourist as it was possible to be.

Rolling her eyes, Angela passed him and the trio walked into the temple.

The vision that opened up before them was remarkable. Though all three had studied the floor plans, history and photographs Angela had provided, nothing could have quite prepared them for the strange beauty of the Temple Church.

Originally dedicated in 1185 to be the capital of the Order's English presence, the Temple Church had begun as what was now called the 'Round Church' at the west end of the complex. With its visible reflection of the Holy Sepulchre in Jerusalem and link to the Holy Land, it had become the protectorate of the Templars after the victories of the First Crusade and the establishment of the Order. The Round Church and its environs became the 'little Jerusalem' of England and a place connected not only with Templar prayer, but Templar commerce and social activity.

Later, the attached rectangular, three-roofed basilica had been added, which now accounted for the majority of the church's floorspace. Its three parallel rows of vaulted ceilings, painted an off-white with a darker brown stone spidering out at the arches' angles, were supported by two rows of black stone pillars. Pews filled the rectangular church, an ornate, wood-framed altar at the far eastern end.

'What a sight,' Sean muttered quietly.

'It's actually surprisingly . . . simple,' Jack said, speaking to them both. After all the photographs and the hype that surrounded the place, following its fairly glamorous inclusion in a few popular books of the past fifteen years, he'd expected something more dramatic. What he saw, instead, was a perfectly lovely, well-cared-for and in most ways traditional house of Christian worship. It didn't look that different from the interior of the Episcopalian church down the road from Jack's home in Boston. Not that he frequented his own parish church that often. He was never quite sure how much he fitted in.

But despite the simplicity here, Jack was immediately conscious of something haunting about the place. The main church looked innocuous and plain, yet seemed to smell of the secrets and mysteries of its past. Jack couldn't help but notice the effect it had on him. The place provoked suspicion, curiosity, speculation . . .

'It's that section that most of the tourists come here to see,' Angela said suddenly. She motioned to their left, to the west end of the rectangular church. It opened into the original Round Church, the two now forming a single space.

The Round Church, however, had an entirely different character. As the three moved into its space, glimpses of the ancient world that had produced it seemed to shine through the modern renovations and even more modern historical display cases and informational banners.

A circle of six Purbeck marble pillars supported the hexagonal dome, fabricated of parquet woodwork, high above them. The wooden roof was new, and the pillars were reproductions of the originals – all casualties of the Blitz that had destroyed so much of the Temple Church on 10 May 1941. But the church's restorations, repairs and recreations were extraordinarily well done, and the feel of the original managed to remain. Rows of smaller arches, each supported by small pillars and surmounted by a row of gargoyles, ran at eye level round the whole space, and far above them, high atop the central arches of the church, ran another row with miniature pillars all in black. Arches, pillars, spires, repeating with increasing frequency as the round temple reached towards the vaulted dome of heaven.

But it was not what was above that was the focal point of the Round Church.

'I almost refused to believe the photographs,' Sean said as they stepped fully into the centre of the space. 'But they're here, right in the middle of the floor.'

The objects of his attention, as well the attention of every tourist packed into the small space, were eight effigies set into the floor of the Round Church. They were not merely its focal points: they were the only things in the strange, mysterious space.

The Round Church had no altar, no shrines, no pulpit, no pews. Only the tombs of eight knights and nobles, preserved beneath ancient carved monuments, staring through stone eyes towards the domed arches of paradise that their own Order had crafted.

20

Meetings of the security teams at the US Capitol were never unscheduled. And more importantly, they were never held with unknown participants. Special Agent Tom Arbuckle's job was security, and more specifically, the security of one of the most significant landmarks of American political power. The Capitol was a fortress, a castle on a hill and a sign of the majesty of the nation. As its chief guardian, Arbuckle insisted on protocol in everything, and protocol never, ever allowed for what was happening today.

Beyond the white-washed wooden door before him was *someone* with an agenda item as absurd as the meeting itself. Not only must the man who had called him here have Washington seniority to rival the president's, he must also have balls fit for an ox.

Tom Arbuckle pulled open the door. But there was only one man within, and it was absolutely the last person he expected.

'I'm Arbuckle,' he said curtly, stepping into the room, 'head of Capitol security with the Secret Service.' He spoke with authority, recognizing immediately that the man before him was not only not Washington nobility, but barely more than a political freshman. What the hell was he doing here? How had he managed to get this face-to-face called?

'I was told you wanted to discuss something about a scheduling change?' he said. He deliberately let the question sound like an accusation.

'That's right,' the other man answered. He seemed uncomfortable – that much, at least, was good. Proper. But the younger man pushed forward all the same. 'I do realize it's unprecedented, but –'

'Unprecedented!' Arbuckle all but laughed. 'Unless I'm confused, the "event" you want to reschedule is the State of the Union. You're goddamn right it's unprecedented!'

The man cowered slightly at Arbuckle's raised voice and unconcealed contempt, but he didn't back away. Swallowing and reclaiming his courage, he stared at the table between them as he spoke.

'What we're suggesting won't alter the State of the Union address itself. We just want to combine it with something else. Make the activity part of a joint-event evening.'

Arbuckle chortled out another mocking laugh. 'The State of the Union doesn't get *combined* with anything, son.'

Finally, the man appeared to gain a little confidence, taking a step closer. 'As I said, Agent Arbuckle, I recognize the unusual nature of our request. But I, and several others, feel it is in the best interest of our nation.' Now he looked up squarely into Arbuckle's eyes, a power to his expression that hadn't been there a moment ago. 'And we, as I am sure you will understand, are in a position to know.'

Arbuckle caught his tongue before he could reply on impulse. The change in the man's confidence was a retort, as clear as anything that could be verbalized, and Arbuckle pulled himself back into line. *Protocol.* As pitiful as he looked, this man clearly had power beyond his station, and this meeting wouldn't be taking place if he was the only one behind it.

Softening his expression, Arbuckle motioned to two chairs at the table.

'Very well. Let me hear more about your . . . proposal.' He waited for the other man to sit before he took a chair himself.

'We'll need to discuss everything in detail if we're going to move forward, Senator Wilcox.'

21

Unknown Location

The first rule of tactical battle is to eliminate expertise. The training and knowledge accessible to your foe are as important as the weapons they carry. Eliminate the men with training, and you eliminate your opponent's deepest force.

These lessons were drilled into every initiate, whose tonsure into the Order's holy ranks would lead one day to the fulfilment of their office in battle. There were many classes of holy men, many types of monks, but those of the New Order were called to something greater than mere self-denial and devotion. A knight bears a sword, and swords are meant to be drawn.

Eliminate those who know your weakness, their military instruction had drilled into them, *and you route out your enemy's tactical power. Then they are simply men who fight, but they do not have a focus to their steps.*

Words of wisdom.

And practical guidance.

The divine charter for the course ahead had been produced by the convocation. The whole Order, assembled as one. Only the Grand Master himself had been absent, but that was as it ought to be. He sent the Seneschal in his stead for such gatherings so that none might ever be tempted to suppose he ruled by his own will, rather than the will of God. And the Seneschal was a venerable man, old and experienced, powerful and held in high esteem by all. A man who commanded loyalty.

Loyalty was everything. But it, like so many other things, had to be honed in the strange circumstances of modernity. Who would ever have expected that the Order would include military enterprise, businessmen, family. All these were strengths, but they were also challenges that the Grand Master had to manage. To keep the body together in the face of such strange diversity.

The charter lay before him, written out in perfect calligraphy on a broad sheet of parchment, a crimson seal cooled in wax now imprinted with the Order's ancient crest. The charter bore the signatures of all the senior knights, its contents having received the unanimous acclamation of the whole assembly.

It is time for the knighthood to fulfil its calling, and to do its duty.

The Grand Master called one of his most trusted knights to his side.

'There is only one man among the ranks of the enemy who has the potential to know our tactics and approach. A man with training, with expertise. With hands-on access.'

He produced a dossier, opened it and allowed the other man to read through the contents.

'I trust you know your duty.'

The knight looked up into his eyes – those horrible, haunting eyes that seemed to contain so much darkness, yet radiated so much intoxicating power. He nodded. There was only one thing duty demanded in such a case.

Eliminate those who know your weakness.

Folding closed the dossier, the man slid it under his arm. Patting the pistol that was holstered reassuringly at his hip – the sword of the modern generation – he moved towards the door.

22

Temple Church, London

The search of the Temple Church was made systematic, and simple, by two facts. First, the church in its entirety was not large, and it was made even smaller if Angela, Jack and Sean restricted themselves to the older Round Church that was by far the most likely section to contain any authentic Templar signs.

The second fact was the plainness of the interior. Just as the Round Church was a single room without pews or an altar, it was also simply decorated, without more than a modest level of adornment.

Which had Angela worried.

The chances of anything at all being hidden in such a stark, open space seemed more remote the closer they looked at it. More accurately, it seemed all but impossible. Especially in a site as heavily visited, photographed and well known as this.

The more Angela surveyed, the more there seemed to be no chance whatsoever that a set of runes similar to those she and Sean had unearthed in Nova Scotia would be found here – unless, like there, they were buried. And that meant beneath the church, which posed a set of problems Angela didn't even want to contemplate.

She forced herself to the task, as pessimistic as she was

suddenly feeling. Unlikely as it was, they couldn't come this far and not at least try to find something.

'Despite their obvious crowd appeal,' she said to the others, 'the effigies on the floor seem like the wrong place to focus.' They were the appealing focal points of the room, but that was precisely the problem. 'As the most famous elements of the structure, the chances of them containing anything hidden, anything that people haven't seen before, is slim.' Yet there was nothing else on the floor. It was the walls, then, that had to hold at least the possibility of hope. She motioned Jack towards them. More arched niches than she could readily count ran in a ring round the room, and between each pairing a carved visage stared back at her from just above eye level.

Faces staring out from history. Angela felt the slightest impulse of optimism.

She stepped closer to one of the arches, scanning its hand-carved surfaces. White pillars supported it, with a slightly rounded stone bringing the arch itself to a point just above her head. Bricks alternated solid and hollow space above the supporting stones themselves, creating a beautifully three-dimensional depth to the flourishes. The archway itself was set about a foot into the wall, the small recess inverted by a deep groove that ran above it.

Remarkably beautiful, if fairly simple. Suddenly, all of Angela's inbuilt love of the past took hold of her. Some time, centuries ago, stonemasons with knights for bene-factors and crusades as their cultural context had taken tools to formless rocks, producing the beauty she could now reach out and touch. She could almost smell the smoke from the fires they would have burned to light and heat the space for their task, the stench of work animals out in the courtyard where lawyers and tourists now walked with mobile phones and all the technology of the present. Angela reached out and ran her fingers along one of the niche's arches. She could feel the slight indentations of each chisel track – imagined the bulky, muscular arms of the man who had worked the stone, a man who lived in a world that still believed the sun orbited the earth and the stars were controlled by the winds.

Yet for all it did to evoke the sensuality of history, Angela could find nothing hidden away in the small space. She looked to the gargoyle-like face carved above it, just to the left: a face with a long, flowing beard. It reminded her of busts of Plato or Homer, and Angela strained to examine it more closely. Well executed, nicely proportioned, clearly restored once or twice in its history. But nothing beyond the ordinary. No line of Templar runes carved along the rear slant of his beard or behind his ears.

As if there would be, Angela chided herself.

One archway down, and no discovery. She took a few steps to her left to face a second. At this rate, the search was going to take them a while.

Minutes passed, Angela lost track of how many, and she had yet to set her eyes on anything of note. Her only observation was that the stonework had been restored remarkably well, and certainly not everything she was looking at was original. The fact that the Temple Church served as home to two of the Inns of Court that were the backbone of the London legal system – the Royal Courts of Justice situated just across the Strand and almost every intervening building the chambers of one firm or another – meant that restorations following the destruction of the Second World War had not been limited by lack of funds. Good for history, but bad for this particular historian. It might well be that whatever they were here to find had been destroyed in the damage of the Blitz, or eradicated in the restorations that followed.

Angela glanced across the round space to Jack, and noticed that he had chosen to focus on the same features as she: he was nose-forward into the second archway from the edge of the eastern entrance to the Round Church, examining the walls in careful detail. Sean explored the sarcophagi on the floor, squatting and trying to get as close as he could while avoiding tourists posing for photos before the monuments.

Frustration was mounting, but Angela couldn't allow herself to be dissuaded quite yet. Not until they'd searched everything at their disposal.

She stepped into a fourth archway, so much like the three before it. Smooth stonework, faces carved above.

No sign of anything hidden.

No sign of anything at all.

It took another forty-five minutes of searching before Angela was forced to admit what had become obvious to all three of them.

'I don't know how to say this.' She held her breath, hesitating, but then released her next words before she lost her resolve. 'There's nothing here.' And that was it – the words were out. But Angela couldn't keep the sense of frustration and defeat from crawling into her features, distorting her face in disappointment. She'd held out such hope; it was hard to admit it now looked to have been in vain.

Sean shook his head, as if unwilling to believe that the encoded text that had brought them here had led them astray.

'It's just not a good hiding place,' Jack said, nodding in agreement with Angela. 'For all the hype about this church, there's not much to it, physically speaking. And the restorations have left almost nothing of the original.'

The fact tore at Angela's resolve. Everywhere they had looked, they had stared at new stone. She couldn't even be sure the stone over which she'd run her fingers was original. What they were standing in was a structure that dated more from the 1950s than the 1200s.

If anything had been hidden here, it had almost certainly been lost.

'So . . . that's it?' Sean asked. 'We're left with nothing?'

Angela couldn't answer. She was no more eager than Sean to admit they'd made their way through so many hurdles, only to arrive at a dead end.

'There was nothing at all on the effigies?' she finally asked, though she knew what the answer would be.

'Nothing. They're beautiful, but plain – and there are no nooks or grooves in which something could be hidden.' Sean's voice sagged. 'Of course, even they're not original, but restored versions fixed up and re-worked from fragments. They were damaged in the bombings, just like the rest of the church. Fairly well destroyed. So we have no way of knowing what might have been on them before the plaster and new masonry used to piece them back together.'

A long, frustrated lull came over both of them.

But Jack's face was suddenly bright, and Angela could see the excitement in his features even before he spoke.

'That may not be entirely true,' he said.

Sean eyed him. 'I'm telling you, Jack, there's nothing on the effigies.'

'I believe you. On these restored versions. But you said we have no way of examining what might have been on the originals, before they were damaged, and that . . . that might not be true.'

Sean could not share Jack's optimism. 'I don't see how. Not unless you're able to step back in time and get a look at them before the Blitz.'

Jack smiled broadly.

'I think we can do just that.'

23

Victoria and Albert Museum, London

The car ride from the Temple Church to the Victoria and Albert Museum in Cromwell Road took just over thirty-five minutes in the late-morning traffic, and Jack used the time to fill Angela and Sean in on the change of venue he had spontaneously recommended.

'You said we can't go back in time and stand before the original effigies of the Round Church,' he said to Sean, who sat in the front of the limousine next to the driver, 'but there's a very real way in which we actually can.'

'If I say I don't follow you, I hope you won't be surprised,' Sean answered.

Jack smiled. 'We obviously can't go back to the years before the Blitz, when the eight effigies in the church were still in their original forms, but we *can* stand before them.'

He swivelled to Angela, seated to his left in the back of the car. 'What was one of the great conservation crazes of the nineteenth century, which Victorians loved as the promise-holding future of museum life?'

Angela stared at him blankly.

'Plaster of Paris,' Jack announced dramatically.

Sean's eyebrows rose and he stared back at Jack, looking unimpressed, waiting for more.

'It might not sound like much to us today, but plaster of Paris was a new invention in high Victorian society, and for many years they went around the world making plaster casts of some of the most famous objects of history. Remarkable things, sometimes almost indistinguishable from the originals.'

'Such as?'

'Such as famous statues. Monuments. Whole church altars. Hell, they even made a full-sized plaster cast of Trajan's Column in Rome, which was a far more attractive sight than the real thing until the Italian government finally cleaned the soot and smog stains from it a few years back.'

Angela was with Jack now. 'The Victorian interest in casting was widespread,' she said. 'A real cultural phenomenon.'

'It was a period when most people couldn't travel, and so could never see the originals.'

'But a plaster cast,' Angela added, 'was a way of bringing the monuments of history from the far corners of the world into the heart of London.'

'And not only from those far corners,' Jack added, 'but even monuments within the country. Even *within the city.*'

Suddenly, Angela's face beamed with recognition. 'There are plaster casts of the Temple Church effigies at the Victoria and Albert?' The words came out half question, half pronouncement.

'I confirmed it by a quick search on my phone back on the Strand,' Jack answered. 'All eight had precise casts made of them in the late nineteenth century, and they've been housed in the V&A ever since.' He paused, turning towards Sean. 'Exact reproductions, made well before the originals were damaged.'

'And though the V&A was hit in the Blitz,' Angela added, 'it didn't suffer the same degree of damage as the Temple Church. Much of their collection was unscathed.'

'They've kept a few of the pockmarked walls to show the damage from the war to visitors today, but the artefacts inside don't bear the same scars.'

Jack looked directly at Sean. 'We're going to be able to stand before the unrestored effigies, after all.'

Few façades in the impressively façaded heart of London could compare with that of the Victoria and Albert Museum. Sprawling out over twelve-and-a-half acres of land in the heart of Brompton, a section of the city sometimes known as 'Albertopolis' for the sheer number of monuments and structures affiliated with the memory of Queen Victoria's beloved husband, its strange appearance was the result of many generations of construction, design and renovation. Aston Webb's eye-catching main entrance, with its open-crown tower surmounted by a statue of Fame, poked up from the busy street in a style that was Gothic yet classical, Renaissance yet medieval. The only thing the V&A's façade was not was unremarkable, and even local residents never quite failed to gawp at its form as they drove through Kensington towards the bustle of Parliament and the West End.

But Jack, Angela and Sean hardly noticed the dimensions of the remarkable structure as they darted out of their car and up the steps leading to the double-doored entrance.

Inside the museum, they spent their first ten minutes at the information desk, situated in the middle of the gargantuan central foyer, from which the museum's extensive wings spidered off in every direction. A resident curator proved only too eager to assist the constant queue of interested visitors who came to his position at the desk, and when the trio finally stepped up to the round counter he made quick business of locating the cataloguing information and room details for the Temple Church effigies they were seeking. They were all gathered together in the Cast Courts, room 46a, together with hundreds of other monumental Victorian-era examples.

Jack led the group in the direction the curator had instructed, and they turned right from the main entrance and information desk, walking alongside the vast hall containing monuments of the European late Middle Ages on their right and Asian and Chinese imperial pottery on their left. Even with all the excitement and focus of their task, it was hard not to slow down and gape at the majesty of the collections on either side of them. Some of the finest treasures of two continents, from two sides of the planet, gathered together and open to the world – all for free. Even the teenage visitors, clearly forced here at the pleasure of their parents and schools, looked dazed with wonder.

But Jack, Angela and Sean couldn't slow down. The awe that they were feeling was compounded by the possibility that they might be about to discover something truly new among these treasures of the truly old. At the far end of the immense corridor, an unassuming door to their left opened into the Cast Courts, and they joined the steady flow of visitors already inhabiting the space.

The hall was an overwhelming sight. Trajan's Column

stood monumental at the centre, spiralling up to the ceiling with its thousands of images of soldiers marching into battle, recreated in two sections in order to fit beneath the glass roof. It was surrounded on every side by larger-than-life sarcophagi, statuary, church façades and spires, all fabricated in plaster – all 'fake', though just as stunning as any original. They were works of art in their own right.

'It should be just over there,' Sean said, staring at the floor plan the curator had given them. Behind Trajan's Column on the far side of the room was a collection of funerary effigies – a suitable home for what they had come to see.

Now it was Angela who stepped forward first, Jack and Sean following suit as they weaved through freestanding objects and placards, through picture-perfect casts of noblemen in courtly dress and dust-covered bas-relief capitols of ancient temples.

And then, suddenly, there they were.

Lying in repose on pedestals that raised them up to thigh-height, rather than flat on the ground as the repaired originals had been, were the Temple Church effigies. They were black in colour here, rather than the faded white of ancient stone, but they were, as Jack had promised, in perfect condition.

Jack glanced at Sean, both men's eyes alight with new energy.

'What's say we start our search again?'

24

Outside Troyes, France, AD 1324

Progress had been halted by, of all things, hunger.

De Faulke had sent his squire from Troyes to Paris to retrieve the encoding device – a trip that should have been brief and simple, launching them into an immediate excursion east. The footsteps of Jacques de Molay were waiting to be traced out. All he had needed was the device to decode the locations that the late Grand Master had encrypted in his notes.

And things had begun well. Alvain had returned to the estate at Troyes in the spring, bearing the device well and good, but nature and fate had conspired against an immediate journey. The Great Famine that had swept into the empire in 1315 had caught them, and everyone else, by surprise. The rains, the cold – they had rendered fields and crops fruitless throughout the land. Everything had changed with the pangs of universal hunger. State benefactions of grain from royal storehouses had at first increased as an act of goodwill, but then trickled down to nothing as the supplies were fast depleted. As a consequence, cities began to lock their gates and country villages set guards at the perimeters, allowing none in. Feeding their own was hard enough. No one was willing to take on the responsibility of adding neighbouring mouths to satisfy. This meant trade and travel diminished, then seemed to stop almost entirely. The famine stagnated the empire, rooting its people to an earth that was less and less able to support them.

An abandoned estate at his disposal notwithstanding, de Faulke had been forced to scrounge for sustenance, just like the peasants of the empire. For that is what the knight had had to become: no longer a living emblem of noble ancestry and spiritual fortitude, but a beggar, seeking hand-outs and enough scraps to make it through another winter.

But at last things began to look better. In the spring of 1318, crops had started to grow again, and there began to be food enough for the populace. The gold that de Faulke had in his possession, which for years hadn't been worth more in practical terms than the rocks from which it had been taken, began to reclaim its value. It could now buy him food, and a horse to replace the one he'd lost. Then, in due time, another mount, supplies, provisions. The world was slowly coming back to Arnaud de Faulke.

But another five years had been required before the possibility of a major excursion east had become realistic. Five years. Far longer than he would have liked, but at least those years had not been wasted. De Faulke had put them to good use. With the decoding device in hand and time at his disposal, he'd been able to pore over every line of the Grand Master's notes. The details were captivating, and he now knew with absolute certainty that the curse uttered from the pyre was meant to point him here – for what Jacques de Molay was helping him to find would bring a curse indeed.

So powerful was the gift towards which de Faulke was

being drawn that the Grand Master had been unusually circumspect, even beneath his layers of encrypted text. There was no direct path indicated in his notes, much to de Faulke's frustration. But there was guidance. Pointers, however enigmatic. And de Faulke had had ample time to research the notes and come up with a plan.

And it was time, at long last, to depart.

25

The search of the effigies in the V&A at first seemed to be as fruitless as that at the Temple Church. Angela, Sean and Jack now had a delimited area to scrutinize – solely the eight casts gathered before them – and they began by each taking a different effigy.

Angela's anticipation was bridled to desperation. The smooth, black-grey surface of the cast was intricately detailed, and yet there didn't seem to be anything out of the ordinary. Nothing unexpected. And what she wanted to find, more than anything, was the unexpected.

No, Angie. Focus. There has to be something here. She had come to believe too strongly to give up.

She examined the cast more closely. The stockings covering the knight's legs were carved in a hash-sign design shaped by an intricate etching of the plaster by its Victorian artisans, who were known for their diligence in ensuring that their casts retained every mark, every hash, every scratch of the original. Angela's hopefulness flared: there could easily be something hidden away in the thousands of slightly bent lines that fashioned the pattern up both his crossed legs – the crossed position a sign that this knight had fought in the crusades.

Angela bent in close, angling her head to allow the

natural light flowing in from above to bring the carving into sharper relief, leaning as close to the effigy as she dared. They were, after all, here simply as visitors. A single touch to the monuments they were studying and museum security would swoop down on them.

But Angela's scrutiny, as close as she could make it, revealed nothing. The pattern on the legs was intricate, but hid no secrets. And the knight's other garments, in contrast to the intricate carving of the stockings, were smooth and his shield was plain. Angela almost despaired as she reached his helmet and the top of is head – the whole effigy, with nothing to disclose.

She looked up to Jack, who was finishing his examination of the cast next to hers, but he shook his head with an unmistakable aura of defeat.

Angela forced herself, against a growing pessimism, towards a third effigy, passing Sean who was still focused on his first.

This time the cast, marked by a placard as that of Robert de Ros, had a lion beneath its feet and a decorated shield – apparently a knight of higher standing than that of the first effigy. More possibilities, and Angela examined every feature of the remarkable monument.

Every cross.

Every ornament on the winding belt.

Every swirl of decorative embellishment. Right, again, to the top of the head.

She almost couldn't bring herself to say the word, even silently. But it was the only one to be said.

Nothi—

But the desperate thought was interrupted.

'Angela, I think I see something.'

'What is it?' Jack asked before Angela even had the chance.

'You need to take a look at this,' Sean announced, pointing towards the effigy he'd been studying.

'That's thought to be Robert de Vieuxpont,' Angela said as she moved towards the cast, taking note of a placard at the base of the effigy. 'A landowner who left his estates to the Templars at his death, becoming one of their major benefactors during the last century of their existence.' De Vieuxpont had become High Sheriff of Nottinghamshire, Derbyshire and the Royal Forests in 1204, and was later given oversight over York, Durham and even Devon and Cumberland. At his death in 1228 he had left not only his full estates, but also his mortal remains to the Poor Fellow-Soldiers of Christ and of the Temple of Solomon, earning himself a burial in the Temple Church and a lasting place in Templar lore.

Sean crouched down, pointing at the chest of the monument. The requiem figure of Robert de Vieuxpont lay in full stately attire, shield included, looking every bit the nobleman in his eternally unchanging stone memorial.

'I don't see anything,' Jack noted, attempting to follow Sean's line of sight.

'There, on the underside of the shield,' Sean answered. He leaned in closer, bringing the tip of his finger to a point just above the cast's left arm.

Just as Sean was about to touch it, the object of his attention finally registered with Jack.

'There's something scratched there.'

'It's not a scratch,' Sean answered. 'Come closer. It's a carving. Or an etching.' He indicated the inverted slope on the underside of the shield, couched in shadow and angled downwards.

Angela crouched down next to the two men. 'I can't see anything at all.'

Sean reached into a pocket, extracted an iPhone and spent a few seconds fiddling with its touchscreen. A moment later, the flash LED on its back panel lit up.

'Flashlight app. God knows what we did before these things.' He pointed the light towards the underside of the plaster shield.

'My God,' Angela allowed the slight exclamation to escape her lips. 'I see it now.'

Etched into the shield was a single symbol.

26

'Have they talked to anyone, anyone at all?'

'Only to a curator at the museum's entrance, sir, and just for directions. They went directly from the Temple Church to the V&A in the company car. No sign of any interactions since their arrival, except to get themselves pointed to the right hall.'

The Seneschal tapped a gold-plated fountain pen against the edge of his desk, assessing the information carefully. There was no room for error, and absolutely nothing could be left to chance.

He leaned back towards the speakerphone. 'Where are they now?'

'Still inside. In the Cast Courts,' Michael Wyatt answered. 'We've got microphones aimed at them from a side balcony.'

'They won't be there for long. They'll find whatever it is they're looking for and head for the airport.'

'My assumption, too.'

The Seneschal breathed deeply. The recent expansion of the group had been a concession, and one that seemed increasingly unnecessary, despite Sean's requests. Decisive action was required.

'Eliminate the curator, the one they spoke to when they arrived,' he commanded. 'And keep on them to the airport. And, Wyatt –' the Seneschal leaned into the phone '– let Sean know you're following them. Make him understand this isn't the time to play explorer. Light a fire under the boy.'

A pause, then: 'As you wish.'

'One other thing,' the Seneschal added.

'Yes?'

'As soon as they're airborne, eliminate the driver, too. We can't allow for any chance of a leak.'

27

Victoria and Albert Museum, London

'Is that symbol what we're looking for?' Jack asked, his gaze still on the strange, tiny carving on the underside of the effigy's shield.

Sean turned to face Angela. 'I don't know. The lady's the expert.'

Angela's gaze was fixed on the unique inscription. 'It's definitely old,' she muttered. 'It's a part of the casting and not a later addition, so it would have been on the original carving.'

'But does that mean it has any connection to our text from Oak Island?' Sean's impatience couldn't be fully concealed, though he appeared to be trying. 'It's not a symbol we've seen among any of the other runes. And it's alone, not part of an encrypted phrase.' He let his last words linger. 'It's nothing like our Templar tablet.'

'The fact that it's an old inscription doesn't, by itself, connect it to the Templars,' Angela confirmed, 'but I think the symbol does.'

Jack was taken by the sudden confidence that came into her voice. 'You sound awfully sure about that. This could be almost anything. A craftsman's trademark, a bit of ancient graffiti.'

Angela smiled gently back, but shook her head. 'It

could be, but it isn't. Not when you view it in light of the text we decoded from our tablet.'

'*To Henry's donation*,' Sean recited aloud.

'We already determined that, in the opening phrase, "Henry's donation" was meant to point us to the Templar church built under the endowment of King Henry II.' Angela's words were coming more quickly now. 'But we've not known what was meant by the second half of the phrase.'

'*The tiered palace of the lord of the dance*,' Jack repeated from memory.

Angela pointed at the small inscription. 'Now examine that closely, and tell me what you see.'

Jack scrutinized the small etching. 'I suppose the outer shape looks something like a ziggurat –'

'A palace of many tiers,' Angela interjected, reinterpreting his statement and nodding her head, urging him to continue.

'The image beneath it I can't decipher. A male figure surrounded by an aureole of flames. He's got a leg lifted in some sort of pose.' He shook his head. Jack couldn't think of an interpretation for the strange caricature.

'He's not in a pose,' Angela responded. Her chest expanded with excitement. A realization had hit.

'He's not posing,' she repeated, standing up and facing the two men. 'He's dancing. That stance, it's one of the classical poses of traditional dance.'

'Dance poses?' Sean asked, confused. 'Christian knights had a prescribed index of . . . dance steps?'

Angela wagged her head. The excitement on her face was vivid despite the grey light of the museum hall.

'If either of you knew anything about Hindu iconography, you'd know this image isn't Christian. It's Indian. The jagged shape above him is a multi-tiered palace, and the figure within it is Nataraja, better known as Shiva.'

She fired her stare directly into Jack's eyes.

'Shiva-Nataraja. The Lord of the Dance.'

28

Angela's energy radiated from her, and though Jack and Sean were enthusiastic about the small find etched under the effigy's shield, that excitement didn't compare to Angela's near exuberance.

'Seems this would tend to vindicate your theory that the Templars were connected to things eastward,' Jack said. He nodded also to Sean. The two men had raced to confirm that this was, indeed, the only such image on the casts, and had returned to Angela's side out of breath.

She nodded back at him. 'If this really is a symbol of a Hindu deity, carved by a Templar on the underside of a tomb in the Temple Church, then it's clear evidence that the Order knew something of cultures far further east than just Jerusalem and the Holy Land. Of course, it depends on whether it's really as old as we're assuming.'

As quickly as her energy had come, a look of apprehension started to consume Angela's features. 'All we know for certain is that this was here when the cast was made. But that was hardly the Middle Ages.'

'It's older than that,' Sean stepped in. 'It has to be. If it were just the carving itself, I wouldn't be as certain. But we have a reference to this image on our tablet from Oak Island, and my team have dated the carvings there to between 650 and 700 years old. I'd be shocked if this carving didn't date from the same period.' He looked up to Angela. 'I think you've got your evidence.'

'But where does this actually get us?' Jack posed the question that really mattered. 'We already know the Temple Church has essentially been whitewashed over the past century. If this symbol was originally on the effigy there – well, we've already determined there is nothing left in the church for it to be pointing to.'

'Not in the church,' Angela answered. 'The church is irrelevant, apart from this.'

'But this tells us nothing,' Sean said.

'No, it tells us everything we need to know.' Angela looked energetically back to him. 'Think back to our tablet and its message. The instructions from the island weren't pointing us here, they were pointing us *beyond* here. The language is important. The guidance was *to* Henry's donation, and *then* the tiered palace of the Lord of the Dance.' She looked towards Jack, hoping to see recognition cross his features.

'The stop here was to clarify the location,' Angela continued. 'This carving gives meaning to the last half of the tablet's instruction.' She turned directly to Sean. 'Now's the time to pull out your laptop.'

Confused, Sean did as she instructed, powering up the small device that automatically used an internal satellite modem to connect to the Internet.

'Shiva, the Lord of the Dance,' Angela said as Sean found a place to crouch and placed the computer on his knees, 'type that into a search engine and read what you discover.'

Sean worked for a moment, clicked through his search

results to a page towards the top of the listing, then read aloud: '"Shiva, also known as Nataraja, dances to destroy the universe, making it ready for a new creation."'

'A Hindu creation myth?' Jack questioned.

'Not just a new creation,' Sean continued, 'a better one. "Nataraja's dancing makes the way for Brahma to manifest the beginnings of an enlightened creation."' Sean looked up from his screen. 'This is all fascinating, Angela, but I still don't see where it's getting us.'

'*Where?*' she pushed, persistent. 'Read further. *Where* did Shiva dance and defeat the broken universe?'

Sean wrinkled his brow and let out a sigh, but returned to the page on his screen. '"Nataraja's cosmic dance",' he said a moment later, '"was danced at the heart of the world, the centre of its body".'

'And where is that?'

Sean's face was a question, Angela's probing sounding more and more mystic. 'It says that Hindu worshippers venerate Nataraja's dance at the symbolic centre of the universe, a place called the Thillai Nataraja Temple in south-eastern India.'

Jack could see the excitement and determination building in Angela's expression, and it was he who gave the next instruction to Sean.

'Call that up in your search,' he ordered, 'the temple name. See if you can get us a picture.'

A few clicks later and Sean's eyes went wide.

'Shit,' he said. He swivelled the computer so the monitor faced Angela and Jack.

'Shit, indeed,' Jack whispered as he looked at the display.

On the screen was an image of the Thillai Nataraja Temple, nestled in the centre of populous Chidambaram, India. Highlighted in the centre of the photograph was one of the temple's main towers.

A seven-tiered structure, covered in images of its main deity.

'The tiered palace of the Lord of the Dance,' Angela said, her eyes like lights. She allowed her gaze to rest on the image a few long seconds, then stared at the two men.

'It's been a short visit, but we've been in London long enough. It's time we head for India.'

Fifteen minutes later, Angela, Jack and Sean were outside the Victoria and Albert Museum and settling themselves back into the black Mercedes that had brought them there from the Temple Church. Blackburn Enterprises was sparing no expense on their excursion.

'Back to Heathrow,' Sean instructed the driver. He sat again in the passenger seat, his computer open on his lap, leaving Angela and Jack to converse in the back. Sean's attention was on booking three tickets on the next available flight to Tiruchchirapali, the nearest airport to Chidambaram.

'Do you know anything about this temple?' Jack asked Angela as the car moved away from the kerb.

'Nothing, but we have the next few hours to learn,' she answered. Her eyes, however, betrayed less confidence. Hindu theology was vast and complex, and the temples that grounded its worship even more so. She could only imagine, from what little she'd seen of the Thillai Nataraja complex on Sean's screen within the museum, that they were heading into something far more extensive than the relatively small structure of London's Temple Church.

'But you're sure we're meant to go there?' Jack asked.

'You saw the symbol, you saw the image of the temple. You suddenly have some doubt they're connected?'

'I don't doubt they're connected. But it could just be a sign of influence, or familiarity. Using foreign imagery to throw off would-be pursuers – imagery that wouldn't be clear to devout Christians of the fourteenth century.' Jack allowed his words to resonate a few moments. 'It doesn't necessarily follow that it's meant to direct people to the imagery's source. And besides, there has to be more than just this one temple dedicated to Shiva in all of India.'

'None like this. Not with the emphasis on Shiva's dance and this peculiar form of architecture.'

Even as she said it, shooting down Jack's worry, Angela was impressed. Not for the first time, Jack's cautious scepticism surprised her. A day ago, she would have imagined him as a man ready to fly to the far corners of the world on a whim, if only for the sensationalism of standing in exotic locales and filling out the appealing image of the world explorer. But it was Angela, not Jack, pushing to travel to the Indian subcontinent. He was measured, careful, and over the morning had proved himself altogether a far more compelling individual than she'd formerly given him credit for.

Though, in this moment, the same scepticism that impressed Angela also frustrated her. With this news, with these possibilities, she wanted him to be excited, enthusiastic. Eager! Eager, like her.

Like me.

Her gaze fell casually to his hands, folded across his lap. For the first time she noticed the absence of a ring. And for the first time, that information interested her.

No. Snap out of it, she commanded herself. As swiftly as they had drifted downwards, she raised her eyes again to the seat-backs in front of them.

'I really think the symbol means more. You were right, Jack, back on the flight, when you said the remnant Templars would have been smarter to travel east. I've been trying for years to prove they did. There are signs here and there in the historical evidence – the odd mention of far-eastern architecture or city planning that could only be gained first-hand; references in late journals and chronicles to ritual practices that are far too close to Hindu and even Buddhist ceremonies to be simply coincidental. But all this evidence has been slight. Possibilities, rather than certainties.'

'But it's convinced you that the move east was a reality.'

'I've been ninety-five per cent certain for years. But this, this raises it to a hundred per cent, doesn't it? With the inscription on the tablet encoded in a Templar cipher pointing here, and then a symbol engraved on the effigy indicating a specific temple dedicated to a specific deity in India . . . aren't you curious to probe a little further?' She cut off her words, and found herself desperately hoping he was.

Jack seemed to stare through her for a few long moments, but just as the silence threatened to become awkward, he spoke.

'I guess we can't really come this far and not see what's next, can we?'

Jack smiled, and Angela reached forward, clutching his hands in a familiar gesture of relief, gratitude and excitement.

And for an instant longer than the gesture required, she let her hands linger.

29

Heathrow Airport, London

Ninety minutes after they'd left the V&A, Sean, Jack and Angela were through security at Heathrow Terminal 5 and settled into the Galleries Lounge South awaiting their flight to India. The lounge was predictably full and pretentiously elegant, but at least offered comforts and concessions during their wait; and as Thomas Blackburn's diplomatic connections had ensured that entry visas for India were waiting for them on their arrival at the airport, they had little to do but pass the time until departure.

Sean sat back in a dark blue chair, sipping a neat Scotch and watching the BBC news on the television opposite him. The afternoon's events cycled across the screen as newsreaders highlighted the key stories.

Sean fiddled with his a drink, disinterested. Until, all at once, his interest was wholly captured.

'Oh, hell.' He set down his drink and rose, walking towards the slender television mounted on the lounge wall. A newsreader in a red blouse craned her head slightly to the side as she listened to something being broadcast in her ear. The breaking-news headline at the bottom of the screen flashed red, and had already grabbed Sean's complete attention.

'We're just receiving word,' the woman announced, her speech halting as she tried to listen and speak at the same time, 'of a murder in the main entrance hall of the Victoria and Albert Museum in central London.'

Sean's skin went cold.

'Witnesses are reporting the single victim was a white male, aged between forty and sixty, who apparently worked as a museum curator.'

Cold skin began to sweat. Sean's mind raced back to their arrival at the museum, to the resident curator who had helped them locate the room where the Temple Church casts resided.

'Reports differ on the precise number of shots fired,' the newsreader continued, 'but it seems that a gunman, male, fired either four or five rounds from a handgun while standing just inside the rotating doors of the main entrance. At least two of the shots were delivered towards the museum's unarmed security guards, who in the chaos that ensued were unable to apprehend him before he fled.'

Sean stepped backwards and fell back into the chair, his eyes stuck on the television. The woman continued to relay the sketchy details as they came through, but Sean could no longer hear her voice.

The only man to whom they had spoken at the museum: executed. Publicly. In a way meant to be seen. Which could only mean one thing.

He, Angela and Jack were not alone on their journey. They were being followed, and whoever was following them wanted Sean to know they were there.

He swallowed hard. Certain decisions had to be taken, and taken immediately. He could tell Jack and Angela. But at the very least, doing so would cause worry and fear. Could derail all their work. But perhaps it wouldn't be necessary. That depended on entirely on what those who were following him wanted.

He was cut out of his racing concerns by a soft female voice wafting down from speakers in the ceiling, commanding them all into motion.

Their flight was being called.

30

The grainy video image took a few seconds to load, but the encrypted stream soon became clearer and the face on the other side of the camera recognizable.

'Senator Wilcox,' the man said, his face wearing the same calm, controlled expression that it had in Preston's office when he had first confronted him with the shattered reality of his new life. His wife, dead. His children, taken. His world, collapsing.

'I'm here, I'm here,' Preston answered. He'd already closed and locked his office door. The video connection was coming through on a laptop the man had given him, across lines he had been ensured were untraceable. Not that he would have tried such a manoeuvre, or told anyone about the contact. He'd watched the video of his wife being killed, and he harboured no doubts that these men, whoever they were, wouldn't hesitate to do the same to his girls. He wasn't about to give them any reason to so do.

'You've had the conversation?' the man asked, his voice slightly delayed over the transmission, not coming through in synch with the movement of his lips on the screen.

'Yes, with the man in charge of security.'

'And?'

'He told me they'll do what they can to see if the alterations can be made to the evening's programme.'

There was a disturbing delay in the other man's reaction.

'The programme revision is non-negotiable,' he finally said. '*Possibilities* are not good enough.' His voice went hard, his eyes harder. 'You were only instructed to do one thing, Senator Wilcox. And you've failed.'

'I was as persuasive as I could be,' Wilcox pleaded.

The man on the display nodded off camera. A moment later he reached to his left and pulled a young girl into frame. Her hands were tied, her mouth covered in grey tape, her face dirty and eyes terrified. The man held her by her hair, making a show of not being gentle.

'Bella!' Preston shouted.

The man let Wilcox's daughter rest in frame for a few seconds, then forcibly thrust her aside.

'You're going to have to do better than this, Senator. Remember, where your wife has gone, your daughters can still follow.'

31

Chidambaram, Tamil Nadu, India, the Next Day

The drive through the inner streets of Chidambaram was as stark a contrast as could be imagined to the London that Angela, Jack and Sean had left less than fourteen hours earlier. While central London was hardly a city of the balanced, evenly toned architectural symmetry of Paris or Venice, its moderate eclecticism was nothing in comparison to the inner corridors of India's Tamil Nadu.

All around them, outside the pleasant but cramped car, hardly as luxurious as the Mercedes they'd had in London, narrow streets were filled to the brim with wares for sale, laid out in piles and stacks before brightly painted buildings that blatantly favoured primary colours over the nonetheless frequent bold pastels. Bicycles weaved with abandon between rickshaws and minuscule buses, the garments on the mob of pedestrians as colourful as the storefronts. Tea shops and restaurants served meals on balconies, while every conceivable surface was draped in advertising, from Sanskrit mobile-phone adverts to Coca-Cola banners that didn't bother publishing in anything but English. Parked motorcycles formed only marginally neat rows intermittently along the streets, and over everything hung the tickling potpourri of petrol exhaust and cigarette smoke, and the heavy scent of spices, on sale at almost every step.

The structures of the city were a strange mixture of new-build with old wood- and metal-frame warehouse buildings, standing side by side on streets in a manner that made it impossible to determine whether any given section of the city was poor or rich, a business district or residential quarter, upper caste or lower. And though none of the buildings were terribly high, never more than four or five storeys at the most, the congested infrastructure of Chidambaram meant that Angela, Jack and Sean could never see more than a street or two ahead of them.

That is, until they turned off East Car Street on to East Sannathi. Then, suddenly, the seven-tiered *gopura*, or gateway tower, over the Thillai Nataraja Temple's eastern portal appeared majestically before them.

At the end of the small road, which was more a bazaar of shops and market stands than a passible thoroughfare, the great *gopura* at the eastern edge of the temple complex seemed to loom over everything, painted in teals, pinks, blues and greys. Moustached avatars clung to the tiers in nearly 800-year-old stone relief, holding lotus flowers, gazing down on the throngs below. There were fourteen of them, situated in pairs, running up the central edifice itself, each reaching a little closer to heaven, each slightly different in shape, in size and colour and form. The *gopura* as a whole housed over thirty additional statues, and was famed throughout India for containing panels depicting all 108 *Bharatanatyam* – the traditional postures of classical Indian dance.

And that was one thing all the statues on the eastern tower had in common. They were dancing, and in fitting tribute they beckoned the world outside to the temple of Shiva-Nataraja, the Lord of the Dance.

A cup of coffee landed on the table in front of Angela, deposited by a smiling waiter who placed similar cups before Jack and Sean. They had left the car at the corner of East Sannathi and walked by foot along the busy street, stopping for a coffee at a small collection of tables outside the Hotel Akshaya Darshan. The sweet scents of spices and flavoured tobacco were mixed with the stench of heat, rubbish and the waste of a uniquely Indian poverty that blended rag-clad, filthy children with silk-suited businessmen in Ray-Bans. The strange mix of rich and poor was as eclectic as the mixture of scents in the air, at once as inviting as off-putting. And certainly overwhelming. The potent fumes from the spiced coffee filled Angela's nostrils and for a brief second cancelled out the sensory overload.

She stirred two lumps of rough sugar into her coffee and drew in a mouthful. The liquid was thick, potent and precisely what she needed.

She glanced across the table to Jack, who appeared mesmerized by the bustle of life. His eyes took in the motion of every cyclist, every pedestrian, every bargained transaction for beer or phone cards or breakfast supplies. And something within Angela admired his ability to be taken in so completely by the culture around him.

She shifted her attention to Sean, who appeared equally interested, yet visibly more suspicious of their surroundings. He'd had a nervousness about him since London that she hadn't been able to pinpoint, but he hadn't been overly talkative either, so she'd left it alone.

'Are you sure *this* is where we're meant to be?' he asked, catching Angela's glance. Sean's emphasis on 'this' left little doubt that, whatever his other misgivings, he was having trouble coupling the strange madness of urban India with their work on Templar history.

'Look behind you, Sean,' Angela answered, pointing towards the monumental *gopura* at the end of the street. 'Can there be any doubt that this is the shape we found in London?'

Sean looked again to the tower as Jack turned his attention back to their table. He brought his eyes to Angela's, waiting for her further thoughts.

'I didn't know about this temple, or even this location in general,' she started, 'but my hypothesis on a Templar migration after the dissolution of the Order in Europe, and the trials that followed for the next two years, always pointed in this direction. Until we found the marker in the Temple Church, I had no concrete evidence to help me sort out exactly where they went, but India was definitely on my list. It's a perfectly sensible option.'

'Sensible?' Jack questioned.

'It would have had two things going for it. First, it was east of France, Spain, and the other European centres in which the Templars had become *personae non gratae*. The natural route would have been for them to travel north and west, into the regions of the empire where there was still some degree of toleration and where they had connections; but that would also have been the expected route.'

'Meaning that if they feared persecution, it would be a route they would want to avoid.'

'I think you and I both share that as a principal criticism of the theory that the Templars moved to England and Scotland after the purge. They knew persecution would follow, and ultimately those lands wouldn't have been any safer than central Europe.'

'So they travel east,' Jack followed. 'Understandable. Anything east of the Outremer was foreign territory to the empire.' He reflected a moment. 'That's one reason why India might be sensible. You said there were two.'

'The second is the religious background here. India is east of the empire, but it's also Hindu.'

'You think the Knights Templar had anything in common with Hinduism?' Sean asked incredulously.

'It's not that they had anything in common with it, rather that it wasn't Islam. Many of the territories east of Europe would have provided suitable distance from Paris, but most of those immediately east of the empire's borders were under Muslim control, and no member of an Order that had fought against "the infidel" during the crusades would have ever made a home in Islamic lands.'

'But to a devout monk, is Hinduism any better?'

'It would have still been seen as barbaric, blasphemous and tantamount to idol worship, but it wouldn't have had the stain of the anti-Christian feuds of the preceding centuries. It would have been . . . tolerable.'

Jack digested Angela's thoughts, then glanced back out at the busy street and temple beyond. Sweat had long since coated his skin, his shirt clinging to his shoulders and chest.

'So it's possible that some remnant group of the Order could have come as far as here, and seen – experienced – all this.'

'The Thillai Nataraja Temple was constructed in the twelfth and thirteenth centuries, but not adorned until the fourteenth. That puts its zenith right about the time of the Templar purge. So they would have seen almost exactly what we're seeing now.'

As Angela spoke, all three had their eyes back on the colourful, mystifying tower that stood so close by. Smoke from incense burning within the temple compound poured out into the street, curling grey wisps floating over the brick walls with an aura of tranquillity, into a city that buzzed with anything but.

'If there was ever a good place for a group of Templars to hide something, whether it was treasure, or knowledge, or even just themselves,' Angela finally added, 'this is it.'

32

Thillai Nataraja Temple, Chidambaram

'You're already in the temple?'

'I've been here for the past two hours, but our men have been on site for the past twenty-four,' Michael Wyatt answered. He stood within the temple surroundings, trying not to appear as foreign and out of place as he felt.

Though Wyatt couldn't see it, the Seneschal smiled on the other end of the phone. He'd been proven right in telling his men to focus on the second half of the Oak Island inscription. Sean and his group had gone off to London, seeking the meaning of the first segment, and it had been necessary to have them followed in case there was more there than expected, but the Seneschal had sensed that the guidance towards a tiered palace was the most significant.

And he hadn't needed a ridiculous picture etched on the back of a shield to figure it out. He'd sent a group of two ahead to Chidambaram immediately.

'Have our men found anything?'

'Not yet. They've done a fairly thorough search during the temple's opening hours, and there's a contact just outside the city who knows the administration and was able to give them a few extra hours this morning.'

'Fruitless hours.'

'Not fruitless.' Wyatt was resistant to the phrasing

without being disrespectful. 'Elimination of possibilities is productive. We've ruled out most of the upper complex and the other three *gopuram*. We believe that whatever's here is somewhere in the smaller, underground shrines beneath the east tower.'

'Very well. But Sean's group has arrived in the city. They'll be on the grounds momentarily. You'll need to keep out of sight. Let them do their work. Then take what they find for your own.'

33

Thillai Nataraja Temple, Chidambaram

The interior of the Thillai Nataraja Temple was as colourful and other-worldly as the tower that faced the street. The great eastern *gopura* was itself only a small portion of a much larger complex that included three other similar towers to the north, west and south, together with a central reflective pool and four distinct temple units sprawling across the vast, tree-lined grounds.

'This place is enormous,' Sean gasped as the trio entered fully into the grounds, a few American dollars poorer for the privilege. The exterior walls formed a great rectangle, the short side over 300 yards in length and its north–south span half that size again. All around them within the enclave, another world seemed to open up. Colonnaded walkways surrounded the glass-like pool at the centre, each pillar a strange mixture of oddly angled shapes interspersed with bas-relief flowers and vines. Every sandstone and granite surface was an exercise in interlaced geometry, and carved avatars of the gods – above all, Shiva – were everywhere.

What struck Angela most, though, were the colours. The natural stone was accented at every turn by bold shades that seemed to clash against western aesthetic expectations. The green of the water ran up against the whites and reds of the colonnades; rust-red and orange frescoes dotted the walls; while teal, green and yellow clothes adorned the carved status of the Hindu deities. Bold golden lettering pronounced oversized quotations of the scriptures in positions high above the footpaths. Angela realized that it sounded neither erudite nor particularly respectful considering the place's religious significance, but it looked for all the world like a box of wax crayons had been left out in the sun, their contrasting tones melting and swirling into a melange of colour that incorporated the whole spectrum in a bright, almost playful way.

'I've never seen anything like this,' Jack whispered to her. She smiled gently. Angela had read Shepherd's dossier, she knew he had seen much of the world. But much is not all. It was nice to think he was as awestruck as she was.

And good to know, too, that he didn't know everything. 'You don't have to whisper,' she said. 'It's perfectly acceptable to speak inside a Hindu temple.'

Jack nodded but, with an accidental tinge of irony, said nothing further.

Before them, signage in multiple languages provided basic orientation and key facts for visitors, and even through the broken translations the uniqueness of the Thillai Nataraja Temple came across. Situated at the precise centre of the magnetic equator, the complex's nine entrances symbolized the nine orifices of the human body, with the temple's 'heart', its innermost sanctum, positioned over what was believed to be the heart of the universe. That central shrine, known as the Ponnambalam, was a work of symbolic architecture of the highest order: twenty-eight pillars accounting for the twenty-eight methods of worshipping Nataraja, sixty-four roof supports symbolizing the sixty-four forms of classical Indian art. The ceiling of the Ponnambalam was composed of 21,600 'breaths', each one a golden tile on which was inscribed a sacred incantation, held in place by 72,000 golden nails, corresponding to the same number of *nadis*, or channels of energy that traditional Indian medicine identified in the human body. Nine ceremonial pots on the roof corresponded to the nine forms of energy in Hindu spiritual science, and the six pillars supporting the inner dais of the sanctum represented the six sacred Sanskrit *shastras*, or holy texts.

All three of them were taken in, and for a long while they stood still, silent, completely overwhelmed. Eventually, it was Sean who brought focus back to their visit.

'It's amazing,' he interjected, 'but we're not here for the sight-seeing like the rest of them.' He motioned towards the throngs of people crowding the courtyard, milling about between the shrines. 'We're here to find something. And I might just remind you both that we don't know what it is, or where, or how we're going to get to it.' The nervousness was back in his voice.

Jack answered before Angela. His face was a broad smile. 'Sounds about perfect.'

As they made their way deeper into the temple, the surroundings became no less awe-inspiring but incrementally more mysterious. As bizarre as the exterior surfaces of the towers and other buildings were to inexperienced eyes, they paled in comparison to the interiors. Room after room was stone-cut in carved relief, chambers alternating from vast floorspaces with high ceilings to tiny cubicles, barely able to hold a few pilgrims. Each was dedicated to a different avatar of Shiva-Nataraja, or to various scenes from the tales of his life. In one, Nataraja danced the Dance of Bliss, a cobra dangling from his hand, a moon and skull above him while he moved within a circle of flames. The painted statue was so lifelike, its surface textured and shiny with thick paint, that it seemed to sweat with the pilgrims, bearing the heat in its eternal pose. In the next room, the *mudra* of creation was symbolized in the beat of a drum, clasped in the god's hand. In another, Shiva danced over the body of Apasmara, the demon of ignorance, preparing the world for creation. His skin glistened in the candlelight, muscles carved with such realism that they almost appeared to twitch as he held up his leg in the dance, and it seemed as if one could hear the plucked music that possessed him to sway to its rhythms and bear the world to creation.

In each chamber, the images of veneration were visited by throngs of the devout, peppered by tourists with their cameras. Garlands of fresh flowers were strung over statues, floral and fragrant, and before them burned candles and oil lamps, incense offered continually. Some of the statues were drenched in milk offerings, others with honey, all mingling together in the increasingly tight spaces to create a unique and unrepeatable sensory experience. The sentiment aimed for seemed somewhere between trance and ecstasy, and it had its desired effect on no small number of the pilgrims.

Jack had his eyes on full alert as they made their way deeper into the interior. The interconnecting rooms seemed to descend, and he was nearly certain they were now below ground level – though without windows it was impossible to tell.

Angela spoke softly to the two men. 'We're looking for something similar to what we saw on the cast from the Temple Church. A message left from one group of Templars, meant to be found by another. It would have to be something visible, but not obvious. Something that would have little meaning, and would attract little notice, to others.'

Though what she said was perfectly sensible, Jack couldn't help but think it seemed as unlikely here as it had been in London. There was a constant flow of people through each and every room they visited. Every surface was seen. It would be next to impossible for anything here to remain hidden, especially over a span of centuries.

They arrived at the far end of a small room and entered a narrow corridor leading to the next. The deeper into the temple they went, the smaller the chambers and the more convoluted the tiny connecting passageways – and as vivid as the shrines were, with their lamplight, colour and decoration, the corridors between them were bare stone, grey and cold. It was as if the rooms here were sculpted around the natural hollows of the stone beneath the monuments above, and there was an earthiness to the atmosphere that increased the deeper they travelled.

Where, in all this, would a visiting group of Templars have been able to conceal anything at all?

As they emerged from the passage into the next room, Sean stopped them.

'We could wander about like this all day. We need to be more systematic if we're going to make progress.' He looked as if he had a plan, or at least an idea.

'What do you suggest?' Angela asked.

'Let's start from what we saw in London. Where did we find the inscription there?'

'On the sarcophagus of Robert de Vieuxpont,' Jack answered.

'A sign by the last of the Templars,' Angela added, 'left on a location that paid reverence to one who had supported them in their prime.'

'But what if it wasn't that at all?' Sean responded. He looked up, saw that he had Jack and Angela's full attention, and continued. 'What if it wasn't respect for a benefactor, or for older knights, or anything at all to do with the Templar past, that caused them to choose that place for their inscription?'

'If not that, then what?'

Sean took in a breath and exhaled his answer. 'Death.'

'Death?' Jack and Angela eyed him curiously.

'What if it was simply death? The inscription was on the shield of a burial sarcophagus, originally situated in a portion of the Temple Church dedicated to burials and the memory of the dead. It may have had other purposes earlier in its history, but what did the Round Church ultimately become?'

'A burial site,' Angela answered. 'A memorial to the reposed.'

'Exactly.' Sean looked intently at her, then at Jack. 'We're not likely to find any buried knights or anything else Templar-related here, but I think we'll be on the right track if we try to find the section of this temple that deals in the same symbolism. We need to find a monument to death.'

34

Unknown Village, India, AD 1326

'You must drink the liquid, mister.' A short man held the wooden bowl up before Arnaud de Faulke's face. The paint on the stranger's cheeks and forehead was bright, a contrast to his dark skin and the darker surroundings.

De Faulke wasn't sure how many others were in the antechamber with them. He could make out the faces of at least eight, but the strange, droning chant emerging unseen carried the tone of more voices. And the place stank of far more sweaty bodies than his eyes could see.

The wooden bowl was again nudged towards his mouth. He looked down at the reddish liquid it contained, watery, smelling of earth and minerals and spices he could not identify.

'You cannot enter unless you drink.' The short man's face betrayed little emotion, but the painted decoration gave him a fearful countenance.

Sweat dripped from de Faulke's brow. The room he had been permitted to enter was underground, yet it was surprisingly hot. Hot and dank. The air was sticky, and the scent of bodies mingled with some type of incense that reeked of sandalwood and musk. His clothes clung to his body, his hair a damp stack atop his head.

Everything about the surroundings seemed – sinister. For an instant, de Faulke's defences rose. These men could be armed. He could be trapped, the iron grate that barred the way to their meeting place closed and locked behind him. He had no way of knowing, and de Faulke was not a man that enjoyed being at the mercy of anyone but God.

He forced away the sudden blush of fear. It was for this that he was here. Initiation. Entry into the unknown. The unknown that he desperately needed . . .

For days, the skin of those that de Faulke and his squire had passed on the roads and in the villages as they headed east had been growing darker. The tone of their colouring was not the charcoal black of the Africans, which had made the knight so uncomfortable when he had travelled there as a child. The barbarian races in this region bore a different complexion. Their skin was oily, almost olive, as if it had been burned by the sun into a reflection of the strangely coloured earth on which they walked.

It was unnerving, yet reassuring. Jacques de Molay's notes had described just such features, which meant they were on the right path.

The deeper they travelled into these unknown lands, the stranger their surroundings became. Surely the One God had created the whole earth and all that is in it, but how dreadful and garish it became when the borders of the Holy Roman Empire gave way to the dark fringes of the civilized world. Food smelled and tasted different; clothing, housing, even colours themselves seemed bold and foreign.

And then there were the shrines and idols – the blasphemous worship of false gods. All the flowers and incense, spice and milk offerings poured over them couldn't hide the fact that they were an abomination upon the earth. The very thought of their existence was an offence. The actual sight of them, so close, all around, was a challenge to the very core of the knight's soul.

Yet it could only be from the realm of darkness that darkness itself would flow. He would bear the stench, the offence, the blasphemy, so long as it led him towards that realm and that promise that de Molay had recorded.

A promise that was known in the local language most often as उत्रास, *uttr'Asa, 'The Terror'.*

De Molay had written of them with a peculiar circumspection. A group of men, educated in all that their dreadful religion found most terrifying. Death. Pain. Suffering. Illness. Agony. Forces, in reality, that were untouchable to the rest of society. Men who did their fellow man a favour by living apart, taking the knowledge of such things to themselves, so that no others needed to go near it.

They were the most feared and outcast group in the local culture – men that the natives preferred never to speak of, and hoped never to see. But the late Grand Master had written that it was these same men who had led him towards the discovery that had haunted him for the rest of his life, and that meant that Arnaud de Faulke wanted nothing more than to stand in their midst.

The bowl was pressed firmly against his lower lip, the fumes rising from it now almost nauseating. He had no way to know what it was, or what it would do, but it was clear that the men of the Terror would not let him enter further into their mysteries unless he drank it.

De Faulke looked forward, directly into the black hollow eyes of the painted man before him. In a single motion, an act of faith, he downed the full contents of the wooden bowl, the strange concoction within burning as it rolled over his tongue and down his throat.

The painted man smiled, and a murmur of approval came from those seated in the darkness.

'Now, you come. You come with us,' the little man said, grabbing de Faulke by his elbow.

He leaned forward to rise, and the lights from the flames swirled in his vision. The moans of the chanting seemed so sorrowful, the world slipping away from reality, as if he were being beckoned into the belly of hell itself.

35

Thillai Nataraja Temple, Chidambaram, India

Angela, Jack and Sean were now deep within the subterranean environs of Thillai Nataraja, having long since passed through all the major halls and shrines for which the temple was known. Sean's idea had given them focus, and that focus had set them in motion. They had walked quickly through the Chit Ambalam, or inner sanctuary, that housed the primary statues of Nataraja and his consort upon a golden stage. They had swiftly passed by the thousand-pillared hall of Raja Sabhai, which was opened only on feast days. They had transversed through the 'golden hall', the Ponnambalam, where the daily rituals of offering and reverence were carried out. The sights could have absorbed them all day, but as soon as they determined a room wasn't somehow connected to death or the dead, they swiftly moved on.

Now, deep in the temple complex's belly, there were still pilgrims in a steady stream, but their numbers here were far fewer. The lighting was dark, mostly lamplight, and the constructed glamour of the large halls had given way to the stable atmosphere of antiquity.

It had been Sean who had stopped to purchase a guidebook from a kiosk before they had entered, anxious to have something concrete to guide their search. And it was he who now led them through the small passageways from chamber to chamber, a focus on maps and directions seeming to help counteract the occasional jittering that both Jack and Angela recognized as the signs of a mild claustrophobia.

'It should be the next one, after this,' he said as they passed through a room that couldn't have been more than twelve feet square. At the far side the next passage was barely wide enough for a single person, its raw stone walls slightly damp, twisting nearly ten feet through stone before opening into the room they wanted.

As Sean emerged, followed by Angela and then Jack, optimism immediately surged in all of them.

'This is it,' Sean said, his voice only a whisper in the small space. 'The lesser shrine to Kali.' By the flickering light of dozens of candles he could just make out the lettering in his guidebook, and read aloud to the others.

'Kali, whose name means "death" and "lord of death", is the Hindu goddess of change and destruction. Originally the annihilator of evil, depictions of Kali often portray her, as in this shrine, in violent terms, with bloodied sword in hand. She holds a place of significance in Thillai Nataraja Temple veneration due to the mythic confrontation between Kali and Nataraja, commemorated chiefly in the Nrithya Sabhai hall, where Nataraja's supremacy was confirmed as he outperformed Kali in a contest of dance.'

'The goddess of death, outdone by a dance –' Jack muttered. Something of his disdain for legend was seeping back into his voice.

'What's important for the moment,' Angela said, stopping him, 'is that this shrine is dedicated to a memorial of death, in one form or another. And *that* is promising territory.' With her final phrase she motioned past the small statue at the tiny room's centre, to the walls that surrounded them.

Those walls were covered, floor to ceiling, in writing, symbols, paintings and carvings. But these weren't the carefully crafted adornments of the other rooms. The inscriptions here were ramshackle, random, from the hands of what appeared to be dozens or even hundreds of different scribes. It looked for all the world like a room full of graffiti, painted and scratched in layer after layer, one text written over the top of the last for who knew how many centuries.

'The guidebook says the walls of the shrine are covered in tributes,' Sean announced.

'Tributes?'

'*The goddess of death ultimately symbolizes time, change and new birth for Hindus.*' Sean's eyes scrutinized the guidebook's pages. '*She is worshipped not for the end of life, but for the end of certain times of life and the beginnings of others. The tributes lining the walls are words of thanksgiving, memorials written, carved or painted there by pilgrims grateful for the transformation of their lives that they attributed to the goddess.*'

Jack's brows lifted, and Angela caught his look. The Templars at the time of the purge were undergoing radical change. If they were to hide something in a Hindu temple, a room dedicated to change and transformation seemed appropriate.

'The tradition of inscribing tributes on the walls was kept here for almost 750 years,' Sean said, looking up from his book. 'It was only banned in the twentieth century, when the increased flow of tourists meant that the number of new inscriptions threatened to destroy the old.'

'That puts it in our timeframe,' Angela said, doing some quick maths. Pilgrims and visitors would already have been inscribing their tributes on these walls in the period after the purge, when any Templars fleeing the empire might have arrived here. 'This is where we stop and search.'

The search began in earnest, but the challenging parameters of the task made themselves apparent immediately.

'Most of these are indecipherable,' Jack muttered as he studied one of the walls in the shrine to Kali. He and the others had each taken a candle from the votive collection before the central statue and were scrutinizing the thousands of memorial tributes left in the room. Some were carved into the sandstone walls, others painted on its surface, while some were barely more than scratch marks.

'You'll know it when you see it,' Angela answered from the other side of the chamber. 'I'm willing to bet than any Knights Templar who got this far in the fourteenth century didn't know Sanskrit any better than you or I do. Don't worry about deciphering the unfamiliar.'

'Look for the familiar that you can't decipher,' Sean added. He paused at his comment, then released a nervous chuckle, apparently calmed by his own wit. 'Damn, that was good. And I wasn't even trying.'

Jack and Angela each winced.

'Sean is right, though,' Angela finally admitted. 'We're almost certain to be looking for a text encoded with the same rune-based cipher we saw on Oak Island. It will look familiar, even if we won't be able to read it outright.'

'I've brought everything with me for that part,' Sean

responded, tapping at the pack on his back. 'We can uplink whatever we find to Seattle, and they can throw it on to the central computer the moment we do. With two texts down, they're convinced that the computer's virtual model of the original encoding device is largely complete, and confident that the time needed to decode a third sample will be significantly less than even the second.' Again, the technical language seemed to distract him from his nervousness over the enclosed space.

Jack let his attention depart from Sean's technical commentary. He ran his fingers along the wall, holding the candle close with his other hand. The swirling, strangely linear Sanskrit inscriptions overlapped one another, the centuries providing for more gratitude than there had been space on the walls. Lines of text came at different angles, written with seeming indifference to the emotive phrases beneath them. Then there were the tributes painted in thick brushstrokes atop the inscriptions, covering two- and three-layer deep carvings with as many different layers of paint. Deciphering one tribute from another was not easy work. Jack found himself staring at a single patch of wall without moving, trying to adjust his depth of vision to sort out one from another.

Several layers, several inscriptions, but nothing remotely Templar.

He moved a step to his left and brought his line of sight up by about a foot. Another patch of wall, just as densely covered as the one he'd left.

'Anything?' Angela asked from her position. The question was for both men, and both muttered responses in the negative.

Jack re-focused his eyes. The orange light of the candle was not helping, the colour making it harder to trace the edges of letters cut into stone of a similar shade. Some of the tributes included small pictures: faces, deities, even stick-like figures that Jack assumed represented the individuals leaving their thanks. He'd only been studying the wall a few minutes, but he already felt as if he were going cross-eyed before the mishmash of words layered over images, scrawled on letters, etched over symbols.

He moved his gaze slightly to the left once again. It was only then that something caught his eye.

Out of the corner of his vision, a few inches above the segment of wall on which he'd been focusing, a symbol stood out. A small diagonal bar running downwards from left to right, with two small, apostrophe-like marks above and below it.

The Hebrew *aleph*. It was a letter that did not belong to the Templars alone, by any stretch of the imagination, and stretched back thousands of years before them. But even without a working knowledge of that language or the one used here, Jack felt certain about one thing: the Hebrew *aleph* had no counterpart in Sanskrit.

'You'd both better come over here,' he quietly announced to Angela and Sean. 'I think I've found our marker.'

36

L Street, Washington, DC

A murder outside a bar as seedy as the Mill House would hardly amount to front-page news in the crime-riddled DC quarter of L Street Southeast. Even if the victim was military. Soldiers had bad habits just like other men, and society was ready to overlook their weaknesses more readily than others. They dealt in difficult realities. They could hardly be blamed for their human weaknesses and the troubles they got them into, especially in a neighbourhood that had been listed as one of the twenty-five most dangerous in the country.

The seasoned knight of the New Order would make the Grand Master proud. He had phoned Petty Officer Second Class Rick DiMaggio earlier in the day, setting up the arrangement. The knight had passed himself off as a friend from their grade-school days – he'd taken a name suitably commonplace and forgettable that the soldier wouldn't be surprised he couldn't quite place or remember it – who had managed to track him down through mutual friends. He and two others would be gathering tonight at the Mill House to reminisce over old times, and if DiMaggio didn't mind slumming it with the low-brow scrum that hadn't gone on to bright military careers, he was invited to join them. It hadn't taken much convincing. A chance to exercise bragging rights over fellow small-town boys, even if the man couldn't quite remember who they were, was an opportunity not to be missed.

The knight had stood him up. The soldier had arrived in the bar at the time they'd arranged, the seedy surroundings and even seedier look to the establishment itself not seeming to deter him. He'd pulled open the metal door on the windowless concrete box of a building and slipped inside in his civilian clothes, and had remained there, alone, for twenty minutes.

The Grand Master's devotee was ready. Twenty minutes was about all any man could take in such a setting without company, which meant Petty Officer DiMaggio would be emerging at any moment, frustrated and annoyed. The knight would act quickly. The attack needed to happen in close proximity, before the soldier could put any distance between himself and the bar. Bar fights happened outside bars.

The moment came only a few minutes later. The door swung slowly outwards, a cloud of heavy smoke emerging from within, and DiMaggio stepped out on to the street. His face bore the frustration the knight had expected to see. The man tightened his coat and turned left on to the small alleyway that would connect him back to New Jersey Avenue.

Stepping quickly to a position just behind the soldier, the knight said in a friendly voice, 'Are you Rick DiMaggio?'

The soldier's answer began even before he started to turn.

'Maybe I am, but who the hell are y –'

He didn't finish his question before a powerful fist

connected with his face, landing squarely between his eyes as the man turned. DiMaggio's head slammed backwards, colliding with the grey concrete brickwork of the bar as the knight brought a knee up to his groin and then delivered two hooks, one to each side of the man's head.

The crunch of bone echoed down the narrow street.

A moment later, the fulfiller of the Grand Master's will walked calmly into the darkness, massaging his knuckles. Behind him, the battered body of Petty Officer Rick DiMaggio lay crumpled on the oily pavement, his last breath already a thing of the past.

Eliminate their expertise, and the enemy will be powerless.

The first phase of his mission was accomplished.

37

Shrine to Kali, Thillai Nataraja Temple,
Chidambaram, India

It took less than a second from Jack's announcement for
Angela to reach his side, and Sean was there almost as
quickly.

'What have you found?'

Jack pointed at the *aleph* etched into the wall. It was at
just above his shoulder level, carved lightly into the stone.
A Sanskrit inscription had been carved later at an angle
across it, and since that time the whole area had been
painted over with the alternating blue and red lettering of
a yet later memorial; but when the candlelight was held at
an oblique angle, the Hebrew letter beneath could still be
made out.

'Is there more?' Sean asked impatiently.

'Yes,' Angela answered, her voice a whisper, already
identifying the extent of what Jack had found. She
moved her candle along the wall, working to reveal more
lettering. 'There is the symbol of three triangular dots,
and there . . . a small cross. This is it. It's definitely our
code.'

'Hold on just a minute.' Sean's voice was a puzzle. He
had taken two steps back from the wall, his back almost
flush against the statue at the room's centre.

'Step back here, Angela, right beside me. Jack, you stay there and keep your candle where it is.'

Angela moved to Sean's side and turned to face the wall.

'Don't look right at the letter,' Sean instructed. 'Broaden your vision a little. Do you see it?' His voice was now filled with an obvious wonder.

Angela scanned the wall, looking for more lettering or portions of the code, or segments of –

She froze, suddenly seeing what had captured Sean's attention. In the faint flicker and shadow of the candle, the runes became more visible, and so did something she had not expected. A rectangular frame, obviously etched by whatever tool had carved the runes, enclosed them, but it also contained something else. Two pictograms, the likes of which Angela had never seen.

It took only a few moments for Sean to open up his bag and extract the various pieces of equipment he would need for the task ahead. With discovery suddenly real and tangible, the nervous impatience that had marked out his demeanour since their arrival in India seemed to dissipate.

'The first requirement is a few high-resolution photographs to transmit.' A Canon EOS 5D Mark III camera was in his hands a second later, a high-powered flash affixed atop it. Sean positioned himself at a slight angle to the etching, and quickly shot a series of images. The powerful flash lit up the dim room with almost blinding intensity.

After taking a series of shots from multiple angles and examining them on the small digital display, Sean seemed satisfied and set the camera down next to his laptop. Transferring the images to the computer took under two minutes by USB-3, and he quickly set to work at the keyboard.

'My team back in Seattle is on standby for these,' he muttered to Angela and Jack as he typed. 'They're as keen to test out another set of encoded data on their virtual recreation of the Templar cipher as we are.'

'But how will you get the images to them?' Jack asked, motioning towards Sean's equipment. 'We're in a stone shrine, Lord knows how deep beneath this temple. You can't be telling me your cellular dongle gets reception down here.'

Sean peered up at him. 'Don't forget what Blackburn Enterprises is all about, Captain Shepherd.' He forced a smile at Jack, the sudden mention of his rank all the reminder that should be necessary. The company was, after all, one of the US military's primary engineers of high-grade technology.

'We developed this for the army a few years ago,' Sean

continued, motioning towards a black box appended to the back of his laptop. 'BSBR, or Boosted Satellite Broadcast and Reception capability. This little contraption allows satellite modem connectivity through up to fifty feet of bunkered earth or, in our case, the stone walls of a temple.'

Jack sensed this was all the detail he was going to get out of Sean; the engineer's attention was already back at his display and his fingers raced across the keyboard.

'What do you make of these?' Angela asked, drawing Jack back towards the images on the wall. Her hand was extended towards the two pictograms beneath the runes. The first was a triangle, precisely etched. A small impression marked each of its angles, and bisecting lines met at a fourth depression carved in its centre.

'Have there been images like this associated with any of the other runes you've found?' Jack asked.

'None. This is the first time I've ever seen this kind of pictogram on any Templar source.' Angela traced over the triangle with the tips of her fingers. She seemed entranced. Jack watched her hands glide along the shallow grooves of the ancient carving, noticing how delicately she touched them, almost with reverence.

Then, all at once, the expert was back at work. 'There are single-word runes marking two of the three points on the triangular pictogram,' Angela noted. 'You're having those decoded, too?'

'On it,' Sean answered, without looking up.

'Impossible to make sense of this until we know what those markers indicate,' Angela added, speaking to herself.

'What about this other image?' Jack asked. The carving

to the right of the triangle was by far the stranger of the two. 'The main shape itself looks almost organic.' It wasn't angular or precise like its partner.

'It looks like a . . . a heart.' Angela's words were soft, confused.

Jack agreed. It wasn't the romanticized, childish heart of love letters and Valentine's greetings: what was carved into the temple wall was a fairly accurate rendering of the lopsided, amorphous shape of a human heart.

And a word resided at its centre.

'That word isn't encoded,' Jack suddenly added, taking note of the detail for the first time. All the other text in the combined etchings was in the encrypted banking cipher the Templars had developed nearly a thousand years ago, but the singular word written in the centre of the heart was in a language that long pre-dated the Templars.

'It's written in Greek,' Angela affirmed, staring at the classical lettering with focus. '*Thanatos.*' The word had only one translation. 'Death.'

As Sean continued to work at his small computer, both Jack and Angela stared at the strange carving. In this shrine to the goddess of death, a Templar, centuries before, had enshrined death at the centre of a human heart.

It was a vision as chilling as the statue of the goddess behind them, bearing in her hand the bloodied dagger of destruction.

38

'This request comes with the full backing and support of the Senate Defence Committee. It represents an opportunity to advance the cause of American military might into the remainder of the twenty-first century, and beyond, with new capabilities and a cost model that will, quite literally, transform the way defence spending correlates to military activity.'

The special committee meeting took place in the US Capitol behind locked doors, its participants summoned with urgency and the promise of great opportunity for the nation – and these men were patriots, even if they were politicians. Senator Anthony Graves spoke to the committee with a confidence that came from many years in the chairman's seat. He was a seasoned statesman and elder, and he sat alongside his young counterpart and close associate, Senator Preston Wilcox.

Below the curved bench of the committee room's front table were two rows of military, security and executive office leaders assembled for the discussion.

'That may be the case,' one of the representatives of the West Wing interrupted. This was a closed-door meeting and formal protocol was understood by all to be relaxed. 'But the State of the Union is an evening that focuses on the presidency. Sharing the podium is an unheard-of shift in practice.'

Graves had anticipated this line of resistance from the first moment Wilcox had approached him with the possibility. Wilcox was young, bold, and the idea had first seemed impossibly brash. But then it had seemed intriguing, and then exemplary. At least the junior senator had been wise enough to know he could never have influenced these men alone. Graves's seniority was a necessity to get something so unusual pushed through, and so quickly. He'd thought through the potential challenges carefully, and he had responses at the ready.

'No one is suggesting that the president share the podium. The address will take place as it always does, and the usual filmed rebuttals by party representatives following the speech can all go ahead as normal.'

'Then I don't fully understand the proposal.'

'We're suggesting that the address be followed by a second event, outside the House Chamber in the Capitol building's Statuary Hall. After the speech and its immediate post hoc announcements have finished, we migrate the two Houses of Congress to the hall for a presentation on the transformation of military protocol in the decades ahead.'

'Why on this night?' one of the representative Secret Service agents present in the room queried. 'Security's a bitch enough for the State of the Union in its own right. Tack on another multi-branch activity and we've got a major event on our hands.'

'It should be on this night for precisely that reason,'

Senator Graves answered. 'How often do we have both Houses of Congress in one place, together with the head of the executive? We should take advantage of the opportunity. Holding a separate convocation would be far more work, cost and trouble.'

'But why is such representation required for a military presentation?' asked a general, seated in his full formal attire.

'Because military spending has been the most divisive issue in both houses over the past three years, if not longer. It's been something the president has struggled to control. The country is facing more enemies than ever before, and the cost of defence has skyrocketed. Spending has more than doubled in the past eighteen months, and that's following a doubling in the previous three years. The people are upset. The houses are upset. The West Wing is upset.'

'And you think this gathering, after the State of the Union, is going to help appease them?'

'It's sure as hell going to take a step in that direction,' Senator Graves said. 'We've got one of the most patriotic contractors in our history offering a contract for the next fifty years that will put new technologies in the hands of our armed services for a contracted rate that is seventy-five per cent cheaper than our current expenditure.'

Numbers rarely excited, but at the dropping of this figure the room went still.

'Seventy-five per cent?' the general finally asked. 'That's unheard of. It could calm the political and public waters over military spending.'

'And give your men some of the best technology in the

world to boot,' the senator added. 'Some of which will even be on display on the night.'

'Gentlemen,' he said a moment later, 'we all know that we're living in a militaristic age. Blackburn Enterprises is offering us a way forward. The technology all of us want, at a price we could never have dreamed of – and all they want is a PR op to show it off. Everyone wins. My Republican friends get more military might, we Democrats get smaller military spending, the president gets to capstone his State of the Union address with bipartisan good news that will soar him up the opinion polls. So tell me, what the hell are we discussing here? It's time to put questions of protocol to one side and talk logistics. This is a presentation that's got to happen.'

39

Thillai Nataraja Temple, Chidambaram, India

The chime of Sean's messaging system broke the silence that had descended over the shrine to Kali.

'Damn, that was faster than I thought,' he said, startled, as he looked down at his computer's display with renewed focus. The small instant messaging window on the right side of the screen blinked with new activity, and he clicked the focus to bring it to the forefront.

Decryption complete, read a single-line message. He read it aloud to the others, the next message following only a few seconds later.

Decoding accomplished in almost real time. Latin contents here, like former two. English translation of main inscription follows.

Apparently, their team had decided to translate themselves for expediency. There was a slight delay, and finally another ping chimed through the small room.

Where silk no longer travels: Xuanzang's workplace.

Sean stared at the screen, mystified. Leaning over the keyboard, he typed a brief reply.

That's it? Nothing else?

The message in reply evoked a sigh.

That's the full text of the main inscription.

'Ask them about the two markers at the corners of the triangular image,' Angela pressed. Sean typed out his message, and a moment later the response flashed on to his screen.

Two names. Hui'wanxiang and Fengizhen.

Sean looked from the screen to Angela. 'Do those names mean anything to you?'

'Nothing.' She shook her head. Jack's shook, too. The names rang no bells.

Sean waited a few moments, and saw that nothing more was forthcoming. Thanks, guys, he typed into the chat. You've been great.

A few seconds later, the connection went dead and Sean folded his computer closed.

The decoded text in hand, Angela walked back to the wall and gazed again at the original. Her mind raced to interpret the strange material, but nothing in either her research or expectation could make sense of the phrase that was only marginally less cryptic in its decoded form than it had been as a set of encrypted runes.

The two pictograms stared back at her. They were there to convey something, that much was certain.

Suddenly, Jack was at her side. He held a tiny digital camera in front of his face and snapped stills of the inscription and the room as a whole.

'I'm sure Sean's got plenty,' Angela said, bemused but with warmth. Jack's travel camera was hardly professional kit.

'These aren't for our study,' he answered. 'Just a few keepsakes. I took some at the Temple Church, too.' He smiled at her. 'Despite my reputation, this isn't the sort of thing I get to do every day.'

Angela was about to reply, but with a definitive suddenness she became aware of a curiosity that didn't have anything to do with the carvings on the walls or Jack's photo memorials.

They were alone. The room was silent.

There had been a constant flow of pilgrims all around them since they had first set foot in the Thillai Nataraja Temple complex, and though the crush had diminished as they worked deeper into the smaller shrines, they had never been without a decent stream of fellow visitors. Until they arrived here. The two tourists who had been in the small room when they'd entered had departed a few moments later, but no one else had entered behind them, despite the fact that they'd now been in Kali's shrine for at least twenty minutes.

Alone. Uninterrupted.

Angela was suddenly uncomfortable. She was probably being overly sensitive, and there was undoubtedly a good reason for the sudden lull in traffic, but she felt a strong desire to depart that welled up quickly.

'Is there anything else we need in here?' she asked the

two men. Sean was already packing his equipment away and Jack shook his head in the negative.

'Between the two of us we've photographed the whole room,' he noted, 'but I doubt there's anything more to be found.'

'Then let's go,' Angela announced, moving towards the small passageway at the far side.

'Not a second too soon,' Sean answered, relief in his voice, anxious to get back into open space and edging Jack towards the small exit.

Angela pushed past the two men, the spring to her step driven by something more than enthusiasm.

'It won't be but a few more minutes.' The announcement came in English, which few of the men and women at whom it was aimed understood, but the message seemed to get across all the same. The sheer bulk and presence of the man issuing it left little to the imagination.

The pilgrims and tourists penned in the small corridor between the two subterranean shrines were growing fidgety. The blockade that the New Order's men had erected in the narrow, stony space was makeshift – a bit of red rope, its ends fixed to either side wall, the men standing just beyond it and the small but growing crowd behind – but so far it had held.

The men, of course, had no authority to stop traffic at the temple, or to play any other role than the visitors they had registered as when they entered; but such restrictions were not about to stop them from their necessary work.

The trio ahead of them were not to be interrupted.

Their privacy was to be protected, guarded, so that nothing would hinder any discovery they might make.

One of the men standing guard at the rope twitched slightly as the speaker in his ear scratched to life.

'They're finished,' a business-like voice confirmed. Sir Michael Wyatt, one of the newest knights of the New Order and the man who'd been put in charge of the operation by the Seneschal himself. 'They're leaving the shrine now. Give them thirty seconds, and you can release the crowd.'

There was a slight click to the audio, then Wyatt's voice returned.

'They've found something on the walls. Once the crowd passes, photograph everything.'

Michael Wyatt let the microphone in his sleeve slip away and pulled his mobile phone to his ear. The connection to the Seneschal was made in a matter of seconds.

'They've found a second inscription,' he began immediately. 'In the underground shrines, just as we'd anticipated.'

'You've got it?'

'It's being photographed as we speak. I'll send you the images as soon as we're outside.'

The Seneschal allowed a silence to pass, and Michael waited anxiously.

'This inscription, it is encoded like the stone on the island?'

'That's what our monitoring picked up from their conversation,' he answered. 'But this one includes pictures.'

'Then we've no further need for this group's work. We

can decode the material ourselves and find whatever's next.'

Wyatt didn't respond. He was unsure what the Seneschal's words implied.

His confusion vanished swiftly.

'Kill the two men,' the older man's voice suddenly commanded.

'Both?' Michael swallowed. 'But it's Sean . . .'

The Seneschal almost hesitated, and his next words came more softly, but still with commanding authority.

'Be merciful with Sean. Make it quick. And take the woman. We need her.'

'What about the other one?'

'Do what you want with him,' the Seneschal answered. 'I have no further interest in Captain Jack Shepherd.'

40

The Distant Countryside, India, AD 1326

The trance had not gone well.

At the very least, it had not yielded results. Not of the kind that de Faulke needed. The urge towards anger had been strong in response. So much planning, journeying, so much store set in what was to be received, and then – nothing. Or so it had seemed.

Jacques de Molay had learned something from this strange people, but perhaps the trance had not been the way that knowledge had come to him.

The draught provided by the tribesmen had been effective in its own way. Whatever strange concoction the wooden bowl had contained, it had a profound influence on the human mind. Perhaps it was a poison, perhaps some alchemical potion, but it had driven de Faulke's mind far from its normal operations. His vision opened up to strange colours, to sights that seemed half-real and half-imagined. His ears had not been able to make out normal sounds, their tones shifting and fading and escaping his recognition; yet he had heard noises that ears normally did not hear. Deep, guttural moanings that seemed to come from within the earth, from within his own body. Strange, mysterious, confounding.

These must be the wallowings of the mystics, he had pondered hours later, as the draught began to wear off and normal thought slowly returned to him. The thought was riddled with condemnation. Mystics were not to be admired. Men, and worse, women, who lived only in their own minds, calling their thoughts divine and always chasing one 'experience' or another. *Experiences that cannot be far from these, whatever they are.*

The tribesmen had been helpful, welcoming, and with the draught consumed had led de Faulke deeper within their enclosure, into old rooms, corridors and tunnels normally reserved for their elect. There the walls had come alive. Each was painted in bright colours, which his intoxicated vision saw as yet bolder than even the strong pigments demanded. Strange beings, drawn by thumb-strokes in bold shades – beings of many arms, with the bodies of men and heads of animals, contorted in postures inhuman and impossible.

Demons, to any man of godly soul, de Faulke reflected. The men worshipped them like gods, but that did not alter the fact.

And yet, what demons! Each had been more sinister than the last, the lingering look of evil present with more clarity in eyes that gleamed, yet haunted, in peaceful-looking beings that danced upon the severed heads of the unfortunate. Incense was burned before the strange paintings, flowers placed around them. Evil, yet evil venerated.

Still, to his disappointment, there had been nothing more. Nothing beyond the paintings, the myths, the strange rituals, that was of any immediate relevance to his needs.

India had held such promise. But it seemed that promise would go unfulfilled.

Then, as he was about to depart their compound, something caught de Faulke's eye. A painting, one among many, staring out at him from the stone walls.

'What is that?' he asked, pointing to the image and drawing the small leader of the mystics to his side with a powerful hand on his shoulder. The man looked at the image and shuddered.

'No good, that,' he answered, shaking his head. 'Den of evil, a place of death.'

The description fitted the image. Painted on the wall was a yawning, black cavern from which strangely radiant lines protruded into a forest scene. All around were men and women, even small children. A population whose many members all had one thing in common.

They were all, to a man, dead.

'Where is this?' de Faulke persisted, pointing towards the painting with renewed zeal.

'You no go there,' the tribesman answered, shaking his head vigorously. 'Is place of death, far from here. Bad place. Everyone who goes near dies the death.'

De Faulke pointed again, but the man resisted. Even the others around him began to shout, 'No! No!'

In the end, it had taken de Faulke's knife, drawn from his hip and held to the man's throat, to finally draw from him the information the knight required. Directions. Instructions. A path that would lead him to the fountain of death itself.

He had found the next step in de Molay's journey.

41

Chidambaram, India

'If our first instruction was cryptic, this one is utterly bizarre.'

Sean spoke pointedly, and Angela agreed entirely.

A small gardened green outside the central temple complex allowed visitors with families to rest on benches and at small wooden tables, and she, Jack and Sean took a perch at one of the latter to address what they had found.

'What's a man supposed to make of "where silk no longer travels"?' Sean continued, 'and who the hell is –' he looked down at the small piece of scrap paper on which he'd written out the decrypted translation the Seattle team had sent them '– *Xuanzang*?'

'If what was being relayed were meant to be obvious,' Angela answered, 'they wouldn't have gone to all the trouble to encode it. Let's quit looking for a clear-cut treasure map.'

Sean grunted his displeasure, but Jack turned to Angela from across the table.

'Do you know the name?' he asked. 'This Xuanzang?'

Angela shook her head. 'It sounds distantly familiar, but I can't place it. It's obviously not Indian.'

'Sounds Asian,' Sean noted.

'It sounds Chinese,' Jack added, more precisely. 'And it rings Buddhist.' He thought for a moment. 'My familiarity with Buddhism is only as extensive as the intro course I took back in college, so I might get this wrong, but I think that name's connected to Buddhist history in China.'

'Buddhist?' Sean replied. 'First our Christian monks are turning to Hinduism, and now Buddhism? Just what was going on with these Templars?'

Angela mulled over Jack's recollections. Then, suddenly, she turned to Sean.

'Pull out your computer again, Sean. We haven't got a library here for any serious research, but the Internet's better than nothing.'

Jack lifted a brow as Sean reached for his laptop. 'Seriously, Angela? Our resident scholar is going to chase out the mysteries of the past with, what, Wikipedia? Aren't you afraid your next-door-neighbour's thirteen-year-old dropout might have written whatever you're going to read?'

Sean chuckled, and even Angela was prepared to take the jibe. 'We're not going to find the mysteries of anything hidden on the Web,' she answered, 'but it's perfectly suited for surveying some bare facts.' She reached across the table and rotated Sean's computer towards herself.

A few seconds later, an encyclopaedia entry on Xuan-zang filled the screen. Jack moved round to Angela's side of the table, eager to read along with her, but after his sarcasm she wasn't about to give him the satisfaction and shoved him away, smiling, her eyes remaining on the screen.

'Xuanzang was a scribe in seventh-century China. He was a Buddhist monk and traveller, famous for ...'

Angela's voice trailed off, and she looked up over the screen at the other men.

'For?' Sean pressed.

'For his nearly two-decade-long journey through India.' She paused, allowing the incense-laden, heavy Indian air to swirl around them. The connection was tangible, immediate.

'*Xuanzang dictated the details of his travels to a disciple called Bianji*' Angela continued, her gaze returning to the screen, '*who compiled his notes into a book known as* The Great Tang Records on the Western Regions, *which became a Chinese classic and an important text on the history of relations between the two regions. Thereafter, Xuanzang dedicated his life to translating over 650 Sanskrit scriptures into Chinese.*'

'The Chinese were interested in Hindu scriptures?'

'There are Buddhist works written in Sanskrit, too,' Jack noted. 'That's where I remember his name from. Xuanzang's translation of the Heart Sutra became a model for devotions and commentaries for centuries. I think I read an English translation of it at Duke.'

'So this monk makes his home here in India, writes a travelogue and translates the scriptures. He's our man, if our text is correct.' Sean tried to make sense of the perplexing swirl of information. '"Where silk no longer travels: Xuanzang's workplace". 'We need to find his "workplace", then, yes? His Indian home, where all this industrious work took place?'

'Xuanzang didn't write here in India.' Angela scanned quickly through the details on the computer. 'It says he was in India for seventeen years, but all his writings were produced afterwards, including his translations. He was an intrepid traveller, by the sound of it. The list of towns, monasteries, districts and peoples he visited is extensive.'

'So where are we supposed to look?'

Not for the first time in their working relationship, Angela was reminded of just how different her and Sean's approaches were. He was a man of practical ingenuity and technical know-how. He saw a course, he plotted his action, and he ran with it. Hurdles represented frustrations. Angela's style was more bookish. The hurdles were the interesting parts, and the mysteries not points of frustration but of immense and growing curiosity.

'Let's think back to the text from your island,' Jack said, breaking through her thoughts. 'That phrase was also in two parts, and both of them were required to lead us here. Now this text is in two parts. We've got some sense of the second half. What do we make of the first, "where silk no longer travels"?'

Angela eyed him. Jack was as macho a man as Sean, and obviously just as action-minded, yet at every turn he seemed measured, reflective. Not qualities that she'd often found came packaged together in a single person, and certainly not in men.

'I hadn't got that far yet,' she answered, 'but that reference seems . . . less oblique.'

'I agree. It's almost certainly got to be a reference to the Silk Road.'

'The Silk Road?' Sean asked. 'The old travel route?'

'The very one,' Jack answered. 'The Silk Road was a, was *the*, major trade thoroughfare connecting the Far East to Europe and Africa during the Middle Ages and long before. It was a network of independent trade routes that eventually gained autonomous international status. A kind of ancient international freeway.'

'It connected India with China?' Sean asked, gaining some hope of a link.

'Among many other locales, yes. But it also stretched west, and south, and had interconnected sea routes. The Silk Road network was vast.'

Sean appeared almost ready to heave a sigh of exasperation, but caught himself. 'I guess this is better than nothing. It gives us a target zone to search.'

'It might just do more than that,' Angela interjected. She had listened to the two men's exchange with interest, and admired seeing them work together.

She was not able to complete her thought. As Angela opened her mouth, the wood of the table in front of her exploded into splinters that flew at her chest and face.

The sound of the gunshot came a millisecond later.

'Angela, get down!' Jack ordered, leaping from his seat and throwing himself on top of her.

She fell to the earth as gunshots began to fill the air.

42

Chidambaram

The second and third gunshots brought the peaceful air of the temple courtyard to an abrupt end. The screams of the pilgrims transformed the atmosphere into one of panic, and dozens of bodies were simultaneously in motion, running for an exit or cover or simply to get out of the way.

Jack's mind was instantly thrust back into the instincts of his military training, assessing the scene around him as fast as he could.

The people's movement, he realized, was going to be their biggest asset.

'We've got to take advantage of this panic,' he shouted across to Sean, who was crouched beneath the splintered table and clutching his equipment to his chest.

'Who the hell is shooting at us?' Angela cried out. Jack looked down at her, still partially covered by his chest. Her face was white, her eyes wide, but she retained a control that Jack knew might mean the difference between life or –

Another gunshot exploded through the air, a thud on the grass near Jack's head the only sign of the missed shot.

'Questions later,' he answered, pulling Angela up so they were both on their knees. 'Right now, we have to move while there are still others here. Unless they're willing to risk killing random visitors, whoever's shooting isn't going to fire blankly into the crowd.'

'All evidence to the contrary!' Sean shouted, tucking his computer back into his bag. But he looked to Jack for instruction, the ex-Marine exuding authority.

Jack surveyed the surroundings. There was an exit through a stone wall about sixty feet to the west of their position. A crowd was already clogging the small doorway, pushing for escape. Their best option was to join the crowd and make it to the busy city exterior as fast as possible.

The problem was the thirty feet of mostly empty space between them and the crowd.

'We've got to move. Now.'

He pulled at Angela, positioning himself between her and the general area from which the shots had come. Sean was immediately with them, and Jack grabbed one of the wooden benches from the table and held it up on his right. Whether the two-inch thick painted bench would stop whatever calibre bullets were being fired at them Jack had no idea, but it was better protection than nothing at all.

'Run. A straight line to this side of the crowd,' he instructed. Angela and Sean obeyed, and Jack ran at their side.

He glanced round the side of the upright bench, searching for the source of the attack. People were in motion everywhere, running in circles in a mayhem that only a random unleashing of gunfire in a public space could create.

All except one man who stood perfectly still, well over

200 yards away, his arm outstretched directly towards them.

The bench in Jack's hand lurched as another shot rang out through the courtyard, and the shattering wood sent a numbing shock through his grip. He could no longer hold the board, which fell at his side as they kept moving.

'Damn, that was close!' Sean shouted.

'Just get to the exit,' Jack answered. There was nothing he could do for cover now, until they were in the crowd.

The seconds that it took to move across the space seemed to last far longer, the danger stretching them close to eternity. They were moving too slowly, but Jack didn't want to push ahead at a faster pace than the other two and remove himself from the line of fire. Right now, he was the only thing between the shooter and Angela and Sean. Not a comfortable position to be in, but it was better than leaving them exposed.

More shots echoed, and in a quick glance over his shoulder Jack could see their pursuer running after them; but the distance was vast and the act of running made his aim wild. A bullet thumped into the grass twenty feet to Jack's left. Another, a second later, was thirty to his right. Still, far too close for any sense of comfort.

At last, they arrived at the throng. 'Quick, into the crowd!' he ordered. 'Push!'

Everyone in the mêlée was jostling to get through the narrow doorway, but Angela had an agility that had her darting through the bodies quickly. Jack felt a rush of relief as he watched her disappear, and he shoved Sean in after her. Only when he had gained ground in the crowd did Jack himself thrust his muscular arms, his right hand still smarting, into the crush and shoulder the panicked pilgrims aside. Their angry shouts were as terrified as they were enraged, but Jack's instinct told him that the man with the gun wouldn't fire randomly into the crowd if he didn't have line of sight.

Jack pushed towards the exit, the going painfully slow. But there was no gunshot. No explosions of stone or flesh around him. His theory seemed to be holding good.

A moment later, he was through the doorway and stepping out into the crowded street that ringed the temple complex.

'Jack, over here!' Angela shouted from his left. Sean was at her side, and was already pulling her across the street.

'We have to get to the car,' Jack said as he ran to their side. They would have only seconds before the gunman made it out after them.

'Take that side-street,' he ordered, leading Sean and Angela away from the crowded main road. The alley ran in parallel, drawing them towards the intersection where the driver had parked and promised to wait.

'Where are we going to go?' Sean asked, breathless as he ran.

'Do you have any contacts here?' Jack asked.

'No.' An interruption of heavy, racing breaths. 'At least, not without making a few calls.'

'Then we go to the airport,' Jack answered, shaking his head. 'We need to travel anyway, and there's not likely to be any place as secure as that in the city. They won't be able to get inside with weapons unless they've got a hell of a lot of power.'

'And if they do?' Angela asked.

Jack kept his eyes on the end of the alley before them, his feet in motion.

'If they do, then I'm afraid we're pretty well screwed.'

The car was parked where they had left it, the driver asleep with a still-smouldering pile of cigarettes in the ashtray.

'Wake up, brother, it's time to go!' Jack smacked his fist on the driver's window as they arrived, startling the man to alertness. The rear doors were already being opened as Sean and Angela threw themselves inside, and Jack took the passenger seat.

'What's going on?' the driver asked. 'I thought you'd be –'

'Just move. We're being followed,' Jack answered, leaning across and putting the man's hand on the keys. 'Someone's in the temple with a gun, and he's coming after us.'

That was all the convincing the driver needed to get the car in motion.

'Where are we going?'

'Back to the airport. Fast as you can, and stay on fast-moving roads.' Jack turned round to Angela and Sean. 'Stay crouched down, at least for a while. If the shooter's got transportation, he might still take a shot at us.'

They obeyed without questioning. The engine roared as the driver kept the car in a low gear and forced his way into traffic.

Jack closed his eyes, controlled his breathing. They'd escaped the temple. He had no idea who'd been shooting at them, but there would be time for that question. Right now, another was more pressing.

He opened his eyes and turned to face Angela in her back-seat crouch.

'Finish your thought,' he said, 'from before.'

'Excuse me?' she peered at him, baffled.

'Before the gunshot, we were talking about the Silk Road. You were about to tell us how you thought the inscription in the temple fitted together.'

Angela gained her own breath and made to sit up.

'Stay down,' Jack ordered. He tried to smile reassuringly. 'Just talk.'

'I . . . I was about to say that the inscription in the temple doesn't simply make reference to the Silk Road. It says something more specific. "Where silk no longer travels".'

Jack stared back at her, his eyes probing hers. 'Where silk no longer travels,' he repeated. 'You mean, where the Silk Road ends?'

'That's my thought. The road's network may have been extensive, but it would have had fairly few end-points, right? One in the west, one in the east, and a few at the terminal points of its southern extensions.'

Jack's look intensified, but it was Sean who spoke.

'Put A and B together,' he interjected. 'If we're looking for a terminus to the Silk Road, and a place where this monk Xuanzang laboured at his translations, we need to search for a place that correlates to both.'

The car lurched round a tight corner, flinging their bodies to one side.

'That's just it,' Angela added, regaining her balance. 'The entry on the computer said that Xuanzang's main literary works were written while he lived in the Xi Ming Temple in Chang'an, or modern-day Xi'an.'

She stared at Jack with a knowing determination.

'Do you want to guess which city served as the eastern terminus for the Silk Road?'

43

'He is dead?' The Grand Master asked the question with his usual severity, his eyes accusing.

'He is dead,' the knight answered. 'I saw to it myself.' He rubbed his knuckles, still sore from the fatal blows he had delivered to the unsuspecting petty officer's face.

'And his death will not attract scrutiny?'

The knight bid for humility, trying not to smile at his ingenuity and keeping to the facts. 'The poor soldier was visiting a bar in a sketchy neighbourhood. He'd had a few drinks, got into a fight, and it didn't end well.' It was the kind of scenario they needed. 'The kind of thing that happens every day.'

'And you left no marks? Nothing that would point to you, or to anything other than the scene you've described?' the Grand Master demanded.

'Nothing. No one saw me. It's a death that won't move past initial reports. Straightforward. Sad, but not unexpected.' He couldn't contain a small comment of self-satisfaction. 'Sometimes bad things just happen to good soldiers.'

Finally, the Grand Master appeared to smile. The deep wrinkles in his face became more severe with the gesture, and the greenness of his eyes seemed all the more probing.

'You have done nicely. I've just been informed that the powers that be have approved the event. The showcase following the State of the Union is now on the official schedule, and a live demonstration of our latest toy is to be at the centre of it.' He peered into the eyes of the knight. 'Petty Officer Rick DiMaggio was the only one of their men certified to operate it. They won't be able to go through with a live demonstration without him.'

'But they won't be willing to cancel the demo either,' the knight answered. 'Not with all it's taken to get it staged.'

'Precisely. Which means they'll need to come to the source, to reclaim the expertise they've lost.'

The man now fully understood the New Order's intentions. 'They'll need a new man. Someone with training and technical understanding.'

The Grand Master grinned broadly. 'And there's only one place they'll go to find him. They will have no choice but to come to us.'

44

In Flight, Between India and Xi'an

The scents of India seemed to linger in the interior of the C-17 military transport jet, and Angela clutched the strangely reassuring solidity of the hard plastic arms on a seat clearly not designed for comfort.

Sean had been able to phone Seattle from the car, demanding to be put through directly to his father's line. The lopsided conversation had struck Angela as odd, but her heart had been racing at an almost uncontrollable rate. Thomas Blackburn had been surprised to hear from his son, demanding to know precisely what had happened to them. When Sean had shared the details of their ordeal, his father had demanded that they avoid public flights and had arranged for a chartered aircraft to be readied for them. A company-modified Air Force customization of the Boeing C-17 was already at a private airstrip near by, and they'd diverted their course en route.

The travel time for their flight to Xi'an Xianyang International Airport, twenty-five miles outside Xi'an, China, was six hours. Six hours. Angela wondered whether her pulse would return to normal by the time they landed.

Jack had wanted to talk the moment they got on the plane, to 'debrief' their experience, as he worded it, and figure out just what it was that had happened. But Angela needed a few moments to herself.

A bullet, inches from my face. Her mind replayed the scene in the courtyard. *So close to death.*

The thought came quickly, powerfully. *Death.* It was a reality that always stirred up her deepest emotions. Angela's childhood had not been easy, and in many ways had been framed entirely by death. So many that had known her – her mother included – had been anything but circumspect in predicting a tormented and troubled life. Her father, so dear and wonderful a man, had been ripped away from her by illness when she was only eleven, and her world had seemed to fall apart. Death, claiming the one person she truly loved. Depression had followed, rebellious teenage years passed, uninterested in school, life, work or a future. 'A failure, through and through,' her alcoholic mother had pointed out in one of her traditionally non-lucid rants. It was a characterization that Angela had taken to heart for too long.

Death, bearing its mark on those who were left when it had passed.

Then Angela had changed. One day, sitting in the back of a car with two friends, drinking the same beers they'd drunk the night before and which they would undoubtedly drink the next night, and the next, the pointlessness of such a wasted life had hit her. Her mother was a drunk, her father was gone, but, by God, Angela Derby wasn't going to settle for this.

The change in her life had been dramatic. A long-hidden intelligence had begun to emerge, together with a wit and brightness that had been suppressed for years. Angela flourished, finished her schooling and earned a place at university – a place that took her away from her mother, away to college, and towards a future that had, at last, begun to hold promise.

Her father, in the years before his death, had taken pride in pointing out to Angela how old their family was, how it, like so many others, stretched back through history, connecting her to the great network of the past. He had loved his family history. Angela was constantly motivated by the hope that she was making him proud of the latest generation.

Her breathing gradually slowed. *Funny*, she thought, with emotions that were anything but, *how it's death, more often than not, that teaches us how to cherish life.*

As another patch of turbulence jostled them both out of a thoughtful silence, Jack looked across the aisle to Sean. Angela needed time with her thoughts, but Jack needed to know what had happened to them.

'Do you have any idea who that could have been?' he asked. 'Who would want to open fire on us like that?'

Sean swallowed and shook his head. 'I don't know. I've never been shot at before.'

Jack leaned his head back against a plastic headrest. 'It was too focused to have been random. We were deliberate targets.'

'I didn't get a look at him. I was too busy running.'

'Why would anyone consider us targets? Is the hunt for history really that cut-throat?'

Sean swallowed again, then turned towards Jack. 'There's something you need to know.'

Jack lifted his head and waited expectantly.

'The BBC, as we were leaving London. I caught it at

the airport. It reported a shooting in the Victoria and Albert Museum.' He hesitated. 'A curator working at the entrance.'

Jack sat stoically. The museum. A shooting. A curator. He ticked through the data.

Then, a click. 'The man we spoke to?'

'I can't be sure, but . . .' Sean hesitated. 'I have a bad feeling.'

'You've known about this since London? Why the hell didn't you mention it before?'

'I wasn't sure,' Sean answered, his face red. 'It could have been anything, disconnected. Still could be. I didn't know if it was worth spooking everyone. But, well . . . I'm telling you now, Jack.'

Jack didn't have the strength to challenge Sean's actions. These were new facts he had to find a way to understand.

'If the shooting there is connected to what just happened to us, then our situation just got far worse. We're being pursued.' He paused. 'It would have been easy to shoot at us in the museum. Why would they take out a curator, but not come for us?'

'Maybe the shooter didn't have a chance there. Or maybe his priorities have changed since then.'

'To priorities that aim the guns away from the people we interact with, and point them at us.' *Not a good trend*, Jack pondered. One more thing to add to the laundry list of things that didn't make sense about every step he'd taken since first getting involved in this mess.

Suddenly, he turned back to Sean.

'You know, I never got to ask you my questions, back

in Seattle. The ones I'd been saving up for our lunch meeting.'

Sean hesitated. 'You're thinking about lunch, at a moment like this?'

'Not lunch, questions. There's still one overarching question that I can't quite understand, about this whole project we're on – which has suddenly become a little more dangerous than the historical-curiosity sell you gave me back in Seattle.'

Sean tried to smile at the sarcasm, but his nerves were ill-equipped. 'What's the question?'

'All this – the research, the expeditions, your find and these travels – it's all to carry out your father's wishes and locate the Templar legacy. But now that guns are firing at us, I have to ask the one question I should have asked at the outset: what's the nature of his interest?'

Sean peered at him from his seat silently.

'What's the origin,' Jack continued, 'of your father's zeal in pursuing a treasure hunt at which hundreds have tried their hands over the years, and every one of them failed? He seems like a smart man, and he's clearly been successful in the business world. So why does a smart, successful man start flooding money into a side project that's got absolutely nothing to do with his line of work and has no more credibility behind it than any other conspiracy theory racking the madness of the lonely, confused and gullible?'

When he looked up at Sean's face, Jack saw an expression that suggested this was far from the first time the engineer had faced such a question.

'You're not the only person to question my father's

motives, though in fact very few people know of his interest in the Templars, and even fewer of our project itself.'

'And?'

'And his interest goes a lot deeper than a passing fad or educated curiosity. My father's interest in the Templars is personal.'

'Personal?' It was the last word Jack had expected.

'In the blood. Whether he's right or wrong about it, my father is convinced that our family is connected to Templar history. A family whose bloodline includes knights of the Order from back in the day.' He raised a brow as he spoke, though whether it was in acknowledgement of the strangeness of what he was recounting, or simply familiarity, was hard to determine. 'A long story, mind you, but one my father firmly believes in.'

'Your father believes that he's, that you're, *related* to the Templars?'

'It's not so far-fetched, really. We come from a European family that, like most European families, goes back for centuries. Years ago, my father did "a little research" –' Sean made a gesture that suggested something far more vast and far-reaching '– and discovered that among the generations back up the family tree were no fewer than seven Templar knights. That knowledge spawned an interest.'

Jack tried to make sense of the information. 'So your father wants to know more about, what, his family history?'

'Wouldn't you? Think about it: he's made his name in defence engineering. The tools of war. The mechanics of the battlefield. And along the way, he discovers he's descended from the families of some of the most famous warriors in history. Wouldn't you have a little curiosity, too?'

Jack nodded, pensive. 'It's not just wishful thinking, this family connection? It could sound a little ... convenient.'

'As much as anyone can know of a family that far back, my father knows. Our family emigrated to the United States in my great-great-grandfather's generation. He was Polish, his wife Italian. My father has been able to trace out both of their family trees for fifteen or twenty generations before – back through Spain, France, Germany, even the Holy Land. All territories associated with the Templars. And in the family lists he found names of known knights. That means that the generations since – my grandfather, my father and his brother, and even me, I suppose – have that same lineage.' Sean looked into Jack's eyes, his expression one of self-justification. 'There may be plenty of legends around about the Templars, but they *were* a historical order that genuinely existed, there's no doubt about that. Not that remarkable that modern-day people might have Templar family members in their past.'

'But the Templars were a monastic fraternity,' Jack protested. 'They were celibate.'

'Sure, but their parents obviously weren't, and those parents had other children.'

Jack sat back in the tight seat. The story that he had so quickly become a part of suddenly looked quite different to how it had in Blackburn's office. A man curious to explore the endless cultic speculations of the past in their own right was one thing, but a man keen to delve into his own family's past, to know more of his origins and how they interacted with one of the more mysterious stories told of medieval antiquity – that was something different.

But how it led to being shot at in an Indian temple courtyard was still entirely unknown.

'Do you know what exactly it is your father is looking for?' Jack finally asked.

'No more than you,' Sean answered. He looked strangely uncomfortable. 'Nor he, I would imagine. It's all speculation and hope. But one thing I'm fairly confident of. We're closer to it than anyone has been in centuries. And after this afternoon, I don't think we're the only ones who want it.'

45

'Tell me where we stand. I need a progress report.'

The boss was hovering over them, lingering in their terrain like some great omnipotent overseer, setting everyone on edge.

'The principal agents will intermix in the central chamber, here. Careful not to touch, it's sterile until loading.'

A laboratory scientist signalled a thin aluminium chamber, just over an inch in diameter by six in depth. 'The pressure inside will be a key factor. We're running a number of tests to determine optimal yield.'

'The effective range?' the director asked.

'Given the small size parameters we're working with, probably not more than 150 yards. Maybe 200.'

It wasn't much, especially in the world of modern capabilities, but the project did not require either high yield or wide coverage. Distribution would be managed by other means.

'One hundred and fifty yards will be fine. More than necessary.'

In all the months that the team of scientists had been at work on this project, the lead laboratory manager had only set eyes on their director once, at the very outset of their clinical research. Since that time he had interacted solely by emails, voicemail and the occasional telephone call. But over the past weeks the boss's presence in the laboratory had become more frequent, and over the last few days had been almost constant.

Within the lab, half a dozen scientists were at work on the preparations. Bio-engineering was a fast-growing field, and the minds in the overly lit room were some of the best in the world. They worked as part of a larger collection of specialists whose research was inadvertently part of the project; though with all those dozens and even hundreds, the actual nature of their work was always an unknown. They were kept in the dark, given details only of their compartmentalized tasks.

But the four men and two women working in the confines of this particular laboratory were special cases. They knew the full scope of the project, and they had been chosen for their absolute discretion, common vision and loyalty to the greater purpose.

'The potency tests, they're in order?'

'We now have several models tested and prepared. Eleven of them, to be precise. They're ready and waiting. We've done all we can do to prepare, but we're confident one of them will produce the right carrier strength when intermixed.'

'This is critical, critical,' the director answered. He looked even more intense than usual, his eyes wandering about the laboratory, scanning every piece of equipment. 'Soon we'll have the agent, the agent and the blood. You'll have to be ready to create the compound at a moment's notice.'

The scientist delivered a firm nod. 'We'll be ready, sir, of that I can assure you.'

The director stared back at him, his features commanding, then turned and walked out of the door.

All the lead laboratory technician could hear as he departed was a muttering under his breath, 'The agent and the blood. The agent and the blood.'

PART THREE
Discoveries

46

The agent and the blood. The agent and the blood.

Thomas Blackburn approached his office, the thought still running through his mind as if on continuous repeat. The agent and the blood. They would be in his hands so soon. And then, and then . . . action.

The immense door swung open before him as he approached. Blackburn was alone, but in an instant he was not. There, on the far side of the room, hanging above his desk in oversized form, was the image that constantly inspired him. Bartosz Blaszczak, his great-grandfather. A good and noble man.

How the mighty have fallen!

The lament poured violently into Thomas Blackburn's mind, as it so often did. His whole life had been shaped by it. The legacy of his family was an appalling tragedy that so few could understand, and there was no moment of his life when it did not eat at him like some inescapable disease.

His family had been made up of good men, noble, honest. Men of integrity. Polish on his father's side, Italian on his mother's, they had never been the upper crust of society, but they had lived moral, dignified lives. And when life in the region had become more difficult, the promise of the New World had drawn them overseas.

Generations of Blackburn's ancestors had desired the journey, wishing to be stirred into the melting pot of American opportunity, but it had finally been his great-grandfather, Bartosz, who had plucked up his courage and done it.

He and Thomas's great-grandmother, Beatrice, had arrived via the customary route at Ellis Island. There the foreign-sounding Blaszczak had become Blackburn, Bartosz and Beatrice had become Blaise and Bea, and the hope of new beginnings had arrived at a soil fertile enough to foster it.

Or so had been the intention. Reality had been a far different beast.

The poverty that Thomas's ancestors discovered in America had been far worse than that they had left behind. A family that had never been rich, but had never been poor, found themselves nearly destitute. The savings they brought with them were exhausted within months, and work was nowhere to be found. Blaise, who was a skilled craftsman, could locate no employment in a nation brimming with advancement. His English was poor, his accent thick and his clothes visibly old-world, and the combination shut every door he tried to open. A man of ample means had found himself with none, and a man with usable skills had found himself in a world that wanted those skills only if they didn't come from him.

But that had not been the worst of it. Thomas walked through his office, the thoughts aggravating his passions and stirring up his blood as he moved closer to his great-grandfather's portrait. While his family had never had wealth, they had at least always had pride. Dignity. Self-respect. But this, too, had been ruthlessly stripped away. Arrivals from overseas were not only condemned to lives of poverty, they were mocked as social outcasts, blamed for the plights of society. Theirs was not 'good company' and it didn't do for men of decent standing to be seen with the Polacks and the Wop-skis. They were marginalized, despised.

Blackburn clenched his fists, his manicured fingernails digging into the palms of his hands. How the memories infuriated him.

A land of promise, a government of freedom, that had taken a family of honour and cast them into the dirt. An injustice of the worst sort.

He sat, controlling his breathing and forcing the fire in his chest to cool. *Control, Thomas.* The pain of the wrongs done to his family burned strongly in him, as it had since he'd been a young boy and he and his brother had heard the stories of their past from their father. They were hard realities to swallow, but one realization soothed the resentment.

Retribution is closer than ever before. The last judgement has not yet been pronounced.

47

'If you don't stop squirming, this is going to hurt.' The man grabbed Anna's chin in his powerful left hand and forced her to stare straight into his eyes. He'd already re-applied the tape over the seven-year-old girl's mouth, and the act had sent her into new spasms of panic. He compelled her to meet his gaze and glared fiercely into her eyes.

'Just sit still, kid, and it doesn't have to get any worse. You've had your hands tied up before.'

Anna seemed to understand and stopped her writhing. The man spun her round and pulled her hands behind her back, clasping them together and locking them at the wrists with a plastic tie. Bella had already been handcuffed in a similar fashion, and she sat next to her older sister.

'Your father's been cooperative so far,' their captor continued, finishing the tie on Bella's wrists, 'but he's going to need a little extra ... persuasion ... for what comes next.'

The tie was done. He took a step back and his gaze fell over the pair of bound girls. For an instant, they were something other than his captives. Staring back at him were two children, small and vulnerable, afraid. Tender. Completely oblivious to the reasons for their distress, innocent of anything and everything.

Parker was too well trained to submit to emotion. The sentiment flickered, lingered less than a second, and was gone, the more important reality reclaiming its place. Before him were the two bargaining chips they needed to compel the senator into action – chips that so far had paid out precisely as they'd hoped. But he, together with his men, had been made directly aware that the event they'd helped to secure was nothing without an assurance of the guest of honour being in attendance.

The girls had another bargain to barter. Parker was ready to do what must be done to ensure that it was successful.

Reaching into his pocket, he extracted a syringe and removed the plastic sheath from its inch-long needle. Priming the fluid within, he stepped forward without hesitation.

He plunged the needle through Anna's skin as if it weren't there, and Bella's just as easily. He expelled half its chamber's contents into each arm so swiftly that the girls had little time to react.

And if they had tried, it would have been too late. As he watched, the girls' motions weakened, faltered, and after a few seconds stopped altogether.

They lay motionless on the cold concrete floor.

48

Xi'an, Ancient Chang'an, China

The triangular pictogram seemed to taunt Sean from the table top. He stared down at the simple shape, the two translated names marking its upper and lower left points. He'd photographed the image in the temple, and this morning had carried it with him to the hotel restaurant on his iPad, where it glowed up from a position between a plate of croissants and a jug of orange juice. The puzzle kept his mind from his worries and the fear that had gripped him since their full-speed departure from India yesterday. From the questions he couldn't answer. *Who? Why?*

But the puzzle was there. A strange mix of the ancient, modern and mundane, it was an enigma, but one he had every chance of solving. Recent events provided that work with a new urgency.

'Not much in the way of local fare,' Jack noted, surveying the breakfast offerings as he took a seat at the small table with Sean. 'I don't know what authentic Chinese morning cuisine is supposed to look like, but I'm fairly sure this isn't it.' The scar above his left eye wrinkled as he offered a sarcastic smile. His mood had clearly improved with a night's sleep, though he still appeared upset at Sean's having withheld his knowledge of the murder in the V&A for so long.

Blackburn Enterprises had put them up in the Grand

Soluxe International, a European brand with branches throughout China, so they'd have the 'comfort' of something normal after their 'adventures'. Gunshots soothed with French coffee and western décor.

Sean was hardly interested in the breakfast offerings. 'This damned pictogram is teasing me, Jack,' he said as Shepherd sat down and began pouring himself a mug of coffee from a bronze-coloured plastic carafe. 'This is the one, I'm fairly sure of that.'

'The one?'

'The marker that leads us to our goal. The end-point.' Sean slid his fingers over the tablet's display, zooming in and out on the pictogram's details. 'The other signs have all been guidance towards a subsequent piece in a puzzle – directions towards the next reveal. But this, it just feels like something different. Something significant.'

Jack took a long sip from his coffee and popped a mini-muffin into his mouth. His eyes followed Sean's to the iPad.

'It's certainly different,' he said round his food. 'No enigmatic phrases or puzzles about temples or history.' He chewed, swallowed. 'But if it were a marker, as you say, then why attach it to a phrase sending us on another journey?'

'I think it's incomplete.' Sean pinched his fingers together and zoomed out, revealing the whole pictogram.

'Two points of the triangle are marked, but the third, and its centre-point, are still empty. However this drawing is meant to be read, I don't believe we have all of it, or that we'll be able to find our way to what it's marking without the remaining data.'

Jack pulled the tablet towards himself and eyed the pictogram with a new interest. 'The two encoded words at these points, what were their translations?'

'Names,' Sean answered. 'Not of people, of villages.'

'Actual village names . . . of places that still exist?'

'They're Chinese, and there are similarities to some points on the map today, but they don't precisely correspond to any towns or villages we've been able to identify yet. Angela's having her people do a little research to see if they can find any connections.' Sean looked over at Jack and saw how his features had tightened. He hadn't known the other man long, but he could recognize a mind at work.

'What is it?'

'It just occurs to me that you could be right. This might well be a marker.'

Sean leaned in, waiting.

'If these really are village names, and if they could be located and plotted on a map, then you've got two out of the three points you'd need for triangulation.'

Sean stared at the image, his eyes suddenly seeing it differently. Sometimes the most obvious solutions were those that got overlooked.

'Damn it, that makes sense. Know three points on a map, and you've got the keys to a fourth.'

Jack motioned towards the pictogram. 'This image has a point at the centre, carved into the temple wall by the same hand as the rest of the picture. Presumably that's what it refers to.'

Jack's observation boosted Sean's enthusiasm. They

were seeking a location, after all, and basic triangulation was a way of providing just that.

'But it won't work without a third point,' Jack added, motioning towards the blank corner of the triangle and popping another mini-muffin into his mouth. 'Without that, there's no way of finding a centre.'

'Then that's what we're here for.' Sean's voice was more confident than he would have expected, but he'd learned long ago that the way past nerves was action. He reached over to his tablet and lay a finger on the image, looking resolutely up at Jack. His new sense of purpose was coupled with the lingering effects of yesterday's attack.

'Whatever's at the final point on this marker has been hidden there a long time. But I don't think we have long to find it.'

49

The decision to let Jack and Sean explore the Xi Ming Temple without her had been difficult to take, but Angela knew it had been the right one. She was convinced, given their successes at the previous locations, that the two men would be able to locate whatever was there without her to guide them. The immediate need was for her to begin making sense of the huge amount of material they'd uncovered already, and that required some quiet time alone.

It wasn't that Angela was trying to avoid another encounter, or wanted Jack and Sean to face it without her if it came. But the nuanced analysis of history went a little better without bullets flying past your face or your legs at full sprint, and understanding the history was as important as finding whatever was concealed here in China.

After Angela had calmed her nerves with a few drinks and a midnight workout on a hotel treadmill after their arrival, her mind had started to analyse what they'd learned. She had to admit she was surprised by how far east the Templars had travelled. She'd always suspected Persia, even India, but China was, pardon the cliché, a world away. The meaning of the inscription in Chidambaram had taken her unawares. Angela had thought they'd found the much-anticipated end-point of her hypothe-sized eastward trek to the remnant Templars. In fact, they'd only found a mid-point.

That journey seemed almost incomprehensible. The Templars had been disbanded in 1312 and had had their fate sealed with the execution of the last Grand Master in 1314. However, Angela could now confidently proclaim that there had been two sets of travels that followed, each almost as remarkable as the other. The one that had been hypothesized by scholars before – north and westward, across the Channel and into England and Scotland, had in fact reached as far west as the Canadian islands. Templars had landed at Oak Island in Nova Scotia. Had alighted there. Had made a mark there.

And then, a separate track: eastward from Paris, most likely avoiding the volatile Outremer and Muslim lands as much as possible, finding refuge in India before continu-ing east as far as inner China. This was territory no one had theorized before.

The strangest fact of all: the two routes were con-nected. It was the marker on Oak Island that had pointed her towards the Indian subcontinent, and from there into the heart of the Far East. These weren't two separate strands of post-dissolution Templar history. Somehow, in a manner that she couldn't yet identify, Angela knew they were one and the same story.

A truly extraordinary extent to which to go . . .

The thought came, but then with surprising immediacy was followed by a moment of recognition. *Is it really so extraordinary? That a group of men, hated and hunted by the world they had tried to serve, would flee to the far corners of the map to preserve . . . themselves.* How far *wouldn't* a people, any people, go to preserve their own existence?

Could that be what had spurred on the Templar migration they were tracking – the impulse of self-preservation? Of protecting, not so much what was theirs, but who they were?

As Angela was suddenly only too aware, when you're being chased, you run. Speed and distance are minor obstacles when confronted with the possibility, no, the surety, of death.

And there it was, again. That word, *death*, provoking its customarily deep, emotional response. The face of her father suddenly filled her memory. He had seen death coming; he had tried to run. But when he knew he would not outpace his fate, his focus had shifted: preservation. He would be gone, but he wanted his family, his heritage, to thrive.

How proud he had been of the long lineage of the Derby family. Of course, they hadn't always been called Derby; the family name had changed throughout history multiple times. But her father had been so proud of the *who* of his family. He loved the memory of all their ancestors, just as he loved those that surrounded him in life.

When he had been diagnosed with terminal pancreatic cancer, he had done everything in his power to ensure that line continued. He had set up trusts for his daughter, and sought to prolong his life to help her grow and mature. The fact that he'd had to spar with a medical system that, knowing the ultimate outcome of his condition would be death, seemed actively to battle his will to fight, had been one of the greatest sources of the bitterness that had gone on to consume so much of Angela's teenage life. But her father had fought with everything in him . . . for her. And Angela had almost rejected all of it.

Suddenly she realized the extent of the Templars' travels was not surprising at all. Faced with extinction, with termination, with a lineage being wiped from the face of the earth, a human would do almost anything, go almost anywhere. *Like her father* . . .

Love was a powerful motivator in life, but survival was a greater one.

The only thing that ever seemed to trump it was hate.

50

Mountainous Region, Inner China, AD *1334*

Sir Arnaud de Faulke could almost smell the death in the air. Every step through the strangely dense forest brought him closer to de Molay's sacred legacy. His squire, Alvain, kept pace a few steps before him, their mounts only just able to make their way through the undergrowth of the steep forest floor. Soon, de Faulke suspected, they would have to dismount and follow the example of their local guide, the diminutive translator whose services they had secured with enough gold to set up his family, who walked ahead by foot.

De Faulke and Alvain had travelled for eight years since they had departed the ritual of the Indian tribesmen. Their progress was far slower than would have been possible were they allowed to take main roads or enter significant cities, but this was not the only reason for their slow movement. Each segment of the intervening journey had required work to discern the meaning of de Molay's notes, and to work through the reality on the ground. They'd had to spend eighteen months in one village, becoming familiar and trusted to the locals before one family had finally passed along the information they needed – information about which they were forbidden to speak. Then de Faulke had been taken by illness, terrible and debilitating, which had caused almost two years of delays during which travel was impossible. Alvain had fallen ill a year later, adding seven months of further delays.

Delays, delays, delays. Yet finally they had advanced, and now they were here in a forest that de Faulke felt was close to the terminus of their journey. There was not much further they could go.

They had crossed the threshold of the small village of Tianbaoxiang two days ago, and de Faulke had spent the days since working his way through the village population, until finally he'd been shown to the small wooden hut that housed its elder. De Faulke didn't recall his name now, and wouldn't have been able to pronounce it if he had. He'd only wanted information, and it was information the old man had.

The imagery of forested death and darkness de Faulke had encountered on the wall painting in India had its origins in a local tradition of this village. The elder spoke of a legend of a great evil, buried in the earth. He had waved towards the hills beyond his hut as he spoke, his strange tongue finding its way into broken French through a younger translator – a man who had obviously travelled.

Out there, somewhere.

The elder's gestures made his description all the more tantalizing. A cave. Tunnels. Death, wormed beneath the soil, terrifying and untouchable. 'A place we do not go, and things we do not touch.'

De Faulke had rarely felt more elated. He had secured the young translator's services the following morning, with instructions that he and Alvain be taken to the site of this buried evil. Taken there quickly, and with no other followers.

The site waited for him now. Within the earth, the curse called out to de Faulke, the last Grand Master's voice singing from the soil. The knight walked towards it, the fog heavy in the trees, fallen twigs crackling beneath his feet.

51

Xi Ming Temple, Xi'an, China

In the mid-morning mist, the Xi Ming Temple looked positively haunting.

'The photos made it appear more welcoming,' Sean noted as he and Jack crossed through the ceremonial wooden entrance. The scent of a fresh coat of red paint on the old timbers crept through the heavy air.

'You didn't think TripAdvisor was going to draw out tourists' snapshots of the foggiest, ugliest days of their visits, did you?' Jack responded. Both men's weak humour was an attempt to conceal the wariness that came from being on full alert. They were in new surroundings, with no idea whether whoever had pursued them in India had followed them here.

Before them, a courtyard that in every guidebook and every online photograph was bright with primary reds, the silver and white of world-renowned statuary and the bold green of carefully tended plant life, was instead a hazy grey that revealed only an allusion to the strange shapes present all around them. The red brick of the temple walls and structures was indistinguishable from the black stone that capped their roofs, and the tall pine forest behind the complex made its presence known only by a slight, jagged darkening of the grey as it touched the horizon.

'At least the fog's kept most of the visitors away.' Sean motioned around them. The mist lowered visibility dramatically, making them feel quite alone.

'I'm not sure that's a good thing,' Jack replied. 'We're here to snoop. Other people are cover.' He hesitated, but then added, 'and last time, it was the presence of a crowd that saved us.'

Sean nodded, acknowledging the implicit warning.

Jack led the way deeper into the complex. The Xi Ming Temple was substantially smaller than the Thillai Nataraja Temple, but the restrictions on visitors were also more severe. No photographs. No departing from designated visitor zones and paths. No food, no drink. Talking in a low voice only. Respectful dress to be worn at all times.

'It's like the fascist take on a spiritual welcome,' Sean muttered, his nerves sounding through in his voice. Jack smiled back. It was good to be in the presence of another man who responded to tension with wit. Or, at least, attempts at it.

'It's not that bad. If you were a monk seeking the quiet life of contemplation, you'd probably want a few rules in place to keep tourist chatter at bay.'

Sean shrugged his shoulder. 'Do we need to apply for permission to scout around inside?' He motioned towards a small admissions booth, with its schedule of entrance fees listed in multiple languages.

'I don't think we'd be likely to get it, even if we did apply.'

'Then what's the plan?' In the fog the courtyard felt more haunting than spiritually enlightening, and Sean appeared to want to get on with their exploration as quickly as possible.

'There are a few tour groups scattered around,' Jack answered. Though the number of visitors was slight, they weren't altogether absent. He could see the outline of one group a few feet before them, and the sounds of another flowed out of the amorphous grey to his left. 'Let's get ourselves tickets and join up with one.'

'And then?'

'We cross the threshold to the inner temple as good tourists, then take advantage of the fog and find the first opportunity to disappear.'

The opportunity to disappear came quickly. The tour group to which Jack and Sean had joined themselves was conducted entirely in Mandarin, and it was clear to the guide and everyone else involved that they understood not a single word of what was being said. As a consequence, they were both left politely to trail at the back of the group, prepared to feign gawking at the sights as the group moved through the complex.

Those sights were more than enough to earn the admiring looks of all the visitors, including Jack and Sean. The Xi Ming Temple had not long ago been largely restored from near ruin to the glory of its seventh-century foundation by Tang Gaozong, and though neither Jack nor Sean could understand the narrative being provided at the head of their small group, the occasional signposts revealed a history as glamorous as the renewed surroundings. An urban monastery at the eastern end of the Silk Road, right at the heart of the Tang Dynasty, Xi Ming had been famed in its glory days for housing one of the best Buddhist libraries in the world. Jack and Sean already knew it had been the home of Xuanzang, who had translated a collection of foreign scriptures from his Indian travels, but monuments in the complex also commemorated a host of other great names in Buddhist history. Kukai, a Japanese monk, had studied Sanskrit in the environs, tutored by the great Gandharan pandit Prajna – one of many Indian connections the temple bore. Shubhakarasimha was another, an Indian monk who introduced a number of tantric traditions to Chinese Buddhism while there. Ximing fashi, a monk whose original Korean name was Woncheuk, had introduced important teachings into the Buddhist legacy from within these walls during the seventh century.

All from within a complex that, while beautiful, was hardly immense. It radiated a traditional Chinese spiritual architecture: graceful pagoda-style buildings in red brick with slate roofs; ornamental square gates made out of ancient wood; porticoes of white walls with red pillars – and connecting all the buildings, an interconnecting series of courtyards of grey stone, accented by statues of elephants, depictions of Buddhist legends and carefully curated plant life. Still, the overall size of the Xi Ming Temple was only a fraction of what they'd experienced before.

Which meant that, when they disappeared from the group, Jack and Sean would have to act quickly if they were to avoid being tripped over by others in the temple, quite apart from the possibility of someone deliberately trying to track them down.

'This way,' Jack whispered to Sean as the small bulk of their tour walked ahead of them, blurring in the mist. He pulled at Sean's sleeve and the two of them veered silently to the left.

It took only a matter of steps before the others were completely hidden from view.

'There's an entrance just over here,' Jack said, retracing their steps from a few moments ago. 'The signpost at the door indicates it leads into the Hall of Heavenly Kings. At the very least, it'll get us indoors.'

Sean followed him to the entryway, doorless and oversized, and the two men stepped inside. Before them, the gloom of the exterior was replaced with the immaculate, studied colouring of the central shrine. Whereas the Indian temple had been colourful in a seemingly ramshackle, almost flagrant manner, the artistry here was of a different tenor altogether. Alternating colours were balanced along careful lines of symmetry, creating a series of interconnected bands and beams that served to make the shrine seem at once both intimate and vastly larger than the actual space it occupied. And it had the obvious, unmistakable feeling of sacred space, even though Jack knew almost nothing about the Buddhist symbolism that occasionally punctuated the largely empty expanses.

'It's . . . stunning,' Sean whispered, and Jack felt himself nodding in agreement. There was something majestic, attractive and inviting about this place. If Thillai Nataraja had been a place that evoked ecstasy and entrancement, Xi Ming was a spot that seemed to breathe silence into its visitors' souls. Despite all that had happened, despite the tension of their current task, Jack felt strangely calm within these walls.

Sean suddenly spun towards him. 'Do you have a plan of approach?'

'There were no guidebooks this time around,' Jack answered, 'and we both know that the information online about this place isn't detailed enough to guide us along.' They had searched the Internet for a floor plan before arrival, but had been unsuccessful in finding anything useful.

'But I think your same insight from India will apply here.'

'A portion of the temple dedicated to death,' Sean replied.

'Or to remembrance of the dead, more specifically. It's a custom common to most religious traditions. The Christian knights entombed their dead beneath stone effigies in London.'

'The Hindu shrine to Kali reflected on memories of death and new life in Chidambaram,' Sean said.

'And somewhere here I bet we'll find a hall of remembrance, or something to that effect,' Jack concluded. 'We'll just have to go exploring for it.'

Sean looked ponderous, then moved back to the entrance. A moment later, his expression was stronger.

'It looks like each complex here is marked with a plaque indicating the shrines it contains. This building contains the Hall of Heavenly Kings and the Bodhisattva Hall.'

'Not what we're after.'

'No. But this isn't the first building we've passed.'

Jack was already in motion as Sean waved him outside.

Across the small courtyard, a square grey hulk with an angled roof indicated another building thirty feet in the distance.

'Mind if I lead the way?'

Sean didn't wait for an answer, but peered into the haze to be sure they were clear of spectators and darted towards their new destination.

The second building contained the Main Hall, reconstructed to its full, colourful glory. Three statues of Buddha sat between immense blue pillars, painted orange flames surrounding the seated golden figures, which were perched above a sea of flowers.

'This looks more like India,' Jack noted as they walked briskly through the space. The colours here were bolder, the scents of the floral and incense offerings more noticeable.

There were no monks in the hall, and they had successfully avoided being reconnected to their tour group. But that meant that they would stand out all the more if they were spotted, and both men were keen to keep moving.

'The exit's this way,' Sean said, motioning. He led Jack to another doorless exit leading back to the foggy exterior, and stopped to examine the signage on the wall outside.

'Finally.' He released a sigh of relief.

Jack approached and saw the cause: a floor plan of the Xi Ming complex – the first they'd encountered. The whole series of thirteen buildings and courtyards was outlined and labelled in Mandarin, English, German and Russian.

'Tourism must not be doing as badly as I thought,' Sean muttered, running his finger along the plastic sign. 'But at least it means we can read this.'

A few moments later, he'd planted his finger on a building marked Great Hall. 'Here we are now.'

He looked over his shoulder, taking in the relative position of the buildings near by. 'Which means that must be the refectory.' He pointed to one red hulk made grey in the fog, and then to another. 'And that's the library.'

'Look,' Jack said, pointing to a label in the upper right-hand quadrant of the plan. 'I think that might be our spot.'

Sean followed his finger. 'Hall of Ancestors.' He nodded. 'That sounds about right.'

'Think you can lead us there in the fog?'

Sean smiled. 'No problem.'

52

Digital Connection to Xi'an

'You have the final marker in your possession?' the Seneschal demanded impatiently.

'It was no trouble at all. At least, not the way we approached it, and knowing what we were looking for.'

Michael Wyatt had directed a group of ten men on the mission to obtain the final triangulation coordinate. The New Order had adherents in China – highly placed and influential – who had been only too honoured to be of assistance. They had money, power and technology at their disposal.

'A fabricated government inspection was all it took to close down the temple for two hours,' he explained, 'while we scoured the interior. With a little . . . persuasion . . . the monks allowed us to work unencumbered.'

'I'm not interested in your methods, only the results.'

Wyatt swallowed the scolding.

'The results were what we'd hoped for. It was the right temple. The full coordinates are now in hand.'

He could hear a long, satisfied breath flow from the Seneschal's lips on the far side of the globe.

'Very well done, Sir Michael.'

The sting of rebuke had passed, replaced with the swell of affirmation.

'You'll send me everything,' the Seneschal continued.

'You should already have it.'

'Then you must now do what you failed to do in India.'

The sting, back again. His success was marred by his inability to take out the two men in Chidambaram. And the woman was still free. Neither situation could be allowed to remain any longer.

Michael Wyatt rose as he concluded the call with a knight's vow.

'I won't fail again.'

53

The Hall of Ancestors was as elaborate as the temple's Main Hall, though the statues were smaller and there were more individual shrines filling the space.

'How old do you think these are?' Sean asked as they stepped inside. For the moment they had the room to themselves and could speak freely.

'Old, I'd think. There's no reason to think this room doesn't date back to the seventh- or eighth-century foundations of the place.' Jack scanned their surroundings. He suddenly felt an intruder, aware that this was a place of remembrance and that he wasn't here for memorial reasons. He didn't know precisely how the small statues commemorated the dead, but there was a reverent air that affected him.

'So, within our timeframe, at least.' A flash of pessimism crossed Sean's face. 'But this isn't looking as good for us as the shrine to Kali in India.' When Jack didn't answer, he motioned to the walls. 'No layers of tributes and etchings here.'

He was right. The walls themselves were either whitewashed, or in a few locations painted a solid blue. But there were no texts. No inscriptions. Nowhere to nestle a foreign message amidst a mess of others.

'Then we need to look for a different type of hiding

place,' Jack said. The room had six niches, each of which contained a small statue and tables for offerings of flowers, fruit and other memorials. He walked to the niche nearest his position and examined it.

'There's not going to be anything in the offerings. They're all perishable.' The tables on which they sat were wooden, so not likely candidates either. The walls here, too, were solid and smoothly painted. Empty slates that would give them nothing.

'Check the statue itself,' Sean suggested, stepping close to him. 'When we were in London, we looked at the effigy carvings first of all. Perhaps there's something here.'

A small statue of the Buddha shimmered golden in the candlelight, round bellied and eternally content, but it didn't seem a plausible place to carve anything. Surely any defacement of a shrine statue would have attracted notice, especially as the golden figure was a focal point. Such alteration would have been addressed long ago.

But as Jack examined the statue more closely, he could see that the gold covering it was a thin leaf, well worn and thin in some places, applied in layers that were more resilient and bright in others.

'It looks as if it's been re-gilded several times,' Sean noted, his face close. 'Probably over centuries, whenever Buddha's belly needed a new shine.'

Jack shook his head expressively. Cultural sensitivity was not Sean's strong suit, but the engineer's observation was on point. The multiple layers of gold leaf applied over the statue meant that the figures weren't solid metal. And that, in turn, meant there could be something carved beneath the gold leaf.

'It's worth us taking a closer look.' Jack left Sean to the first statue and moved to the second shrine. Another figure was seated in similar form, almost identical in features to the first. The pot belly and rounded face were inviting, warm, and for an instant Jack wished he knew more about the traditions the statue represented.

But what he really wanted, at this moment, was to know if it contained evidence of another tradition altogether. As unlikely as it seemed, every fibre of Jack's being hoped that beneath the golden skin of the Buddha was the inscription of a long-dead Christian knight.

The statue in Sean's niche yielded nothing, and despite Jack's careful scrutiny, his search of the second was no more successful. Frustration mounted quickly, and dread almost as fast. If they were on the right track and a marker had been carved into one of these statues centuries ago, the very fact of their continual re-gilding could mean it was now lost, buried under gold leaf that would make the ancient message invisible, even if they were staring right at it.

Jack shook off the worry and moved to another shrine, beginning his examination anew. The rounded head, the swollen belly. The neatly folded hands and gently crossed legs. The lotus flower beneath. All shimmering. All smooth. All message-less.

Sean was now at another statue and his mutterings revealed a similar frustration. That was four down. There were only two shrines remaining in the Hall of Ancestors.

They each moved to a final niche, the room suddenly seeming quieter, filled with a tension that tugged at them both.

Jack examined his statue, which looked almost identical to the two he'd already seen. He walked to its left side, then back to its front, straining to see something his eyes had missed at first glance. He stepped to the right. His eyes were aching in the poor light.

He then walked to the rear of the statue and passed his gaze over the Buddha's back. He could feel the disappointment rising in him like a frustrated cry, pressing into the back of his throat, and –

And then his eyes tricked him, or seemed to. He stepped closer.

The Buddha's back was smooth, like the rest of the statue, its flowing lines artful and serene. The statue was clean, unmodified. But it was its base that was drawing Jack's attention.

At the very bottom of the statue, where the gold form met the wooden surface of its support, a faint ring of dust marked its outline in the dim light. A ring that was askew. Or, rather, a ring that showed the statue itself was askew. The outline of its normal position was clear, but the Buddha was sitting off his mark – by no more than a tiny fraction of an inch.

As if it had been moved.

Jack's heart started to pound. It could be nothing but an accidental nudge from a worshipper or a careless pass of a dusting wand by a monk-cleaner. But it could also be something more.

Hoping that he wasn't about to unforgivably disrespect a tradition he did not understand, Jack reached out both his hands and firmly grabbed the statue. When he lifted it, the figure was surprisingly light and came away with almost no effort.

Jack looked down at the surface beneath, his hope surging. But the Buddha had not been hiding anything. The wooden pedestal beneath the statue shone back up at Jack in pristine condition.

Then, almost on impulse, he flipped over the statue in his hands, staring at the bottom of the figure itself.

Jack's world went silent. And then, only two words came from his lips.

'Oh, fuck.'

54

'What the hell did you do to my girls?' The tears streamed down Preston Wilcox's face, and it took two men to hold him in place, keeping him from the bodies tucked into the boot of the grey Chrysler. 'We had an arrangement, you bastards!'

The man standing closest to the car faced Wilcox and allowed him a few moments of rage. Rage was good. It would be necessary to fuel his action.

The father lunged for his children, and Commander Parker could almost see the torment in his mind. He would be reliving the video clip of his wife's murder, and he would be wondering just what torment had been unleashed upon his daughters.

Parker needed Wilcox to feel that terror. To gather a taste of what real loss and horror could feel like. If only, for the moment, so that he could relieve it.

'Our arrangement still stands, Senator,' Parker said softly but firmly. 'Your girls are fine.'

Wilcox's wild eyes spun on him, uncomprehending.

'They are just . . . asleep,' Parker explained, motioning towards them. As Wilcox's eyes spun back to them, his face seemed to register recognition. Gently, the girls' chests were rising and falling. They were breathing.

'What the hell is this about?' he pleaded. 'I did what you

272

asked. I arranged the meetings, spoke with the right people. Your event is happening. They're doing up the fucking seating charts, for Chrissakes!'

Parker waited for the anger to quiet, then answered calmly.

'You've done well, but we need something more.'

Wilcox didn't respond, just stared into his eyes, waiting, worrying.

'Get it done, and you'll have your girls back. Safe.'

The senator gazed down at his daughters, drugged and tied in the back of a car, and the resigned sag to his shoulder revealed everything. He knew he had no option but to comply.

'What do you want me to do?'

Parker smiled cordially. 'It's something minor, really. But there is one guest that you need to make sure gets on the list.'

55

Xi Ming Temple, Xi'an, China

Jack had never before experienced quite the mix of emotions that suddenly ran through him. Exultant relief, because what stared up at him from the underside of the statue was clearly another sequence of Templar rune encoding.

But with it, dread, because the runes were carved into the fabric of the statue itself, beneath all the layers of gold gilding.

All of which had been crudely scraped away, and recently, by the look of it.

'Sean, get over here.' The words came with an unexpected alertness to how loud his voice sounded in the hall. Jack hadn't noticed before, but suddenly felt very exposed.

Sean arrived at his side a few seconds later. He'd already searched the final niche. If there was nothing in Jack's, there was probably nothing to be found.

'What is it?'

Jack pointed out the underside of the statue to him, and Sean's expression immediately reflected the same mixture of relief and surprise that Jack felt inwardly.

'What does this mean?' Sean asked.

'The carving? It means we've found what we came here for.' A line of encoded text stared up at them. Beneath it, a symbol was clearly visible, its shape familiar. 'And that we've got part three of our triangulation marker.' Jack pointed to the encoded text carved next to the triangle.

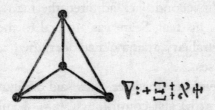

Sean's head nodded, but his eyes expressed no relief.

'I meant, what does *this* mean, Jack?' He pointed to the absence of gold over the carving, to the rough and recent signs of scraping, with fragments of gold leaf still fluttering at the edges of the uncovered area.

'It means someone was here before us,' Jack answered. 'That someone else knew what we were looking for, and where we were going to find it, and got here before we did.'

Sean's eyes moved quickly from side to side as he appeared to trace back through his memory and connect the dots.

'The gunman in India, the one who tried to kill us . . .'

'He must have found what we found in the shrine to Kali.'

'But how would he have been able to decipher it?' Sean asked.

'I have no idea. But it pointed here, and someone's been here since. Maybe even during the night.'

Suddenly, Sean's face went white. He spun on his heels, his eyes darting randomly to the nooks and corners of the room.

'If they've got what they want, and they know we want it, then –' Sean didn't finish this thought. His face betrayed his fear. *We're predictable targets.*

For a split second, Jack admired the man's instinctive alertness. In his fear, Sean was attuned to the same risk that Jack's military training had identified and already begun to assess.

'Sean, there's no one here,' Jack said firmly, willing him back to a state of self-control.

'How can you be sure?'

'Sean, breathe. I spent my military career trying not to be hunted down by ground insurgents. It's one thing to be taken by surprise in a crowd when we had no reason to believe we were being followed, but I've been paying just a touch more attention since then.' He released one hand from the small statue and placed it firmly on Sean's shoulder. 'There is no one here.'

Though for the life of him, Jack couldn't figure out why. Sean's fear was reasonable. If someone was trying to kill them, and had been able to make their way here in advance of their arrival, the most logical thing to do would have been to sit in wait and corner them right here. But Jack hadn't been speaking platitudes when he'd reassured Sean. He'd been on full alert since they'd landed in China, and even more so – if that were possible – since they'd begun their outing here to the temple. And he was as certain as he possibly could be that there was no one following them. And that didn't make any se –

'Oh, hell.' The realization hit him suddenly, terribly. He spun towards Sean, holding out the statue.

'Take this, quick. Get whatever photos you need, but

do it fast.' Sean didn't have time to respond before Jack reached into his pocket, grabbed his small camera and passed it to Sean's other hand. 'Take a few with mine, too. We should have back-ups.'

'Jack, what is it?'

'Just do it, Sean!' Jack snapped. He was reaching for his mobile phone, taking a few steps away.

'And just what the fuck are you going to do while I'm standing here snapping pictures like a tourist?' Sean asked, his nervousness now fully apparent.

Jack raced through his contacts, found the entry and hit dial.

'I have to warn Angela.'

56

Grand Soluxe International Hotel, Xi'an

'You can relax. I'm not going to hurt you. At least, not unless you make me.'

The snub nose of the gun pointed at Angela's face did not ring with the same tone of comfort as the words of the man who held it.

'Who are you?'

'You can keep asking, and I will keep declining to answer,' the man responded. He had tied Angela's hands behind the back of the hotel room's desk chair and bound her ankles. He sat on the edge of the queen bed calmly, keeping the gun steadied on her position.

'You won't tell me who you are, or why you're here, but you keep saying you won't hurt me, despite tying me up and holding me at gunpoint.'

The man's face looked almost bemused. 'Exactly.'

Angela's defiant tone belied the terror that ached in her chest. She'd seen guns before, of course. It was impossible to work for a defence contractor, however sidelined her project was, and not catch sight of firearms and worse. But there they had always been products, produced and packaged for a reality that took place far away.

She'd never had one pointed at her.

At least, not until yesterday.

'You're the one who was shooting at us at Thillai

Nataraja.' The words rushed from her throat. They were a frightened realization, but came out sounding like an accusation.

'Maybe so.'

'You didn't seem to mind hurting me there, did you?'

The man peered at her curiously. 'You weren't harmed, were you?'

Angela could feel the pain in her joints that came from too much adrenaline coursing through her system for too long.

The man had taken her entirely by surprise. She had been sitting at the desk, working over her notes, pondering history and interpretations and broad strokes of meaning, when the soft bleep of the door indicated the electronic lock had been released.

He'd had a keycard.

The door had swung open with full force, and before Angela could take in the scene the man had been on top of her, crossing the distance from the door to the desk in only a few steps. The gun had been at her temple before she'd even seen his face.

Then the threats. The ties. The man settling on to his perch, sending a text message to an unknown recipient with his gaze always on her from the corner of his eye, and the gun unwavering.

Angela had never known such fear. Yet she'd also never known such anger. This man had tried to kill her, and Sean, and Jack – despite what he said. Death, that reality Angela so despised and dreaded, was something this man was ready to mete out without hesitation. And for that, she hated him more than any man she'd ever known.

On the glass table before the television, her mobile phone began to vibrate. She turned her head towards it, and the man's followed.

'Don't,' he instructed, before she could be so foolish as to try to move.

'It'll be –'

'I know who it will be,' he said. 'And it's better that Sean and Jack don't hear the fear in your voice.'

57

Mountainous Region, Inner China, AD *1334*

The darkness stared openly at de Faulke now, so close that he could touch it.

The knight and his companions stood before what appeared to be little more than a small gap in the natural rock formation before them. Moss hung from the upper edge and the lush ground cover reached up towards it, creating a green curtain that almost shielded the blackness beyond from view. Almost, but not quite.

'This is it, you are certain?'

'I am certain,' the translator said, answering the knight. 'We never come here. It is forbidden. This is a . . . terrible place.'

He shuddered, clipping his words, and de Faulke could understand the fear that gripped him. Though the surroundings were no different from the jungle scenery they had been walking through for hours, the afternoon sunlight shining through the thick green foliage above with an orange glow, not strong enough to fully eradicate the wisps of fog that clung to the ground, there was something different about this spot. Something immediately, tangibly . . . sinister.

'We go in,' de Faulke announced, the statement betraying nothing but unyielding confidence. He glanced towards his squire, and Alvain searched through a leather pack to find two torches and a large blade. The darkness would need to be breached, and neither of them knew whether the thick overgrowth at the entrance would continue inside. He hitched the blade to his belt and lit the torches from a flint, passing one to his master.

'You are coming with us,' de Faulke added, noticing their guide's obvious hesitation. The boy edged away from the entrance, petrified of whatever lay beyond, but de Faulke's stern glare seemed to terrify him almost as much.

'We don't know what we'll find,' the knight continued. 'If there's text, you'll need to translate.'

The boy swallowed hard, but recognizing that this was a demand and not a request, nodded in acquiescence.

A moment later, a strong sweep of the blade cut through the greenery that blocked their entry. After 7,000 miles of travelling, Arnaud de Faulke stepped into the darkness.

58

'Sean, wait a minute.' Jack reached forward and grabbed Sean's hand before he could slide his plastic keycard into the lock. Angela was in 422, just next door to the side-by-side rooms Jack and Sean had taken.

'I thought you wanted to check she was all right?' Sean protested. They had run here from the Xi Ming Temple at full bore, Sean somehow managing to work at the keyboard of his tablet as they moved, uploading the images of their discovery in the Hall of Ancestors to the decryption team in Seattle. Jack hadn't been able to get through to Angela, though he'd been ringing her mobile constantly. He'd even rung the front desk and asked to be transferred, but there was no answer there either.

'Just . . . hold on,' he instructed. His voice was suddenly at a whisper.

Sean took a step back from the door. 'What is it?'

Jack waved aside the question impatiently. 'Let me think a second.' Angela's silence meant one of two things. Either she was out, or she was still inside the hotel room, and couldn't answer. Which would mean she was not alone. Or that she was –

No, he pushed the thought from his mind. It might be irrational, but he chose simply to refuse to believe that Angela could have been killed. Instead, he prepared himself for a situation that he suddenly realized they were entirely unequipped to handle.

He looked to Sean. 'You don't happen to have a weapon on you, do you?'

Angela and the intruder had both heard the voice outside the door. She knew it was Sean's, but whether the man with the gun could identify him she didn't know.

The voice had suddenly gone silent, but they were both now on alert, and the faint ruffle of whispers could just be discerned.

That meant Jack was with Sean. Angela felt a sudden surge of hope.

The man at the edge of her bed stood up. When he turned from the door to look at her, his face was a broad smile.

'It looks like your partners have finally come to find you,' he whispered, and began to move to a position behind her.

'You said you wouldn't hurt us,' Angela protested.

She heard the draw and click of the gun's slide action being readied.

'I'm afraid you misheard me, Miss Derby,' the man whispered in her ear, kneeling down so that his body was shielded by hers.

'I said I wouldn't hurt *you*.'

'Of course I don't have a weapon!' Sean answered. 'I have a laptop, my camera, a wad of cables, my torch –'

'Give me the light,' Jack ordered, holding out a hand.

Guns they did not have, but a metal Maglite was better than nothing.

'Now, hand me the key.' Jack's whispered command was authoritarian, but Sean hesitated.

'I'm going in with you.'

'It'll be a cold day in hell, Sean,' was all Jack answered. He grabbed the card from Sean's clutch and shoved him to the side of the doorway.

A gunman expecting someone to come through a door would be expecting him to be standing, which meant chances were good he'd have his weapon readied at chest height. Jack crouched down, as low as he could go and still retain the ability to move quickly on his feet. The torch was in his right hand. He'd have to thrust open the door, assess the position of anyone inside, and charge them with whatever degree of surprise he had. All while staying low, dodging whatever bullets might be flying over his head.

It was an absurdly insecure position and an entry that was wrong on almost every tactical level – no idea who was inside, where they were, what firepower they had.

But Jack had no choice.

Positioning the keycard in his fingers, he raised his hand to the lock.

There was no way Jack and Sean were making it into this room alive. Angela knew nothing about combat or gunfights, but two things she knew absolutely. The first was that the man positioned behind her intended to kill both of them, and the second was that there was no cover once the door opened. They moment it swung aside, Jack and Sean would be dead.

And that Angela Derby would not allow.

She didn't have time to develop a plan. As the realization hit, the tiny red light on the electronic lock flashed to green, and the tone signalled the input of a valid card.

Click.

The lock opened, and with a speed that matched the intruder's when he'd made his own entry, the handle swung and the door burst inward.

But this time, Angela knew it was coming.

The moment she saw the tip of the door handle start to move, she leaned forward as far as her bonds would allow. The man with the gun was still crouched behind her, peering out from beyond her right shoulder, and she could see his firing arm extend with the motion of the door.

With every ounce of her strength, Angela swung backwards and crunched the muscles on her right side. As the door swung, the side of her head came back and she slammed it into the forehead of her captor.

The impact was like nothing she had ever felt. Her vision exploded, and a sound louder than she'd ever experienced trumpeted through her head. The room went white, then black, and for an instant Angela thought she'd been too late – that the man had fired his weapon, that she'd got her head in the way and the bullet had smashed through her skull. She could feel herself careening downwards.

But then, another sound. A shout, from a voice she recognized. When Angela blinked her eyes, vision began to return in a blur, but she could make out Jack leaping over her, something black and oblong in his raised right hand.

He landed on the intruder before the other man could raise his gun, and Jack's hand came down. The sound of metal meeting forehead was gruesome.

And as quickly as it had begun, the commotion ceased.

Angela saw Jack push a finger against the fallen man's neck, then turn to her. He was rising, coming towards her, panting heavily from the action but with a look of relief on his face. He had saved her. Or she had saved him. She couldn't be sure. Maybe it was both.

Angela lolled her head down on to the thin carpeting of the hotel-room floor, and allowed the scene to fade away.

59

Washington, DC

Anthony Graves peered over his desk at his colleague's face.

'You've gone mad, kid! It's absurd for you even to make the request, after all we've already had to push to get this far!'

The young gentleman from Arkansas stood before him, clearly at his wits' end. Graves had worked with him, had gone along with him, but this was a step too far.

'If the Man wants to be there,' Graves said, 'he'll be there.'

Senator Wilcox paced the luxurious office. He'd heard Graves's words, but seemed unwilling to accept what his colleague was saying. Wilcox's lips moved silently, deliberating with himself, then he turned to Anthony and spoke with rapid stress.

'I'm told by our sponsors that his presence is essential. They're threatening to change the terms of the contract if they can't present to him. Say it would amount to a waste of money and effort.'

'Threatening about the terms?' Now Graves sat forward, his mild annoyance at the other man giving way to surprise and anger. 'God help them, I'll castrate the bastards if they try it. After what we've done for them!'

'Surely, Anthony, there's something you can do.' Wilcox

stopped his pacing and stared straight at Graves. The older senator checked his anger, surprised by the sight before him. Preston Wilcox looked tired, even beleaguered. There was more red in his eyes than there should have been, and the worry marks of stress were everywhere on his face.

Poor kid. Maybe he can't take the stress of politics after all. Anthony Graves wasn't entirely surprised. It was a hard game. The pressure was something a man could either bear or couldn't. Sometimes you never knew until you were tested.

'Fine, fine,' Graves finally relented, sighing. 'I'll have a word.'

'Thank you, thank you so much.' Wilcox's relief was dramatic. He stepped forward and reached across the desk to grab Graves's hand, shaking it furiously.

'No problem, son. He'll have just given the biggest speech of the year. What else would the president of the United States be doing at that time of evening, if not attending our little show-and-tell?'

60

Thomas Blackburn made it from a filing cabinet to the phone on his office desk by the third ring.

'Blackburn.'

'It's Sean.' The voice of his son had the slightly distant, digitized timbre of an encrypted call, but it was still clear enough to shock Thomas Blackburn to his core.

'Sean, I . . . wasn't expecting to hear from you.' He hesitated, trying his best to determine what this meant. 'I thought you were pushing ahead with the expedition. You weren't scheduled to update me until later.'

'Things have fucking changed!' Sean yelled into the phone.

Thomas Blackburn's breath was getting shorter, his nerves causing a familiar ache in his hands and joints.

'Language, Sean.' He forced out measured words. 'What's changed?'

'The gunman in India, it wasn't a lone event. He followed us here.'

Blackburn didn't answer.

'Actually, he got here before us. He knew where we were going and uncovered the final piece of the puzzle before we even got to it. Then the bastard tried to take us out.'

'You have obtained the final segment?'

'Are you listening to me? This man tried to kill us!'

'But he obviously didn't,' Blackburn snapped back. He took a breath to control an anger he hadn't been expecting.

'I'm sorry,' he finally said. 'What happened?'

Sean explained the situation as clearly as his emotions would allow.

'So you've taken this man out?' Blackburn asked when he was done.

'He's lying unconscious on the hotel-room floor.'

'Do you know who he is?'

'I've never seen him before,' Sean answered.

Blackburn pondered whether it was necessary, or a distraction, but finally gave an instruction. 'Send me a photo, let me see if I can find out.'

Sean acknowledged his father's request, then went quiet, allowing his breath to return to normal.

'Having taken down this man,' Thomas Blackburn said after his son had calmed down, 'have you been able to decrypt what you found in the temple?'

'The results just came through on my phone,' Sean answered. 'At this stage our computer can decrypt the Templar sequences almost in real time.'

'So they have made me aware. And . . . what does it read?'

'There was a single line of text. Decoded and translated it reads "Where my heart is also".'

Blackburn grated his teeth. 'What is that supposed to mean?'

'We don't know. Angela's working on it.'

Blackburn leaned forward, holding the phone closer. 'She's all right? Nothing happened to her?'

'She's got a sore head and bruised wrists, but she'll be fine. The woman is resilient.'

Blackburn breathed a sigh of relief. 'Let me know when you sort through the text's meaning. But I can assume you found the final coordinate?'

'The final village name has allowed us to plot out a triangle over our map of south central China,' Sean answered. 'The centre-point is at a set of coordinates I've just sent to your email.'

Blackburn swivelled to his computer, tucking the phone into his ear. His fingers trotted over the keyboard with the speed of a much younger man, locating Sean's message and entering the coordinates into a satellite-mapping application. A few seconds later, he was zooming in on heavy, green foliage covering the one spot on earth he had dedicated his life to finding.

The ages were crying out to him. His ancestors, his past: *Well done, our son!*

'You have done well, son,' he echoed the sentiment aloud into the phone, his eyes clinging to the image before him.

Thomas Blackburn sat straight, command taking over emotion. 'As soon as you've all recovered, I want you to travel there. As quickly as you can. Spare no expense. Take everything and anything you might need. I'll have a full excavation crew on its way to you from our China branch in Shanghai within the hour.'

'You've got it,' Sean answered, the course of progress

seeming to charge him out of his shock. 'We'll need a bit of time to get ourselves ready, but I think we can be in motion within a couple of hours. It's still late morning here. The site is only two hours away by helicopter, so we can be exploring it by late afternoon.'

'Make sure you are,' Blackburn replied. Then he allowed his paternal sentiment a moment to return. 'And be careful, Sean. What you're dealing with it's ... just, be careful.'

There was a slight delay. 'I will, Father. Don't worry.'

A longer pause, then, in tones that came out almost like an afterthought, Thomas Blackburn added, 'I'm going to ensure the crew packs a special crate in the supplies they bring with you. It'll be locked, and marked with your name. I'll text you the PIN to open it, but you're not to do so until you're on site, at the threshold of discovery. Is that understood?'

'Understood,' Sean answered.

'Not before you arrive,' Blackburn repeated. 'But once you're on site, don't take another step until you've got hold of what's inside.'

Michael Wyatt's failure was intolerable. The Seneschal had expected so much more from him. A newly consecrated knight was meant to serve with the power of God, not to fall at the hands of some woman. The fact that she'd been tied to a chair when she'd felled him added insult to what was already a festering injury.

The New Order's contact in the Chinese police force had relayed the full findings of their investigation to the

Seneschal almost as they happened. Wyatt had been clubbed unconscious by Jack Shepherd after being knocked to the ground by the woman, and Sean had called in the officers a few minutes later.

'You must release the three of them,' the Seneschal had instructed the contact.

'That will be difficult,' the police officer replied. 'Police procedures are strict here. They should be detained for further questioning.'

'Find a way.'

The officer had not protested further. Police procedures were one thing, the will of the New Order another.

'Do you want us to finish the job on the two men once they're free?'

'No.' The Seneschal pondered the change of direction as he spoke. The resilience of the group had surprised him, as had their efficiency. His plan to eliminate them from the path would no longer provide an advantage. They'd already identified the end-point – they might as well collect it safely and secure what he needed. Besides, killing Sean was never going to have been easy. He would have let it happen, of course, but it would have haunted him for as many years as he had left.

'Let them go, and then keep them safe.'

'Safe?' The knight in China sounded surprised at the 180-degree shift in the mission.

'We can ensure they collect the treasure unharmed,' the Seneschal answered. 'Then they can deliver it, and the key, together.'

He set down the phone. He would have to decide how

to deal with the comatose Wyatt later. But after his fall, the man no longer mattered.

Just like the Grand Master's involvement, the new knight was no longer required.

61

Xi'an, China, Heading to Airport

Jack kept his eyes on Angela as they sat in the back of the expansive car, making their way towards the airport. She had borne being captured, and fending off her attacker, better than many people he'd known in his life – including trained soldiers – but he was still worried about her.

'Angela, are you sure you don't want to take a little more time?' he said, his voice supportive. 'A couple of days, to get ourselves grounded again?'

She looked up at him, her expression stern.

'Jack, I've told you already, I'm fine. The head is pounding, but it's nothing that requires recovery time.'

'I wasn't thinking so much about the physical trauma as the –'

'That man, whoever the hell he was,' Angela interrupted him, 'didn't *traumatize* me, Jack. He attacked, and we fought back. Plain and simple.'

Jack hesitated, but smiled. 'I didn't realize how much fight you had in you. Not exactly what one expects from a bookish type.'

Angela's eyes warmed. 'We've known each other all of three days, Captain Shepherd. Nice to know I can still surprise you.'

'Not to mention take him down a peg or two,' Sean interjected from the front.

Angela's smile turned into a grin. 'An added perk. Couldn't wait for the Marine all day. I had to take a little action for myself.' She forced a wink at Jack, then winced from the pain it caused at her temple.

'Still no word on the man's identity?' Jack asked, allowing her the jibe.

'He was carrying no identification,' Sean answered. 'I snapped a photograph and sent it to my father. Maybe it'll turn something up. Otherwise, the Chinese police will make a match eventually.'

'What's your best guess?' Angela asked.

Jack thought through a few silent moments before answering. 'If someone believed we were actually getting close to real treasure, something as big as the Templar treasure has been mythed up to be, it might be something they'd kill for.'

'Men certainly did in the past.'

'But it doesn't explain how this man was able to get to the temple before us,' Jack added. 'India was a matter of following, but here he was pre-emptive. And that means he must have known how to decode the runes.' He gazed into Angela's eyes. 'Who else, apart from the two of you, would be able to do that?'

'No one,' she said flatly. 'People have been trying to break the Oak Island codes for generations, and never made any progress. And then to link them to the Templars, to India . . . that's work that's taken us years.'

'And a hell of a lot of computing power,' Sean added.

'Well, somehow this man was able to figure it out. If he couldn't have done it from the outside, perhaps he was . . .' Jack let his voice trail off.

Sean shook his head vigorously. 'I told you already, I've never seen him before. If you're thinking it's an inside job, I can guarantee the man we stopped has never worked in our Seattle complex.'

'Maybe it wasn't him,' Angela suddenly said. Both men turned to her.

'There was someone else?'

'Not with him,' she answered, 'but he sent a text message from the hotel room, while he had me tied up, waiting for you. He was in communication with somebody.'

Jack glanced forward at Sean, but the other man only shrugged. 'I can't imagine,' he finally said. 'Everyone on the team works for Angela and me, and they're vetted and constantly monitored.' He paused. 'But I'll phone and check that no one's gone on sick leave suddenly, all the same.'

Sean turned away from them and began working with his phone.

'I want to say it again,' Jack said to Angela, 'there's no need for us to rush. Until we know just who this man was connected to –'

'We're so close,' Angela interrupted. 'We're at the end of the journey, Jack. This next step, it's going to take us to what people have searched for for centuries. We can't stop.'

'I'm not suggesting we stop.'

'And I'm starting to think I understand what the secret is,' Angela continued, her energy suddenly brimming. 'I think that whatever the Templars hid here, so far east, was less about riches and power than it was about self-preservation. They ran, and ran far. Their life at home was over. They wanted to survive.'

Jack was thrown by the sudden assertion. 'What does that have to do with hidden treasure?'

'What is more to be treasured than something that will keep you alive? What's really worth more: gold, or the ability to stay among the living?'

It was a question that didn't seem at all out of place in their current context.

'I'm not sure, Jack. It's just a theory. Maybe I haven't quite figured it out yet. But I don't think the treasure we're chasing concerns wealth. I think it's about something else.'

She reached forward and placed her hand on Jack's arm.

'And we're not stopping until we find it.'

62

Fewer than three hours after leaving their hotel and the unconscious body of their attacker in the hands of the Chinese police, Jack, Angela and Sean were airborne once again, this time in the belly of a modified Kazak Mil Mi-17 helicopter – one of a trio flying together towards the coordinates they had triangulated from the ancient runes.

'Any sense of what our target will look like?' Sean asked, speaking to the other two through interlinked headsets. The sound of the helicopter's massive rotors was reduced to a gentle thumping through the noise-cancelling technology.

'Probably not like much,' Jack answered. Beneath them, the hilly, mountainous terrain of inner China extended as far as any of them could see. 'Or anything at all. It was obviously chosen for its remoteness. This isn't Indiana Jones – I wouldn't expect to round a bend and find a massive temple concealed in these forests.'

Angela smiled from the other side of the chopper. The panic and shock of the morning had given way to an anticipation years in coming. Outside her window, the two other aircraft advanced with them in loose formation. They were packed with equipment, ranging from a small jeep to every sort of search-and-retrieval technology imaginable, including ground-penetrating radar units, thermal scanners, even a portable drone that could be used to raise a camera high above for aerial surveillance once they themselves were on the ground. All that, alongside a full excavation crew of eight members, with tents, provisions and enough kit to make this a week-long expedition if necessary.

Thomas Blackburn wanted them to have everything they needed.

At Angela's instruction, the supplies included digging equipment, as well as chainsaws, axes and other resources that might be useful in what amounted to an Asian jungle scenario. They need be prepared for whatever unknowns might lie ahead of them.

'Touch us down there. See if you can get all three birds together.' Sean motioned towards a small clearing in the forest, only a hundred feet or so from the spot his GPS unit indicated was the exact point they had triangulated. It was as close as they were going to get the bulky helicopters, and it was near enough to make their way by foot.

Jack felt the familiar *thud* of the craft's wheels making vertical contact with land. He didn't mind flying – in aeroplanes. Helicopters, however, were a different story. They had always struck him as particularly flagrant attempts by mankind to flaunt the laws of nature. *Not enough that humanity should fly . . . now it wants to hover.* Or perhaps that was merely the rationalization he'd always offered for something more basic: a rumbling stomach and sense of nausea brought on by the strange sensations of lift and drop that only helicopters could effect. He'd disliked it in the military, and he disliked it now.

The roar of the twin-turbine engines came suddenly, like an assault, as the noise-cancelling headsets went offline and Sean slid open the door of their craft. The massive rotors slowly transformed from a blur of motion and noise to a swirling vision of blades slicing the air above them, gradually winding down towards a halt.

'Out we go,' Sean shouted, jumping down on to the grass and leading Jack and Angela to a free zone in the clearing.

Safely away from the motion of the helicopter, Jack turned back and watched as the other two craft touched down a few feet apart. The pilots were experts: he estimated there were only a few arm-widths between the rotor-tips as the helicopters landed together in the condensed space.

'The crew will off-load the gear,' Sean said, calling Jack and Angela closer towards him. 'It'll take them a bit of time, but there's no reason not to get started while they work.'

Sean had not put away the GPS unit he'd had with him on board, and glanced down now at its small display.

'It's close?' Angela asked.

Sean reorientated the device, looking up to the forest at the north-western edge of the clearing.

'That way.' He reconfirmed the direction, and a second later led them from the open knoll into the forest that surrounded them like an endless green sea.

63

'What do you mean, the man is dead?' Special Agent Tom Arbuckle already felt uncomfortable with the last-minute arrangements that had to be put in play for the post-State of the Union event. Surprises like this aggravated his dissatisfaction.

'We got word this morning,' a fellow Secret Service agent reported.

'I thought the guy was stationed here at home, on base. How does a soldier die on his own base in the nation's capital?' Petty Officer Second Class Rick DiMaggio was a US Army specialist in anti-landmine and bomb-disarmament robotic technologies, and was the Defence Department's choice to operate the new Blackburn Enterprises XRX-450 unit at the demonstration following the State of the Union. The technology behind the motorcycle-sized robotic contraption was new – not even yet in its release stage – and DiMaggio was the only man who'd yet received training on its operation.

'He'd gone off base, into the city for some sort of action at a bar,' Arbuckle's man reported. 'Wound up in a brawl outside the premises. Local PD found him dead on the pavement, his face smashed in pretty bad.'

Arbuckle rubbed his chin. This was not good. 'Anything suspicious?'

'Nothing. I spoke with Captain Kevin Hawks at the reporting precinct. It's the third death in two years outside the Mill House, and they're almost always fist fights. Petty Officer DiMaggio chose to go to the wrong sort of place. Paid for it.'

Arbuckle shook his head. This figured. A high-pressure addition to a national event, all to showcase new military technologies that could transform the coming generations of defence exploits, and now the one man capable of operating the flagship piece of show-and-tell was dead.

'They'll have to cancel that portion of the presentation,' he noted, speaking mostly to himself.

'Negative,' the other agent replied. 'The supplier considers it a key feature. They're unwilling to remove it from the programme.'

'I'm not about to allow anyone to operate a piece of futuristic *military engineering* in a room seating both houses of Congress, who hasn't been fully trained!'

'The company isn't suggesting that,' the agent noted. 'Blackburn Enterprises is going to supply one of its own men. The device will be operated by one of the team who designed it.'

Arbuckle drew in a long, slow breath. A change of operators. Not ideal, but then nothing about these circumstances was.

'One of its own men?' he questioned. 'With security clearance?'

'Design team, fully cleared. Probably safer hands than the military tech.'

Probably so, Arbuckle thought. And that was, at the end of the day, what he most needed in a room with so much political overhead. *Safe hands.*

64

Mountainous Region Outside Tianbaoxiang, China

The woods were dense with growth, and Jack immediately felt as if he had crossed the threshold into another world. Massive trees were as tall as their trunks were thin, with knee-high ground cover and a canopy above that let in little light. Those rays it did permit were coloured an alien green that accentuated the reds and browns of the rest of the vegetation. It was like something out of a film set, and for the first time in his life Jack questioned whether the surreal atmosphere of so many high-end Chinese martial arts films was really as far-fetched as he'd always assumed.

Sean's small device emitted periodic blips as they made their way towards the target point, the sharp sounds gradually growing shorter and more frequent.

'Does this look like . . . like what you were expecting?' Jack asked, nudging Angela as they stepped round bushes and branches.

'I have no idea what to expect,' she answered. 'But I won't pretend this isn't all new to me.' A few inches of mist clung to the ground, spreading in flurried wisps as they walked.

'It shouldn't be much further,' Sean announced. He kept a few steps ahead of them, absorbed in following the guidance of his equipment.

'You'd better keep your head up, and not pointed down

at that machine,' Jack urged. Branches stuck out at odd angles, bamboo stalks shot up in the odd rays of accentuated sunlight. It was a marvel Sean hadn't walked into something already.

'I don't think he heard you.' Angela smiled at Jack. 'I've never seen Sean concentrating so hard. Maybe we would have got here three months ago if he was this focused all the time.'

'You do realize I can hear you both,' Sean said, not turning back to face them.

Jack laughed, pushing his way through a pack of fern leaves. The pings from Sean's tracker were a constant pattern of rapid, short bursts now. And then, as Jack watched him take another two steps forward, the beeps merged and became a solid, dramatic tone.

'We're here.'

It took Jack and Angela only a few seconds to reach him.

'You want to shut that off?' Jack asked, motioning towards the whining GPS device. Sean flicked a small switch and cancelled the tracking tone.

The quietness of the forest suddenly overwhelmed them. There were the usual sounds of nature – the breeze in the leaves, a few calling birds. But the overwhelming quality, following the shrill, technical tone of the tracker, was silence.

Which fitted the surroundings perfectly, since the device had led them to a section of forest remarkable for presenting Jack, Angela and Sean with the surprising find at the end of their multi-continent trek.

Nothing.

65

This emptiness has to be misleading.

Angela's mind refused to accept what her eyes beheld. She did not doubt that Sean's computers and GPS equipment had led them to the precise point they had triangulated from the Templar runes. They were too well teched-out and careful to have made a mistake. Which meant that the spot where they were standing . . . *mattered*. Despite the fact that it was entirely unremarkable, indistinguishable from any other section of the forest through which they'd walked from the small landing site.

There is more here. There has to be.

'We need to make a thorough sweep of this section of forest,' she announced. She kept her tone strong, knowing that Jack and Sean would be feeling the same sense of deflation.

'Remember, the members of the Order would have been here sometime after the purge in the early decades of the 1300s. That's almost 700 years ago. Things could have looked very different back then.'

Sean peered into her eyes. His expression was profoundly discouraged, with eyes that accused her of trying to avoid the obvious.

Jack observed the locked gaze and spoke before Sean had the chance. 'I don't know about either of you, but if

308

I don't weed my garden for two weeks, the thing's completely overgrown. I can't imagine what it would look like after 700 years.'

Angela smiled and exhaled with relief, breaking Sean's defeated stare. Whether or not Jack sincerely still believed there was anything here to be found, at least he was feigning optimism. She didn't have both of them openly resigned to failure.

'If that's the spot marked out by the coordinates,' Angela added, pointing towards Sean's feet, 'then I suggest we start to examine everything within a hundred-foot radius, as a way to begin.'

Voices began to break through the branches behind her, and Angela turned to see the excavation crew making its way towards their location. The eight men and women of the team carried large packs, as well as crates filled with equipment.

'A hundred-foot radius sounds good,' Sean said, returning to life. The appearance of people bearing tools and technology seemed to give him a renewed burst of enthusiasm.

'And we've got equipment here to help us do more than just strong-arm our way through the bramble.'

Within fifteen minutes, packs and cases had been opened to produce three metal detectors and Blackburn Enterprises's own portable ground-penetrating radar unit. Unlike most GPR systems, which looked like push lawn-mowers and required a fairly flat surface to operate, the company's research and development branch had found a way to mitigate data interruption from a radar burst to a receiver held several feet above ground, allowing the device to be fastened to a mount on an operator's waist and walked over any type of terrain. One of the excavation crew flown in from Shanghai, a Missouri-born Blackburn Enterprises researcher, wore the unit now and began pacing the area Angela had indicated.

Their packs had also contained an array of clippers and branch-cutters, and several of the team set to work clearing the foliage.

Sean was in his element with the technology and worked with the team, while Jack appeared content to put his hand in with the clearing, taking up a large set of cutters and setting to the task of snipping through bamboo stalks and vines.

Angela left the technology to the technicians, and there were plenty of the team working on clearing without her joining in. Eyes and hands – these were her preferred tools.

We still don't know exactly what we're looking for, she reminded herself, pushing away branches to gaze down at the forest floor itself. They obviously weren't going to find a structure here. No matter how overgrown, there was no chance of revealing a hidden chapel or temple or house. But what could hold a treasure that had required so much effort to conceal and so much care to protect? A chest? A vault? Or were they only here to discover another set of instructions, with guidance on a further leg of travels?

Don't analyse. Just look.

There were more than just trees and bushes around them. The hilly, uneven forest floor was broken up by mounds of earth, together with large stones, well over her height, poking up from beneath the soil. *Plenty to search. Plenty of targets to scope out. Plenty of sites to . . .*

Angela couldn't believe what she was thinking. Her inner voice had almost said the words she had rebuked so many others for speaking aloud. *Plenty of sites to hide a buried treasure.*

Treasure. In the end, Angela realized, she'd been swept up in the same quest as so many others, no matter how she had tried to deny or redefine it. She had chided Jack in Seattle for talking about 'Templar treasure', yet here she was, all the same, digging through the forest. It may have been a triangle, rather than an 'X' that marked the spot, but that seemed largely, discouragingly semantic.

Angela's pulse started to increase and her skin felt the cold tingle of anxiety. What had her life become? She was a scholar, or at the very least a scholar-to-be. An emerging expert in her field, she hoped. She'd formulated theories that had found concrete historical support; and yet she was reduced to, to what? To becoming the very sort of sensationalist treasure-seeker she'd so lamented all her life.

A treasure-seeker, with millions of dollars of other people's money to spend, wandering through the forest with clippers and toys and ancient signs, all of which were bringing her ever closer to . . .

Angela blinked firmly, and took a clear look at her surroundings.

To an empty patch of forest with a few rocks and too much bamboo.

Shit.

She could feel the sweat tingle all over her body, not from exertion. From the anxiety of a deep, instant awareness. Her work was –

At that moment, a voice tore through Angela's interior crisis. A voice pronouncing words odd enough to call her to attention.

The crew member operating the radar unit spoke with a sense of confusion all his own.

'There's something not right with this tree.'

66

Mountainous Region Outside Tianbaoxiang

It took twenty minutes for the roots to be cut away from the tree in question. The radar unit operator's announcement had been odd, but it was the only way he could describe what the display on his live readout was showing. The massive tree that rose before him had an above-ground root system that gnarled its way down the sides of a great mound of earth and rock in an almost solid lattice-work, itself covered in other vegetation.

'Everywhere else, I get standard feedback,' he added, explaining the readout to Jack and Angela while Sean directed the others to begin cutting through the root system. 'Stone and soil behind the roots. But just there, I get, well, nothing.' He pointed towards the section of root where the team members were now at work. 'It's like the roots have a space behind them. A hollow.'

That word had sparked the energy of the team, and twenty minutes into their work, Sean instructed the crew to step back. They had used a chain saw to cut through the roots in a tall, rectangular pattern, five feet high by two-and-a-half wide. The cutting complete, all that remained was to move away the disconnected section – though even with the roots severed, it still stood securely in place.

Sean took a sideways stance and readied himself. It was

clear from the look on his face that he was not at all unhappy to be the one to remedy this situation. He leaned hard on his left foot, then kicked his right into the centre of the rectangle.

The roots gave slightly at his kick, but there was no more dramatic result. Sean kicked again, but as far as the roots moved at his blow, the rubbery vines quickly snapped back into place afterwards.

'Wait a moment.' Jack interrupted Sean before he went for a third blow. He took his pair of cutters and walked to the right-hand incision made by the saw.

'When you kicked, I saw another root, a little deeper. I think it's holding the whole segment in place.'

He wedged the cutters deep into the incision until he could feel the hard, snake-like wood against the blades, then pulled the handles together. A distinct snapping sound marked out success.

'Try it again now.'

Sean positioned himself once more, drew up his leg and kicked hard at the roots. This time, his foot did not spring back. The cut-out portion of root work gave way, and the sound of snapping branches and scraping wood filled the air for a sharp second.

The rectangular portion of root they had cut fell inward, into the hollow the crew member had described from his radar display.

Only now, they were not facing a black mark on a digital monitor. Behind the rectangular cut in the root outcropping was a real space, black and cold: a hollow in the rock beneath the tree, leading back and downwards.

Framed by centuries of vegetation, they had found the entrance to a tunnel.

In the last minutes Angela's thoughts had been filled with such a sense of frustration and defeat that the sudden, definitive realization of success was difficult to absorb. Yet there it was: a hole in the earth, apparently a natural formation in the rock that stuck up from the forest floor, well overgrown yet at precisely the spot the Templar markers in India and in the Xi Ming Temple had indicated.

There were no more doubts about the validity of their search. The only question that remained, having now found the location of the Templars' hiding place, was whether anyone else in the past seven centuries had found it before them. Discovery of the tunnel, by the means they had employed, was remarkable enough in its own right, and Angela knew she could jump-start her career publishing papers on the eastward linkage of the Order, that now had such concrete support. But she also knew that, in this moment, discovery of an empty tunnel was not what she wanted. She wanted to find what had been hidden inside.

'We've got torches,' she said, grabbing three from one of the plastic bins the team had carried from the helicopters. 'Let's see what's in there.'

She passed a torch to Jack and made to toss another to Sean, but he stopped her with a wave of his hand and a peculiar look.

'Not just yet.' Angela couldn't read his expression, but Sean's words were unexpected and unwelcome.

'Not yet? Sean, this is what we've been working towards for years. Why wouldn't you want to see what's inside?'

Sean's peculiar expression deepened.

'I do, and we will. But there's something we need to do first.' He beckoned Angela and Jack to follow him as he stepped away from the newly revealed entrance to the tunnel.

Fifteen feet back the way they had come, towards the clearing, the excavation team had left a metal crate beyond the edge of the work zone. It hadn't been opened, and Sean waited until Angela and Jack had joined him before it. 'My father packed this for us, and ensured it was brought out by the crew.'

Angela examined the crate more closely. It was not a simple carrying case like the others. This one bore digital locks and an electronic keypad.

'He gave me the PIN to unlock it when we last spoke, but said that I wasn't to do so until we had found what we were looking for. "Until you're at the threshold of discovery", was the way he put it.'

'What's inside?' Jack asked.

'I don't know, but I think that where we stand now definitely puts us at a threshold, so I think it's time we find out.'

He reached down to the keypad and entered a ten-digit code he'd previously committed to memory. Angela watched as the numbers appeared in sequence on the red LCD display above Sean's fingers. When the code was complete, a sharp click announced the release of the interior locks.

Sean grabbed the front edge of the lid and lifted, swinging it back on its hinges.

'Holy shit,' Jack announced the moment his eyes caught sight of the contents.

Angela stared on in baffled silence. The crate's contents included a number of items she couldn't identify, but those on the top she recognized perfectly well.

The items staring up at her were gas masks.

67

'The tunnel stops just ahead, but you're goin' to want to see what's at its end.' Alvain looked into his master's eyes as he returned to de Faulke's side with the report. The knight had sent him ahead to scout the darkness as de Faulke himself moved more slowly. The walls of the natural stone tunnels were covered in images – signs warning of death, of torment – and he scrutinized each of the images as he passed.

At his squire's report, he hastened his step and followed.

'By God's grace,' he exclaimed, suddenly reaching the end of the tunnel. His eyes were wide in the torch-lit darkness. 'It looks like a shrine.'

The tunnel terminated in a natural chamber. The subterranean room was rectangular in shape, its ceiling almost vaulted by the arched bearing of the stone, and at its far end the wall curved to form a natural apse. Had the saints themselves deigned to carve a chapel from the stone, they could have done little better.

De Faulke's eyes adjusted, and then his heart felt like it might burst.

At the far end of the chamber, situated in the natural apse, were three stone chests. Each was covered, closed, and bore markings on its sides.

This is it, his mind all but shouted. *We have found it, by the Lord's mercy!*

He stepped forward to the chests, running his fingers over the pitted stone surface of their lids. They were old – very old, plain and unembellished. Each was simply a rectangular box of no more than an arm's length on its longest edge. Their stone lids were fixed tightly and sealed with tar. Only a single word was written on the front side of each chest, in a language de Faulke could not read.

'Boy, come here,' he ordered their interpreter. The young man cautiously stepped forward, but even in the darkness the paleness that drained his face was evident.

'What does it say?' de Faulke demanded, pointing towards the word painted in black lettering on the first chest.

The boy's response came as a whisper. 'It says ... death.'

The fire in de Faulke's heart flashed bright. 'And this one?' He pulled the boy to the second chest.

'D-darkness.' The translator was shaking now, pulling away from the sight, but de Faulke clenched his shoulder and forced him to the third stone receptacle.

'And the final chest? What is written there?'

Tears started to flow down the young man's face. He shook his head wildly, trying futilely to get away from the knight's solid grip.

'No,' he cried, 'I cannot. I will not! We do not say that word.'

He writhed to escape, but de Faulke was seemingly possessed of a new strength. He drew his sword, pushed the translator towards the chest and thrust the side of his blade against the man's neck.

'The word. Tell me what it means.'

'Sword or no sword, sir,' the native replied, 'I will not utter that word. But in your language it means . . .' He seemed to struggle to say it, even in a foreign tongue. But finally, his mouth opened.

'Annihilation.'

PART FOUR
Deceptions

68

The phone rang once, twice, and Senator Preston Wilcox's hand clasped at the receiver. He was already out of breath, having raced to lock his office door before answering.

'Wilcox.' He slid into his seat. His voice was as anxious as it had ever been.

'It's Harry Hanks here,' a voice said, 'from the White House Office of Public Engagement.'

Preston exhaled a nervous breath, short as it was, closing his eyes. It wasn't the kidnappers. Thank God. If they'd rung first, before he'd been able to confirm arrangements . . .

'Thank you for calling me back,' he forced himself to say, as calmly and professionally as his nerves would allow.

'No problem. Just wanted to confirm that the president has gratefully accepted the invitation to be present at the defence-technologies exhibit planned for the evening of the State of the Union. I'm liaising with the Department of Scheduling and Advance to work out the details.'

Preston's heart soared. Whatever favours Anthony Graves had called in, they had worked. His girls would be safe.

'That's, that's just wonderful news,' he answered as best as he could.

'I have to say, he was surprised at the timing of the event. I don't think we've ever done anything so big on the same night as the address. But he and Thomas Blackburn have been friends for years, and to be honest, being able to say he's walking from the House Chamber to a presentation that will revolutionize defence spending . . . well, that's going to give him some nice fuel for the speech itself.'

Preston commanded himself to offer a polite laugh. 'We did think he might avail himself of the opportunity.'

Harry Hanks laughed back. 'Just wanted to let you know. We're all a go.'

A moment later the handset was back in its cradle and Preston Wilcox's relief surged through him. He'd done it. Everything the kidnappers wanted, from arranging the exhibition to ensuring the president's attendance. Everything.

They'd have to let his girls go now.

The Grand Master was filled with a rare rage. The two knights who stood before him cowered visibly at the scorn and anger he allowed to flow freely with every syllable that came from his lips.

'I have been betrayed! Turned on by someone within our ranks!' He spat out the words at full roar.

'Not one, but two attempts on the research team that I myself instructed was to be protected at all costs!'

He slammed a fist down on the round table that stood between him and the other men.

'I want to know who is responsible for this betrayal!'

'Master, we have only just learned of this fr —'

'Don't make excuses! Get out of my sight, and don't come back until you know who ordered the attacks. I will not have betrayers in our ranks!'

The Grand Master pointed towards the open door, and the knights marched through it with fear clinging to their faces.

He breathed hard, long, furious breaths.

He would wait for the answer, but he already had suspicions as to who had dared to challenge his authority.

69

Gas masks had not been the only equipment in the crate Thomas Blackburn had provided for the expedition team.

Beneath the masks had lain a collection of full-body suits, the type worn by hazmat teams when dealing with chemical spills or infectious agents, complete with self-contained, internal oxygen supplies. Bio-protective sample containers were packed beneath those.

And nothing else. No note of explanation, no instruction.

'What the hell is your father up to?' Jack asked. He seriously contemplated ignoring the box and its contents; that was, until he saw Sean climbing into one of the plastic suits and Angela following his example.

'We're meant to be locating the Templars' treasure,' Jack persisted, 'not crawling into a chemical warzone.'

'Who knows what lies ahead of us down there,' Sean answered, pulling on the various zippers and clasps that bound up the suit. 'We're military contractors. Better prepared than not.'

Jack begrudgingly took up one of the suits and began to step into the rubberized legs.

Angela was obviously anxious. They had come, literally, to the far side of the world, and even just being here was a discovery. But the feeling that Jack was getting from this 'find' was not the exuberance of one walking towards a treasure trove.

'You're secure? The oxygen's on?' Sean asked, looking over Jack's suit. Jack fidgeted with a control on his arm, and the airflow hissed to life.

'As ready as we're going to be.'

It was all the confirmation Sean required. He turned on his booted heels and headed for the entrance to the tunnel.

In the darkness of the underground passageway the sounds of nature that had filled the forest behind them went silent. Apart from the soft hiss of pressurized air flowing into his mask, Jack could hear nothing at all.

They each had a powerful torch in hand, which transformed the darkness into a surreal shade of LCD white. Stone, soil and moss covered the walls, with the amount of vegetation clinging to the edges receding rapidly as they moved further into the depths. After they had walked perhaps fifty feet down the tunnel's surprisingly straight path, it had disappeared altogether and the walls were bare stone, moist and dripping in the torchlight.

'Watch your step.' Angela's voice whined into Jack's ears, a sudden, jolting reminder of the radio system built into the helmets. 'The passage begins to veer to the left down here, and the footing is less even.' She was several paces ahead of Jack, with Sean at their head.

Jack watched his feet as he navigated the bend, which was followed by another.

And it was then that he began to see the art.

Painted on to the natural stone walls of the tunnel

were – he wasn't sure how to describe them. They weren't symbols so much as figures, some life-like, some stylized. Some were men, some clearly women; and there were natural surroundings. Trees. Mountains. Rocks. And a cave.

Or rather, a tunnel.

Suddenly, Jack realized that the wall paintings were describing scenes related to this place. His stomach began to ache.

'Have you two been paying attention to these paintings?' he asked. Sean didn't seem to lose pace at the front of their column, but Angela hesitated slightly.

'They look old,' she said. 'Some are annotated in what looks like Late Middle Chinese. But look at this one.' She motioned towards a painting and allowed Jack to approach behind her.

'Latin,' Jack noticed. His stomach was beginning to feel worse.

'There's going to be enough here to study for years,' Angela said through the radio, the excitement evident in her voice.

But Jack was not feeling anticipation. He couldn't read most of what was written around him, but the imagery was not hard to decipher. These were not paintings of victory, triumph, treasure or power.

They were images of pain. Of agony and suffering.

And they were lining the passageway he, Angela and Sean were walking down, like foreboding warnings in the darkness.

70

The Tunnels, Mountainous Region, Inner China, AD *1334*

It was time to know what the trove of death de Faulke had entered really contained. Alvain stood beside him, their young translator-guide cowering in the corner of the chamber.

It is time to claim what we have come for.

De Faulke prised open the lid to the first chest, breaking the tar seal and sliding the stone cover aside. He instructed Alvain to remain a few steps behind. This moment should be savoured, kept sacred to a member of the Order's highest ranks.

He pushed the stone lid further, until finally the centre of gravity shifted and it fell to the floor behind the chest. De Faulke stared down in wonder.

Within, cradled in carved indentations, were ten small vials. They were of fine porcelain, well crafted and shiny, though with no artistic adornment or decoration. Each was nested on a small bed of straw, closed with a stopper that, like the chest itself, had been painted over in tar, sealing it in place.

Ten tiny glistening gems in a box marked 'Death'.

Sir Arnaud de Faulke had found what his heart most desired.

Still, there was a need for certainty. The long quest eastward meant just as long a return journey, and before he made it he wanted to know, beyond any doubt or question, that the means of effecting his master's curse were now in his hands.

De Faulke stood tall, contriving a test that would remove any doubt. On the way through the tunnel to this shrine, they had passed a small cleft in the stone – a cleft that created a tiny side chamber. Minuscule, with the narrowest of entries. Barely enough to fit a man, standing. *That will do nicely.*

Taking one of the ceramic vials from the chest, he held it reverently in his hand, then placed it in a pocket and turned towards his squire.

Speaking in Latin, rather than French, so that the translator would not understand, he gave his instructions. 'Grab the native. Take him to the small side chamber we passed, just before this room.'

The squire took a moment to register the instruction, then complied without questioning. He grabbed the translator by the arms and pushed the confused man up the tunnel. The young native was confused, but appeared relieved that he was being jostled away from the find. He put up little resistance.

That was, until Alvain pressed him into the cleft. In an instant de Faulke had his sword unsheathed and pressed against the man's neck.

'Don't. Move.' He mouthed the words dramatically, then he instructed Alvain to take stones from the floor and seal up the entrance. As the squire worked, the local's face began to register what was taking place. He saw himself being enclosed, and his colour, already depleted and wane, completely drained from his features. But de Faulke kept the sword pushed against his Adam's apple until the stones were so high that he could not escape. The man began to yell as the last stones were lifted by Alvain and de Faulke together.

Finally, he was wholly sealed in, but for a tiny gap at the top of the new wall they had constructed. Alvain prepared to lift a final stone to seal the entrance, but de Faulke prevented him.

'Wait.' Reaching into his pocket, he extracted the small vial he'd taken from the chest. Glancing at it a final time, he reached up and threw it forcefully into the small chamber with their entrapped guide. The sound of porcelain shattering echoed out of the space.

'Now!' de Faulke ordered, and his squire raised the final stone, positioned it, and sealed the small room closed.

The man inside began to shriek, and Sir Arnaud de Faulke's heart filled with joy.

The Tunnels, Mountainous Region outside Tianbaoxiang, China

Jack's mutterings about paintings and symbols continued behind him, but Sean had come to the conclusion that ignoring the other man was his best option for the moment. They were more than a hundred feet into the strange tunnel system, and Sean was not interested in Jack's questions or concerns.

The tunnel, unlike the pit Sean had dug out on Oak Island, appeared to be natural and not man-made. However the Templars had found this place, they had come upon a resource that was ready and waiting for their use.

Seems about right. The Templars were always keen to see the hand of God in everything. *Must have seemed like true proof of Providence, finding this.*

He pushed his way forward, deeper into the earth. The gas mask covering his face fogged slightly at the edges, the plastic suit wrapping his head and forming a tight seal. It gave the whole underground environment a mildly blurred, hazy aspect.

Another bend. 'It keeps going,' he spoke softly into the small microphone mounted in the mask.

Going and going. Sean's blood stirred hot. Every step further seemed a validation of the importance of this place, and meant he was closer to the goal he and his father had sought for so long.

Sean still did not know what the Templar treasure was, and to be entirely honest he did not care. It could be a crate or two of gold. Maybe it actually was a relic discovered under the Temple Mount in Jerusalem, like some of the theorists said, or even something to do with the Church. Maybe he'd round a corner ahead and be faced with the True Cross, or the Chalice.

What would matter would be that he'd found it, whatever it was. That he'd have taken his father's wish and run with it, and that he'd located what history had said could not be found. He, Sean Blackburn, would have conquered history itself. It would mark him out for ever – an accomplishment to prove to the world his worth, at an age far younger than his father. The old man had worked for over three quarters of a century to reclaim his family's name from the shit hill it had been cast on to when they came to America. Sean hadn't yet hit thirty, and he would make the Blackburn name famous throughout the world.

Fuck 'em, Sean thought, the words punching through his mind with the force of pride. He'd never had the kind of bitterness against the world that his father harboured – Sean had been born as Blackburn Enterprises was already growing in stature and reputation. But his father had instilled in him enough awareness of their family's past for Sean to know what hurdles they had faced. That, and he had seen the way some of those bastard politicians had looked at his father when they spoke. Sure, they were happy to take his technology, to use him for cheap power and reliable toys, but they always had that look in their eye. That look that said, 'Look at the immigrant boy, all grown up and playing with the big kids.' These men who had never done anything, never made their mark on anything, judging *him*.

Fuck 'em all.

Ahead, the tunnel banked sharply to the left. Then, as Sean rounded the far corner, he came to its end.

Only it wasn't merely an end. The tunnel's terminus broadened into a wider, taller space. A room. He stepped inside, and noticed how the stone above his head formed a natural vault, the far end rounded.

He was standing in a shrine.

A minute later, Angela and Jack entered the cavern. Their lights combined with Sean's to illumine the small room brightly.

'What are those?' Angela shone her torch to the far end of the space. Jack followed the beam, and the three of them walked to the objects of her attention.

Standing before the curved rear wall of the cavern were three stone chests. They were clearly ancient, pock-marked from centuries of moisture and mould, though black patches of now unreadable markings on the front indicated they had once born titles.

The stone chests had flat lids, cut to a precise fit.

And two of them were already open.

72

The Tunnels

'Does this look anything like the treasure you were expecting?' Jack's voice was tinny and muffled through the headset Angela wore inside her gas mask, making the question sound all the more perplexed.

'I've never known what to expect,' she answered. 'But this . . . this surely was never it.'

Before them, the two open chests each contained ten carved niches. Within each, a small ceramic vial lay enshrined, each one with a ceramic stopper that had been sealed in place with hardened tar.

That is, except that one vial was missing from the first chest, and three from the second.

'What are they?' Jack asked.

Angela's mind sped through the possibilities, but this find was entirely out of her range of expectation. 'I have no idea what we're looking at.' The tightness in her stomach added a few silent words: *but it doesn't feel good.*

'Sean, anything?'

'Not a clue,' he answered, his voice just as tinny. 'The containers are tiny. Whatever they're holding, there can't be more than a few grams in each.'

What could be of such value, in such minuscule quantities? Angela wondered. Gold wouldn't come close, or gems, or currency. And none of those things would be kept in these sorts of containers.

Suddenly, her vision caught Jack turning towards Sean. Even in the plastic suit, his body stance was accusatory.

'Your father seemed to have some idea of what we'd find here,' Jack said. 'He sent us out for treasure, but he knew enough to pack these suits, these masks.' He thumbed his gloved hands towards their protective apparel. 'And now we find ourselves in a tunnel containing unknown vials of *something.*' Angela could barely see Jack's eyes through the misty plastic of the mask, but they looked angry.

'How did he know?' Jack demanded. Then, leaning forward into Sean, 'Did you?'

'I didn't know anything!' Sean answered, taking a step back from the suddenly imposing ex-Marine. 'Don't start pointing a finger at me just because we're not sure what we're looking at. My father is a clever man, always thinking ahead. I'm sure he had his reasons for packing this kit.'

Jack shook his head. 'It's feeling more and more like your father knew where he was leading us all along. Have we been sent on some farce of a chase, Sean, just so we could help your father get a hold of this – whatever it is?'

Angela's stomach tightened again. No, that couldn't be the case. She'd helped them find their way here through real research, real investigation. They'd followed the clues of history.

Hadn't they?

'I guarantee my father's never seen this before, and that he didn't know where we'd end up,' Sean answered. 'I've been working on this with him for years. I'd have known.'

Jack went silent. After a moment's stillness, Sean took a step towards him and raised a hand to Jack's shoulder.

'Listen, none of us knows what this is. Let's not get angry or suspicious. These masks, these suits, they're just good preventative measures. Caves and tunnels can be filled with natural poisons, gas, even simple oxygen deprivation. We plan for those kinds of scenarios for the forces. Rather than be suspicious, let's be grateful my father had us ready for anything, *especially* since what we've found is so out of the ordinary.'

Jack said nothing, but finally nodded his head in acknowledgement, his body language shifting from angry to frustrated. Within her suit, Angela breathed a small sigh of relief.

The moment of reassurance did not last. A second later, a voice crackled through their headsets, coming from one of the excavation crew members in the tunnels behind them.

'Mr Blackburn, Miss Derby, Captain Shepherd, I think you're going to want to come see this.'

More noises behind them. Angela turned and walked back up the tunnel, retracing her steps. Ten paces behind the entrance to the chamber a huddle of their team members stood, staring at a small hole in the wall.

'It looks like a small side chamber,' the voice announced again in her ear. Angela's peripheral vision caught Jack standing to her left, Sean a step behind him.

'Appears to be a natural formation, just like the rest of this place,' the man continued, 'though the entrance has been walled up. These stones have been laid here by hand.' He motioned towards the rocks surrounding the hole.

'Anything inside?' Angela asked.

'That's why we called you over here. You'd better take a look.'

Angela stepped closer and poked her upper body through the tight space. It took a moment's work to bring her right arm through after her head, allowing her to shine a torch into the chamber.

'Down towards your right,' the crewman instructed. Angela angled her torch in that direction, and immediately she saw it.

'Hell of a lonely place to die,' she whispered. Compressed into the tiny chamber was a skeleton, slumped down on its knees, its flesh and organs long since gone to dust.

'What is it?' Jack's voice came through her earpiece.

'Bones,' she answered. 'A full skeleton. Someone died in here, and not recently.'

'It's not just the bones we wanted you to see.' The crew member's voice was back on the headset. 'Shine your light on the walls behind him, and then at the stones near the hole you're leaning through.'

Angela transferred the beam of her torch. It took her a moment to make anything out, but gradually another sight started to come into focus. Short white lines etched in the soft stone. They came at different angles, different lengths.

Angela's mouth went dry. The lines all came in sets of four. Like the fingers of a hand, pulling its nails along the rock face.

Scratch marks.

The man whose bones lay in the corner had died here. Buried, entombed, alive, trying to escape.

73

'I want you to put two men on him for his protection.' Senator Anthony Graves spoke to two senior agents from the Secret Service with a tone of familiarity. He had known these men for years, had them over to receptions, helped their careers. He knew they would indulge him the favour of a personal project. And Graves needed their help.

'Senator Wilcox has asked for this?' one of the agents questioned.

'No, Preston's not to know. Tell your men to be discreet. He hasn't asked for help. This is my call.'

Preston Wilcox hadn't asked for anything, in fact. To the contrary, he'd seemed evasive and out of sorts on each occasion he'd spoken to Graves over the past several days, and no more so than at their last meeting. The two of them had put in a tremendous amount of work pushing the defence exhibit forward. But at their last discussion, Wilcox had looked more than merely stressed. He'd looked afraid.

At first, Anthony Graves had thought his younger colleague might simply not be up for the stress that came at the crest of Capitol Hill. But stress and fear were two different things, and Graves had been around long enough to spot the difference.

'With your men on his protection detail, I'd like the two of you to look into what's going on in Senator Wilcox's life,' he ordered the two agents in his office.

'What's our scope?'

Graves nodded appreciatively at the fact that the men didn't ask for details on authorizing powers or raise the question of jurisdiction and command authority – neither of which permitted a senator, however senior, to command the Secret Service to undertake personal investigations.

'Everything,' he answered. 'Check out everything. His office, work, family, friends. Check his calls, his emails, all his records.'

He ran through various scenarios in his mind. He had no idea what he was actually dealing with, but to have Preston so spooked, just days before an event they'd been at the forefront of coordinating, it couldn't be good.

He gazed up at the two agents. 'Something has scared the shit out of Preston Wilcox. I need you to figure out what it is, and fast.'

'I'm not using a gun on a kid.' That had been the pronouncement of Commander Parker's assistant an hour ago. He'd made it emphatically, then stormed out of the room, shaking his head, disgusted.

I can't blame the man, Parker thought. *It's hardly a noble task*. A man didn't renounce the world to follow a divine calling, only to go around killing children.

But wars demand casualties. Even holy wars.

Parker watched the twin camera feeds on the monitor before him. They'd brought Anna and Bella Wilcox back to the house after the excursion in the back of the car to make the final demands to the senator. It had worked like a charm, as Parker had known that it would. Bastard had been so sure of himself. The first glance at his girls unconscious in the trunk – that had sure as hell whipped the cocky out of him.

The drugs were now wearing off, the girls slowly coming back to life. Bella roused first, shaking off the deepest sleep she'd ever known. She tried to stand, then saw the chain once again fastened at her ankle. Though there was no sound on the monitor and the foam-padded walls prevented any from travelling up the stairs from the basement, Parker saw her begin to cry.

'I'm not using a gun on a kid.' His fellow knight was right. There was something unthinkable about that level of violence against someone so young. He wasn't sure he'd be able to do it himself.

So he'd have to come up with another way. Because one way or other, the girls would have to die.

74

Outside the Tunnels, Mountainous Region
Near Tianbaoxiang, China

The dead man in the side chamber had really done it for Jack. This place was evil, an environment of death, where the only other sign of visitation were the claw marks on tunnel walls left by a man entombed alive in its depths.

What was more disconcerting was the unshakable feeling that whatever evil had plagued that poor man of so long ago had never really left this place. Jack had the strangely superstitious sense that they were traipsing on sinister ground. The fact that they'd almost been killed getting to it compounded the sentiment.

And I damned well want to know why. Thomas Blackburn's interest in funding their explorations had been hard enough to justify before, but what they'd found put the stop to any suggestion of unearthing treasure or riches. And Blackburn had somehow seemed to know what they would discover – at least enough to equip them with suits and masks. Despite Sean's offer of an explanation, it wasn't exactly standard kit for unearthing hoards of gold or ancient bones.

Stepping closer to Angela as Sean disappeared into the woods with his phone, Jack faced her with conspiratorial seriousness.

'I don't know about you, Angela, but I want to know exactly what it is we've just unearthed.'

Angela gazed into Jack's face. He seemed capable of holding so many emotional states together at the same time: enthusiasm, kindness, aloofness. But the curiosity that so often marked his features was no longer just that. There was something in Jack's eyes now that troubled her. *Worry*.

'What's wrong?'

'The more we discover, Angela, the more uncomfortable I become. This tunnel. That chamber.' He hesitated. 'Whatever those vials contain, it isn't treasure, Templar or otherwise. It's something bad. And I'd bet good money it's tied to the death of whoever that was, walled up inside.'

Death.

The word clicked in Angela's mind. That single term, the vivid reality that had been too often in her head over the past days. Only this time, the response it evoked wasn't emotional. She snapped her gaze up to Jack's.

'Say it in Greek.'

'Excuse me?'

'Death. In Greek.'

Jack stared at her blankly, but Angela's mind was now two steps ahead. She motioned anxiously towards his pack.

'Let me see your camera. The small one you've had with you the whole trip.' Jack silently complied, reaching into his pack and extracting the tiny digital camera.

'Do you have all your photos on this?'

'Everything I've taken since we left Seattle. No time to download them.'

'Good.' Angela pressed her way through a few touch-screen menus to get to the photo viewer, then began rapidly moving backwards through the flash drive's contents on the two-inch screen.

'What are you looking for?'

She didn't answer. The photos retraced their steps: the chests, the tunnels, a whole series on the Xi Ming Temple that Jack and Sean had explored together. Then, finally, they were in India, in the belly of the Thillai Nataraja complex, in the dark shrine to Kali.

A few more clicks, and Angela found the photograph she was looking for.

'There. There it is.' She passed the camera to Jack. 'Take a look.'

He pulled the small display close to his face and examined the image. It was the second pictogram from the inscription they had found at the temple. To its left was the triangle with the first two encoded landmarks.

The engraved image was a human heart, containing its single word. *'Thanatos.'*

'Death, in Greek,' Angela affirmed. She could feel the familiar tingle of discovery back in her veins. The pieces were coming together.

'This picture hasn't been of any use to us until now,' she said, 'only the triangular pictogram.'

'The one that ultimately pointed us to ... this.' Jack motioned to their surroundings, then sighed. 'A far cry from treasure.' He looked as deflated as Angela had felt not long before.

But not any more.

'Quite the contrary,' she answered. 'I think this second image proves that we *have* found the Templar treasure.'

'From an inscription of death,' Jack asked, confused, 'in a human heart?'

Angela grabbed back the camera and moved forward through the photos until she found one from the Xi Ming Temple.

'This last inscription. You remember its decoded meaning?'

Jack glanced down and the words immediately came to mind. *'Where my heart is also.'*

Angela's pulse raced. 'Exactly, Jack. And I finally think I know what it means. It's a paraphrase from the Bible, right there in Matthew's Gospel: "Where a man's treasure is, there his heart will be also."'

Jack nodded that he knew the verse, but he didn't appear to see how the biblical passage answered their question.

'Put it together, Jack. Treasure is that which man holds in his heart. And in the drawing of the heart . . .'

Finally, Jack saw the connection. 'Death,' he whispered, 'treasured in the heart.'

Angela nodded. 'The treasure the Templars were hiding is death itself.'

75

Outside the Tunnels

Sean pulled the mask from his face and took in a long breath of the wet forest air. The canned oxygen he had been breathing in the tunnel was a clean mix, but this was fresh, and nothing beat fresh.

The plastic suit still covered his body, but Sean would remove it in a few moments. There was something he had to do first.

He walked a few paces into the woods for privacy and removed a satellite phone from one of his bags. It took a few minutes for it to power up, dial and connect, but the line to his father's phone was crystal clear when he came through.

'You found it?' Thomas Blackburn asked his son. The old man's voice sounded as excited as a child's.

'We found it. Just where the runes and pictograms said it would be.'

There was a moment of ponderous silence. Sean could envisage his father, frozen, eyes closed, offering up a word of thanks that his life's work had taken such a leap forward.

'You were ... careful?' Thomas Blackburn finally asked.

'We wore the suits you provided. There's a tunnel here, in the middle of the forest. Well concealed, but extensive.

You should have seen it, Father. The walls have been painted – remarkable images. Who knows how many centuries ago. And a shrine at the end.'

'Tell me exactly what you found there, in the shrine,' Blackburn persisted. He seemed uninterested in stories of paintings and tunnels.

Sean recounted their discovery, as awestruck as his father.

'Just as he said, down to every detail,' Blackburn muttered on his end of the line.

Sean straightened and pulled the phone closer to his ear. 'As who said?'

Thomas Blackburn hesitated, as if pondering how much to reveal to his son. Then he began to speak of things Sean had never before heard.

'A knight, from the end of the Templar reign. It's his life we've been trailing for years, his guidance that has led me, and you.'

'Me?' Sean asked.

'He said there would be a tunnel, and within it three chests,' his father continued. 'They're what we've been looking for, Sean. They're what we need.'

Another longer pause. Sean was mystified.

'I want you to have the team unseal the third chest and bring its contents back to me. I've provided containment cases in your supplies. Tell them to be fully suited up throughout, and to use extreme care.'

'Will do,' Sean answered. At least these were concrete instructions, not ruminations on the guidance of ancient monks. 'We'll scope out the area for other materials as well.'

'No, your excavation is over.' The elder Blackburn's tone did not allow room for questioning, but Sean was not merely an employee, he was his son.

'But we've only been here a few hours. There could be more. We should at least have a look.'

'I said you're done!' Blackburn's raised voice was frightful. 'Pack up the contents, seal the container, and get all of you back to America immediately.'

Sean could hear the slamming of the phone, and the line went dead.

Thomas Blackburn felt like a prophet whose visions had come true. His son had located that which only he had known existed. It was no longer a myth or legend. It was reality, being boxed, sealed and flown back to him.

Everything the knight had said had been proved accurate. Every comment, verified through their explorations. The signs, the path, the resting place.

And the power. Thomas Blackburn had every confidence that the treasure they'd found would do everything the ancient knight had promised.

76

The tormented screams of the young man still echoed in de Faulke's memory. They had lasted only an hour, at most, coming from behind the sealed entrance to the chamber where he and Alvain had secured him. An hour of shrieks, cries, pounding fists and clawing at the walls in the hope of freedom. Then the cries had become sputters.

And, finally, they had stopped.

The native had gone silent, and de Faulke and his squire had waited another hour, perhaps two, before knocking a hole through the stones. A hole just large enough to pass through a flame and a head, to survey the treasure's effectiveness.

Now they were once again on the move. The tunnel, the room and the body of the departed translator receded into the hilly forests behind them.

That body, covered in the most horrible torments. De Faulke had a high tolerance for the sight of grievous affliction. He'd been required to supervise the torture of heretics before. He'd seen the symptoms of hot oil, of iron pans and spears. He'd witnessed digits pulled off rather than cut, he'd watched men torn apart on the rack.

Yet what he had seen in the tunnel had truly chilled de Faulke. The way the man's skin had seemed to have boiled, without any heat. The way it had gone black in places, like darkness had eaten at his very flesh. The way the blood had flowed from his eyes, his ears. It was a torment unlike any he had beheld before.

All caused by the single vial de Faulke had thrown into the chamber. A vial from the first chest. A vial so similar to the three he now carried with him, padded in straw cushioning and contained within the satchel at his waist.

Only these were from the second chest.

If the contents of the first were able to do . . . *that* . . . to a human being, then de Faulke had no doubt that what was in the second chest could accomplish bringing the Grand Master's curse to life. Just as the Indian tribesmen had said, out of this cave would come a darkness that would terrify the land. He would unleash a pestilence that would make de Molay's dying words a reality.

As for what was in the third chest, de Faulke shuddered at the thought. The second, he felt, would have more than enough power for his purposes. He hadn't even unsealed the stone chest marked 'Annihilation.' Some power should be left only to God.

The time had come to return home. But rather than depart directly west, back to the empire on a straight path, de Faulke directed his squire to lead him towards the great temple and trading centre in Chang'an, a few hours' journey to the south-east.

There was a new project that needed to be begun.

77

In Flight, Between Shanghai and Seattle

Angela, Jack and Sean were once again in the air. Four hours after their discovery in the tunnel, their trio of helicopters had taken them from their excavation site directly to Shanghai, where a Blackburn Enterprises Dassault Falcon 7X had already been fuelled and was waiting on the tarmac. It took under an hour for their find to be loaded into its cargo hold, the paperwork for their flight filed and the engines throttled up for departure from the Shanghai Pudong International Airport.

The flight back to the United States would be long. It was not the length, however, that upset Angela as she sat in the jet's luxurious interior. It was the strange juxtaposition of peace, extravagance and calm on a day that had been filled with confrontation, dirt, darkness and mystery. Suddenly to be cushioned in leather and served drinks out of crystal felt uncomfortably awkward.

'Sean, can I use your computer?' she asked after they'd reached a cruising altitude and their orders for supper had been taken. Sean offered up the laptop without questioning, then walked to the back of the plane, slipped on a set of headphones and settled down to watch a film on the seat-back entertainment. Everyone had his own way of coping with the pulse of the day and the length of the journey ahead.

'We can get Internet up here?' Angela asked before he had wholly immersed himself in his digital world.

'Wi-Fi's up. No password.' Sean answered quickly and disappeared into his seclusion.

Angela positioned the laptop on the wooden table in front of her seat and powered it up. The Mac connected to the aeroplane's Wi-Fi network automatically, and a few moments later she had an Internet browser open.

It was time to figure out what the Templars' treasure of death was really all about.

An hour later, his supper finished and his threshold for boredom apparently at its limit, Jack rose from his seat and stepped across the narrow aisle to Angela. She was still at work on the laptop, her face a portrait of focus and attention. As Jack took the seat opposite her at the table, he had to nudge the monitor to attract her attention.

'What's keeping you so occupied over here?'

The Blackburn Enterprises stewardess appeared and put a Scotch on the rocks on the table before Jack silently, before Angela could answer.

'You've been glued to that computer since we left Shanghai,' he added, lifting the drink.

Angela's features were sharp, yet they looked drained.

'Is everything all right?'

'I've been researching any connection between the Templars and Xi Ming, or even China itself,' she finally answered.

'Whatever you've found, looks like it has you worried.'

'I haven't found anything. There's nothing to find. The

reason that no one has ever posited a connection between the Order and China is that there never was one. At least, none of record.'

'We know there has to have been some connection,' Jack protested gently. 'We saw the evidence with our own eyes, and we've got artefacts to prove it secured in the cargo hold.'

'Right. But any group of Templars who travelled to Asia would have had to be small, to wind up there without their presence being known or recorded. A group that wanted to remain hidden.'

'Fair enough. If they were trying to lie low, they wouldn't have travelled in large groups, and they wouldn't have wanted their presence known.'

Angela nodded, but she still appeared troubled. She looked more deeply into Jack's eyes.

'If you're right, and I'm right, that would put the Templar visitors in China at what time?'

'You're asking for a year? Well, probably a year or two after the execution of the last Grand Master. And that was in 1313?'

'Thirteen fourteen.'

'It would probably have taken a good few months to travel, maybe even a year. So they would have arrived in China in, I don't know, 1315 or 1316.'

Angela shook her head. 'That's too fast, Jack. It would have taken years, and that's only if they'd left Europe immediately. But there was a massive famine that decimated most of the empire, literally, in the decade that followed. Ten per cent of the population down. Chances of anyone having the means of mounting an expedition when there wasn't enough food to live day-to-day are pretty slight.'

'Okay,' Jack answered. 'So they left later.'

'Probably by at least a decade, maybe more. And then a journey that may or may not have been direct. In secret. So one that would have kept them off the main roads.'

'All right, I'm getting your point. It would have been a much longer trip.'

'Maybe as many as five or even ten years.'

'That would put them in China around,' Jack paused to do the maths, 'around the mid-1330s.'

As he said the dates, Angela's face whitened.

'Angela, what is it?'

She looked directly into his eyes. 'Jack, how much do you know about the Black Death?'

78

In Flight

'The Black Death?' The question felt like it came from left-field. 'You mean the plague?'

'The Great Plague,' Angela answered, nodding. Jack looked completely confused.

'Angela, I'm not sure what you're –'

'What do you know about it?' she cut him off. Then, her face serious, almost pleading, she said, 'Please, Jack. Just go with me on this for a minute.'

Jack sat back and sipped from his drink before answering.

'It was one of the worst pandemics in history. It devastated Europe, reaching all the way into Russia and the Near East.'

'It killed off close to sixty per cent of the population of Europe,' Angela elaborated. 'Maybe as many as 200 million people.'

'Spread by rats, right?'

'That's the most popular theory. More particularly, from the fleas that lived on the rats.'

'And that allowed it to travel by ship, and then across land.' Jack shuddered. Even a cursory knowledge of the Black Death was enough to stand one in awe of the death and destruction it had wrought.

'The speed with which it travelled is shocking.' Angela

turned back to the laptop and glanced at the details. 'Those 200 million deaths that spread across the whole of Europe – it took less than three years.

Suddenly, Jack seemed to remember Angela's initial question, and he sat forward. 'Which years?'

'Between 1348 and 1350.' Angela's face was white again.

Jack worked through the maths in his head. If a group of Templars had journeyed east from France in the time-line Angela had outlined, that would still have put them in China a decade or more before the Great Plague hit Europe. And that was another issue.

'The Black Death was a European plague,' he protested, though his face showed worry mixed with his surprise. 'What does it have to do with the connection here?'

'The plague *affected* Europe,' Angela answered, 'but it didn't originate there. It is believed to have been caused by a form of the Yersinia pestis bacterium, which recent studies indicate originated in the east.'

'The east?'

'There is some evidence to suggest that the bacterium was first encountered in Kyrgyzstan in the early four-teenth century. And from there, trade routes are suspected to have brought it to China.'

Jack sat silently, taking in the details.

'From China, it would have travelled west, along the Silk Road.'

Jack set down his drink. 'China. The Silk Road. The dates.'

Angela stared at him knowingly. '*That's* why I look wor-ried, Jack.' She folded closed Sean's laptop and leaned towards him, her voice barely more than a whisper.

'The best theories to date have the bacteria causing the plague making their way quietly through China at the same time our Templars might have been here, hiding their strange treasure. They hide it, they leave, they make their way back towards the empire.'

'And you think they may have brought something back with them.'

'Jack, it's just possible that they were infected while they were in China – that the Templars we've been following east, unbeknownst to them, returned west carrying the plague that destroyed most of Europe.'

79

No mere mortal could do what I have done.

This was the thought that reassured and inspired Thomas Blackburn in equal measure as he sat in his office, waiting for his car to arrive. The successes of the past weeks were the culmination of years of work.

Higher powers guide those who seek righteousness.

That was a line he had read when all this had begun, and which today's events proved true. There was a higher power at work in his life, as there had been so long ago. That same higher power would see him through to the end.

When he thought about it objectively, it all seemed so remarkable. A pathogen so old, older than the very concept of biological warfare, tucked away for centuries. Hidden and removed from modern history, known *only* to history, and connected to history itself. And the key that might turn sickness into a plague: a pathogen given new strength by blood.

Just as in those final days.

So many had mocked him for his interest in the Templars. They had scoffed at him for his claim that there was a family lineage, even though he could prove it beyond a doubt from annals, registers and records. 'So what?' invariably came the response when he'd pushed far enough to show that the connection wasn't merely imagined. 'What does that matter?'

It matters for this. Blackburn clenched his fist, as if his old fingers were already wrapping round the small ceramic vials he had sent his son and his team to recover. *It matters for this, and for what is to come.*

Whenever he doubted – in those rare, fleeting moments – that this was the right course for his life, the signs came and reassured him. Locating the journal, tracing out the nature of the secret, even finding the bloodline that could activate the treasure's fullest power.

The key.

That was the most remarkable feature of his genius, though whether his success in tracing it out had been skill or divine accident he would never know. Blackburn had put all the skills of a worldwide quest into finding what he needed. Sponsoring research. Tracing historical registers and European family annals. Using legitimate employer blood tests to sample for other purposes. He had the ancient sample; he had everything he needed for a comparison.

And finally, one sample had matched. Years in the hunting, and a small blood test had at last confirmed success.

Higher powers guide those who seek righteousness.

He had found the descendant. The key. The blood, waiting to bring the curse to life. Others were trying to rip success away from him – the fiasco in China was unforgivable. But Thomas Blackburn was not a man to stand idly by while his purposes were thwarted by ineptitude or deceit.

It was time to bring his designs to fulfilment.

80

Unknown Location

The Seneschal glared at the men across the room. 'There have been developments' – a word that always meant more than it said – 'with the security and reliability of those who bear the treasure.'

A hush overtook the men. Everything depended on the treasure's discovery and safe delivery.

'They've taken possession of the material,' the New Order's second in command continued, 'and now we must ensure they don't fall into the wrong hands.'

He knew he would need to give his men a stronger impetus for action.

'They're also too close to learning what's in their possession. Once they know what the treasure really is . . . the risk is great that they'll determine what we intend. We might be deprived of its power for good.'

That seemed to do the trick. The ranks of knights stood taller, duty and purpose straightening their stature.

'The Grand Master's already re-routed their flight,' one of the Seneschal's men replied. He shrunk back after the words had been uttered, seeming to sense the reaction they would evoke.

The Seneschal's face reddened, his fists clenched tightly. But he'd anticipated that action, as much as it angered him. The Grand Master was easy to read. 'Impatience.

That has always been his problem. If we don't control it, he will make it our downfall.'

The knights' affirmation was silent. They had joined the Seneschal in resisting the Grand Master's approach because they already agreed with the second-in-command's position.

'You must prepare yourselves immediately,' the Seneschal suddenly ordered. 'Personal drives can no longer dictate action. The group must be intercepted on arrival and the two men done away with once and for all. You'll take the material, and the key, and bring them to me.'

He eyed his subordinates, noting the ferocity in their expressions. He knew they would not forsake their vows.

'The Grand Master will have men waiting for them already,' one of the knights said. 'They'll have different instructions. How do you want us to handle that situation?'

The Seneschal let his deep eyes drill into the man for a long, commanding moment.

'Confrontation has always been inevitable. Deal with it however you must. Just ensure that when the bullets have stilled, you've got what we need.'

81

Chidambaram, India, AD *1335*

'One cannot be too obvious, Alvain, even with the text encoded.' De Faulke spoke to his squire softly, not desiring to attract any undue attention. They were alone, but there were others near by and he didn't want their solitude disrupted.

They worked by candlelight in the small room beneath the hideous temple. He would have called it a crypt, but de Faulke did not wish to defile that term by assigning it to a shrine dedicated to the wretched goddess carved into a statue at its centre. Blasphemy and idols everywhere. These dark-skinned tribes were as horribly pagan as the Greeks or the Egyptians long before.

Alvain held a candle, the sole light source illuminating his master's work. He scratched gently at his armpit as he maintained the light.

The small wooden box de Faulke held propped on his knees was barely more than a handspan in width and the same again in height, three levers on its front and two dials at its side operating the encoding mechanism the Order had crafted to protect their most valuable communications. They'd developed this unbreakable means of securing their correspondence seventy years before, and it had effectively ensured that none ever knew of the real extent of their work. When Emperor Baldwin II had used the True Cross as collateral on a loan the Order had extended to fund one of his wars, this system had ensured that Christendom – which would gladly have skinned the emperor alive for such impiety – never knew what their ruler had done. Business required secrets.

And so had Jacques de Molay's notes. And so would the instructions de Faulke intended to leave for future knights, when the Order rose in glory once again.

There were only eight such devices in existence, kept under guard at all times at each of the Order's chief centres of commerce across the empire. Those who protected the devices had taken an oath to destroy them before they fell into the hands of others. Better for secrets to be lost for ever than exposed to those who should not know them. But one could never be certain.

'No, Alvain, we must go a little further than just encoding our directions. We must speak in terms that would not be obvious to all, should someone ever break through our system.'

De Faulke had already left his mark in the Xi Ming Temple at Chang'an. He wanted to ensure that future brethren seeking the treasure could find it, without allowing for the possibility of it being located by any others. What he had discovered belonged to the Order.

'"The Silk Road" is too obvious,' he continued. 'The name's not used by everyone, but people could figure it out. We need another way to point people to its eastern limit.'

The squire held the candle firmly, his other hand, having left his armpit, now stroked the stubble at his chin.

'What about "where silk no longer travels"?' he finally

asked, then screwed up his face as if he'd been foolish to offer his own thoughts.

In the orange light, de Faulke's smile was unmistakable. 'That's not bad, Alvain. Not bad at all.'

A moment later, the knight was passing each letter of the Latin text through the encoding sequence on the device. As the first symbol appeared, he picked up an awl and began to carve his instructions into the tribute-covered wall of the heathen sanctuary.

When their task was complete and he had left the grounds of the temple, de Faulke instructed Alvain to find a suitable spot outside the village limits and make camp for the night. The sun had not yet set, but he was weary and they both could use the rest before the long days of travel ahead.

Noble work required effort. Perhaps that was why his body seemed so worn and depleted. It would have been quicker just to return and not consume extra days of travel leaving enigmatic instructions for the future, but the great spirit of noblesse oblige drew de Faulke to his duty.

At his side, Alvain coughed a deep, guttural cough. It had been plaguing him for the past two days and seemed only to be growing worse. The poor man didn't complain, of course. De Faulke had never heard him utter so much as a single word of dissatisfaction in the twenty-one years he'd known him. Yet the man's health was clearly failing, and de Faulke didn't like the sounds coming from his chest.

PART FIVE
Disasters

82

In Flight, Between Frankfurt and Seattle

Sleep had not come easily, and when it finally arrived it was anything but restful. The past four days of nearly non-stop travelling had left Jack exhausted, though the pace and excitement of their discoveries had made it difficult to stop, relax and get the rest his body needed. But once he and Angela had finished their troubling conversation about China, trade routes and the Black Death, sleep had finally taken him. Sleep, and a depth of dreams that stole at his rest and ate away at the peaceful respite the flight should have been, adding to nightmares he'd known for too long.

A small child, that child, at play and at peace. A tiny, innocent smile on his face, the sun beaming down into the open courtyard. A thousand stories of good and evil, told to keep the boy on the right path, free from wrong or harm. They come like voices now, texturing the strangely heavy air.

The mortar shatters, and the child's body falls into Jack's arms. It is covered in blood, and he rolls it over . . . he must see the boy's suffering face. Only it is not the boy's face that stares up at him. It is his own, bloodied and broken, pleading for an end to all of this.

He recoils, pulling his eyes away and looking up, but the burnt orange of the desert light is gone. It is replaced by darkness, cold and angry, scented of earth and decay. He feels himself enclosed, the space restrictive, tightening. Before him is a chest: grey, old, terrible. On it a single word, 'Death', painted in a strange hand. And then the edges of the letters begin to sway and change – and then they are pouring with blood, seeping down the stone, to the floor and to his knees, where he has collapsed in sorrow and regret and –

Jack was startled awake by a sudden change in the aeroplane's balance, the sharp, banking turn enough to pull him from the dream. His eyes blinked, adjusting to his surroundings in the dimly lit interior, and he felt something unusual on his face. Brushing a hand to his forehead, Jack slid his fingers along a thick layer of sweat, and realized from the stickiness of his shirt that his whole body was covered with the same.

He'd had the nightmare about the child a thousand times before. More than that, more times than he could possibly count. And his own face staring up at him – that had been the image tormenting him since those final days of his active duty. *I have done this, not them. It is my fault. I am responsible.*

But the addition of the chest, of the blood, these were new since their find in China and Angela's talk of plague. An additional torment to add to the old.

Jack used the bottom edge of his shirt to wipe the sweat from his face. Dreams were just dreams. Reality lingered on, even after they were gone.

Reality. He'd been woken from his restless sleep by a change in the plane's direction, and in his ears Jack could now feel the sensations of shifting pressure that marked the beginning of their descent. Jack had been surprised when the pilot announced that they would be flying to Seattle on a westerly route from Shanghai, which made the journey over twice as long and would require a refuelling stop in Germany. Sean had told him that this was probably due to customs concerns, which made entering American airspace easier, with restricted cargo, if the originating flight came from a friendly nation in Europe.

But the flight to Seattle from Frankfurt was still a solid eleven hours. Jack had tossed and turned for an interminable length of time, he'd paced and he'd tried to read. Sleep was prone to be light and unrestful, but at least his nightmare, when it had finally come, had burned through a bulk of the remainder effectively.

He lifted the shade on his window and stared out into the night sky, just beginning to shift from black into the dark blues of morning. The tip of the small jet's wing dipped as the pilot banked another sharp turn in their descent.

And then Jack saw something that banished any remaining traces of sleep. Something that shot his mind full of new questions.

Beneath them were not the mountains of Puget Sound, and no Space Needle poked up at them from the skyline. Instead, the shape looming up at him was unmistakably that of a very different monument. Round, broad, well lit and standing atop a megalithic structure that could have been dropped out of ancient Rome, it was surmounted by a bronze statue of Freedom vast enough to be seen even from their height.

The United States Capitol, in all its federal glory.

They were not landing in Seattle. They were landing in Washington, DC.

83

Statuary Hall, US Capitol, Washington, DC

In the Statuary Hall of the US Capitol, preparations for the defence-technologies exhibition were now in full swing. Row upon row of folding white chairs were being assembled in two parallel sections towards the centre of the vast semi-circular space, which had once been the meeting place of the House of Representatives, but which since 1857 had gone through various functional shifts before becoming a focal point for a hundred cultural statues, two from each state, pedestalled into niches along the walls. A respectful space was observed in front of each statue to prevent any damage, while the showpiece technologies for the exhibit were being off-loaded from trucks and crates through a network of service entrances and into display positions. In one corner stood the pride of Blackburn Enterprises's R & D department: a full-size yet fully pilotless fighter jet. The model had been tested extensively and could hold its own in a dogfight with the best the US Air Force currently had at its disposal, all without risk to pilot or the possibility of depleting tactical expertise through airman casualties. Shoot down one of these, and the operator – from a safe location up to 8,000 miles away – could simply enter a few keystrokes and in seconds be in command of an identical aircraft already in the sky.

On the opposite side of the hall, the latest in stealth concealment for tank warfare; and on platforms at the sides, equipment that ranged from the familiar to the never-seen-before. And at the front of the amphitheatre-like space, in pride of place, the Blackburn Enterprises XRX-450, the very latest in robotic bomb-disarmament, which now came with the offensive capability to enter enemy compounds and place explosives behind combatant lines, was being unpacked from an oversized stainless-steel transport container.

Eight independently suspended wheels gave the small device the ability to scale stairs and obstacles up to four feet in height, while an array of six different cameras provided remarkable operational vision and control. Three robotic arms sprouted like antennae from the top of the unit, two with nimble 'hands' capable of lifting up to 500 pounds while at the same time manipulating single wires to an accuracy of less than a sixty-fourth of an inch. The third arm was mounted with an array of testing equipment: scanners, probes and a collection of scientific tools that were, thus far, entirely classified.

As the technicians unpacked the device and lifted it out of the box, the only surprise was how light it was. Four men could easily carry it.

It was as if the device, despite its sturdy appearance, were almost hollow.

84

In Flight, Over Washington, DC

'I don't know anything about this,' Sean admitted after Jack prodded him out of his rest, demanding an explanation for their change of course. 'The flight plan was for a direct path to our private airfield next to Sea-Tac.' He looked towards the front of the cabin, but the metal door to the cockpit was closed, a small red light indicating that it had been locked for descent, as required by the aviation authorities. 'Maybe it's another fuel stop? Something mandated by air-traffic control?'

'I'm not happy about this,' Jack answered. 'We haven't been told anything about a change of course.'

Angela rose from her seat and walked over to peer through Jack's window. The view from her own was obscured by the right wing. The white city seemed to glisten beneath them.

'If you could all please take your seats and fasten your safety belts –' the captain's voice came over the clear Bose tannoy – 'we're about to touch down at a corporate airfield in Washington, just outside the capital.' There was the slightest delay before his voice continued. 'We've encountered a minor signal-light error with one of our cockpit control panels en route. Nothing at all to worry about, probably just a burnt-out bulb, but we thought it best to get it sorted before continuing the journey. We shouldn't need to be on the ground more than forty-five minutes.' The announcement ended with the chirp of the pilot's microphone cutting off.

Sean released a satisfied sigh, sitting back in his leather seat. 'See, it's nothing. Only a technical delay.'

Angela moved back across the narrow aisle and fastened herself into her seat. The first direct rays of morning sun cut through the cabin.

Jack watched the earth rise closer in his vision, unable to stop himself wondering why a signal light was worth grounding a private jet.

Landing at the private airstrip was quick business, the small dedicated-runway establishment accustomed to political and business travellers who were rarely in the mood for holding-pattern delays or traffic backlog on the tarmac. The wheels of the Blackburn Enterprises's company jet skidded against the ground as the aircraft threw up its spoilers and reduced its speed to a strong taxiing pace, then made its way directly to the paved square in front of the small metal-and-glass private terminal.

Through the windows, Jack could see an entourage already assembled to meet them. No fewer than three black sedans, a small cluster of men standing outside them, their suits ruffling in the wind.

'Border control takes place right here on the plane,' Sean said, noting the crew outside. 'Homeland Security and customs will check our paperwork before we deplane.'

They had handed over their passports and paperwork to the stewardess as they boarded, and Jack could now see her descending the small staircase she had folded out of the side of the craft, handing the documents over for inspection. A few moments later they were returned to her and the spritely woman stepped back up into the plane.

'Miss Derby, Mr Blackburn, Captain Shepherd,' she said, 'you're welcome to disembark the aircraft for the short stay here in Washington. There are coffee and refreshments in the terminal lounge.'

Jack wasn't interested in leaving the plane, but the others were already rising.

'I could use that coffee,' Sean said, stepping towards the door.

'And I could use a stretch,' Angela added, nudging Jack as she walked past him. 'Come on. It's been a long flight.'

There was no point grumping in his seat alone. Jack undid his belt and rose.

The breeze at the door was strong as he followed Angela down the stairs and stepped off on to the tarmac. Then, as his feet left the metal of the steps and pressed down on the asphalt, the situation changed dramatically.

Four of the well-dressed men from the cars stepped forward, two taking up positions behind their group, and two in front. Two others remained nearer the cars, but Jack's military experience had long ago made him sensitive to the details of his environment, and that sensitivity was telling him something he didn't like. They were being surrounded.

'If the three of you would kindly come with us,' one of the men said, 'we've been given instructions to drive you to a meeting near the airport.'

Angela cast a confused look at Jack, but his face was

hard on the man who had spoken, his suspicions coalescing. 'We've not been informed of any meeting. With whom?'

'Sir, I don't know the details. But you'll need to get into the car.' He motioned to one of the sedans.

Jack instinctively moved closer to Angela, something protective taking over inside him. But Angela shoved him aside and stepped forward.

'We're not going anywhere,' she said. 'Not without knowing where or who we're going to meet.'

Jack watched the man scan Angela, mentally sizing up the situation. He then returned his eyes to Jack's, and the look he bore was unmistakable. It telegraphed a single message: *You're coming with us. It's only a question of how.*

Jack touched Angela gently on the arm and spoke to the men surrounding them. 'Very well. We'll attend this . . . meeting.' He glanced at Angela. *Don't react. We'll talk in the car.*

The man who had spoken nodded politely and opened the door of the nearest sedan.

'The two of you in here,' he said, motioning to Jack and Angela. Then, to Sean, 'there's room for you in the second car.'

As they reached the open door and Jack allowed Angela to slide on to the leather bench seat ahead of him, he caught a close-up glimpse of the lapel of the nearest man. His skin went cold, and as he quickly surveyed the others, it went colder.

Each of them wore the tiniest of lapel pins. Round. Enamelled white.

With a red cross at their centre.

85

East Bank of the Tigris River, AD 1335

'Alvain, rise up. We've rested as long as we can.' De Faulke stared down from his mount at his squire, who sat on an exposed tree stump. The unfortunate man's illness had grown ever worse as they travelled, and Alvain now needed to stop and rest almost hourly.

The squire coughed deeply, waving an arm upwards at his master. He required another few minutes.

De Faulke gazed down over the gently flowing waters of the river that tradition held flowed out of ancient Eden. The undulating earth that surrounded it was mystical, sacred, like their very Order. Here, lost centuries ago, Adam had walked nobly on the earth, prefiguring the Saviour in all His glory. This river, this land, they had been beautiful. They had been the gifts of the Creator to a Christian creation.

How pitiful, how truly loathsome, to have to cower now, unseen, at the banks of so sacred a site. The machinations of politicians and church diplomats had allowed the heretic to claim what was rightly Christian soil. This land was no longer God's, it was the property of the Mohammedans. *The blasphemy!*

'My God!'

Alvain's exclamation tore de Faulke from his reverie. He looked down at his squire, whose words were overtaken by a fit of heaves and coughing the like of which de Faulke had never witnessed. 'Alvain, are you all ri—'

The squire convulsed, falling from the small stump on to his knees. A spray of blood shot through his teeth, staining the yellow grass beneath him.

'Alvain!'

The squire tried to speak, but words would not come. Another massive convulsion racked his body, and then, with a long gasp rasping out of the depth of his lungs, the man who had stood faithful at de Faulke's side for over twenty years breathed his last. Alvain's lifeless body collapsed at the edge of the plain.

De Faulke dropped down from his horse and went to embrace him. Rolling Alvain over, he saw the familiar face, marked with the sores that had begun to plague him as they had travelled, now stained with the blood that ran from his mouth. *And from his eyes*, de Faulke noted with a revolted surprise.

He knew the squire wore a small silver cross round his neck. It had been a gift from de Faulke when Alvain had made his profession and joined the Order. The knight would now bury his companion's body, paying what tribute he could, but while Alvain would have to suffer the indignity of resting in heathen earth, it would not be fitting for the Lord's cross to remain in apostate soil.

De Faulke grabbed at the ties of Alvain's tunic and pulled it open. As the fabric parted, he involuntarily thrust himself backwards, falling on to the ground and pulling himself away in horror.

His squire's chest was a mire of boils, of blackness, of

open sores – as ghastly a thing as de Faulke had ever seen. It was obviously related to the effects of the poison on the man they had killed in the tunnel, but this was far, far worse.

In the squire's body, death had become a far more terrible plague.

86

'Have you ever seen any of these men before?' Jack whispered to Angela. He was sat to her right in the sedan, and she wasn't embarrassed to admit that she was comforted by his presence. The car moved swiftly through the streets that wound away from the extensive airport complex.

'Do any of them work with you, back in Seattle?' Jack pressed.

'I've never seen them before,' she answered.

'Angela, did you see their pins? On their lapels?'

She shook her head, and Jack looked straight into her eyes as he silently mouthed his next words. *Templar crosses*.

'Templars?' Angela whispered back. Jack shot her a look, silencing her before she could continue. But he nodded solemnly, whispering, 'A small pin; the Templars' red cross.'

Her eyes widened, her thoughts straining for an interpretation. 'That's not the emblem of the Templars as a whole,' she whispered back. 'The cross was the mark of Templar crusaders, worn on their albs. Warriors.'

'Well, whoever these men are,' Jack answered, 'it's become a sign for them. They're all wearing it.' His look implored her for more information. 'Do you have any idea why?'

She shook her head honestly. 'Jack, the Templars have

been gone for centuries. The past may be interesting, but it's the past.'

Jack slowly returned his gaze forward. The two suited men in the front seats were silent, their eyes forward. Militant. *Warriors*.

'Someone doesn't seem to think so,' he whispered, as the car turned sharply left.

The building before which the small troop of sedans came to a halt was inconspicuous: white stonework, modern but not artistic. An edifice like so many others in the city, notable only for the fact that the single-storey structure had only two windows. But in a city that prized secrets and secrecy, this could hardly be thought abnormal.

As the car carrying Angela and Jack pulled to a stop, the driver and his companion quickly exited and opened the rear doors. They did not speak, simply motioning towards the single entrance to the building while Angela stood upright on the hard ground of the car park. Now that she was looking, the tiny and otherwise inconspicuous pins fastened neatly in the button holes of both men's lapels shone out at her like beacons.

Once inside, she and Jack were led through the first door off a short central corridor. The small room beyond was empty, save for a plain wooden table and three plainer chairs. Except for the fact that there were no cameras and no large mirror to complete the stereotypical scene, it looked like the interrogation room in any fictionalized police precinct. On the opposite side, another door led to an unknown space beyond.

'You'll wait in here,' one of the men said as Jack followed Angela inside. 'It won't be long.'

Behind Jack, in the corridor through which they'd entered, Angela could see Sean being led off by another duo of cross-bearing suits. Sean was turned to his left, into a room that, as far as Angela could see, looked identical to the one she and Jack now occupied.

'What are you doing with Sean?' she demanded, moving towards the door. 'Why isn't he with us?'

A suit stepped forward, blocking her path. 'He'll be fine, Miss Derby. Please simply wait here a few moments.'

That was it. No explanation, no extrapolation. The man stood his ground while his colleague exited, then backed out and closed the door behind him. The distinct slide and click of a bolted lock followed a second later.

Jack was already at the far side of the room, trying the handle of the second door, but it wouldn't budge. 'This obviously isn't the hospitality suite.'

'Why have they separated us from Sean?' Angela asked. 'Why are we being kept apart?'

Jack walked to the table, slid out one of the chairs and sat down. His eyes kept tracing the walls, examining the space.

'This is an interrogation room, Angela. These people want something from us.'

'But Sean has been with us all along. Why not include him?'

'My guess is that they want to separate the witnesses, so they can't concoct a common story.'

'Witnesses? To what?'

'I don't know. I really don't know.' At least she and Jack were on the same page on that, without any need to concoct common stories.

A set of noises from the lock on the door at the far side of the room interrupted their conversation, and a moment later the door opened. One of the men who had led them in now stepped through.

'If you would please come with me.' The request, Angela thought, was expected. What came next, however, was not.

'The Grand Master will see you now.'

87

The surprise Angela felt at hearing the phrase 'Grand Master' was surmounted only by the sight that awaited her and Jack beyond the room's far door. The suit stood slightly aside, beckoning them forward. Angela crossed the room as Jack got up from his chair and followed.

As she entered the room beyond, Angela froze. Her world seemed to shrink, to collapse in on itself, things foreign and mysterious colliding with someone she had come to know so well. Her tongue seemed unable to move, to vocalize the barrage of questions exploding in her mind.

'What the fuck is this?' Jack's voice suddenly blurted behind her, his shock less stultifying than hers.

In front of them, standing tall and self-confident, was Thomas Blackburn.

'I'm sorry to have called you here in this manner,' he said calmly, 'but it was important that we meet.'

'We weren't "called here",' Jack answered, anger fiery in his voice, 'we were forced out of the sky and into cars at the airport.'

'Don't be so melodramatic, Captain Shepherd. You were flying in my jet. If I need to alter its course, I have every right.'

Angela wasn't able to concentrate on Jack's protests. Two words echoed through her mind and would not leave.

'Grand Master,' she said aloud. 'They called you the Grand Master, these men who are wearing pins with the Templar crusaders' cross.'

Blackburn smiled paternally, deep wrinkles creasing his face. 'There is no reason to conceal things from you any further. You've done what I hired you to do.'

For an instant, Angela's focus shifted. *Done?*

'We haven't *done* anything,' she protested, taking a step forward. 'Nothing is finished. We've discovered so much – material that opens whole new doors on history. We've crossed a milestone, but in terms of the bigger picture we've only just begun.'

'I'm afraid not,' Blackburn answered firmly. His tone betrayed no consolation. 'Learning has never been my goal, Angela. I am a man of action. Of purpose. And you've been helping me with those very things, though you haven't known it.'

'You still haven't told us why these men called you their Grand Master,' Jack interrupted. 'What sort of game is this you've wound us all up in?'

For the first time, Thomas Blackburn looked angry. The eyes that so easily broadcast fatherly care turned hard and glared into Jack's.

'This is not some game, Captain Shepherd. Games are what lesser men play. This is an end to games. A rallying together of men of like mind and common conviction.'

'I knew it,' Jack answered, 'I felt it from the very first. All this talk of Templars and treasure . . . you're as mad as every other treasure-hunter who's wasted his life on this nonsense.'

Now it was Blackburn who released a bemused snort.

'A comment that doesn't do you justice, Jack. For one so intent on seeing past the public face of things, I'm actually rather surprised you haven't figured out what's going on.' He walked closer to Jack, leaned into him, his face only inches away. 'I have not been seeking the Templars, Captain Shepherd, I *am* the Templars!'

Angela watched the exchange with disbelief. This was the man who had funded her work, who had given her a home for scholarly enterprise. He had always seemed so in control, so careful, so . . . sane.

'Jack was right,' she muttered, 'you did know what we were out to find.'

'Of course I knew, Miss Derby.' Blackburn spoke to her softly. 'Ever since I founded our New Order, twenty-four years ago, I've known our legacy was out there, waiting for us. Waiting to be rediscovered and claimed.'

'A "New Order".' Jack repeated the phrase with distaste. He scanned their surroundings. 'Men who wear Templar emblems, who call you Grand Master. Christ, you're not just mad, you're a cultist as well.'

'Call it what you will, Captain Shepherd. The first Templars were maligned in their day, too.'

Angela took another step towards the man who, until this moment, she had considered an honest, if eccentric, boss. 'So you knew we would be going east. You knew my research –' She felt the worth of her pursuits slipping away in the confusion of this new reality. 'Everything I did, it was just a show.'

'Not so,' Blackburn countered. His words softened as he moved from Jack to her. 'I knew you would go east, and further east than you anticipated, but the specific locations of the journey were unknown to me. I needed your assistance for that.'

Angela shook her head, overwhelmed. 'All this, to find –'

'Treasure,' Jack interjected. The word was an accusation.

This time, Thomas Blackburn gazed at him with a look of pitying condescension. 'Yes, Jack. For treasure. But not the kind of treasure you are thinking of – something that ought to be clear to you now, having found what you did.'

'You need to be careful of it,' Angela interjected. 'Whatever it is . . . I suspect you know. But there's something about the history you don't'.

Thomas Blackburn eyed her curiously. 'The history?'

'Angela, don't bother,' Jack protested. 'It's not worth it.'

'Returning from their travels in China,' she persisted, 'we have reason to believe that the Templars were infected with the bacteria that caused the plague. There's a chance that the treasure itself might be infectious.'

Jack took a step towards Blackburn, recognition crossing his features. 'But you knew that already. The gas masks. You knew.'

The Grand Master smiled. 'The world around us is so foolish, Jack. Always seeing treasure in terms of gold, or riches, or secrets, or power.'

'But if the treasure's infected, then that puts you at as much risk as –'

'The treasure is not infected with plague, Jack. The treasure *is* the plague! Or rather, something far worse than the plague.'

Angela blanched. Her next words were only a whisper. 'You're . . . you're mad.'

Blackburn broke Jack's gaze, stared at her a moment, then straightened himself and turned his back on them both.

'Take the descendant's blood,' he ordered, walking to the far side of the room. 'The key is the last ingredient we need.'

At the instruction, two members of Blackburn's New Order stepped up to Jack. They were fierce, bulky and severe, and Jack would have a fury of a time breaking the grip of either.

But it was towards Angela that three other men moved. Two were clones of the burly men guarding Jack.

It was the third man, however, that terrified her. His hands were already sheathed in latex gloves, and he carried a small steel tray on which lay a syringe, three empty glass vials, a cotton swab and a length of surgical tubing.

'Please hold still, Miss Derby,' the man said, setting down the tray of equipment on the table beside her and pulling a surgical mask over his mouth and nose. 'This will only take a moment.'

88

Someone was holding Senator Preston Wilcox to ransom. The facts were clear. The only questions were who, how and for what reason.

'Has anyone gone in or out?'

None of the team of four Secret Service agents used one another's names or any other form of identification as they spoke. They were concealed in a small van, disguised as a cable-repair service, watching the house through camera feeds.

'No, sir. Since we've arrived, nothing. But there are definitely at least two persons inside. They're not talking much.' He signalled to the unit recording the sound input from the suite of laser microphones they had trained at the house. 'Consistent background noise. Probably watching television.'

Inconspicuous. There was nothing telling about the house or its occupants, in fact, except for one thing. Whenever anyone went downstairs, they disappeared. That is, the sound went silent. Their microphones should have continued to pick up movements – the scuffling of shoes, the moan of floorboards, occasional speech – even from the partially underground storey; but when they descended the steps, the men inside vanished from any audible tracking. And there was only one way that happened.

Somehow, for some reason, the basement had been soundproofed. And that was, in these circumstances, anything but inconspicuous.

The unofficial Secret Service team had already searched the home of Preston Wilcox. No one had been present at the senator's house – nor, they had discovered, anywhere else. His children had not reported for school in five days, and his wife had not called into her office at SJ&A Realty for just as long.

Another sign.

The house had been clean, with no obvious signs of anything amiss. But they had not gone there for a casual search. The team had scanned Wilcox's house with a number of tools, including an ultraviolet wand – a standard resource for picking up evidence of . . . mischief . . . that was invisible to the naked eye. And it had worked. No signs of distress anywhere but in the master bedroom, but there they had found blood spatter on the headboard. It had been wiped clean and given the once over with some kind of cleaning agent, but traces remained. And that had led them to spot the tiny bullet hole in the headboard and the walls. They had been filled in and were barely visible. Someone had gone to great lengths to cover up what had happened there.

That had been enough to validate Anthony Graves's concerns. The Secret Service unit began monitoring Preston Wilcox's electronic traffic, tailing his visits and visitors at the Capitol and his office off the Hill. Several calls he received were encrypted, but the Service had planted bugs, allowing them at least to hear the senator's side of his conversations.

He was being held to ransom. They still didn't know why, but his family was being used as bait. And whoever had taken them had come here. A tail on one of the visitors to Wilcox's office had led them to the house in the Washington Highlands, and since he'd entered, there had been no further movement.

They were inside, in a run-down house in a poor neighbourhood, with a soundproofed cellar.

'Get a larger team together,' the surveillance leader said to one of his companions. 'We need to get inside that house.'

89

'I'm sorry you had to go through that, Angela.'

Jack was sincere, and the look in his eyes betrayed more than a desire to comfort. He clearly felt guilty that he'd not been able to stop what had happened to her. Though he'd been pinned down by two men, each substantially larger than himself, Angela could see in his face the pain that registered from not being able to help her.

But Jack was not to blame. The violation Angela felt was as strong as her outrage. There had been nothing painful in the way the members of Thomas Blackburn's 'New Order' had extracted her blood, whatever their reasons for wanting it. Apart from the men who had held her firmly in place, there had been nothing brutal, nothing violent, though it had been clear that she had no choice but to cooperate.

Yet it was still a violation. They had taken something from her, *of her*, at the command of a man she had trusted. And she still didn't know why.

Angela Derby, however, was no schoolgirl with hurt feelings. She was still a woman who took charge, and she intended to reclaim that charge, even if circumstances suggested a rather different situation.

'Don't be sorry, Jack,' she said, answering him, rubbing the crook of her elbow where a small plaster covered the site of the syringe's entry, 'be angry, and use that anger to help me figure out what we need to do next.'

Jack leaned forward. He allowed his look of guilt and compassion to linger a moment longer, and Angela was grateful he wanted her to see it, but it quickly shifted to an expression of deliberation. He was keen to work through their current situation, and that encouraged Angela all the more.

'I'm sure the room is just as securely locked as it was before our meeting,' he said, nodding his head towards the two doors. They'd been returned to the small interrogation room after their encounter with Blackburn and his troop. This time, they'd been stripped of their phones, and a large jug of water had been set on the table. 'It looks like they plan on leaving us in here for a while.'

'Blackburn is obviously out for some kind of revenge,' Angela said. Her mind was less on their surroundings than on their broader situation. 'The way he spoke, it wasn't just ideological. It felt . . . personal.'

'We know he believes himself to be connected to the Templars through his own family history. I think he sees his own life as a mirror of what happened to them.'

'Parallel histories?'

'It might explain why he was so keen to fund your research.'

Angela nodded. It made terrible sense. 'He hired me right out of university. Because he felt I could help him bring a story to light that he believes is somehow connected to his own.'

Suddenly, she looked straight into Jack's eyes. 'I was wrong before. After Xi'an, when I suggested what the

Templars were hiding in China had to do with self-preservation.'

Jack had been waiting for a re-interpretation of her theory since they had made their discovery.

'I think it was the opposite,' Angela clarified. 'They probably knew it was over for their Order, at least for the time being. What they were out for was revenge.'

Jack nodded, his expression telegraphing the bewilderment that he was ready to agree with her. 'If Blackburn is right about what we found in China, it looks like they managed to work out a hell of a plan for it.'

The click of understanding fired in Angela's mind. Blackburn had sent them to find a trove of poison, of death, not simply to understand his past. He wanted the fruits of that past – the revenge the Templars had wrought on their generation – to give him the means to extend that revenge into the present.

'I still don't understand how it's connected to you,' Jack said. Angela was rubbing the spot on her arm where Blackburn's medic had drawn her blood. 'How are you linked into any of this?'

'I don't have any idea. But let's stay with what we know: Blackburn intends to use what we found.'

'In modern terms,' Jack affirmed, grudgingly going along with her, 'it could be the basis for a biological weapon.'

'And Blackburn's words didn't make it sound like he was thinking about using it months off in the future. It sounded imminent.'

Jack nodded again. 'The fact that he stopped our plane, forced us here . . . He's in a hurry.'

Angela's eyes widened. The thought that had just come into her mind was spectacularly frightening.

'What's today's date?'

He looked down at his digital watch. 'January the twenty-third. Why?'

It took a moment, but her face paled. 'Jack, tonight is the State of the Union. One of the biggest political moments of the Washington year.' *And we've landed in Washington, DC.*

The date, the event and their circumstances; Blackburn's political connections, his talk of revenge, the location of their aircraft's sudden 'signal-light error'; the biological agent he had in his hands. The facts collided into a clear reality.

'In less than six hours,' Angela continued, looking at her watch, 'both Houses of Congress will be assembled in the same room, together with the president and the vice president of the United States. If Blackburn is intent on enacting revenge on the government . . . could there be a better location? Or opportunity?' It was hard to believe the words were coming out of her mouth.

'I'm not sure he could weaponize what we found so quickly,' Jack answered. 'And how could he get it on site? The State of the Union has to be one of the most secure events in the world. How would he deliver it?'

Even as Jack listed his questions, Angela could see in his face a growing certainty that they had identified the right target.

'Big questions, Jack, and I don't know the answers. But Blackburn has been a step ahead of us all the way along.

We'd be foolish to think he hasn't thought these things through long ago.'

She leaned across the table towards him. 'Captain Shepherd, we have to get out of here.'

90

Unknown Location

The only possibility for escape that Angela could see was the air vent on the ceiling in the far corner of the room. There were no windows.

'That looks like our only option,' she said, pointing towards it. Jack followed her finger, then surprised her with an almost teasing smile.

'An escape artist now, too? Does that go hand in hand with developing historical theories and plotting migration patterns?'

Despite herself, despite the circumstances, Angela laughed. Given what they now had to do, a little humour was a welcome stress relief.

Jack smiled. 'How do you expect us to get in there?'

'You're a Marine, aren't you? Can't you make a screwdriver out of your credit card, or a pair of pliers from a pencil?'

'Of course,' Jack answered, 'but there's just one problem.' He let a brief silence linger. 'I haven't got a pencil.'

It felt good to laugh. Angela's fear receded, if only slightly, and her optimism rose.

The credit card was, in the end, precisely what was required. The six screws securing the vent cover had a coat of paint sealing them into position, but no locking mechanisms, no welded reinforcements. Within ten minutes, by standing on the table, Jack had been able to loosen and remove them all.

He lowered the grille away from the ceiling and set it on the floor. 'This obviously isn't a secure building,' he said. 'Any proper holding cell would have had potential escapes thought through and things would have been a hell of a lot harder.'

'We're not out yet. We still have to get up there, then work our way out.'

Jack pulled a chair towards the table, creating a make-shift set of steps leading up to the vent.

'Ladies first?'

Angela grinned at him. 'On this one occasion, I think I'm going to allow you to take the lead.'

Jack smiled back, then tucked in his shirt and looked up towards the vent.

A moment later, his feet were dangling in mid-air.

Jack hoisted Angela up into the air duct from her perch on the table top, and as she drew herself fully into the metal tunnel that ran above the ceilings of every room in the building, the first thing she noticed was how utterly filthy it was. Jack's movements had already displaced much of the dust immediately round the opening, but his shuf-fling only accentuated the deep layer of dirt, fluff and who-knew-what-else that lined the entire length of the passage before them.

'This is what was delivering the air we breathe?' Angela asked as she lay flat on her belly in the filth. 'Surprising it takes a plague to kill us. Breathing this ought to do the trick.'

'Follow me.' Jack began to pull his body forward. With their position in the ducts there was no option but for him to take the lead, and Angela pulled herself along behind him. Recognizing that tight spaces were ahead, and she'd need her hands free, she'd removed her wallet from her handbag and stuffed it in her back pocket, leaving the Tory Burch bag in the room below.

A few moments later, the darkness of the tunnel was broken by thin streams of light shining up from beneath. Another vent opened into a room below, and as Angela passed over it she saw it was where they'd been led to meet the Grand Master. In the corner, now at the edge of her vision, was where she'd had her blood drawn by members of Blackburn's New Order.

Three men stood there now. One of them had been there earlier, but the other two were faces Angela didn't recognize. She did her best to keep silent, sliding herself forward inch by inch.

'I thought I told you to bring them to me.' One of the men below – by many decades the eldest – spoke to the others. 'How could you let this happen?'

'The Grand Master arrived before you. He took her blood.' One of the younger men spoke towards the elder with an air of the humiliated servant.

'I told you to confront them! And yet you let them slip away! Do you disobey the Seneschal of the New Order so lightly?'

'We were prepared to disable the Grand Master's men,' the third man interjected, 'but . . . did you expect us to go after your brother?'

Angela froze. She peered down at the old man, wanting

more than anything to see his face, but all she saw was the silver top of his head.

Brother. Her memories were spinning. Thomas Blackburn had spoken so often of his family – his great-grandparents, his own father and mother. *'And we, the current generation, with children of our own.'* He'd spoken of himself and a sister. Then Angela's memories clarified.

A brother. He'd spoken of a brother also. Paul? Pavel? Piotr?

'Where are the captives now?' the old man below her suddenly asked, ignoring his man's question.

'They're locked in the first holding room. Sean Blackburn's not with them.'

'And the Grand Master took the descendant's blood?'

'Three full vials. Far more than will be needed.'

The old man appeared to think. His words, when he spoke them, were cold.

'Then neither Angela Derby nor Jack Shepherd matter to us any longer. Kill them both.'

Angela's skin went icy. Below her, Thomas Blackburn's brother rubbed a hand at the side of his neck, leaning back his head in an effort to relieve whatever kink was there, his eyes gazing vaguely towards an invisible point in space.

It was at that moment that Angela caught a glimpse of his face. His sunken green eyes, his deep-set wrinkles. Even the way his carefully cared-for hair was combed.

The man who had called himself the Seneschal was the spitting image of his brother.

Suddenly, with a force that convulsed her whole body, Angela sneezed. The layer of dust along the bottom of the duct burst into a cloud that filled the space, and she sneezed again.

Beneath her, the three men's gazes immediately snapped to the vent above their heads.

'They're in the vents!' the Seneschal announced. 'Shoot them!'

'We don't know who's up there. What if it's all three?' one of the younger men asked, already reaching for his weapon. 'Sean could be with them.'

The Seneschal seethed anger, but seemed to accept the man's point. 'Then move them along to the nearest access point, and kill them there.'

In front of her, Jack rolled on his side and looked back. His face showed he had heard everything Angela had. 'It's time to move.'

The gunshot that burst through the metal duct behind them reinforced his point. Wiping her nose and eyes and pulling herself along after Jack, Angela moved as fast as she could into the constricting, deepening darkness.

91

Unknown Location

The Grand Master of the New Order of Knights Templar watched over the procedure as if he were a father attending the birth of his first child, his eyes gleaming with wonder.

'Be extraordinarily careful,' he said to the lead chemist, his voice little above a whisper. The man's arms were inserted into the two gloved access ports in the sealed laboratory containment unit. Within, the vials that had been retrieved from the third chest in China lay on foam supports, while a glass platform provided a workspace on which sat a number of Petri dishes, glass tubes and precision equipment. The entire unit was sealed, providing access only through the gloved arm slots and a vacuum-negative chamber that could be used to extract objects from within without allowing the air inside the unit to leak into the laboratory environment.

'If this is like the others,' the technician replied, 'the contents will be reduced and thickened.' He used a small laser cutter to slice the ancient porcelain vial in half lengthwise.

The contents of the other vials they had opened had all been similar, and by this stage in the process they were expecting the same. What was inside had very likely once been a liquid, but over the centuries had reduced down to a thick brown paste that clung to the insides of the tiny containers.

'Quiet, quiet!' Blackburn ordered as the cutting came to a conclusion and the thick gloves the technician manipulated picked up a set of tweezers and a scalpel. Slowly, with an elegant gentleness, he prised apart the two halves of the vial, flipping one over and laying them side by side on a Petri dish. The pasty contents within clung to the ceramic halves thickly.

Picking up a small scraper, he scraped the contents of each side of the vial away, depositing the brown matter into a test tube that already contained a gel-like agent with a slightly yellowish tint.

'This growth agent, the thirteenth we developed,' he said softly as he worked, 'is the one with the highest yield. More powerful by a fourfold measure.'

Their tests had confirmed with scientific accuracy what Blackburn had already hypothesized from history. These vials, taken from the third chest, contained a far more aggressive biological agent than that which had caused the Black Death in Europe. It was a related bacterial strain to *Yersinia pestis*, but this one had never been identified before.

'When we add the blood from the sample you obtained,' the technician continued, 'the mutation to the bacterial strain is almost instantaneous.' Blackburn had provided them only three hours ago with the two ingredients they had been without in their previous research: the biological agent itself, together with the blood sample from the descendant. She'd been kept safe from harm, which meant that Sean's insistence that they bring on Jack Shepherd for 'a new perspective' hadn't been a total waste of time, as Thomas Blackburn had once feared. He'd protected her well.

'Something in the blood chemistry affects the agent. We're not quite sure how – we'll have to study that later. But the end result is one of the most aggressive biological agents I've ever seen.'

'How aggressive?' Blackburn asked impatiently.

The technician capped off the test tube within the containment unit. 'If you're using *Yersinia pestis* as a point of comparison, then I would say that this is at least twenty, or even thirty, times as aggressive, and far more contagious. We've not had the time to do any tests yet, but I would suspect this begins to have a visible effect on living tissue within a matter of minutes from infection. That's something the Black Death never did.'

He carefully set the tube in the airlock chamber of the unit, then withdrew his hands from the access points. A few seconds later, the vacuum swoosh of reverse airflow hissing through the room, the technician had removed the test tube. He held it carefully before Blackburn's gaze.

'To put it in the vernacular,' he said, 'this is some scary shit.'

Blackburn's eyes twinkled.

A moment later, the technician had inserted the tube into a Taitec SE-08 mixing unit and set it spinning.

'Have the compound in aerosol form within an hour,' Blackburn instructed. 'And in the canister I provided.'

'It won't take me half that long.'

Blackburn watched the small test tube spin, and saw the glory of centuries coming to fruition before him.

92

Angela and Jack raced as best they could through the duct system, navigating corners carefully and trying to control their breathing. They only advantage they had against the Seneschal's two men was that the branches of the air ducts led in multiple directions, and it wouldn't be obvious to their pursuers which route they would follow. If they could get far enough ahead, into a room the men weren't expecting, they might be able to escape.

They pushed round another corner. A 'Y' in the ducting gave them the opportunity to veer to the right, and they moved as fast as the space would allow.

Beneath them, every fifty feet or so, a vent looked down on an empty room. Angela kept waiting for Jack to stop, but at each vent he hesitated, examining, then moved on. He seemed to favour distance over immediate opportunity.

Another long tunnel, then a ninety-degree bank to the left. Angela's elbows and ankles were starting to protest at the unexpected abuse they were taking.

Finally Jack's motion, a few feet ahead of her, came to a halt. He peered down through a square vent that looked exactly like all the others they'd passed.

'What is it?' she whispered as softly as she could.

Jack scrutinized the scene below him.

'A glass door, and the light streaming in is blue. Natural light. I think we've found an exit.'

Angela's excitement tingled. They'd made it this far. Escape was in sight.

'There's just one problem,' Jack said, rolling slightly on to his side so he could look back at her. 'The vent is screwed on just like the one back in our room.'

'So? You unscrewed that one easily enough.'

He shook his head. 'From the other side. All these screws are fixed from the bottom.' He lightly tapped the edges of the vent.

'The only way we're getting this off is by force. And force is going to make enough noise to make your sneezes seem inconsequential.'

Their pursuers would be notified of their exact position. But there was no other choice.

'We'll just have to be quick,' she said back. 'You pound out the vent, then we both drop and get through the door as fast as we can.'

Jack looked back at her again. 'I drop first. You follow, and when you're down, you go straight for the door. If those men have caught up with us, I'll do whatever I can to cover your exit, but you just run.'

'Jack, I'm not leaving without y—'

'This isn't a negotiation,' he answered. He bore a commanding stare, but then his eyes softened. There was emotion there, something new . . .

'And we don't have any more time to talk about it.' Jack broke the stare, adjusted his position and brought his elbow forward. The space only allowed him a few inches of vertical motion, but it would have to be enough.

Pulling in his breath, he slammed his elbow down on the centre of the vent grating.

The sound came like an explosion, the metal ducting shaking and reverberating the noise along its length and into the darkness behind them. Angela's ears hurt, the sound overwhelming and the shifting air pressure pushing at her eardrums.

But when she opened her eyes and looked forward, there was no more light than before. The vent cover was still in place.

And she could hear yelling from some distant part of the building. They'd been heard.

The next explosion of sound surprised her. She hadn't expected Jack to move again so quickly, but his elbow slammed into the grating a second time – and then a third and a fourth in quick succession. The overlapping bangs merged together into a sustained, metallic roar, and Angela brought her hands forward to cover her ears. The vibrations were also causing the thick layer of dust to dance into the air, and the air duct was fast becoming a clouded, choking, deafening constraint. She coughed, then tried to cover her mouth and nose with the neckline of her shirt to filter her breathing.

It was the fifth blow that finally burst the grating from its hold, and the noise of the strike was followed by the clattering of the vent against a concrete floor below. Angela opened her eyes, and through the stinging of the dust she saw a square column of light shining upwards.

Instantly, Jack was in motion. He pulled himself forward until he could lower his legs through the hole, and without a word dropped himself into the room.

Angela crawled forward to follow suit, and when she peered down through the opening she saw Jack waiting below, surveying the room. Then he looked up and stretched out his arms, waiting to catch her.

She didn't dare take a breath before taking the plunge. Instead, Angela closed her eyes, swung her legs downwards and simply let go.

Jack's strong arms caught Angela as she dropped from the ceiling, cushioning her fall as her feet made contact with the floor. He gave her a second to absorb the shock and gain her balance, turning her so that he could look into her eyes and ensure she was uninjured. Those eyes were red and watering, but solid. Angela nodded an okay, and Jack pushed her towards the door.

There were footsteps coming towards them from a corridor beyond the room's wooden internal door. Jack quickly took stock of his options. There was a wooden pamphlet stand along one wall, a small round table supporting a vase full of yellow tulips, and two heavy, wooden chairs.

Not much for cover. He would have to be offensive, rather than defensive. The chairs would have to do the job.

Footsteps slammed against the concrete, and Jack knew the two men, and possibly the older man with them, would burst through the door in a matter of seconds. He took up one of the chairs, moved to the side of the door, and held it high above his head.

At the corner of his vision, Angela pushed upon the glass exterior door, and Jack caught the shadow of her body moving through it. *At least she's safe.* The plan had gone well thus far.

Less than a second later, the wooden interior door burst open.

As a man's body began to follow through it, his hands held forward, clutching a Beretta, Jack was already in motion. He slammed down the chair just as the man's head passed through the doorway, the wooden seat making perfect impact with the top of his head. The gun in his clutch fired as the man's muscles seized, the bullet slamming into the wall on the far side of the room.

The man was going down, but rather than let him fall, Jack released the chair and lunged forward, catching the man by the torso. The limp body was the only shield Jack had against the man behind him, and without pausing for thought he pushed the first attacker forward, thrusting his back into the face of the second man.

The collision brought all three men to the ground, Jack slumped over the top of the unconscious first attacker, while the second sprawled out on his back.

But the gun hadn't been dislodged from his hand. He was still conscious, and as Jack began to right himself, he could see the man's arm rising, his chest beginning to come upright.

Jack threw himself on to the attacker again, slamming his head back to the hard floor. At first the man seemed resilient, the blow knocking a strange expression on to his features – but he continued to fight.

Jack grabbed the man by the sides of his head, then used all his strength to pull back and upwards. The man's head rose a solid eighteen inches before Jack reversed his weight and threw everything he had downwards.

This time, the man's head hitting the concrete was

accompanied by the sickening crunch of fracturing bone, and his eyes stared up vacantly. Jack could feel the muscles in the man's whole body twitch beneath him. And then the second attacker went limp, the first trickles of blood emerging from beneath his head.

Jack released his breath, then his grip. Both attackers were down.

But the man called the Seneschal was nowhere to be seen.

93

Jack emerged from the building that had been his jail only a few minutes ago. He had the second attacker's Beretta in his hand, and the only thing on his mind was Angela.

'I'm here.' Her voice resounded with relief as she spotted him and came out from behind an over-full dumpster a few feet away.

'What the hell are you still doing so close?' Jack asked, shocked. 'I thought I told you to get away.'

'And I told you I wasn't leaving without you.'

Jack tried to beam as stern a look at her as the situation demanded, but the truth was he was glad she was there.

'What are you doing with that?' Angela asked, looking down at the gun in his hand.

'We've been stripped of everything useful, Angela. Those men took our phones, and I didn't have a weapon to begin with, but I don't want to face whatever comes next with only the contents of my wallet.'

Angela shook her head. 'You can't bring that with you.'

'Angela, I'm –'

She cut off his explanation. 'They won't let you in, Jack. Not where we're going.'

She sounded certain.

'And where is that?'

'The same place as Thomas Blackburn, and the same

place as half the population of this city,' she answered, setting off quickly. 'We're going to the Capitol.'

It took only a few minutes of walking before Jack was able to orientate himself and determine just where they were in the city. He'd been to Washington several times in his military career, as opposed to only a single tourist visit on Angela's part, and he was able to figure out the basic route they would need to follow to get to Capitol Hill.

'It's only a fifteen-minute walk, if we walk fast,' he said, scanning a bus route map trapped in the plastic display of a covered stop.

'We can get a taxi,' Angela suggested.

'Evening traffic in central DC, on the night of the State of the Union?' Jack shook his head. 'Faster if we just run.'

'Okay, we run,' Angela answered, 'but first, we need to get our hands on phones.'

'Now?'

Angela looked across the street, at a small shop that sold liquor, newspapers and an array of mobile phones that looked about as black-market and illegitimate as every other hack vendor in the area.

'In there. One for you, and one for me. And make sure they have video capabilities.'

Jack protested as she nudged him towards the shop. 'Angela, you said yourself, we need to get to the Capitol.'

'First this,' she answered firmly. 'You need to phone ahead and warn anyone you can connect with there. And I . . . I want to get hold of Sean.'

94

My skin is my betrayer. Black. Boiling. Turning against me.

The very act of dipping the quill into the ink pot and drawing it along the page brought renewed pain to de Faulke's fingers, but he knew he had to go on – to commit his experiences to paper.

The whole of me is covered in strange black patches, where my skin seems to have died. There are nodules hard as rocks in my flesh, and boils that burst and burn like fire. Every hour my breath grows worse. And the pain. My God, the pain.

Death had been following him everywhere. Behind him, stories of cities dying, of whole populations descending into darkness, caught up with him on his westward travels as people fled their homes to escape the terror. This was wrong, so very wrong.

He dipped the pen again, set it to his notebook. *Something has gone terribly amiss. The power of what we have found, it is far greater than the legends suggested.*

De Faulke swallowed, and he could feel the pus bursting from the sores in his throat. How naive he felt now, thinking back to the desire he'd had to unleash a pestilence upon the empire. How innocent he had been only a few months ago!

Our experiment at the shrine worked. But poor Alvain – somehow my trusted squire was infected during the encounter with the contaminated man. De Faulke paused a moment from his writing, the memory of his squire painful. *I buried Alvain three weeks ago. In his body, the pestilence took on new power. I know not how. That which consumed him, though from the same vial we used on the local, was far worse than anything we saw on that man.*

And now, now I see the signs in me. By God, it comes fast.

De Faulke paused again, looking down at the page. The journal itself was becoming a macabre sight: blood from his wrists smeared along the pages, added to the browning blood of Alvain, which had coloured its contents from de Faulke's hands as he wrote his entry after burying the man. The blood of a dead man, and one so soon to be dead, on pages filled with the stories of death.

The Grand Master's curse is coming true, he wrote, straining to complete his task, *but it is utterly out of control. Perhaps I was wrong. Perhaps I am not the curse-bringer after all. I stand now at the edge of our empire, but I do not know how much further I shall be able to go. I may not make it to France.*

He coughed, and heard from his own chest the great wheeze he had witnessed in his squire.

95

'Damn it, that's another one that's hung up on me!' Jack flipped closed his cheap new phone in frustration. His breath was short as he and Angela kept their speedy pace down Maryland Avenue, but it was frustration more than fatigue that had shortened his temper. He'd been on the phone constantly, trying to call ahead to warn of the threat. But no one was listening.

'Third in a row,' he added, exasperated. He was already dialling the operator again, preparing to seek another connection to someone at the Capitol. 'No one will take me seriously. Thomas Blackburn is well known and deeply trusted.'

Angela held her own phone to her ear, listing to the ringing while she acknowledged Jack's frustration with a nod. Calls from random telephone numbers only hours before the State of the Union, accusing a trusted friend of the government of biological terrorism, were going to be a hard sell.

Suddenly, her line connected.

'Hello?'

'Sean, is that you?' She'd phoned Blackburn Enterprises's main office in Seattle and requested to be transferred through to him. There was always the chance Sean had fared better than she and Jack, and still had his phone. A chance that had paid off.

'Angela, thank God you're all right!' The relief in Sean's voice was powerful. 'Have they let you go? Did they hurt you?'

Angela had a hard time choosing her words. *Had they hurt her?*

'They tried,' she answered. 'They drew my blood. We broke out of the building a few minutes ago. We had to take two of them down to get away.'

'But you're okay? Thank God,' Sean repeated. 'I was so worried about you both.'

'Where are you?' Angela asked, her words clipped.

'They locked me up in a small interrogation room,' Sean answered. 'Grilled me on our discovery in China.'

'They questioned you?' Angela wasn't sure what to think, what to ask. So many thoughts were rolling through her mind. It was hard to know what to make of anything.

'For almost an hour. They only let me loose about twenty minutes ago.'

Angela looked at her watch, trying to sort out the timing.

'What did they tell you about your father, Sean?' She knew the question was abrupt, but she knew she had to ask it.

'My father?'

'Yes, Sean. What did they tell you about his role in creating a Templar Order of his own? Of seeking revenge for wrongs he believes have been committed against your family?'

415

Sean's voice hesitated on the other end of the line. 'Not much,' he finally answered, with what might have been shame in his voice, 'and from the sounds of it, not as much as you. But enough for me to figure out that my father has used us all for something . . . something I can't even contemplate.'

'And there are more forces at work than just him,' Angela added. 'His brother, your uncle. I don't know the details, but it would appear there's a coup in the ranks.'

To this Sean responded only with silence. Angela allowed him his moment, but they didn't have time to waste. 'Do you know anything more about what your father is going to do? How he's going to do it?'

'Only that it's going to take place at the Capitol,' Sean answered. 'I think he's going to attack the State of the Union with whatever it is we found abroad.'

'We're already on our way.' Angela glanced over at Jack, whose frustrated expression told her he still hadn't had any success.

'We'll be there in about five minutes. I don't know how, but we're going to try to stop your father if we can.'

'I'm on my way, too.' Again, Sean's voice seemed to hesitate, as if the words he had to say were hard to force from his lips. 'We can stop him together.' Another pause. 'Find me when you arrive.'

The line disconnected, and Angela returned her phone to her pocket. Beyond, ten or eleven long blocks down the street, the marble dome of the Capitol building loomed over the rooftops.

Jack had already put away his phone. 'No one's listening,' he said. 'Though I'm sure someone at one of the security agencies is tracing those calls, trying to sort out whether I'm the one who poses a threat.' He contemplated the possibility a moment longer, then grabbed his new mobile again and flung it into a waste bin as they jogged by. He'd done the same several blocks back with the gun he'd retrieved from their attacker.

'I'd rather not be stopped at the gate.'

'Sean's out, too,' Angela answered, pressing forward into a run. 'He's going to meet us there. We'll just have to be more convincing in person.'

And Angela knew she'd have to be convincing about one more thing, too. A single fact that she was now certain had to be true.

The service entrance to the Capitol's ceremonial presentation hall opened on to the exterior of the building via a secure door for staff and a wide loading bay. As Angela and Jack finally arrived at the Capitol, it was this point of access – rather than the main entrance to the rotunda and congressional heart of the building – that attracted their attention. In the loading bay were parked two large trucks bearing the Blackburn Enterprises logo, three others queuing behind.

'Over there,' Jack said, pointing to the site as they slowed to a walk. There was a note of surprise in his voice. 'Company crew.'

Angela surveyed familiar faces from Seattle working at the rear of the docked trucks, unloading equipment and talking in what appeared to be a customarily friendly and relaxed manner. *No signs of catastrophe yet.*

'That's the service entrance to the Statuary Hall,' she

said, trying to process the sight before them. 'I heard on a tour, once, that it's one of the largest reception areas in the Capitol.' *But not an area used for the State of the Union.* She and Jack had been out of the country for days. Whatever the reason for Blackburn Enterprises's presence here, neither she nor Jack knew about it – but it only solidified their suspicion that the Capitol was the target.

'This is good, having the company's men at the gate,' Jack said. 'Chances are we'll meet someone we know at the door.'

'It's all going to depend on whether Blackburn's had our security credentials revoked,' Angela pointed out. The entry was now only a few dozen yards ahead of them. Would Thomas Blackburn have had the time to block them out, given the pace of his actions? Or the inclination, believing that both she and Jack were secured where he'd left them?

Either way, we'll know in a second. She straightened her shirt, brushing away as much of the remaining dust as she could and trying to look a little less like a bedraggled escapee who'd just run halfway through the city, then took the final steps to the secure doorway beside the loading bay. In a small booth beside the door a guard watched her approach, and Angela noted the cameras high above them. She also noted the armed soldier just beyond.

'Identification,' the guard demanded. He held out a hand, his eyes on Angela's face. She reached into her pocket, extracted her wallet, and a moment later passed the guard a driver's licence together with her Blackburn Enterprises secure ID.

'You're with the company?' The guard scanned both

documents and awaited the readout on a blacked-out display screen inside the booth.

'Yes. Both of us.' Angela motioned to Jack, who produced his own identification and passed it to the guard.

A seemingly endless silence passed, the guard saying nothing more but staring at his computer screen, tapping keys in intermittent bursts. *This moment either ends with the door opening*, Angela thought, trying not to panic, *or with a very public arrest.* She looked beyond the guard, the muzzle of the soldier's gun looking more frightening than it had a few moments ago. *Or worse.*

Finally, a small bleep emerged from the computer. The guard scrutinized the display, an eyebrow rising.

'Most of your colleagues have been here for hours,' he said, handing back their documents. 'You can go through here, then take the first double doors on your left.'

He clicked a button and a buzzing marked the opening of the secure entry.

Angela nodded, tucking her cards back into her wallet, and stepped into the US Capitol. She still hadn't taken a breath.

Inside the Statuary Hall, Jack and Angela were confronted with the bustle of final preparations for some type of presentation, with row after row of chairs lining the centre, fronted by a display of Blackburn Enterprises equipment. Angela spotted a helicopter, a fighter drone, automobiles, even small mobile robotics. All were emblazoned with US military logos and the crest of Blackburn Enterprises.

'Angela, take a look at this.' Jack handed her a

419

programme leaflet from a stack on a nearby table. Her eyes widened as she read the header line at the top.

The Transformation of American Defence Strategy: A Post-State of the Union Presentation for the Joint Houses

'Blackburn Enterprises is hosting an event immediately after the speech?'

'With presidential attendance.' Jack pointed out a notice a few inches down the page. 'This answers the question of how Blackburn is going to get into the State of the Union. He isn't. Too secure. He's going to make his move here.' He motioned beyond them, at the enormous space bustling with activity.

Angela swallowed. This meant they had to figure out a way to convince the people in this room that the evening's programme included something much more deadly than defence technologies. If they didn't, it was going to become the site of a disaster she didn't want to contemplate.

Angela's vision broadened to take in the whole scene. Men were unpacking boxes, adjusting display boards, ensuring the burgundy cords, blocking off safe distances from the showcase technologies, were evenly hung. So much equipment. So many places a biological weapon could be concealed. *Or*, she suddenly thought, *not concealed*. In this environment, it could be positioned in plain sight. It could be a feature of the evening.

Then, a face Angela recognized. Standing not far from the entrance was a man she'd interacted with at the company before. *Tom? Ron? Maybe his surname was Morecraft?*

The details escaped her, but she knew the man, and remembered him as polite and hard-working.

Angela would have to trust that memory.

'Excuse me,' she said, approaching him. He started, surprised, but smiled when he saw her face. *Good, he remembers me, too.*

'Do you have your phone on you?' Angela asked abruptly.

'Yeah, of course.' He started to fish into his pocket, assuming she was asking to borrow it for a call.

'No,' Angela stopped him, holding up a flattened palm. 'Just tell me your number.' She opened her new phone, typing in the digits as he recited them, a confused look on his face.

'That's great. Thanks.' She nodded briefly, smiled and walked away, her fingers still on the keys, leaving the man baffled.

That's going to have to do, Angela thought, bracing herself. She pressed the last number, then closed her phone.

96

'Go, now!'

The command sent the ten-man SWAT team into a flurry of motion, breaking their covert silence with roars of vocalized identification, followed by the brutal blows of an iron ramming post slamming through the front door of the house at 447 Atlantic Street. Part of the team was at the rear entrance, and the blow there came simultaneously, the highly trained men flooding into the house in perfect synchronicity.

The surveillance of the house had been continuous in the previous hours, and sound-flow monitoring had deemed this the appropriate moment for the breach. All three men on the interior were upstairs, all seated, and all in the same room. The two daughters of Senator Preston Wilcox were, all indicators suggested, in the basement, which would keep them safe in the highly probable case that the incursion required violence.

'What the fu—'

The first man inside the house, seated on a sofa, was not able to finish his surprised exclamation. His hand was in motion towards a Beretta on the table next to him, and that was all that the two SWAT agents with their eyes on him required. Bullets from both their assault rifles landed in the centre of his chest before his fingers ever touched his gun.

A second man was seated in a reclining chair at a right angle to the sofa and was a split second faster than his companion. Rather than rise, he pushed himself forward and down towards the cover of a nearby table. There was a small collection of handguns on its surface, and though the man wasn't at an immediate angle to reach them, his ultimate intentions were clear. An agent at the front of the room modified his aim, tracking the man's motions, and fired three shots at the moving target. The first missed its mark, impacting the carpeting behind him, but the second two burst through the left side of the man's ribcage. He dropped face-first on to the floor, motionless.

'Back away from the desk slowly, your hands where I can see them.' The command was directed at the third man, seated before a computer with his back to the agents. For a few seconds he didn't move, and the tension of ten specialists with their triggers half depressed was almost electric. But when motion finally came, it was of his arms slowly rising, moving towards his head.

'Keep your palms open and bring your hands behind your neck.' The SWAT team leader spoke without removing his sight from the back of the man's head.

The sole remaining kidnapper complied.

'Interlock your fingers behind your head.'

As he did so, two of the agents swept forward and flung him off the desk chair on to the floor. One kept his hands clasped; the other frisked him from head to feet.

'He's clean. Get him secured.' The man was pulled up

by his shoulders, his arms repositioned so his hands could be bound behind his back.

A second later, the team leader spun him round, his weapon still drawn. 'You have precisely two seconds to confirm to me whether the daughters of Senator Preston Wilcox are still alive.'

97

Must not be seen. Must not be known. Must not fail now.

The mantra repeated in the mind of the man whose place in the New Order had been his birthright and inheritance, his lips mouthing the words silently. What it had taken to bring him here was beyond even his comprehension – but he was here now. He would do what honour and duty required of him. His work had formerly been expansive, but it had now all become so simple.

A small cartridge, barely larger than a cigar tube.

A single motion, to slide it into place.

A twist to lock it.

And then it would be done.

The knight ran his fingers over the small module, loosely nestled in his pocket. It was strangely warm, as it was when it had been delivered to him only a few minutes before, handed to him as if it were a precious gem. He had never suspected that this was where his work would lead him. His visions had never included aerosol compounds or quite so much death. Treasure had been envisaged in different terms.

But that had changed. He had finally had his eyes opened to the true nature of their work. No more secrets, no more subterfuge. His heart had stopped at the news. He'd felt all the array of responses: confusion, anger, disbelief. But then, finally, acceptance. There was a cost that had to be paid. The price was high, but it was just.

A suitable moment of quiet arrived. He looked around him: no others were near by, and those in the distance had their attention elsewhere. The invisibility of a busy scene. *Perfect*.

He took a single, long step over to the XRX-450 unit, around which he had been inconspicuously hovering, and entered a lengthy series of keycodes into one of its exposed control pads. At his final button press, there was a tiny pop and the faintest sound of sliding metal on metal. An opening appeared in one of the unit's extendable robotic arms, no more than an inch in diameter, its two-by-two-inch cover retracting slowly.

In a single, smooth motion, he slid the cartridge from his pocket, aligned the proper end forward and pressed it into the chamber. As it entered fully into position, he pressed gently and a sharp click signalled it had locked into place.

Like it was made for it, he mused. Which, of course, they had ensured it was.

He entered a few more keystrokes on to the pad and the cover slid closed. When the metal plate once again covered the chamber's entry, it retreated a fraction downwards, coming flush to the surface metal of the arm. The fit was so precise that even standing only two feet away, knowing precisely where the access point was, he could barely see it.

It is finished.

He felt a slight tinge of guilt at the thought, at those biblical words. God would not be smiling on him now, but his ancestors would be. And that, in the end, would have to be enough.

98

Statuary Hall

'We need to find Sean,' Jack announced as he and Angela started making their way deeper into the vast hall. 'He's got far higher connections than either you or I. If anyone is going to get this threat taken seriously, it's him.'

'He said he'd meet us here,' Angela answered. She surveyed the space, which was brimming with people. 'It could take a while to find him.'

As she walked into the heart of the presentation area, a large chart outlined the plans for the post-State of the Union event. The hall was to be filled with a majority of both Houses, and a special booth had been reserved for the president.

The measure of Thomas Blackburn's treachery, his insanity, was overwhelming, and Angela now knew he had not done it alone. His brother was every bit as mad as him. A family affair, with a recreated Templar Order made up of men willing to help them achieve their aims.

But Angela was increasingly sure that the true level of Blackburn involvement had yet to be disclosed. And that was something she needed to change.

'There you two are.' A familiar voice broke through the tension of Angela's search, and both she and Jack turned to see Sean approaching from behind a large cluster of presentation supplies near by. He looked relieved to see them, rushing forward with a hand extended.

'I was beginning to think you hadn't made it,' Jack said, taking Sean's hand and shaking it.

'I'm so glad the two of you got out. I wasn't sure they were going to release you.' Sean gave a comforting smile to Angela.

'They weren't, and they didn't,' Jack answered, and quickly summarized their encounter with Blackburn and escape from the small building in which they'd been locked.

As the two men began to speak, Angela quietly took a few steps aside. Without letting either of them see her actions, she worked her fingers into a pocket and set the only plan she'd been able to think of in motion.

A moment later she stepped forward, directly into the midst of the two men's dialogue. Angela knew what she had to do, and she put on her most authoritative tone to manage the confrontation.

'Where were you after we were arrested, Sean?' she demanded. Both Sean and Jack fell silent, each surprised by the sudden interjection.

'Why were you separated from us after we'd landed? And how is it that your father, after telling you about this elaborate plot, which you tell me on the phone you "knew nothing about", simply lets you walk free?'

Sean's eyes widened, surprised, and even Jack looked taken aback by Angela's barrage of questions and fighting tone.

'Angela, I'm not sure –,' Sean tried to answer, but she wouldn't let him get a word in edgeways.

'Tell me, Sean, what's your real motivation for all this – for all we've been through, for all we've been doing? It's been hard enough figuring out your father's; I've never really stopped to question yours. What's the source of your zeal for something so oddball and strange as Templar history?' She stepped forward, unremitting.

'Angela, I don't understand why you're asking. We've been working together for two years. You know I haven't had anything to do with my father's activities.'

'I know nothing,' she spat back, 'nothing but what I've been told by your father, and by you. And in the past hours, I've learned that everything he's told me has been a lie.'

'And you're willing to assume the same of me?'

'You conveniently neglected to mention how involved in things your uncle has been.'

Sean looked like he'd been caught off balance. 'My uncle? He hasn't. Uncle Piotr doesn't work for the company.'

'But he knows plenty about your father's plot. About our work. Our travels. Our find.'

'I don't know how that could be.'

'I don't believe you, Sean. You're lying. You're family's too closely knit for you not to know of his involvement.'

'Angela, this is becoming insulting.'

'Be insulted if you want, but there's too much that doesn't make sense. And it's not your uncle's role in this that really concerns me. I want to know yours.'

'I've told you, I –'

Angela was at full bore, unwilling to be interrupted by Sean's protestations. 'We arrive in China, and your father has communicated to you that we need to wear gas masks going into that tunnel. He knew something. You knew something!'

'Ange—'

'Our plane is diverted on return, and you're separated from us. Convenient, Sean. We're held captive, I'm made to give blood for God-knows-what, and Jack and I are left to crawl through damned piping to escape – but you're simply allowed to walk free. And when we hear your uncle talking about being ready to kill us, he and those around him are obviously concerned not to harm you. And you're not involved? Bullshit, Sean! Bullshit!'

He didn't answer, but Angela could see in his eyes what she needed to see. She forced herself to breathe, to control her voice.

'Angela,' Sean finally said, 'why don't you just take a few moments and calm –'

She cut him off. 'Do you know what's the saddest thing of all, Sean?'

Sean Blackburn was too well rehearsed to do anything other than protest his way out of her accusations. But there was one tactic Angela felt he was less equipped to resist.

'The saddest thing in all of this is that you've partnered up with your father, with your uncle, selling your soul and throwing away your life in the process – and all for men who don't show you any loyalty at all.'

For the first time, Sean didn't try answer. His prepared retorts hadn't anticipated such comments, and he looked . . . offended.

Perfect.

'I don't know what's motivated you, Sean. Power?

Influence? The chance to prove yourself? But one thing I do know is that the same deranged sense of family loyalty that's in your father must have been instilled somewhere in you. Yet your life means nothing to him.'

'You don't know what you're talking about.' Sean's face was tight, his expression unreadable.

'The bullets fired in India were fired at all of us, Sean. And the attack in China. Face it, your life was expendable.'

'My father would never harm me,' Sean protested.

Jack craned his head, as if he were trying to take in Sean's reaction.

'Your father doesn't give a crap about you,' Angela spat back, making her words as poisonous as possible. 'Your father's love of family is a joke. You've been a pawn, and nothing more.'

'Fuck you, bitch!' Sean snapped with surprising suddenness into a vicious rage. 'You know nothing about us!'

'You're a joke, Sean! Your father's joke. Only the joke's on you, now that it's over. Your involvement in his plot has been stripped away from you.'

'You'll never know what's been at stake!' Sean shouted. 'How involved I am! Nothing's been stripped away from me. My role is at its peak!'

Angela didn't react. She had known Sean would fold, his Blackburn family pride too engrained and arrogant to face such insult.

Jack's eyes, however, flared wide. A look of betrayal came over him, and was followed in seconds by one of anger. Profound, personal anger.

He opened his mouth, some threat or condemnation ready to erupt, but before he could speak, Sean jolted.

He was far faster than Jack or Angela could have anticipated. The gun was aimed at them before either had a
chance to move, the click of its action shocking them to
attention. Then all either could hear was the panting of
Sean's angry, accusing breath.

99

Statuary Hall

The rage that had been brewing in Sean burst with all the force of months and years of suppression. The small Glock 38 in his clutch moved in spurts between Angela and Jack, but spent most of its time with the snub barrel directed towards the ex-Marine. Sean's eyes burned with a redness to match the anger in his cheeks.

'Finally,' he spat, 'we don't have to dance around any longer. How fucking tiring it's been, having to play charades with the two of you.'

Angela's anger had not abated. But Sean had become like a man possessed, the gun twitching in his hand, and she said nothing to provoke him further.

'So you've made the connections. But you're wrong about my father, and you're doubly wrong about our relationship.' Sean looked as if he were prepared to laugh at her, but only angrier words came. 'Of course I'm involved in his plans! It's only right that a son should share in the glory of his father.'

'Glory!' Jack managed to answer back with condescension, despite the gun levelled at him. 'Your father's planning a biological attack, Sean. Indiscriminately, for revenge that's not even his. He's not one for glory; he's a terrorist with a very loose grasp on his sanity.'

For an instant a flash of doubt crossed Sean's face, but

it passed as quickly as it came. 'You wouldn't understand. Some truths require sacrifice.'

'This isn't sacrifice, Sean. It's murder.'

'You wouldn't understand sacrifice. You're life's been one of privilege. Military career, right up to the top. Accolades in your education, then on to fame and prestige. What the fuck have you ever known of oppression? Of poverty, of being the outcast?'

'*You're* asking me this?' Jack questioned back, incredulous. 'You, the son of one of the wealthiest men in America, born into a life of power, influence, wealth. Shit, Sean, you're not even thirty and you've been given the reins of an R & D programme that would be the envy of anyone in the field!'

'I've told you before, Jack, I'm my father's son.' Sean's eyes seemed distant. 'Sure, now that we have money everyone is keen to know my family, but do you have any idea how hard it is to rise to that position as an immigrant family? Do you know what kind of crap my father had to go through, or my uncle, for that matter, to get to where they are now?'

'Sean, that's part of life. We have to struggle to get where we want to be,' Angela pleaded.

'There's struggle, and there's struggle,' Sean answered. He glowered at her angrily. 'You wouldn't be anywhere if my father hadn't funded your research. But have you ever been spat at in the streets? Have you ever been cast out of social circles, simply because of your background? *That* was the "American Dream" my ancestors came to this country to follow!'

'You really think that justifies terrorism?' Jack asked. 'Mass killing? Jesus, Sean, you've always seemed so down

434

to earth. I can't believe I trusted you, and all this time you've been plotting biological warfare.'

The look of hesitation was back on Sean's face, but he bit down his doubt. 'I haven't been plotting anything. I knew my father had a plan, I knew what we were looking for probably wasn't treasure in any traditional sense. But I was just as surprised by what we found in China as you.'

His face was now a mixture of anger and pleading, as if he wanted Angela to accept him for what he'd done.

'You didn't know what your father intended to do?'

'I didn't. He only told me this afternoon.'

Angela halted. 'But . . . but you're going along with him? He tells you of this "plan", and you accept it?!'

Sean's look went hard again. 'Of course I accepted it. It is my duty. The duty of a knight. The duty of a son.'

'You're not a knight, Sean,' Jack interjected. 'The Templars are long gone, whatever pretend re-creation your family might have fashioned. And whatever wrongs your father feels he's suffered, they don't mean you owe him anything. Nothing that requires this.'

Sean glared at him with pure hatred.

'People today have no sense of family, of lineage. Does it really matter that I haven't suffered my family's indignities myself? Should it? My *people* have suffered – and it's their blood that flows in my veins.'

'You're willing to unleash a plague in the centre of Washington, out of a sense of loyalty to the past?' Angela's face expressed her disbelief.

'Blood,' Sean answered, 'cries out for vengeance.'

Then he turned directly towards her, his face beaming a strange new certainty.

'You, of all people, should understand what moves me. You're a woman of lineage, too, and yours is central to our story.'

Angela's heart suddenly fluttered from more than fear of the gun. 'What do you mean? How am I connected?'

'You're the descendant, Angela. The key. The one my father needed to complete the treasure.'

She shook her head. The words made no sense.

'The key,' Jack said, muttering towards her. 'That's what Blackburn called you, just before they took your blood.'

'You think he's mad,' Sean continued, 'but he's far smarter than even I'd known until this afternoon. Did you know he'd been looking for you for years, tracing out family lines all over the world that connected to the fourteenth century?'

Angela's thoughts spun wildly. Suddenly, she could hear her father's voice, telling her stories of their family's past. Stories of ancestors stretching back centuries. And then, the impossible realization.

'You can't be suggesting that your father thinks I'm a descendant of the Templars? It's enough he thinks he himself is!'

Sean laughed coldly. 'No, Angela, he doesn't believe you're one of us. For our purposes, you're something far more important.'

'This is just madness,' Jack grunted. 'One of "us"!'

Sean ignored the remark, keeping his gun trained on Jack and his eyes on Angela. 'Did it never surprise you, Angela, that my father sought you out the way he did? That the anonymous grant you were given for your master's studies came without your applying for it? That Blackburn

Enterprises approached you personally, before you'd finished, to offer you a job without your ever seeking one?'

'Of course it seemed strange, but –'

'My father had spent months trying to find you, years. He'd found the lineage he needed, and eventually it led to your grandfather, then your father, then to you.'

Angela's mind raced to understand the details. Her grandfather, her father . . . it didn't make sense.

'But I'm not descended from the Templars, Sean. You said so yourself.'

He waved aside the interruption. 'Once he found you, my father nurtured you. Your research, your career. It turned out you had a historical mind – that you could help him in more ways than one.'

'Sean, what the fuck is this about?' Jack demanded, impatient.

Sean raised the gun, keeping him in check. But Angela could only feel the thumping of her heart, beating against her chest. Sean's words gripped her, though she still couldn't understand them.

'My father didn't need another Templar descendant,' Sean said, staring into her green eyes. 'What he needed, more than anything else, was a direct descendant of their servants.'

The thumping in her chest was louder, almost deafening. 'Their . . . servants?'

'In particular, of a squire who had served with one very specific knight.'

The thumping was at its peak, but at Sean's next words it seemed to stop altogether.

'And that blood, Angela, runs in your veins.'

100

Statuary Hall

Sean's revelations were too immense, too confusing. Angela was stunned into silence. The extent of her betrayal by Blackburn Enterprises, and the Blackburn family, grew with every word that came out of his mouth. The tiny pinprick in her arm where Thomas Blackburn's man had drawn her blood flared with a spark of pain, as if to remind her of its presence.

My blood. Blood they believe is connected . . . She wanted to ask what it meant. She had a thousand questions. But Sean was no longer in the mood to let her speak.

'I want you to know, Angela, that I'm sorry about this. I really am. Before today, this wasn't on the cards – but things change.' As he spoke, Sean reached into a pack slung from his hip. 'To be honest, I hadn't intended to share any of this with the two of you, but you quite literally backed me into a corner.'

It was then that Angela saw what Sean drew out from his pack. A small suppressor was gripped in his fingers, and he began spinning it on to the barrel of his pistol.

'But you obviously understand I can't let the two of you live. Not now. Not with what you know, and what's about to happen.'

'How did you get that in here?' Jack asked, motioning at once to the suppressor and the gun itself.

Sean laughed. 'I didn't walk in with it, if that's what you're thinking. For God's sake, Jack, look at this place. It's filled with our equipment. Blackburn Enterprises designs jets that radar can't see and ship coatings that sonar can't detect; you think we can't figure out how to smuggle a handgun in our equipment without being spotted?' He shook his head, as if he were disappointed in Jack. 'Not quite the fresh thinking I was hoping for when I urged my father to bring you on to our team. Ends up it's me thinking ahead, not the bright Captain Shepherd. Not that I necessarily anticipated this particular situation, but it works out pretty well in the circumstances.'

'Come on, Sean,' Jack protested, 'you can't kill us in here. This is a secure facility. You'll be stopped. This whole plan is going to be stopped.'

'Again, you don't seem to see what's in front of you.' Sean shrugged away his reproach. 'Look around. There are storage crates everywhere.' Just beside them was an enormous metal container that had been used to bring in technical equipment for the presentation. 'That one's big enough for you both. It'll stay here throughout the display. The security sweep is already complete. No one will find you until it's all over, and by then, no one will care.'

Angela felt the cold sweat start to rise on her skin as Sean's expression changed. In an instant, all friendliness, all interest, all humanity seemed to leave him. Sean's face hardened, and in that moment Angela was absolutely certain that he would shoot them both without hesitation.

In the next second, she was proved right. Sean raised the gun, the suppressor now tightly affixed, to Jack's chest.

The gunshot when it came, however, was not silent.

The explosion of compressed powder being ignited burst into the hall, magnified by the metal equipment and high space above them. Then another shot, louder than the first. Angela instinctively ducked, lunging to the side, but her eyes caught the explosion of sparks on the metal crate behind Sean's head that marked a bullet impacting the surface.

Behind Sean's head.

Someone was firing at him. *Thank God.*

She pushed herself further aside as another shot echoed into the hall. She could see Sean's face contort in shock. He had not expected return fire, and the last shot had come within an inch of his head. Sean lithely spun on his heels and darted through the narrow space between two containers, disappearing from view.

Angela rose cautiously a few seconds later, looking towards the position where Jack had been standing.

Please, don't let him be dead, her mind roared, with more emotion than she had expected.

'Jack!' she cried out. 'Jack! Are you all right?'

There was a delay that seemed like an eternity, but finally she heard his voice.

'I'm fine, I'm fine.' He rose from behind a display case, ruffled but whole. 'I don't think he managed to get a shot off.'

At that moment, two security agents from Blackburn Enterprises, commissioned to work together with the Secret Service to provide security for the evening's event, burst into the small space, their weapons drawn.

'Where'd he go?' the man in front demanded. His eyes were on Angela. She motioned the way with an extended finger and the two men charged away.

As she heard their footsteps vanish into the depths of the hall, Angela stood upright and walked over to Jack. There was a moment's hesitation, but adrenaline made her decision for her and she wrapped her arms round him. 'Thank God he didn't get you.'

'Or you.' Jack smiled, accepting the embrace and returning it.

'But I don't understand how the guards found him,' he added. 'Are we standing here through the dumb luck of a random patrol?'

It was Angela's turn to smile. 'Not exactly.' She motioned to a nearby crate. It was a few feet behind them, where Angela had retreated to quietly when they had first come across Sean.

On the crate was her phone, open, the video camera pointing towards them.

'I suspected Sean since we landed at the airport,' she confessed as Jack examined the set-up, 'and especially since overhearing Blackburn's brother speaking to his men. It's why I wanted a phone with video capabilities. I established a call to Ron Morecraft, who was on duty at the door. Figured that if Sean tried anything, he'd see it and could respond.'

Jack gazed at her. Angela couldn't read the look. Admiration? Respect? Her heart was still racing. She could easily be reading the signs incorrectly.

The sudden embrace that claimed her, though, was impossible to misread. Jack reached forward, drew her to himself, and pressed his lips into hers. And in a move as surprising as anything else she'd experienced that day, Angela kissed him back.

IOI

US Capitol, Washington, DC

The two Blackburn Enterprises security guards had been joined within seconds by Secret Service agents and Capitol security, jointly pursuing Sean Blackburn, and though the sweep of the building – the entire building – and its surroundings would continue for many hours more, the initial report was not encouraging. Either he'd pre-scouted a means of escape or had simply been lucky in weaving his way ahead of his pursuers, but however he'd done it, suspicions were that Sean had managed to get out of the Capitol.

Angela and Jack spent the next forty minutes filling in the military liaisons and Secret Service supervisors with everything they knew. Thomas Blackburn's intentions, their discovery of a biological agent in China, the shared resentment he and his son felt towards the government and society. And they had the video recording from Angela's phone, which removed any doubt.

The US Capitol went into lockdown. The defence-technologies exhibition to follow the State of the Union could obviously not be allowed to take place.

The head of Capitol security for the Secret Service, a senior agent by the name of Tom Arbuckle, relayed the news to his superiors and to the White House. The calls were brief, concise and commanding.

As he set down his phone, he turned to the sea of agents that had arrived on site. 'There is a biological weapon somewhere in this hall. No one is leaving until it's found.'

The search had been underway for two hours before attention turned to the XRX-450 robotic unit positioned near the front of the display platform. Having scanned all the storage rooms, chairs, crates and other obvious spaces for some sort of offensive device, focus had since moved to disassembling the equipment Thomas Blackburn's firm had brought in. Any one of them could house a biological weapon, and the Secret Service and FBI agents approached with caution, making use of Blackburn Enterprises's own men to assist them in tearing apart the equipment.

The robotic device was taken down panel by panel, until finally the framing of the extendable arms was unscrewed – and there, nestled within one arm, was what they were seeking. A small cartridge, its contents apparently under pressure. A glass tube was at its centre, containing a reddish liquid and attached to a firing mechanism that simply released the contents in aerosol form.

There would have been no explosion. No flames or carnage. Only a fine, gentle mist streaming out into the room and into the lungs of all those present.

'What does it contain?' Angela asked as the agents manipulated the cartridge delicately, placing it into a quarantine containment case that would be taken to the Center for Disease Control for full analysis. She glanced at Jack. They both instinctively knew there could only be one answer. Whatever else had been added to it, this cartridge contained the compound they had discovered in China.

The agent's words, however, wrenched Angela's gut.

'I'm not sure what it is,' he said, 'but it looks almost like . . . blood.'

102

Washington Highlands, Washington, DC

The relief Preston Wilcox felt as he grasped his two daughters in his arms was like a rush of new life. They had been taken, imprisoned, chained up, and there were a few bruises on their ankles and redness round their mouths where gagging tape had been applied and removed several times. But they were alive. They were here, and he pulled them further into his chest.

But their mother . . .

The tears flowed down Senator Wilcox's face. For the first time, knowing his daughters were now safe, he could feel the full grief of his wife's loss. *Oh, Beth . . .*

He pulled Anna and Bella closer still and looked up at the two Secret Service agents who had tracked down their kidnappers and arranged their deliverance. Wilcox's eyes watered, grateful beyond words.

But there were words that needed to be said.

'You know who did this?' the senator asked.

'We don't know all the details.'

'Tell me what you do know.'

'These men all worked for Blackburn Enterprises,' the agent answered. 'The same company whose exhibit they were blackmailing you to sponsor through the Senate.'

'Blackburn Enterprises. Why?'

'We don't know that, Senator. Their motives are unclear.

We only took one of the kidnappers alive, and so far he's not talking.'

Preston Wilcox looked down, released the clutch round his girls with one arm and stroked his fingers through Bella's dirty hair.

When he glanced back up at the agents, his expression was fierce.

'The man you took may not be cooperating, but the head of Blackburn Enterprises is on the guest list for the State of the Union, and if I have to interrupt the president himself to get him to do it, the bastard's going to talk.'

103

Blood streaked down Arnaud de Faulke's face. He could barely breathe, and every movement was now a torment. But he forced the words through his teeth. He had been cursed, rather than given life to the curse. His life was over. He had only days, if that.

Over the past morning, he had written a letter to the members of the Order in England, where he knew a few remnant knights had found refuge and strove to carry on their work. He'd considered them foolish at first, going to territories where the French would know of their presence; but now they were his final hope. They were brothers on whom he would have to rely.

The letter was now folded into the cover of his journal, which de Faulke had tied tightly closed and wrapped in several layers of cloth. He had inscribed everything inside. Everything they would need, to know where to look and how to decipher the instructions he had left.

He wrapped himself in cloths also, despite the agony they caused to his body as they pressed against his sores. He covered as much of his face as he could. He could not allow his disfigured visage to terrify the young courier from the local village he needed to employ.

'Boy,' de Faulke said to him as he approached, limping along the street, 'this parcel must be delivered to the

Jerusalem temple in London, at all costs.' The boy looked at him blankly.

'You know London, in England?' de Faulke asked. A nod. 'Go there. It is a long journey. Ask for the Temple Church and you'll be given directions.'

The boy shook his head. He seemed eager to help, but it also seemed he knew where England was and recognized just how long a journey he was being asked to undertake.

De Faulke reached into his satchel and extracted his money pouch. He had no need for gold any longer. He tossed the entirety of its contents to the boy. It was a sum that would have caused even a wealthy landowner to gawp. The boy saw enough gold to satisfy him for life, and scooped it up eagerly. When his eyes came back to de Faulke, they were committed.

'You must not fail or delay,' the knight commanded, 'whatever the obstacles. Do you understand?'

The boy nodded enthusiastically, and de Faulke waved him off. He had come recommended, and de Faulke was as confident as he could be that his parcel would be delivered.

He knew he could not send along the vials themselves. They were too fragile, and he did not want to kill off his last remaining brethren by some accident in delivery. Instead, he would provide his written account of the discovery, the tunnel, of the effect of the pestilence. And of the clues he had left along the path to find it, so that the Order, when they were ready, could claim what he had found.

PART SIX
Culminations

104

The rage burning in Thomas Blackburn's chest as he sat in the back of the moving car was stronger than anything he had experienced in his life. It tore at him like an unknown fire, consuming his flesh from the inside – straining his threshold for pain and stirring together anger, hatred, betrayal, despair.

A whole lifetime, wasted! His heart almost moaned the unbelievable words. *Wasted!*

His breath was fluttering, and Blackburn had already taken double his usual dosage of Digoxin to strengthen his seventy-two-year-old heart. He wanted to cry out, to scream, to smash a fist into someone or something. Anything to dispel the lifetime of hope that was turning to agony and failure within him.

How could things have gone wrong, so fast?

A day ago, everything had been advancing according to plan. Despite the obstacles posed by his cowardly brother, the ancient biological agent had been retrieved, and then today, even in the face of potential sabotage, Angela Derby's blood had been gathered and successfully compounded with it. Sean had finally been brought wholly into their work – something that had had to wait until the last minute, in case he'd threatened to quit the project – but Sean had responded like a good son and noble knight.

He'd been in position to insert the cartridge containing the compound into the XRX-450 unit only hours ago.

Seven hundred years of history had been at the verge of finding their culmination. And then, suddenly, it had all been ripped away from him.

In the back seat of the blacked-out sedan, Blackburn fingered the small, leather-bound notebook next to him. The personal diary of Sir Arnaud de Faulke had been the source of his greatest hope since Blackburn had sponsored the excavation in England that had located it eleven years ago. The account of the unknown knight, whose life bridged that critical gap between the dissolution of the Order and the disappearance of the Templars, had brought Blackburn a degree of focus and inspiration he hadn't foreseen earlier in his life. The story of the knight's sojourn – how he'd watched the Grand Master fall, heard the curse and spent the remainder of his days seeking to bring it to fruition – had imbued Blackburn's own life with purpose. In the Templars' unjust demise, he had found a foreshadowing of the treatment his family had experienced in the New World, and when he had first read de Faulke's account of de Molay's curse and the lengths the knight had gone to to bring it to life, Blackburn had felt history and his own story collide.

In the years of research that followed, it became clear to Blackburn that the Black Death that had killed off so much of Europe in the fourteenth century was the accidental by-product of the knight's failed attempt. He couldn't be faulted the lack of success – who of the period knew of the power of such biological agents as he'd uncovered in the furthest reaches of the Asian darkness?

But the intervening centuries had changed much. Biological warfare was now commonplace, even if it was despised by the public and by governments – at least in their published statements and on-camera pronouncements. *Doesn't stop them from researching it*, Blackburn thought, *or buying it when we perfect the art*. He'd long ago learned how militaries worked, both in the USA and elsewhere. It was all well and good to hate something publicly, to decry it as inhuman and abhorrent. Just so long as you had plenty of it in your back pocket in case things got bad.

Blackburn had poured vast quantities of his personal wealth into researching the claims of the medieval knight's journal. De Faulke had written that the pestilence he had discovered had caused a certain effect on its own, but in the body of his squire, a man called Alvain de Thierry, it had taken on new strength and wrought terrible agonies. Blackburn's scientific mind had interpreted that to mean that something in the blood chemistry of the squire had reacted with the biological agent, compounding its potency. When, on page 137 of the journal – Blackburn knew the page, its shape and texture, by heart – de Faulke had written that what now appeared as a smear of brown on the left side of the page was his squire's blood, which had got on his wrist as he buried him near the Tigris river, Blackburn had been given the final tool he needed.

He had been sure he could succeed where the knight had failed. And he *had* succeeded, all but for his brother's betrayal and his son's failure at the last moment. Thomas should never have made Piotr, who'd always resisted the anglicized version of his name, 'Peter', the Seneschal of the New Order. His sense of heritage had never been as strong as Thomas's own, and he clearly didn't have the stomach to act when destiny provided the opportunity. 'There is no rush,' was his routine mantra. 'Let's gather the treasure and prepare for a powerful tomorrow.' But Thomas Blackburn had had enough of waiting for tomorrow. The day was today, and his brother would simply have to watch history pass him by.

But Sean . . . Sean had held such promise, and only this morning had received details of their difficult work with stoicism and admirable resolve. Thomas had been proud. Yet his son had still fallen on the battlefield – and it was a pitiful fall. All Sean had to do in the end was insert the cartridge containing the serum into the device and walk quietly away, but the boy hadn't been able to do even that. And now . . . now everything was being torn away from Thomas Blackburn.

He tried to breathe deeply, controlling his frustration and his temper. He stared out of the heavily tinted window, watching the familiar bustle of Washington pass by him like a picture frame in motion.

This is not over. Unlike de Faulke, Blackburn would not succumb, even in this moment of apparent defeat.

In his left palm, he turned over a small object. A tiny glass tube radiated on his dry skin like a precious gem. Within it, the descendant's blood sparkled, mixed in perfect proportion with the growth agent from his lab and the compound from de Faulke's vials.

105

US Capitol, Washington, DC

'The State of the Union simply will not be cancelled,' Tom Arbuckle said firmly. The look on his face bore the determination that came from following orders, however one felt about them. His had come from the White House, after a thorough update on the encounter in the Statuary Hall.

'How can it possibly be allowed to go on?' Jack protested. 'Discovering a biological attack focused on the president and the whole of Congress isn't enough to warrant a delay?'

'A *thwarted* attack,' the director of Capitol security replied. 'The weapon was discovered and removed.'

'And that's . . . that's enough? No thought that there could be another?'

The agent gave Jack a look of distaste. 'Of course we're considering that possibility. Every inch of the House Chamber is being torn apart at this very minute by a team of over seventy-five agents – from the floorboards and the seat cushions to the bulbs in the light fixtures on the ceiling. And we have two hundred more agents scouring the remainder of the Capitol. We know the kind of thing we're looking for now, and so far, there's nothing.'

Angela could see the exasperation in Jack's eyes.

'But the possibility alone,' she interjected, 'isn't that enough to postpone the event for at least a day or two?'

'Our teams are the best in the world, Miss Derby,' came the firm answer. 'There is nothing they could find in two days that they couldn't find in the next three hours.'

'But –'

'No buts.' Special Agent Arbuckle cut off Jack before he could raise any further protests. 'I've already spoken to the head of the Secret Service and the president himself. The State of the Union cannot be cancelled, or even delayed, by a terrorist threat. It is one of the most visible events in the nation's political life. It would be a resonating sign of a government beholden to terrorists, and the president simply won't have it.'

'Even with such a tremendous risk?'

'It is a controlled risk,' Arbuckle replied. 'No secondary device, or any similar unit, is in this building. And security on entry, which was high to begin with, will be raised. No one will be bringing anything in.'

'But Thomas Blackburn is still out there,' Jack protested. 'You can't believe he's simply going to walk away, not after putting so much effort into his designs.'

'Walking away is almost certainly what he will do,' the agent answered. 'As far away as possible. But he's been placed at the top of our terrorist watch list and the whole city is looking for him, with instructions to arrest and detain on sight. He won't get anywhere near the Capitol.'

Angela had heard enough, and the solidity of Tom Arbuckle's tone was clear enough to know that they weren't going to alter the government's plans.

'At the very least,' she said, hoping for the tiniest

measure of influence, 'get a hazmat team on site, just in case.' Before the agent could protest, she added, 'I know your security is thorough, but there's no reason not to have a back-up in place.'

Special Agent Arbuckle looked at her patiently. 'Of course, Miss Derby. We called one in twenty minutes ago. They'll be here within the hour.'

106

US Capitol

Walking directly into the US Capitol was the only option left, and it had the added benefit of being precisely the last thing that any of the security team controlling the building would expect. They would be anticipating that Thomas Blackburn would run, would try to find distance and safety after a failed plot. But Blackburn had no intention of disappearing.

He had every intention of being seen.

He glanced at his watch. It was 7.18 p.m. The State of the Union was now just under two hours away, which meant early arrivals would already be entering the Capitol, the traditional pre-speech receptions and drinks taking place in various quarters throughout the building.

Blackburn knew he was a wanted man. Every Secret Service agent in Washington would have been told to detain him. Which is what he would rely on.

A new plan had formed in his mind, and detention was an integral part.

He'd secured the supplies he would require from the lab, shortly after news of Sean's failure and the shutdown of the exhibition. He pocketed them now: three small syringes, alongside the tiny glass vial that contained the hybrid agent his teams had mixed that afternoon.

Blackburn set de Faulke's journal aside. It had brought

him as far as it could. The final step was one that Blackburn would have to walk alone.

He'd instructed his driver to take him to the northern side entrance to the Capitol, reserved for dignitaries, VIPs and other special arrivals for key events. The drive-up would be manned by a small team of greeters taken on for the evening's event, together with two security agents outside the door, and two more positioned inside. Blackburn knew from experience that just inside the double doors, off to the right, was a small holding cell into which problematic 'visitors' could easily be shuffled if there was any question of propriety or clearance, so as to not interrupt the flow of other high-profile guests. A cell into which Blackburn knew he would be thrust.

His car slowed as it pulled up alongside the entrance, its blacked-out windows preventing Blackburn's face from being seen as the red-coated greeter came to open the rear door. Thomas had hired the car from a large livery company, so the plates – scanned automatically by detection cameras as cars approached the building – wouldn't be linked to him and signal his arrival too early. He didn't want to be stopped any further away than where he was right now.

The young man in the red coat pulled open the door, a welcoming smile on his face. He peered in and caught Blackburn's glance, but didn't seem to recognize him. *Not his job*, Blackburn reflected.

But it *was* the job of the dark-suited agents standing five feet behind, on either side of the door, and as Blackburn stepped out of the sedan, the recognition on their faces was instantaneous.

Blackburn forced himself to act nonchalant as he stepped towards the entrance, two small concrete steps passing beneath his highly polished shoes.

'Excuse me, sir,' one of the agents said as both swooped to his sides. 'Please come with us.'

Blackburn said nothing. The agents' words were polite, but they gripped his arms with rigid strength, their hands locking round him like vices. He was pulled towards the door, and then, just as he had suspected, thrust to the right and through a steel door that closed swiftly behind them. The tiny antechamber housed a series of monitors linked to CCTV cameras aimed at the entry's interior and exterior, and just beyond the control centre another door led into a bare, isolated holding cell.

'Are you Thomas Blackburn?' asked one of the agents as they pushed him inside. They knew he was, and another of the agents was already on his radio, passing news of his arrival and capture up the chain of command, but protocol required verbal confirmation.

'I am,' Blackburn answered. Then, as innocently as he could, playing up the frailty of his age, 'what is all this about?'

The guard looked him over, and for only the briefest instant, Blackburn could spot the glimmer of pity, of disbelief in the man's eyes – as if the gentle little man before him, slightly bent over, wrinkled and grey-haired, couldn't really be as bad as had been claimed.

The glimmer passed in an instant, but it was enough. Thomas Blackburn had his in.

107

US Capitol

The opportunity would last only seconds, and then would be gone for ever. Reaching a hand into his pocket, Blackburn clutched his fingers round one of the syringes and made sure the other two were positioned for easy, and fast, access.

'Excuse me,' he said, keeping his voice soft and cordial, 'before you lock me in here, could I please have a glass of water?' An innocent request. He knew it would be denied, but the few seconds it took for the nearest guard to register the question and utter a polite 'no' was all he would need.

The agent paused, the door half closed. He was already shaking his head as he began to turn towards the captive detainee.

The man never completed the motion. Thomas Blackburn lunged forward with surprising agility and plunged the needle into the carotid artery on the man's neck, depressing the plunger in a swift, unhesitating movement. The sixty cubic centimeters of Novichok nerve agent swept into the agent's bloodstream like an invader.

The effect of the massive overdose was instant. The man in Blackburn's arms, whose weight he could barely hold and who he instead lowered as gently as possible to the floor, twitched only slightly as his nervous system shut down, then collapsed as the drug dropped him into a limp, full-body paralysis for the few seconds before his brain ceased to instruct his heart to pump and he died a silent, inglorious death.

Blackburn released the agent's body as quietly as he could and swiftly stepped into the control room. His hand was already extracting the next syringe as he straightened his body, and he thrust it into the second guard's neck from behind, without the poor man knowing what had hit him. A second later, he, too, was lying on the floor.

The two agents stationed inside were out of commission. But Blackburn knew there were two more outside, and as he peered through the door he could see that one had been moved inside, while the other remained at his post at the exterior of the building.

He drew the third syringe into his palm and edged open the door that led from the control room into the corridor. The steel door, however, was not as stealth-minded as the man behind it, and the groan of metal on metal from the hinges couldn't be missed.

The third agent turned towards the noise, and his eyes widened as he saw their detainee walking purposefully towards him.

The agent might have questioned the seriousness of the threat posed by Thomas Blackburn – or he might not – but he did not hesitate in his duty. His right hand was moving towards the SIG-Sauer P229 holstered at his chest before he'd taken another breath.

But Blackburn had the advantage. He was already in motion, and the space between the door and the agent was no more than three steps, two of which he had already covered. As his foot planted for the third, his arm rose up and swiped sideways.

The look of shock on the agent's face froze on his features as the nerve agent burst into his bloodstream. Blackburn reached forward to support his body as all the agent's muscles went limp. The man's mass was too much for Blackburn, but at least he could direct his fall with some degree of care.

'I'm sorry,' he whispered into the dying man's ear, and in that moment he meant it.

But he was beyond mourning innocent losses. Thomas Blackburn looked up, taking notice of the CCTV cameras monitoring the corridor. He knew full well that the feeds were not only monitored at the entrance station, and that within seconds his actions would be known, if they weren't already.

Stepping over the warm corpse, Thomas Blackburn walked purposefully into the heart of the Capitol, allowing the cameras to trace his every step.

108

US Capitol

Angela stood close to Jack in the operations room where Special Agent Tom Arbuckle had permitted them to observe the final preparations for the State of the Union. Angela had the strong sense that the agent had granted them the concession chiefly as a way of getting them to be quiet, comforted by the suites of video feeds, environmental monitors and troops of investigators completing their sweeps of the entire grounds. But Angela did not feel comforted. She had the terrible feeling that Blackburn would not give up, whatever the obstacles placed before him. She had seen the look in his eyes. It was not the look of a man who would accept defeat.

'It's a tight ship,' Jack noted, observing the complex systems at the fingertips of the agents around them.

'It won't matter,' Angela answered, though she spoke mostly to herself. 'Blackburn believes he's got seven centuries of history pushing him forward. He won't stop.'

The alarm had sounded only seconds later, as if intent on cementing her as prophetess. A light on the central console began to flash, accompanied not by the garish, siren-like klaxons that red alerts yield in films, but only a single light blinking together with a whining tone, which every eye and ear in the room were trained to spot.

'Holding cell eight, at the dignitaries' entrance,' one of the agents announced, reading the alert code off a monitor. Within two seconds, a whole bank of monitors displayed live feeds from the cameras positioned in and near the cell.

'They've apprehended a man matching the description of Thomas Blackburn,' he continued, relaying the information coming to his earpiece. 'Special Agents Cox and Flydale are escorting him into the holding cell now.'

On one of the displays Angela and Jack could suddenly see two agents walk into view. Between them was an older man, who even from the rear they both recognized as Blackburn.

'That's him,' Jack said. 'That's definitely Blackburn.'

'And I want to talk to the bastard face-to-face!' The exclamation came as a surprise from the doorway behind them, and Angela and Jack turned to see a man standing in the doorway. He looked to be in his mid-forties, but his eyes looked a hundred years older and were aflame with anger.

'Senator Wilcox?' Jack questioned, confused. He'd seen photos of the man who had not long ago been appointed to the Senate Defence Committee.

'Thomas Blackburn kidnapped my daughters,' Wilcox answered, taking a step into the room, 'and murdered my wife in order to blackmail me into supporting the addition of a defence exhibit after the State of the Union. I still don't know why.'

'We do,' Angela said. 'He was planning an attack. A biological agent at the exhibition.'

Wilcox's eyes went wide, as if he hadn't anticipated that Blackburn's intentions could have been so much grander than murder and kidnapping.

'The exhibition's already been called off,' Jack assured him.

Tom Arbuckle had taken note of the senator's entrance, but turned his attention back to his agents and the bank of CCTV displays. The three men on the screens walked through the camera's field of view, instantly appearing on another monitor that covered the interior of a small control booth. A second later, they moved on to two monitors that displayed different angles of a minuscule holding cell.

'It's Blackburn,' another agent suddenly announced. Angela glanced at his computer, where a still of Blackburn's face as he'd entered the corridor had been frozen on the screen, a host of facial-recognition metrics now overlaid on the image. 'Identity has been positively confirmed.'

'I told you that already,' Jack muttered, annoyed and anxious.

'Put the building on lockdown,' came Arbuckle's stern and commanding voice. 'No one comes in, no one goes out, until we've escorted Mr Blackburn off the premises.'

With a few keystrokes and fewer than ten seconds of radio communication, the capital of American democracy had gone into security quarantine.

What came next, however, took everyone by surprise.

'Holy shit,' came a rare, unrestrained remark from one of the agents. He pointed a finger at the displays, where the elderly Thomas Blackburn had suddenly sprung to life. With a speed worthy of a man half his age, he had reached for something in his pocket – a syringe, they could just make it out – and lunged for the nearest guard. The man fell in under a second, and Blackburn was already moving for the next.

'Get everyone we have down to that corridor!' Arbuckle commanded.

Even as he barked the order, Blackburn took down a third agent on the screen, laying his body gently on the floor and moving out of the camera's range. He flickered on to another, showing a swift retreat into the depths of the Capitol.

'I don't understand,' Senator Wilcox said, his eyes glued to the monitors, 'he's got to know the whole building is under surveillance.' In fact, Blackburn had made his awareness of the cameras only too clear, staring straight into one as he dropped the third guard. 'He has to know that wherever he goes, he'll be watched every step of the way. And he has to know there's no getting out of this building now.'

Angela watched Arbuckle as the senior agent checked his sidearm and started moving towards the control room's exit with a group of his men, each grabbing heavier weapons from racks near the door.

'I don't think he has any intention of getting out,' she said to Jack and the senator. 'He's beyond that.' She tugged at Jack's arm and led them out, taking up a jog behind Arbuckle's team.

'Blackburn knows only too well that where he goes now, people will follow.'

109

US Capitol

The alert had been sounded. There was no audible tone, no ringing klaxons or sirens, but Blackburn knew the whole building would be looking for him now. But more importantly, the building would be sealed. Contained. Standard protocol. No one would be allowed to leave, from the office workers and support staff to the hundreds of senators, congressmen and guests already on site for the State of the Union.

The leadership hadn't arrived yet, nor the president. They always arrived at the last minute, a focal entrance deemed an important part of the dignity of the former, and a practical security matter for the latter. They certainly would not be allowed in now. But it was all right. Blackburn would have preferred their presence, but he could do what needed to be done without them.

I'm so close, within reach. His mind raced as he moved through the corridors. His eyes closed briefly as he walked, and the grandeur of history was there in the black of his eyelids. If his life had to be sacrificed, so be it. The curse would finally be unleashed, and those responsible for so much oppression, injustice and wrongdoing would die, as had been foretold centuries before.

And all it would take would be the tiniest movement of his jaw.

Blackburn slowed, then stopped. He could hear footsteps running in the distance. They would be upon him in a matter of seconds.

The time was now. He was close enough.

Lowering a withered hand into his right coat pocket, Blackburn withdrew the small glass vial that his scientific team had prepared. As he held it up in the light, it twinkled like the most beautiful of gems, the blood, the ancient biological agent and the growth factor his men had created mixed together in a beautiful, sparkling garnet red. For the briefest of instants he relished the true beauty of the treasure he had found. He had never seen a gem look half as enticing.

The patter of feet was louder now, just beyond the end of the long corridor ahead of him, with others behind.

Reverie and admiration fled. Thomas Blackburn took the vial and placed it in his mouth, clenching it between his teeth.

As he tightened his jaw and bit down, the dying words of the last Grand Master of the original Order of Knights Templar boomed through his mind.

A curse upon you all! Mark my words, a great calamity will befall all those who have condemned us to such a death!

The glass shattered in his mouth, liquid pouring out over his tongue. Blackburn allowed it to swirl with his saliva, along with the blood that trickled from the wounds in his cheeks that the glass fragments caused. Then he rolled back his head, holding the glass shards in place and allowing the liquid to drain down the back of his throat.

He swallowed. He spat out the glass. He swallowed again.

It was done. There was no going back. As he saw the fleet of Secret Service agents round the corner ahead of him, weapons drawn and sealing off any escape, one other fact caused Thomas Blackburn to smile.

There was no way to stop what he had done.

110

US Capitol

'He's round the next corner, on the right, ten yards,' one of the agents whispered to Tom Arbuckle. Angela could hear the whisper like a beacon in the otherwise profound silence with which the group of over twenty agents – she and Jack trailing at the rear, Senator Preston Wilcox close at their side – moved through the ornate marble spaces. An earpiece-link connected the team to a controller monitoring Blackburn's movements via the cameras positioned everywhere in the Capitol, who in turn directed them towards Corridor D-17. There Blackburn had, their earpieces informed them, stopped moving.

Arbuckle whispered to the men closest to him. 'Keep on your guard as we round the corner. Full spotting positions. Team Two will be arriving from the opposite end of the corridor the same moment as us.'

'It's a go,' the man closest to Arbuckle replied. The whole group slowed as they approached the ninety-degree turn as the corridor branched perpendicularly to the right. Then, in a perfect unison, the agents swept forward.

'Stop where you are!' one of them yelled as the whole entourage moved into position, but the command proved unnecessary. Thomas Blackburn had nowhere to go. Before him was the phalanx of Arbuckle's agents, and behind him another team ran into parallel positions. There were no doors at the sides of the corridor, no exits. The old man was trapped.

'I'm Special Agent Tom Arbuckle of the United States Secret Service,' Arbuckle announced, moving forward through his men, all of whom had their weapons trained on Blackburn, 'and you are under arrest for conspiracy to commit an act of terror, and for the murder of multiple federal agents.'

If Blackburn felt anything at hearing the words, he did not show it. He was, Angela thought, surprisingly calm in the circumstances. Close to two dozen gun barrels were pointed at him from the front, as many behind, yet Thomas Blackburn looked almost . . . serene.

'There is no need for the weapons, Special Agent – Arbuckle, was it?' Blackburn finally said, looking dispassionately at the man in charge. 'I am quite unarmed, as you well know.' He held up his arms, extended wide, inviting the agents to confirm the fact anew.

Arbuckle gave a subtle motion, and two agents swept forward to Blackburn, their weapons lowered, and frisked him thoroughly.

'He's clean,' came the verdict from the man closest to Arbuckle, a few seconds later. 'He's got nothing on him. Nothing. Not so much as a wallet.'

'As I told you,' Blackburn said emotionlessly, 'I have nothing in my possession that should cause you any concern.'

Angela glanced at Jack, and for a second she could see doubt creep on to his face. Had they been wrong? But they had seen Blackburn kill the three agents at the entrance. All in order to enter the Capitol with . . . *nothing*? What was he playing them for?

'Put a set of cuffs on him, then escort him downstairs under full guard,' Arbuckle commanded. Unarmed or not, the agent showed no signs of being manipulated by Blackburn's age or feeble appearance.

It was then that Angela heard it. A sound that all at once seemed so innocent and normal, yet at the same time caused her a panic she had never known. In that instant, she knew exactly how Blackburn intended to bring his curse to fruition.

For in that moment, Thomas Blackburn coughed.

III

US Capitol

It was not an ordinary cough. The contraction of Thomas Blackburn's lungs began deep within, and there was a guttural wheezing accompanying the forced breath that convulsed through his throat.

He stood tall, despite the obvious pain the cough caused him and the spasms it seemed to send through his abdominal muscles. When the single, long cough was over, the tiniest spot of blood on Blackburn's lower lip removed any doubt from Angela's mind.

'Don't move!' she shouted out, unable to restrain the panic in her voice. Her words were directed at the Secret Service agent stepping towards Blackburn with the slender tie of the vinyl handcuffs in his hand.

'Don't get any closer to him!' Angela shouted again, pushing forward between two agents. Jack and Tom Arbuckle both swung their heads to her, and Arbuckle reached out an arm to stop her.

'This isn't the moment for you to be interfering with a Feder—'

'Take another step closer to him, and you're dead.' Angela projected her words towards the handcuffing agent, who now looked up at her, surprised, and then towards his commander.

'Listen, lady, I told you not to inter—'

'He's infected,' Angela cut him off. She shook her head, disbelief giving way to what had to be true. 'He's infected himself. The agent he hoped to introduce to the presentation, the biological compound . . . he's got it in his blood.'

Suddenly, the agent closest to Blackburn froze, his eyes expanding in horror.

'How do you know this?'

Then Thomas Blackburn coughed again. Deeper this time, raspy, and another line of blood formed at the left edge of his mouth.

The agent with the handcuffs saw it and leapt back in sudden, comprehending fear.

Blackburn burst into laughter. He wiped his hand with a sleeve, then looked down at the bright crimson blood smeared along the cloth and laughed even more.

'It's too late!' he cackled. 'There is nothing left for you to do! I've already won!'

He continued his laughter as Angela motioned for everyone to take several steps back. The agents now seemed only too eager to comply. Facing a man with a bullet or bomb was one thing. Being exposed to a biological agent that would eat away at you from the inside was another.

'The compound we discovered in China is many times more aggressive than the bacterium that caused the Great Plague in the Middle Ages,' Angela announced aloud.

Blackburn grinned at her. 'How little you really know! The material we've devised, which uses your own blood as a compounding agent . . . it makes the plague look like a schoolyard cough. And as quickly and as far as that plague spread, this is far, far more contagious.' Blackburn squinted his eyes, then burst into a fit of uncontrolled coughing. He made no attempt to keep the blood and spittle from his mouth from spraying out into the corridor, and even craned his neck towards an air vent high above.

'Cut the ventilation system,' Arbuckle shouted into his cuff-mounted radio, his order instantly relayed to agents somewhere in the hulk of the building. 'Seal off the air supply.'

'Too late, too late!' Blackburn laughed, now almost joyfully.

Suddenly, he snapped his head to Angela. The red in his eyes was not just an apparition: blood vessels and capillaries were bursting one by one, and his eyes took on a demonic tone to match his words.

'At last, Miss Derby, all is avenged. The Order is redeemed!'

Blackburn grew more frenzied, his eyes glazing over. Angela couldn't tell if it was from rage or an effect of the infection.

He seemed to sense that his end was coming. His body convulsing, his breath slight and uncontrolled, he bore hateful, red eyes into Angela.

'A final embrace, to seal the curse!'

Blackburn mustered his strength and lunged forward towards her, arms outstretched. All at once Angela saw his aim: he would infect her, cling to her, and in God-only-knew how short a time she would be dying the same tortured death as he, and so would everyone around them.

She tried to lunge away, but an explosion of light and sound transformed the space around her. Bullets flew past her from behind, while the guttural cry of a man tortured by loss filled in the spaces between the blasts.

'This is for my wife, you son of a bitch!'

Preston Wilcox grabbed a sidearm from the waist of one of the agents, whose arms were occupied with a larger rifle, and unloaded the clip in the direction of Thomas Blackburn.

The agents around them opened fire, and the marble floors and walls of the corridor magnified the report of their weapons to an almost deafening roar.

Then, as fast as it had come, it stopped. Temporarily deafened by the sounds, Angela could not tell if Thomas Blackburn's fall to the ground was as surreally silent as it appeared to her, but she saw his legs give way under a torso riddled with bullet holes, each flowering out with rosettes of blood. And then he fell, face forward, on to the cold floor.

The hazmat team burst through the swell of agents and swept up to Blackburn's position as soon as his body was still, covering him with a specialized, clear tarpaulin and sealing its edges to the floor as a short-term containment measure, until it could be properly quarantined. Arbuckle was on his radio, instructing full atmospheric isolation measures to be put into effect. The Capitol might be an old building, antiquated in so many respects, but since the anthrax scare that had riddled Washington shortly after 9/11, its ventilation systems had been upgraded with full anti-terrorist mechanisms that included isolated airflow systems, distinct quadrant ventilation and the ability to pump clean air from storage tanks into various rooms.

They would do everything in their power to make sure that Blackburn's efforts got no further than the Capitol building, and, with any luck, only part of it.

The Secret Service agent nearest Senator Wilcox took a calm step towards the man. Wilcox's arm was still outstretched, the pistol shaking in his grip. Tears streamed down his face and he pulled at the trigger again and again, the empty clip the only thing keeping the gun from firing.

'Senator, it's all over,' the agent said soothingly. He reached a hand out slowly to Wilcox's arm, then removed the gun from his grasp. 'We got him. It's over.'

Wilcox turned to him, his eyes wet, filled with a profound sorrow. Then he nodded his head and allowed the agent to walk him aside. There would be questions and interrogations to follow.

Angela stepped forward as the hazmat team sealed their makeshift containment tent. Beneath the clear tarpaulin, she could see Thomas Blackburn's body, his arms outstretched as if in the shape of a cross. Blood from his gunshot wounds poured out from beneath his torso – and the crimson streams, now among the most deadly substances on earth, seemed to flow in the shape of the same red cross that had been the emblem of the Knights Templar, advancing on crusade, for centuries.

Epilogue

The Seneschal rattled his fingers along the wooden arm-rest of the private jet. Beneath him, land had turned to sea and stretched out to the horizon in a hazy blue.

The Grand Master had fallen. His plans had been too bold, and worse, he had not been able to face the prospect of failure with dignity. Thomas had taken things too . . . personally. His brother had always been like that. A man of noble aims, but a leader of men ought to know that the greater war was more important than any particular battle.

The moment Sean Blackburn had been uncovered at the Capitol, the Seneschal had ordered the immediate retreat and withdrawal of all the New Order's men from Washington. He did not technically have the authority to do so without the Grand Master's approval, but the Grand Master had not made himself available. And the Seneschal, as his closest followers knew, had seen the signs of his fall on the horizon.

The New Order, however, would not be allowed to fall with him. Not so recently after it had truly begun to mature. They would soon have 200 knights, if their recruitment rates kept up. Thomas Blackburn was gone, his company finished, but even through his madness he had created something enduring.

479

Behind the Seneschal, Sean Blackburn sat anxiously, gazing out at the seascape beneath them. He'd barely made it out of the Capitol, but Providence had been with him. The Seneschal could use his presence to call the others back to order after the loss. Piotr had been ready to eliminate Sean, but perhaps he had been prevented from doing so for a reason. Bloodlines were important.

War had been declared. Not the personal, vindictive war of a man who could not see past the struggles of their common past, but a just war against the oppressive world that too often sought evil in place of good and comfort in place of truth. Just as it had done hundreds of years ago, when the Order had been at its zenith and had learned to wield power over an empire that was crumbling at the edges.

The modern world was falling, too, but the New Order would speak into the darkness with the same light that had led their ancestors. There was corruption here, there was innocence to be protected. There was piety to be restored and the corrupt to be destroyed.

It was time for a New Order, a new day, and the rise of a new world.

Outside of Ascalon, Near Jerusalem, AD 1335

Sir Arnaud de Faulke lay on his back, his eyes towards the bright sun. They were open as far as they would go, but that was barely more than the tiniest of slits between swollen eyelids. The bright orange light pushed through, made hazy by the crusted deposits that covered his pupils.

It was true, then, that death could be a mercy. De Faulke welcomed it now, longed for it, as each remaining breath tortured his body with a searing agony.

His brethren in the north were the Order's only remaining hope. If the courier was faithful and delivered them his journal, they would have what they needed for the future. Curse, treasure . . . whatever it was, it would be their inheritance, and it would guide them back to power one day. A new Order, a *novus ordo*, to rise up and reclaim the honour of the old.

But de Faulke could no longer worry for their future, or for the Grand Master's revenge. His body was about to be reclaimed by the earth – a spoil of sores, but still the handiwork of the God of power. He could only hope that, dying here at the fringe of the Christian realms of the earth, he might stave off spreading to his fellow men what the curse had brought upon him. But even there, God would take His own course. It was out of de Faulke's hands.

Blood sputtered at the edges of his lips as he pulled in a last, deep breath, and departed this life with the words that had been his guideposts since the day he had taken up the Cross. The words that led every knight into every battle, even the battle of death itself.

'*Non nobis Domine, non nobis, sed nomini tuo da gloriam*. Not to us, Lord, not to us, but to Thy name give glory.'

A Note From The Author

The territory of Templar history has always been one that, as a storyteller, I've found both captivating and repulsive. Captivating, because there is so much intrigue and mystery to the Templars – so much that is ancient yet modern, good yet sinister, famous yet secretive. But it is also repulsive, inasmuch as generations of half-hearted imaginings about Templar intrigues have too often reduced their stories into little more than fantasy works that happen to take the cover of history.

This may sound strange, coming from an author who's just penned a book connecting the Templars to the Great Plague, but I've tried to rein in my naturally explorative fiction-writer's mind within the contours of some truly fascinating question marks in the historical record, as well as a few coincidences of timing that couldn't help but attract a novelist's attention.

In the first place, I have attempted to keep my descriptions of Templar history – its formation, operation, reach and structure – as accurate as is reasonable in a work of fiction. Perhaps the motivation for Umberto Eco to say that the lunatic is one who, sooner or later, brings up the Templars is because there is simply so much to their history that can captivate and fascinate a curious (or crazy) mind. The Templars really did begin as a charitable order of monk-knights charged to protect pilgrims en route to the Holy Land, and their emphasis on poverty, simplicity and charity was as severe as Thomas Blackburn describes in this book. Yet they grew into something quite different: inheriting the former territory of Solomon's Temple in Jerusalem after victories in the crusades, the Templars grew quickly to heights of power and wealth that historians to this day cannot fully explain. By the time of their demise in the early fourteenth century, they were among the wealthiest and most politically powerful entities in Europe, and this, coupled with their secretive nature, made them suspect in the eyes of political and Church powers. When their Order was disbanded in 1312, their last Grand Master, Jacques de Molay, really was burned at the stake before Notre Dame Cathedral in Paris, his hands bound in prayer, and he really did utter the curse that forms the starting point for our story.

What caused the Templars' rise in power? The simple answer is that no one knows, and Jack Shepherd's suspicions in these pages express only a handful of the theories that have been put forward over the years. Some suggest that the Templars discovered buried treasure beneath Solomon's Temple, which gave them the funding to exercise unparalleled dominance; but others suggest that what they found was far more dramatic: the Chalice of the Last Supper, or even the bones of Christ. Wild speculations, but all grounded in the mysterious reality that no one knows *what* brought the Templars the sudden power and influence they held. And so curiosity abounds, and the myth of the Templar treasure was born.

What we do know is that, in addition to being skilled warriors and devout believers, the Templars were ingenious businessmen and thinkers. Their creation of a precursor to the modern banking system, described in this book by Angela and Sean, is accurate, and the Templar encoding cipher, which figures in the breaking of the clues left by Arnaud de Faulke, is based on real hypotheses about how they encrypted their most secretive messages.

The encoding cipher did not, to the best of my knowledge, utilize the rune-like symbols that I've caused it to employ in this novel, but the symbols themselves are real and are connected to Templar lore through the Money Pit located on Oak Island, Nova Scotia. While I have invented some of the rune sequences in this book in order to provide more material to work with, the Money Pit cover stone text (provided on p. 80) is the actual inscription of a real stone discovered there (photographs of which are easily obtainable online), roughly dating to the post-dissolution Templar period, and which has never been decoded in a manner that can be authenticated. Scholars hotly dispute the degree to which the surprisingly deep, booby-trapped pits on the island, with their encrypted ancient markers, relate to the popular theories of a western migration of the Templars, and most likely these debates will continue for generations. The Money Pit has never been successfully dug out (its traps have thwarted every attempt), and what it contains remains a mystery to this day.

And what of the Black Death? A novelist hardly has to work to make the drama of the plague come to life; the pestilence that reduced the European population by almost 60 per cent in just over two years remains one of the most horrific examples of a communicable-disease pandemic in history. Most readers are aware that the bacterium causing the plague was transmitted by fleas that lived on rats, but far fewer are likely to be familiar with the current scientific theories, given substantial support by genetic studies published in 2010, which place the origin of the bacterium in the Far East, probably in the plains of China, from where it travelled to Europe along the Silk Road and other trade routes. The 'accidental timing' of the outbreak of the Great Plague, only a few decades after the last Templar Grand Master had died uttering a curse of vengeance upon the empire, was the seed of intrigue that led me to this story.

Finally, a word about the rise of a new Templar Order. If the thought of a businessman being part of a secretive organization founded on the principles and legacy of an ancient monastic order sounds far-fetched, the reader needs look no further than the tens of thousands of professionals, politicians and world leaders that belong to countless Masonic organizations the world over, most of which have vivid, abiding roots in Templar lore, history and symbolism. That some of these groups might be tempted towards evil, and spurred on towards it by the power of that ancient lore, is hardly beyond the realm of imagination. Just how far might a new Templar Order, a *novus ordo*, go? Well, this is Book I for a reason . . .

Acknowledgements

A few words of thanks are more than due and will ensure I continue to be friends with some of the wonderful people with whom I've been privileged to work on this book. Among these, Luigi Bonomi is amongst London's finest agents, nicest people, and general treasures of the publishing world, and I'm glad to have him on my side. Alex Clarke, the Publishing Director at Penguin and Hana Osman, Editor, are responsible not only for the keen interest shown in this book and the drive to publish it with energy and gusto, but are also tremendously classy people who have restored my faith in French cuisine and informed me that a New Years pledge of a 'Dry January' can guiltlessly be abandoned (for the purposes of a literary lunch, at least) by January 3rd. I'm tremendously indebted, also, to Sophie Elletson, my Editorial Manager at Penguin, for overseeing the complex, elaborate yet wonderful process that stands between a final manuscript and the published book; and no set of thanks would suffice without notable mention of Jennie Roman – one of the most skilled, pleasant, efficient and enjoyable copy-editors with whom I've had the pleasure to work. I must also mention Thomas Stofer, whose creative eye helped refine my early ideas and bring this story from concept to novel; Miles Orchard, a careful and critical reader who shared superb thoughts early on; and Father I., who provided both historical insights as well as editorial commentary that were greatly appreciated. The beautiful cover is the work of Nick Shah, who I've never met but who I clearly owe a good dinner. There are other people to thank, too, all of whom will make their presence known to me in angry letters after not seeing their name here: but to all of you, my genuine and sincere thanks. Here's looking forward to the fun we'll get up to next.

He just wanted a decent book to read ...

Not too much to ask, is it? It was in 1935 when Allen Lane, Managing Director of Bodley Head Publishers, stood on a platform at Exeter railway station looking for something good to read on his journey back to London. His choice was limited to popular magazines and poor-quality paperbacks – the same choice faced every day by the vast majority of readers, few of whom could afford hardbacks. Lane's disappointment and subsequent anger at the range of books generally available led him to found a company – and change the world.

'We believed in the existence in this country of a vast reading public for intelligent books at a low price, and staked everything on it'
Sir Allen Lane, 1902–1970, founder of Penguin Books

The quality paperback had arrived – and not just in bookshops. Lane was adamant that his Penguins should appear in chain stores and tobacconists, and should cost no more than a packet of cigarettes.

Reading habits (and cigarette prices) have changed since 1935, but Penguin still believes in publishing the best books for everybody to enjoy. We still believe that good design costs no more than bad design, and we still believe that quality books published passionately and responsibly make the world a better place.

So wherever you see the little bird – whether it's on a piece of prize-winning literary fiction or a celebrity autobiography, political tour de force or historical masterpiece, a serial-killer thriller, reference book, world classic or a piece of pure escapism – you can bet that it represents the very best that the genre has to offer.

Whatever you like to read – trust Penguin.